MASSY'S GAME

BY JACK OLSEN

MASSY'S GAME
by Jack Olsen

P♥P

A PLAYBOY PRESS BOOK

LIBRARY OF CONGRESS CATALOGING IN PUBLICATION DATA

Olsen, Jack.
  Massy's game.

  I. Title.
PZ4.04985Mas   [PS3565.L77]   813'.5'4   75–17269
ISBN 0–87223–441–X

For Su and One

MASSY'S GAME

WASPS ROSTER

NAME	HOMETOWN	AGE	HT.	WT.	SCHOOL	POS.
Broussard Massy	New Orleans, La.	22	8′ 2″	245	Des Rocher Inst. of Music	C
Edwin Crowder	Philadelphia, Pa.	28	6′ 11″	220	St. Joseph's	C
Justin Fell	New York City	26	6′ 4″	200	U. of Pa.	G
H. C. A. Manno	Kalispell, Mont.	29	5′ 11″	180	BYU	G
Archibald Jones	Phoenix, Ariz.	28	6′ 3″	225	N. M. State	G–F
Basil McBride (Capt.)	Raintree, Fla.	30	6′ 7″	215	Friendship J. C.	F
Conrad Green	Kansas City, Mo.	23	6′ 6″	205	Kansas U.	F
Abdul Rahman Buzruz	Chicago, Ill.	29	6′ 3″	195	Peninsula Coll.	F
Leon Baldwin	Tallulah, La.	24	6′ 2″	205	Grambling	G
Tyrone Mays	Omaha, Neb.	22	6′ 1″	190	Iowa	G
Woodrow Thomas	Jersey City, N. J.	26	6′ 8″	210	Rutgers	F
Johnny Hawes	Mountain Home, Ark.	24	6′ 7″	225	Ark. State	F
Francis X. Rafferty	Youngstown, O.	52	6′ 2″	190	Ohio State	Coach

I
the beginning

1

There's about forty blowhards walking around now claiming that they knew him well, they understood him, they could see what was coming, but that's baloney. I knew him better than any of the other sportswriters, and I didn't know him at all. It's not easy to relate to an eight-footer. You stand in your hole and look up at his face, and right away you're annoyed—he's turned you into a kid, miniaturized you, made you talk uphill to dad. Who wants to repeat that old trauma? Dulcy felt something similar the first time she saw him up close.

"He makes me sad," she said.

"Sad?" I said. "Jeez, honey, what's sad about him? He's a big, strong, healthy kid."

"Nothing good can come of this," Dulcy said.

Well, she intuits things. She's a psychiatric social worker by trade but a soothsayer by natural inclination. She'll call me up at the paper to ask what day it is, but when it comes to what human beings will do, my wife has an uncanny feel.

She sized Massy up at one of our dirty weekends in training camp, 35 miles out of town on the verdant campus of Battenberg Polytechnic. That was back before anybody knew if the kid would make the club or not, and most of us doubted it. Somebody said he'd been checked out by a dozen pro teams, and the scouts had gone home laughing. Even the scouts from the Eastern League and the industrials. That didn't keep our coach from seeing something in him. There were horselaughs all around the league when we gave the monster a tryout.

Dulcy and I were standing in the hall when he came stooging along, wearing a pair of size 28 Puma shoes for a necklace. I had an urge to ask where were his oars, but instead I just stood and watched him walk, with his neck and shoulders all kind of scrooched together to keep from bumping his head on the ceiling. After the kid passed, I felt a tug at my belt, and it was Dulcy.

"For God's sake," she whispered, "do you have to stare at him as though he's some kind of *object?* Don't you think it's hard enough to be eight feet tall?"

"You're right, Dulcy," I muttered. I try to be a sensitive person, but her antennas are always tuned finer than mine. Why, certainly, the guy must hate to be studied all the time. I made a note to ask him about it at the first interview. It would be a refreshing change from the usual brilliant questions: Do you think you'll make the club? Are you looking forward to the season? Do you put your pants on one leg at a time?

"I'll ask him about that," I said to Dulcy as we walked toward the cafeteria.

"About what?"

"About being stared at."

"Oh, *great* idea!" Dulcy snapped. "Why don't you ask him how's the weather up there? You could say, 'Gee, ain't it raining up there?' Just like Thomas Wolfe in 'Gulliver.' "

"Hey, good idea, honey. Kind of break the ice."

Dulcy walked faster and I rushed to catch up. Sometimes she didn't know when I was putting her on. Sometimes neither did I.

All anybody knew about Broussard Massy in training camp was what we'd read in the papers, and most of that was hearsay and guesswork. When I first heard that the kid would try out for the Wasps, I got a peculiar phone call. A guy with a southern accent told me he had an important message but he couldn't give his name and he hoped I'd take him seriously because if I didn't the most awful things could happen and someone could get kilt and we'd all be sorry but listen, mister, as sure as God made meadowlarks, that eight-foot two-inch free-agent that's trying out for the Wasps is purely loony and nuts, not to mention a real certified psycho case and ought to be in a wet-pack and in fact *once was,* and if I don't believe it, just check the records. What records? I asked, but the man had hung up.

I sent back to the morgue on the off chance there'd be a clipping or two about the kid's college athletic career, but then I remembered that Massy hadn't had one. The librarian sent me two clips—a yellowed AP feature telling how a seven-foot kid was starring in a New Orleans junior high school league and how the scouts were getting him up in the morning and putting him to bed at night and barring unforeseen developments the sports world would be hearing from him in a few years when he enrolled at LSU and made gumbo out of Pete Maravich's stats. The other clip was about two inches long, from UPI. The head was

FROM KEY TO KEYBOARD

and the piece told how Broussard "Bru" Massy, 7–2 center of the De Lesseps S. Morrison Junior High School basketball team, had dropped out of sports to concentrate on piano, "much to the distress of his basketball coach and the satisfaction of Miss Agnes Richardson, the boy's former music teacher." That was our whole clip file on Bru Massy: The first eight-footer in professional basketball was coming in with a whimper.

Naturally the Wasps's press agent jazzed up the kid's profile in the training camp guide. Our PR man was Jack Carbon, a dapper little guy of 63 with pomaded hair slicked straight back, real sharp in 1938. Jack's literary approach was simple: *Never understate.* He must have been a cousin of the guy who invented the sizing technique for cans: "Giant" means small, and "large" means you can see it with a microscope. His bio of Broussard Massy started with the simple facts and figures, like all the rest:

Broussard "Bru" Massy
Center
College: Des Rocher Institute of Music, New Orleans
Height: 8–2
Weight: 245
Birthdate: 6/7/53
Birthplace: Marcilly, La.
Experience: Rookie

3

Then came the "bio" box:

> *Bru Massy, who towers two inches above eight feet, could be the*
> *surprise of the season for Coach Francis X. Rafferty's Wasps. A*
> *superstar (and supertall!) athlete in his adopted New Orleans,*
> *Massy gave up basketball in favor of a career as a brilliant concert*
> *pianist, but with his graduation last year from music school he*
> *found the siren call of the nets too magnetic, and the eight-foot-*
> *two athlete contacted Wasps's General Manager Darius Guile for*
> *a look-see. "With a little more meat on his bones, he could*
> *become a legend in his own time," Coach Rafferty beams. The*
> *early betting on this 8–2 giant is odds on that he'll wind up a star.*
> *"Who knows?" Coach Rafferty laughs. "Hopefully he'll be our*
> *white Wilt!" Keep your eyes on Bru the Brute. At 8–2 and 245*
> *pounds, there's plenty to see.*

Did you catch the subtlety in that bio? *"Superstar* athlete." *"Brilliant*
concert pianist." Check that powerful image: magnetic nets. Note the
quadruple repetition, as though we might forget that the kid stood—
what was it again?—oh, yeh, 8–2. And listen to Coach Rafferty laughing "Who knows?" Did you ever try to laugh "Who knows?" Maybe
I'm a purist, but I don't believe that quotes can be laughed or snorted
or smiled or sneezed. Our sports editor, Tex Pecos, was always inserting
words like that, "brightening the copy," as he'd explain. He'd make it
read: "Captain Basil McBride raised his hands in a victory sign and
belched out, 'Great game, men!' " In real life, all McBride ever belched
was a belch.

But I guess you had to excuse Jack's excesses this time. What was
he supposed to say about Massy? Nobody knew a thing, and the kid
wasn't talking. He'd stand there with his head hanging and answer yes,
no, and ummmmm. I covered his first press conference for the *Blade-
Mirror* (or the *B-M* as we fondly called it), along with four other
regulars on the Wasps's beat: Nick Storen of the morning *Item*, Pete
Tyles of the evening *Herald*, Lucious Johnson of the weekly *Afro-ite*,
and Pennsylvania Morgan of the *Off the Pigs News*. That was the team's
official press complement, although only Storen and Tyles and I made
all the road trips. As senior statesman, I opened the questioning:

"We want to welcome you to the Wasps, Bru. Say, how's the weather
up there?"

I just did it for a joke, but the kid never changed expression, never even blinked. He stood there like the Frankenstein monster without the bolts, except that Massy's head was covered in thick ringlets, whereas the monster wore a crewcut, at least in the movie. Another difference was the kid's white skin, the kind you sometimes see on bone china or circus clowns, except that in Massy's case it was accented by black eyes and black eyebrows and black hair. A handsome kid, for a colossus. You could have sketched him in full color with one lump of charcoal.

"Just kidding," I said quickly. "How've you liked the town so far?" I specialize in deep, probing questions.

Massy lifted his shaggy head and opened his dark eyes wide and moved his lips about a quarter inch. If he hadn't been the biggest human being I'd ever laid eyes on, I'd have sworn he was suffering from stage fright.

"Huh?" I asked.

"Fine," Jack Carbon said hurriedly. "He says he likes it fine."

"Bru," Pete Tyles said, "do you think you'll have any trouble learning Coach Rafferty's system?"

The rookie's leonine head rotated slowly toward Jack Carbon again, and a deep breathy voice came whooshing out like the air ahead of the elevator in a mineshaft. "What's Coach Rafferty's system?" Bru Massy asked. His first whole sentence as a Wasp!

"We'll get into that later," Jack Carbon said. "Next question?"

"Hey, baby, what's shakin' in your life?" It was the squeaky voice of Lucious Johnson of the *Afro-ite*. "I mean like where you live, what kinda vines you into, what kinda wheels you dig?" After a long silence, Lucious pressed on. "I mean, y'unnastan', like human interest stuff, y'unnastan'.".

When Massy didn't seem disposed to answer, the press agent said, "Well, look for yourself, Lucious. You can see how he likes to dress: jeans, tennis shoes. . . ."

The big man reached out and touched Jack's arm and shook his head sideways. It was abundantly clear that the rookie didn't intend that the question be answered by himself or anybody else. For just a few seconds there, I'd been under the impression that Massy wasn't in control of the situation, that he'd been ordered to dummy up, maybe by an agent or the front office, but those few authoritative shakes of the head told me who was in charge. So—we had a reluctant giant on the premises! There'd only been a few in the history of basketball—Wilt (off and on),

Jabbar, Bill Walton, one or two others who stubbornly refused to share their personal lives with the public and did their talking on the court. But there's a difference. The others were already stars when they turned pro; Massy was a big nobody from nowhere. As far as I could determine, he hadn't even played the game in six, eight years.

The more I thought about it, the more I figured we reporters were being made stooges in the Wasps's latest publicity stunt—they would sign the game's first eight-footer strictly for the news value, they'd let him jack around training camp for a week or two, and then they'd send him stumbling back to Louisiana, a couple of hundred bucks in his kick and an innocent look on his face. It didn't seem fair, but then nobody was twisting his arm. And he certainly wasn't embarrassing himself by revealing any personal secrets.

Jack Carbon spoke up. "I'm sorry, fellas," the press agent said. "I thought we made it clear. No personal questions, please! Give the boy a chance to get his feet on the ground."

"Hey, man, fuck you!" Pennsylvania Morgan of the *Off the Pigs News* called out. "Like he's a professional jock, man! He's got a responsibility to the public! I got a responsibility to my readers, man!" Pennsylvania seldom spoke without exclamation points; there was talk on his paper about changing his by-line to "Pennsyl! Vania! Morgan!" But his angry exterior was only a cover for the violent young man underneath.

"Bru set the ground rules," Carbon said. "Don't blame me."

I stepped in again as elder statesman. "Bru, does this mean you'll never share your private life with our readers?"

The big man nodded.

"Why's that?" Nick Storen of the *Item* asked.

Massy tilted his big head to one side and raised his coal eyebrows as though to say, "Who knows?"

"You're adamant?" I asked.

"No, he's Eve," said Storen, ever the smart ass. "Don't you just love his hairdo?"

Massy missed the wisecrack, or else he was the master of the innocent exterior. He coughed lightly behind his fist and said, "I know y'all have your needs, but I just can't help. I'm sorry. I truly am. I just hope y'all try to understand." He tilted his shaggy mane to the side and smiled sweetly and I was reminded of a Great Dane puppy after he tears up the rug.

"Look, Mac, we can understand anything," Storen said in his most

6

officious big-important-sportswriter voice, "but you got to give us a little something to go on. I mean, what's this all about, Massy? What're you, on the lam or something?"

The kid looked down on him serenely, smiling all the time, but not saying another word or even trying to.

"Bru," I said when the scene had become embarrassing, "which do you prefer, high post or low? Run 'n' gun or set plays?"

"Yes, sir, either one," he rumbled, not unpleasantly. I waited for an amplification, but none came.

"Next question?" Jack Carbon said nervously.

"What chew like to eat?" asked Lucious Johnson, doggedly pursuing his "human interest" story.

"Just good food, I guess. Nuts, cheese, milk, stuff like that. I don't eat meat." The kid didn't sound aggressive or sarcastic, just nonverbal. He acted as though he'd given away too much already, and was waiting for the next incisive question.

"Think you can handle pro centers like Orion Halliday and Willie Danielson?" Pete Tyles asked.

Massy smiled again and said, "Yes, sir," and Pennsylvania Morgan said, "Hey, man, I hear you play piano!"

The big man just stood there.

"I mean do you or don't you?" Pa. persisted.

Massy turned to Carbon, and the PR man reminded us once again that there were to be no personal questions. "Well, what the fuck we s'pose to ask?" Morgan said. "Training's not started, none of us ever seen him play. What else is there to ask except personal stuff?"

"Why don't you ask if he expects to make the club?" the press agent suggested.

"Do you think you'll make the club?" Pete Tyles asked helpfully.

"I hope so, sir," Broussard Massy answered.

"Thanks, Bru," Jack Carbon said, and the big man headed for the exit. He bent over to get through the door.

"Great interview," I said to the press agent.

"Well, whattaya want? He's a good kid. Doesn't drink, doesn't smoke, doesn't curse."

"How'd a misfit like that ever get into basketball?" Pete Tyles cracked.

"He *is* a little different," Carbon admitted.

"It won't show," I said.

"What's that mean?" the PR man asked.

"He's a Wasp, isn't he?"

2

The Wasps, for the benefit of nonfans, were a team in the National Basketball Association, but they weren't your everyday team or "five," as we sportswriters call them with deadening regularity. Mostly, the Wasps were losers, although they'd sting you once in a while, as the local press was fond of saying in headlines:

WASPS STING BULLETS

CELTS FEEL WASPS'S STING

More often it was a case of stinger stung, because the Wasps were like all expansion teams, slow at first, and picking up momentum slower than most, even though we always had high hopes at the outset of each season:

WASPS HONE STINGERS

WASPS PREPARE TO DO THEIR STING

I, Samuel Evan Forrester, being of more or less sound mind, do depose and confess that I covered the Wasps from the earliest days of the franchise, right after I fled to the *Blade-Mirror* sports department from the women's page, where I spent my rookie year in journalism. If I'd known what awaited me in sports, I might never have transferred. But working with an all-female cast hadn't been any bargain, either. There were four women and me, and every female was called "Miss," "Mrs." or "Ma'am," but I was called "you," "sonny" and "boy." My copy was slashed and torn and sometimes spiked, and I was made to feel like a sex object, even though I'm not particularly handsome, well-groomed or well-dressed, and my dear wife Dulcy says I usually look like a package of seconds marked down from $1.98.

8

The women's editor ("Ma'am") soon had me reduced to handling the recipe column and writing heads like

POTATOES TAKE THE LIMELIGHT

Then one day a reader sent in a recipe for hot chili pancake batter and I ran it along with her name in boldface: Mrs. S. Tuneros. When the paper came off the press, the managing editor rushed into the women's department. "We've been flummoxed, you dumb bitch!" he shouted at "Ma'am," and when she pointed to me, the big boss ran over to my desk and screamed, "There's no 'S. Tuneros,' you jerk!"

I just sat up straight and looked humble.

"We got *taken* on S. Tuneros, dummy!" the editor went on. "Spell it backwards!"

There was a long meeting in the editor's office, and sports editor Tex Pecos was assigned as my keeper. I became a sportswriter, the lowest form of humanity after child molesters, and from then on I always spelled names backwards before running them. Yes, I did. Me, Mas Retserrof.

That was ten years ago, just before the contest to name the city's new pro basketball team. I ran the contest myself, as my first *B-M* sports assignment. A ton of suggestions buried me and the whole staff for a month. We picked through every conceivable name, including "Totems" and "Rockets" and "Pipers" and "Blue Devils," names so terrific they'd already been taken. From the beginning, team executives insisted that they wouldn't call the club anything that human beings couldn't actually *be*—which ruled out names like "Crows," "Cats," "Coyotes," and "Tomahawks." We also ruled out smart-ass suggestions like "Coons" and "Spades."

The winning entry turned out to be the "Men." The first owner of the team, a nightclub impresario, made it up himself, which saved some prize money. The name lasted for two seasons, during which time the "Men" spent their entire time in the "Cellar." When another owner bought the franchise and hired Darius Guile as general manager, the new management dubbed the team the Wasps, and isn't that a pip?

"Mr. Guile," I said respectfully, "that name is a mistake. What fan can relate to a Wasp? They're the bad guys of the insect world. They don't even give honey."

9

"My boy, the name's perfect," Guile said, throwing an arm loosely about my shoulder. "Exactly what we want for our image. Wasps are light on their feet, and quick to move. And Wasps can sting."

Nice insects finish last.

"Mr. Guile," I persisted, slipping out of his overfriendly hold, "Wasp stands for White Anglo-Saxon Protestant." In those years the club was 50 percent black, and anybody with eyes could see that the pro game was making a sharp change in complexion. Who could identify with a bunch of black jocks called Wasps? "At least call them the Basps," I pleaded.

"Foolish carping."

"Then call them the Carps! *Anything* except Wasps."

"The name'll catch on," Darius Guile insisted. "It's been market-researched and tested. You'll see."

Well, I saw. The name caught on—as a synonym for bumbling basketball. In all, we'd had four last-place finishes in four years, then a stunning rise to next-to-last, followed by four more years of last. The Wasps flitted from bush to bush, light on their feet, more often off their feet, funnier than the Globetrotters. They developed traditions, such as never scoring the opening goal, losing tip-offs, and fouling out at least two players. Wise guys said our slogan was: "Losing isn't anything, it's the only thing." There were local fans who had attended 15 or 20 games without seeing their heroes win. The Wasps were studied by a team of social scientists, and a monograph was written about them: "Defeat from the Jaws of Victory: or The Klutz Syndrome," by T. George Hairston. It was reprinted in *Psychology Today,* and the issue had the lowest newsstand sale in the magazine's history.

Some said the club should have been called the Fats, or the Obese Oblige. The board of directors was overweight to the last man. General Manager Guile was shaped like a beaver, Jack Carbon had a belly of pure Budweiser, and our trainer, Armando "Pasty" Pasticcino, distributed his 250 pounds evenly over five feet six. While the players were being pummeled and massaged and spritzed and steamed to within an inch of their bones, the rest of the staff lived on pasta, beer and mashed potatoes. They were a graceful sight in their plum-and-white blazers, waddling through the lobbies of luxury hotels like the Inner City Plaza in Minneapolis and the South Philly Hilton, little wasps embroidered

10

on their breast pockets, gelatinous ass cheeks wiggling through their slacks. My secret fantasy was to snap my fingers and change the breast designs into sea elephants.

3

Back at the dorm, there was a message for me to call Stacy Shoulders, an insurance man in town. Shoulders was the type who buys tickets in blocks and flies his own Cessna to games and would consider it the crowning achievement of his life if the Wasps made the playoffs. He was the treasurer of the Hive, our booster club.

"What can I do for you?" I said over the phone, hoping to keep it short. The Stacy Shoulderses of this world are the business office's headache, not mine.

"Sam, can you keep a secret?"

"Can I keep a secret? Does a bear make do-do in the woods?"

Shoulders didn't seem to get my clever response. "What?" he said. There are guys like that. All they can do is smile and make money. Stacy had made millions. The poor fool!

"Yeh, Stace," I said, trying to regain my dignity, "I can keep a secret. What's up? You preggers?"

"I'm trusting you, Sam, because I need your expertise. This could be important to the Wasps. This could be important to the whole NBA."

He mumbled and stumbled around for another five minutes, begging me to keep his secret, reminding me that it was a violation of insurance ethics to confide in a layman on a professional matter.

"Look, Stace," I snapped into the phone, "tell me or don't tell me. I got things to do."

"Your new man? Broussard Massy?" His voice dropped to a whisper. *"He just took out an insurance policy with us."*

"No shit!" I said, trying to sound properly amazed, when in fact I was having trouble staying awake. "Took out a policy, eh? Son of a gun!"

"For five hundred thousand dollars."

"Excuse me, Stacy," I said. The antique phones at training camp were hand-crafted by dwarfs in the Black Forest. "Say again," I instructed. "I have a banana in my ear."

"How'd you get a banana in your ear?"

"Massy bought a policy," I said, slowly and distinctly, realizing I had to play it absolutely straight. "For how much?"

"Five hundred thousand dollars."

"A half mil? You're putting me on."

"Putting you on what?"

"You're kidding."

"I'm *not* kidding! I was as surprised as you. A half-million dollar policy. Straight life. Premium seven thousand a year."

"Well, what's worrying you?" I said, trying to collect my thoughts. "You're not afraid you'll have to pay off, are you?"

Shoulders said, "That's the Pru's problem. I'm just the middleman." But he did wonder what was going on. Was the kid expecting to "pass away," as Stacy put it, or was he just a superworrier, or was he the sole support of a hidden family of 18 somewhere in the bayous of his home state?

"I wish I knew," I said. "Did you give him a physical?"

"EKG, barium, X rays, the works. Cost us a hundred and fifty dollars. That young fella is sound, believe me. Doc said he's the strongest human being he's ever tested."

"Did the doc grab his balls and tell him to turn his head and cough?"

"I guess so."

"Well, Massy told me that's the test he hates the most. The doctor always makes him take off his truss and disconnect his Pacemaker."

"What?"

I told Stace I was only spoofing—what a straight arrow!—and signed off, promising to find out what I could. God knows he'd posed an interesting question. How many untried young professional athletes would shell out $7000 a year for insurance? Straight life is something you buy for others, not for yourself, and you pay and pay and pay to protect your loved ones. Jocks aren't famous for such altruism.

Besides, the kid hadn't even made the club yet, and if his performance in the first week of camp meant anything, he'd never make it, and then how would he pay the premium?

Nothing made sense. The kid was earth-simple in his tastes, that was for certain. I'd seen his room and I'd seen his clothes. Blue jeans on his ass and a single framed painting on his wall: A bunch of horses running across a pasture with their manes flying. A regular Woolworth's special, frame included, $1.49. The rest of his room looked like a monastic cell. There was nothing to suggest that the occupant was a man with expensive tastes in insurance.

Then I had a brilliant thought. Maybe the kid really was a mental case, just as my Mystery Caller had insisted weeks ago. And being a mental case, maybe he was planning suicide. Why else take out the policy?

But who'd benefit?

And how? Why? *When?*

I dialed Stacy back, and he shot down my theory. The policy paid off on suicide, sure, but not if the act took place within the first 60 months 60. "We discussed it for quite a while," Shoulders told me. "Suicide and murder—he seemed very interested. A lot of our clients are. I told him, 'Don't bother killing yourself. The Wasps need you, and the Pru wouldn't pay off.' I was just sort of kidding him."

"Then why the hell's he bought that policy?" I said, half to myself.

"That's why I called you," the insurance man said. "I knew you'd come up with the answer."

Sure, I'll come up with the answer. The difficult takes a while, the impossible a little longer. "He tackled the task that couldn't be done —and couldn't do it." The story of my life.

4

You may think that a package of 8–2 requires no special handling, that the kid was just the same as a stretched-out six-footer, but right from the jump I learned otherwise. In the second week of training camp, the general manager yanked me out of a poker game and said, "Sam, do me a favor."

When you hear those words from Darius Guile, master manipulator of fans, dice and player contracts, flinch! I flinched. "Please, please," I said, "no more favors. I haven't got over the last one."

"What was that?" the shiny-pated master of chicanery replied.

"The one where you asked me to line up a date for that redhead from Chicago?"

"Oh, yeh," Guile said, blowing smoke in my face. "Well, how was I suppose to know?" What he hadn't known was that the flame-haired beauty whom I'd fixed up with our bachelor sports editor Tex Pecos was of the male persuasion, underneath her pancake makeup and fox wrap. The editor had got to the nut of the matter about 3 A.M., after a long evening of champagne, caviar and dance.

"No more favors, D. G.," I said. "But thanks for thinking of me."

"Sam, listen," Guile said, grabbing me by the arm. "The kid can't sleep. He's bruised all over from practice, and he hangs two feet over the end of the bed."

"Isn't that the normal number?"

"Two feet in length, not in feet!" Guile said impatiently. "We tried putting a coupla beds together, but his room's too small."

The GM's message was already loud and clear. The senior press statesman on the beat, good old Sam Forrester, was the proud tenant of the only out-sized room on the floor, the room used by the hall proctor during the regular school year, and it had taken me six years of waiting to fall into such luxury.

"Look, pal, this big stiff isn't gonna make the club," Guile ran on smoothly. "I know it, you know it, the whole world knows it. So how long can it last, changing rooms with him? A week? Ten days?"

"Six years? Ten years?"

"If this kid lasts more'n two weeks I'll kiss your ass in Colonel Sanders's parking lot."

"I'm not giving up my room," I said. "Dulcy's coming this weekend."

"Yeh, well, you think about it," the GM said tartly. "But don't think about it in your room. Go someplace else to think about it." He turned and walked off in his customary cloud of busyness and smoke.

I rushed to the dorm just in time to see two big custodians shoving my desk along the hall. My old room had been turned into a repository of size 28 sneakers, used jockstraps and books, and two beds had been joined lengthwise against the wall, providing about 12 feet of comfort. I hurried over to Massy's old room in the rooks' bay. Sure enough, my framed picture of Dulcimer was balanced on the washstand.

14

"Good of you to do this, Mr. Forrester," one of the custodians said as he jammed my desk alongside the narrow bed, exhausting almost the last square inch of floor space.

"I'm a team man," I said modestly.

That night I quit the poker game early, figuring I could use a solid eight hours' sleep for a change. It was raining hard, but the downpour didn't keep an owl from trying to make a connection in the giant oak outside my window. He'd call HOO, HOO, HOO, *hoo hoo hoo,* hoohoohoo, speeding up the tempo toward the end, and from the distance there'd be a coy response: *Who?* as though to make sure this was true love and not just a roll in the leaves.

I entertained myself by listening till the owls flew off to find a motel and then I dropped into a fitful sleep, full of towering granite cliffs and serpents and sports editors; I never sleep well when the bed's lumpy and the room's overheated and my wife's 35 miles away. It must have been three in the morning when I woke up and cried out, "What?" the way I often do, and Dulcy reaches out and pats me comfortingly and I roll over and go back to sleep, only this time nobody patted me so I just lay there with the pillow half wrapped around my sweaty head and peered into the solid blackness and listened to the rain. *Hey, who moved my window from the right side of the room to the left?* Oh, yeh, Massy and I had exchanged rooms. No problem. He'd be gone soon.

Ever since childhood I've had a natural aptitude for terror. I almost enjoy scaring myself and then pulling the sheet over my head and going back to sleep. A grown man! Now I listened and thought I detected movement—a tiny murmur by the door, felt rather than heard.

A mouse? The old building creaking in the storm? Well, there wasn't much point in going to bed early if I spent half the night imagining things. I turned on my side and shut my eyes hard and started counting to myself, one of my old sleep techniques. Usually I'd begin messing up the count by the time I reached a few hundred, and then I'd fall fast asleep. It'd go, ". . . 191 192 193 194 196 197 194 161 *zzzzzzz.* . . ."

But I'd only reached 50 when I was sure I heard breathing.

Without turning my head, I peered toward the dark walls, looking at gradations of black, till I came to an extra-dense patch in the outline of a man, an FBI target silhouette, leaning alongside the door. A bucket of shaved ice slid down my back, but then I told myself to relax. For about the thousandth time, I'd mistaken my hanging bathrobe for an intruder.

Then I remembered I wasn't in my regular room.

I slipped one hand from under the covers and slowly reached toward the floor. My bathrobe was right where I'd left it, alongside the bed.

Then the patch on the wall spoke:

"*Ssshhhh.* Don't talk. I got a gun."

I didn't know the etiquette for talking to prowlers, and besides every cord and nerve in my neck had turned to wire. I couldn't have uttered a peep if I'd tried.

"Look, kid, we been patient," the man went on. He sounded calm and reasonable, like an accountant or a schoolteacher, not especially intimidating, except that any voice coming off your wall in the dead of night is bound to be unnerving.

"Leavin' a little present for you," the voice went on, just above a whisper. He seemed to have a hint of an accent, but I was too preoccupied to figure it out. "Better play it our way, podna." His *r*'s were soft, almost unpronounced. "Next time you get it in the face." The door opened without a sound. "Wise up, kid," he whispered, "or you and Mike and Leon, you're all dead." Against the dull backlight from the hall I could make out the edges of a medium-sized man, and then he was gone. I realized whom he sounded like: Bob Cousy, or a close relative.

My heart rate slowed to a mere 150 and my breath stopped coming in gasps. Then I noticed a stench spreading through the room, like rotten eggs. I snapped on the overhead bulb and saw a wisp of yellowish smoke spiralling toward the ceiling. A puddle of amber liquid seemed to be eating away at the dresser. I reached out to touch, the curious child, but quickly pulled back.

I grabbed a towel from the bathroom and sopped up the fluid, keeping it off my hands, and by the time I could rinse the towel in the full force of the cold-water tap, holes had been eaten in the cloth. I mopped up as best I could, using the old high school chemistry advice: When you can't neutralize acid, drown it.

Then I sat on the edge of my bed and tried to make sense.

Should I call the local cops? By the time they got here the man would be long gone from the campus, and how would I ever identify him? I could imagine the conversation with the local constabulary. They'd be sore that I'd bothered them at—let's see, 3:24 A.M. "Okay, Mac, we understand. Had a bad dream. Now try'n get some sleep."

Maybe I should arouse somebody else. But who? Nick Storen? He'd splash it all over page one the next day:

INTRUDER THREATENS WASP REPORTER

MYSTERY DEVELOPS

AT TRAINING CAMP

Pete Tyles would probably do the same. So would Pa. and Lucious.

Well, I could talk it over with Darius Guile or the coach or the trainer. But what could they do? Good basketball heads, sure, but this didn't happen to be a basketball problem.

So I called the brains of the family. "Are you awake, honey?" I said nervously.

"I am now," Dulcy's cold voice replied. "Sam, let me guess. You've been playing poker and you're twelve dollars ahead and you just had to tell somebody, and I'm the lucky one. Well, *damn!* I was sound asleep. Sometimes you can be so inconsiderate!" Then all in the same breath she rattled on, "Oh, I wish you were here, sweetheart. It's so cold in this bed."

"Listen, honey, I don't want you to get nervous or anything, but a man just poured acid on the dresser and the next time I'll get it in the face and so will Mike and Leon."

"Oh, *sweetheart!*" Dulcy said sympathetically. She sounded as though she were talking to one of the five-year-olds she sees in her social work. "Such a bad dream! Did you have a teentsy-weentsy too much to drink in the poker game? Oh, you're such a baby when you're alone."

"Dulcy, this wasn't a dream. *Dulcy!* Listen to me, I'm wide awake. I'm looking at a big scar on the dresser. I can still smell burning wood and acid fumes."

"What?"

"Honey, I'm a little shook. I'm not thinking straight. So I called."

My dear wife asked me to run through the minute-by-minute events of the evening, and as soon as I told her about switching rooms with Massy, she said, "Tell me again what the prowler said first."

" 'Don't talk. I've got a gun.' "

"And then?"

"He said, 'Look, kid, we been patient.' "

17

"Kid?"

"Kid."

"Who'd call you kid, Sam? You're thirty-six years old."

"Yeh, who?"

"Honey, don't you see it? He thought you were Massy."

She hit on it. "Honey, you're—uh—dead right, you figured it out, go on back to sleep, I gotta rush now, goodbye, sweetheart."

"To call the police?"

"To talk to the kid."

Massy's new room, my old one, was at the far end of the hall, on the corner of the ivy-covered building. I tiptoed down the corridor, and drummed my fingernails against his door. I hoped he'd answer fast, before some light sleeper woke up and asked why the hell I was making house calls in my bathrobe at four in the morning.

No answer.

I knocked.

Still no answer.

I called out in a stage whisper: "Bru! Broussard! *Massy!*" and knocked harder.

There was a stirring inside, and a fuzzy voice said, "Who is it?"

"It's me. Forrester. *Blade-Mirror.*"

"I'm sleeping."

"Bru, it's important!"

"The building burning?"

"No. It's——"

"Then go 'way!"

"Listen to me!" I croaked. "They're after you and Mike and Leon."

The door opened on creaky hinges, and the kid loomed two feet above me in a dashiki that looked as big as a bedsheet. I stepped inside. *"Who's* after *who?"* he asked, flipping on a light and revealing a wrinkled forehead.

I told him the story, only leaving out my fluctuating pulse. At first he appeared alarmed, but as I ran on I got the impression that he thought I was a little nuts. Or was he trying to convince me that nothing I said had anything to do with him? He kept glancing from me to a Christ on the Cross that hung above his bed.

"What's happening, man?" I demanded at the end.

"Who knows?" Massy said, walking toward the door. "Maybe you made an enemy?"

18

"Bullshit," I said. "C'mon, Bru."

"I don't have the slightest idea," the big man said, turning from what I tried to make an intense stare.

"What's it mean: 'We been patient, kid'?"

"How would I know, Mr. Forrester?"

I couldn't believe it. Somebody had a pitcher of acid with "Broussard Massy" written on it, and the kid was trying to act bored. I coaxed and cajoled, but he just stood at the door with his hand on the knob. "Bru, you've got to tell me!" I said. "I *know* that man wasn't looking for me. I *know* he was after you, Bru. Who's Mike? Who's Leon?"

He took his hand off the doorknob and spoke emphatically. "Mr. Forrester, I think you mean well, you surely do, but you're on a bad track. Now please, sir, stop asking questions I can't answer. If I could, I would—honest, I would, Mr. Forrester. You got to believe me." If he hadn't been eight feet tall, I'd have sworn he was about to start bawling.

"Mr. Forrester," he went on, "I'll give the club everything I got. I'll play till I fall down. I *want* to make the club, sir, I *got* to make it. But the personal stuff, that could be the end of it, on the court and off."

"But somebody's threatening to blind you, disfigure you. . . ."

"If you keep insisting, Mr. Forrester," the kid went on, as though I hadn't opened my mouth, "I'm gonna purely have to be rude. I want you to understand, this isn't the way I want it, this is the way it is." He snapped off the bare bulb that lit my old room and opened the door into the hall. "Now, sir," he whispered, "I'd appreciate it if you'd go. I haven't been restin' much lately."

"Sure, kid," I said, thoroughly confused. "Sleep tight."

He'd already closed the door behind me.

I stayed awake the rest of the night. I kept seeing Bru Massy walking toward me.

Here he comes, closer and closer.

What is it about him that's different?

He has no face.

•   •   •

5

Coach Francis X. "Buttsy" Rafferty counted aloud for calisthenics, but after a while Buttsy stopped and Abdul Buzruz took up the count and that meant everybody had to work twice as hard. Buz counted the way he did everything else—efficiently, hup-two, hup-two, hup-two, *zoom! zoom! zoom!* and pretty soon the maple floor was puddled with sweat. Big Massy stood in the rear, probably so he wouldn't bump into the regulars, and he kept up with everybody else through the jumping jacks and the windmills and the squat, but when Buzruz called for the monkey leap and the eagle jump, the big man missed a few beats.

The whistle blew sharply. "Hey, rook, you cain't count or sumpin'?"

Massy didn't answer, just looked at the floor, eight feet below the tip of his thin straight nose.

"Now let's try again!" Buz led the men in whirligigs, increasing the speed till even some of the smaller players were falling behind. Massy spun his lanky frame while the black curls stood straight out from his head, and somehow he kept close to the pace.

"Hup two and *halt!*" Buz snapped. Massy's feet skidded out from under him and he hit the hardwood floor with a dull clunk. Pasty the rotund trainer duck-walked over like a chubby Buster Keaton and said, "You okay?" Massy just climbed slowly to his feet.

"Don't rub!" I said to myself, and he didn't. At least he had some class.

When calisthenics were over, Coach Rafferty put the team through buddy drills and line drills and a light scrimmage. Massy looked so clumsy I didn't think he could find his ear with a roadmap, let alone play an intricate free-lancing game like professional basketball. I sat in the stands with Darius Guile, watching our poor coach try to drub some life into the club, and every once in a while I'd turn to look at the GM out of the corner of my eyes, and he looked like a man who has just reentered the house after the fire. When the kid got knocked on his ass for the fourth time, I said, "D. G., you're not serious about this monster, are you?"

"The coach is," he muttered, leaning forward and propping his head in his open hands.

Nick Storen of the *Item* came over and sat, uninvited. Down on the court, Buttsy Rafferty was running the centers through an outlet drill. On his first attempt, Massy lobbed the ball six feet over the head of Sweet Basil McBride, and Buttsy blew the whistle and hollered, "Lead him, son, *lead* him! That don't mean throw the ball a mile over his head. Everybody ain't eight foot tall."

Massy resumed his position under the basket, and this time when Coach fired the ball at the backboard to set the drill in motion, the big man missed the rebound completely. "Ooo-*ow!*" Red Green commented. "We in trouble!"

Buttsy's whistle chirped. He shook his head from side to side, like a parent with a fractious child. Massy looked at the floor, saying nothing, as usual.

Two seats away, I heard Nick Storen snicker. "Holy Christ, D. G.," he said, "the freak's a menace to navigation. He'll kill somebody."

"Unless the other players kill him first," I said. He was taking a pounding in every scrimmage.

"Give it a chance," Guile said. This time he sounded like someone who's about to abandon all hope.

"That kid can't walk and chew gum at the same time," Storen said.

"He's not running for President," snapped the GM.

Nick Storen was a cynic, one of those reporters who could spot the bad side of Mother Cabrini and hold her up for ridicule. When the Wasps lost, you could count on Nick to describe their errors in enthusiastic detail. He'd write: *The 76ers tried to give the Wasps a Christmas gift last night, but our hometown lads were too shy to accept.* Or: *The Wasps were incompetent, but the Bullets were worse. . . .* Very clever stuff, as you can see: vinegar cocktails. He was like the *B-M* copyreader who'd written a head:

COLD CURE IN SIGHT:
DOCTORS' JOBS ENDANGERED

"The new man'll never make it," Nick told Coach Buttsy Rafferty during a break in the morning work. "Never."

Coach leaned back and said, "Well, basically what'd you expect from this kid? I mean from the standpoint that he hasn't played in like eight, nine years. Do you take and judge a kid on his first days back like that? That's harsh, Nicholas, pertaining to athletes."

This was vintage Francis X. "Buttsy" Rafferty, looking as though he was about to burst into tears and uttering favorite locutions like "from the standpoint" and "basically" and "pertaining to," and his superfavorite, "take and," as in "take and roll off the pick," or "take and order us a beer." At 52, Buttsy had the typical coach's vocabulary, or lack of one, but somehow the players usually understood his Stengelese. I never regarded it as Buttsy's fault that the Wasps were losers. Give us a couple of star guards, a dominating center and a pair of sharpshooting forwards and the whole club could turn around. The coaching was already solid. Though not as solid as the board of directors and the trainer.

"Why bother with this freak?" Nick Storen was saying. "He's a piano player, not a center."

"Listen," Coach said, "pertaining to this kid let me just say that basically he's got the skills, got the ability. It's just that he doesn't have the skills and the ability yet."

We gentlemen of the press remained silent at this gem of paradox.

"With some handling and understanding," Buttsy continued, "this kid can be the greatest that ever played. Take and take a look at him over there."

I took and took a look. Massy's tongue hung like a marathoner's, his black ringlets dangled like wet ebony shavings, and he was slumped against the wall of the gym, in violation of standing instructions.

"I'm looking," Nick Storen said. "All I can see is a big stoop."

"Well, not forever," Coach said. "We'll give him some handling, see how he picks up. He's got the potential, from the standpoint that he used to be a player."

"In junior high," Nick reminded.

"Develop him slow," the Butts said. "Basically it's like handling a bird. Take and hold him too tight, and you crush him. Too loose and he flies away."

"Too long and he'll shit in your hand," Storen added, heading for the exit.

"Whyn't you write about it?" Coach called out. "Don't tell us, tell your readers!"

22

"Yeh," Pete Tyles of the *Herald* hollered at Storen's retreating form. "All twelve of 'em."

A couple of mornings later, Storen's column "A Little Trick with Nick" tore into GM Darius Guile for giving Massy a tryout. Under the subhead

WASPS COURTING DISASTER

Nick had written:

> *When the team should be concentrating on patterns and plays and fundamentals of the game, such as what in the world is that round leather thing bouncing out there, the Wasps are wasting time on an eight-foot two-inch glandular error from Louisiana who plainly wishes he was back in Cajun Country messing up Chopin instead of here in the big city messing up roundball. Broussard Massy hasn't bothered to touch a basketball since junior high, preferring to take part in "cultural" pursuits such as sonatas and fugues, but when you see him on the court you wonder how he ever managed to keep his balance on the piano stool. The Wasps are stuck with eight foot two inches of clumsiness. They should have settled for two good players of four foot one.*

"How sweet!" Dulcy said as she flung down the Sunday paper in my little room at camp. "I just love the human kindliness in Nick's writing. Who taught him, the Marquis de Sade?"

"Nick can't help it," I said. "He's bitter. He's had a hard life."

"He ought to be cleaning toilets for a living," my wife said.

"I could tell you a few things, honey, but I won't."

"You already have."

A few years back, Nick had been a hot prospect on the *Item*, but then his wife left him and married a successful free-lance writer. Nick discovered the solace of sour mash, and before long he wasn't a hot prospect anymore. I'd seen it happen to dozens of journalists: if they fell behind a certain rhythm, they were doomed to work on newspapers the rest of their lives, and who should know better than Samuel Evan Forrester? You either accepted your fate and tried to be the best

23

damned newspaperman around, which is nothing to be ashamed of, or you soured.

Before he pulled himself together, Nick came within a half inch of losing his job, but the *Item* gave him one last chance. You guessed it. The Wasps. A marriage made in heaven. If ever a beat called for a misanthrope, it was the Wasps. The lousier they played, the better Nick liked it. He became the Heinrich Himmler of the sports department, battening on others' errors, wallowing in young jocks' embarrassments. He was also a murderous lowball poker player. No matter what you held, he held worse. That was his karma, and he reveled in it.

6

The team was supposed to work out for a month before hitting the exhibition trail, and "the Terrible Turk" struck six times in the first two weeks, but he never came near Bru Massy. The Terrible Turk was the players' nickname for getting cut, as in "Look out, here comes the Terrible Turk." It was sorrowful enough to make the Wasps, but to be dropped by the Wasps was like being canned as a volunteer fireman.

One morning I called on the GM in his temporary office to find out when Broussard Massy would be cut. "The big guy?" Darius Guile said. "Cut? Why? He's doing as good as can be expected."

"How good is that?"

"Well, we've taught him how to tie his shoes. How to find himself in the dark, using two hands. Which way to face when he takes a leak."

"Sounds like he's almost a Wasp."

"No way. But try to tell Rafferty. He's got some kind of crazy idea."

"Yeh, I heard."

On the face of it, Buttsy's idea wasn't exactly crazy, just slightly ridiculous. Over a beer in the coaches' room, he outlined it to me. "I know the kid looks clumsy out there, from the standpoint of coordination, but did you ever think what he could accomplish if he put it together?"

"Coach," I said, "being a giant's not enough. Look around. There's dozens of big guys, but how many Jabbars? How many Chamberlains or Russells?"

"Sure," the Butts said, grabbing my arm with excitement, "but Jabbar and Wilt, they're fucking pygmies next to this guy. *Eight foot two!* Why, that gives him a foot on the tallest guy that ever played!"

"What good's an extra foot if you keep tripping over it?"

"Sam, basically it's just a matter of retraining the old reflexes. Don't forget, this kid's been banging a piano for eight years."

I'd been wondering about that. "How come he drops piano all of a sudden and comes back to basketball?"

"Hey, you know the ground rules!" Rafferty said. "That's personal." He scratched the back of the salt-and-pepper fuzz that ringed his gleaming dome. "We promised not to release anything pertaining to his private life. So I'm not saying." He hesitated. "Also, I don't know."

I thought about the $500,000 insurance policy and the prowler in my room, and I wondered if the coach had any inside information. Probably not. The kid was a stone wall. When I knew the whole story, I'd write it. Till then it was between Massy and me.

"But you think it'll be worth it in the long run?" I asked. "All this time and energy to turn him into a player just because he's tall?"

"Sammy," Buttsy said, waving his arms like a Roman orator, "basically this kid is the answer to the problem we've been looking for."

"He's what?"

"He can turn the whole franchise around, the whole NBA. Why, if he gets his self together——"

"That's some 'if.' "

"——He'll be a one-man team. They'll have to take and change the fucking rules! With that kid in the middle, you could play Martha Mitchell and Eleanor Roosevelt in back and Truman Kaypote and Henry Kissinger in front and whip everybody's ass. That's the one thing we been lacking all these years—a big, strong, eight-foot center."

"Sure," I said. "Who hasn't?"

That evening Dulcy brought up the subject of the man with the acid for about the tenth time, and for about the tenth time we couldn't get out of the starting gate. "I guess it's just no use," my brilliant wife said. "Massy knows the answer, but——"

"Massy won't talk," I interrupted.

"And if you brought in the police or the front office——"

"It'd just get worse. The way the kid reacts, it wouldn't surprise me if he ran all the way back to Louisiana. What was it he said?"

"Something like if you kept prying into his personal life, it could be the end of everything?"

"Yeh. That takes in a lot of territory." A light breeze lifted the gauze curtain on my dormitory room, and I felt a stirring in my aging bones.

"C'mon, honey," I said, taking Dulcy by the hand. "Let's walk."

We strolled across the big open lawn in front of the dorms and then settled into a lazy pace, hands locked together. We reached the Maxine Peterson Music Chapel just as dusk was beginning to settle over the little campus. The air was light and perfumed, and so was my wife. We had almost the whole college to ourselves. A few of the players were back in the dorms, but most of the regulars had gone into the village to do field work. There was no convenient motel in nearby Battenberg and next to no privacy in the dorm, but there were plenty of convenient greenswards and wooded nooks where lovers could discuss philosophy.

Dulcy and I were headed for one ourselves, although she didn't know it yet. As we walked arm in arm around the empty music chapel she stopped and tilted her head. A quizzical look flickered across her face, and I could tell she was trying to dope something out. That's the way she is—one second she'll be rolling along without a care in the world and the next she'll blurt out something like "Erik Erikson."

"Huh?" I'll say.

"Our new butcher? I was trying to think who he looked like. It's Erik Erikson. What a relief!"

But this time she wasn't thinking about something, she was hearing something. "Don't you hear it, Sam?" she asked.

I listened hard, but all I could make out was a raucous choir of birds in the oak woods just beyond the chapel.

Dulcy held her hand up for silence. "It's piano," she said, "and it's playing—it's playing. . . ." She shut her sea-green eyes and frowned, but no answer came.

"It's playing, 'Hooray, hooray, the first of May,' " I said impatiently.

"Sam!"

She began to quarter the lawn like a springer spaniel, stopping now and then to cup an ear toward the dark brick wall of the auditorium, and then she snapped her fingers and said, "It's Ravel!" You have to understand that my wife is capable of picking music out of the air anyplace, whether music is actually being played or not. She comes from a family of music freaks, and that accounts for her given name, Dulcimer, in honor of the instrument her mother was practicing the night of conception. Lucky it wasn't a French horn.

"Oh, sure, it's Ravel," I said sarcastically, "and as soon as the applause dies down, our lovely songbirds will swing into 'America the Beautiful' while flying backward in formation."

"Listen!" my beautiful wife said, dragging me closer to one of the stained-glass windows. A shaft of sunlight pierced the foliage and shone on the blond hair that hung to her tiny waist. Who cared about Ravel? Let us knit up the Ravel'd sleeve of care and skip nimbly to the woods and. . . .

I caught a note or two, and then a brighter passage, up and down the scales, rapidissimo. Someone inside was playing a record.

"Grieg?" I said.

"Oh, Sam, it's all Grieg to you," Dulcy said, looking at me disappointedly. Well, she was right. The Grieg piano concerto was my style, and proud of it. For 20 years I hadn't even known its title; I'd thought it was Liberace's theme song, because he played it every five or ten minutes. When Dulcy brought home the Artur Rubinstein version, I told her it was nice that the great master had finally recorded the Liberace theme. "Rubinstein has a nice touch," I remember saying at the time.

"Ravel," Dulcy repeated as she balanced on tiptoes outside the music auditorium, her slender ankles tensing below gently curving caives. "It's his—it's his—Piano Concerto in G Major! No wonder it stopped for a few seconds. The pianist was between movements. Now he's playing the presto. Hear? Oh, honey, doesn't it sound jazzy? Catch the resemblance to Le Tombeau de Couperin?"

I furrowed my brow like an expert and said, "I can't get interested in a composer who steals." By now the record seemed to be approaching its climax, which I viewed as painfully ironic. I bit my tongue to keep from admitting it: The pianist was good. Even I could tell. He was slipping up and down the scale in a series of dazzling runs, and he didn't slop the notes together, the way some musicians do. Each note was clear and distinct, and yet they all made sense as a group, like a school of shad.

Suddenly the record was over. That was one of my objections to the far-out composers my wife admired—their music always ended without an ending so you didn't know when to clap.

"My God, Sam," Dulcy was saying, a tortured expression on her face, "that was beautiful! Not just beautiful, Sam. That was spectacular!"

The massive doors of the Maxine Peterson Music Chapel opened a crack and a face appeared just as the last flare of the sun fizzled and died. Blended into the shrubbery, Dulcy and I watched as the door opened wider and a large form shambled down the steps. It was either Samson with poor posture or Broussard Massy.

"Hey, kid!" I called.

At the sound of my voice he jumped all the way to the bottom of the staircase and took off like a scalded elk, not jogging, not loping, but sprinting wildly, his black curls flying behind him in the dying light, as if a thousand demons were on his case.

"Bravo!" Dulcy said after him. *"Bravissimo!"*

The big man never broke stride till he was out of sight.

"For God's sake, honey," I said, "what're you saying bravo about? All he was doing was playing a record."

"A record? Oh, Sam!" Dulcy broke into giggles. "Sam, the Ravel concerto's for full orchestra. All we heard was one piano, running through the parts. It had to be live."

I didn't want to expose my dear wife's ignorance, especially on such a mellow evening, but I couldn't resist leading her inside the chapel. I was dead certain we'd find a slowly spinning phonograph topped by Ravel's Piano Concerto in C Major or whatever it was, the one with the amputated ending.

An upright piano had been wheeled to center stage, and the stool been screwed down till it made me look like a midget when I sat on it. There wasn't a phonograph in sight. "Sweetheart," Dulcy said, a reverent look on her face, "do you realize what we overheard?"

"Massy's first concert?" I said.

"His first! And we were *there,* Sam. We were the only ones! Why, I could hardly tell it from Horowitz. Could you?"

"No," I said in all honesty. "I couldn't tell it from Horowitz." Matter of fact, I couldn't tell Horowitz.

Dulcy looked tired the next morning. She had to get up at six to prepare for the drive back to town, and I walked her out to the parking lot. "I didn't sleep much," she confesssed just before she drove away.

"I know," I said, trying to sound wicked, but just sounding tired.

"Oh, Sam, I didn't think about it till two or three in the morning, and then I kept thinking about it all night long."

"About what?"

"That sad strange boy." She took a deep breath. "I couldn't get him out of my mind."

Dulcy's green eyes were laced with just enough light red lines to make her look sultry and dissipated, a psychiatric social-working Tondelayo. She raised them to mine.

"Haven't you been thinking about him too?" she asked.

I had to admit I hadn't. Maybe I'm just insensitive, but I was becoming inured to Massy's peculiarities. "I'll talk to him, honey," I said as she slid under the leather wheel of our Spitfire. Damn kid! Why couldn't he just be neurotic, like an ordinary jock?

Well, there was only one way to find out what was going on. I'd have to ask questions. Act aggressive. Maybe pay a call on the big man. Who knew? If I kept it up, I might be mistaken for a reporter.

7

After breakfast, I walked to the gym to visit Armando "Pasty" Pasticcino, the Wasps's trainer and gourmand and amateur quack. It was 9 A.M., an hour before the morning work, and Pasty hadn't arrived yet, so I took a seat on the sidelines and waited. Not a soul had been in the gym for maybe 12 hours, but it still smelled of maple and canvas shoes and sweat socks and shower steam and liniment and wintergreen and leather and overheated jocks.

I know people who dislike the smell of gyms—my wife, for one, says it's "gagging"—but I enjoy it, and I even enjoy going into a locker room after a game and doing interviews. How else would an ordinary guy get into a major-league locker room?

Every player has his own distinctive aroma. Sweet Basil McBride sweats pure aftershave. I got up the nerve to ask him about it once and he said he'd taken a lot of "Florida dry baths," quick towel-downs followed by generous splashes of Aqua-Velva. "It last two, three hours after the game," Captain Basil told me confidentially. "By that time you either scored or struck out, so what's the difference?"

Waiting for Pasty to show up, I remembered a time when I'd sat in this same seat at courtside while Buttsy Rafferty was drilling the team, and Justin Fell and Red Green ran up and down the court feeding the ball back and forth at high speed, ending in a butter-smooth lay-up. Swept up in the beauty of their maneuvering, I'd suddenly been taken with an impulse to snatch the ball and put up a fancy shot of my own, maybe a Rocket to the Moon with a Cherry on Top, or the old Snakehip Special with a Twist, Earl Monroe variation. I'd leave my feet at the free-throw line and soar through the air like a peregrine falcon and sneak the ball from one hand to the other in midair. I'd fake those pussies out of their jocks and slam-dunk the ball with one hand, and then as it swished through the bottom of the net I'd grab it before it hit the floor and dunk again just for good measure, the way Wilt Chamberlain did one time. Then I'd holler "In your eye!" and stroll back to my seat.

"I better not do it," I mumbled.

"What?" Coach Rafferty said.

"Oh, nothing. I was just thinking how I'd love to be a player for a few minutes."

"You too?" Buttsy said.

"Don't tell me you feel like throwing away your whistle sometimes?"

"Every day, just about," the coach confessed.

I started to ask if that's why he suited up for Wasp games, with a big number "1" on his back and a pair of Converse shoes on his feet, just like a regular player, but I knew that would be hitting too close to home. Every man is entitled to his own free space, his own idiosyncrasies, and I didn't intrude. Buttsy said wearing the uniform helped him feel involved, and that was good enough for me. There wasn't any doubt that he loved the game; his will specified that he be buried with a regulation Wilson ball in his coffin and dressed in his uniform, complete with sneakers and whistle.

"I don't know what came over me," I said, looking out at the black and white shapes cavorting in front of me, sweat beaded on their backs, dancing from one end of the court to the other as easily as I'd cross a sidewalk. "I just felt this urge, you know what I mean?"

"Completely," Buttsy said.

"Well, I better not do it. I'd just fall flat on my ass."

"Eight, ten years ago it'd been different, huh?" the coach asked.

"Eight, ten years ago I tried it," I said.

"What happened?"

"I fell flat on my ass."

Scratch a sportswriter, even a bitter one like Nick Storen, and you'll find an idolator, the same genus as stadium lizards and bubble-gum-card collectors and little boys who wait outside for a five-second glance at their heroes. Jimmy Cannon said, "A sportswriter is entombed in a prolonged boyhood," and Dan Parker called basketball "the silly business of throwing an inflated bag through a hoop." Why, certainly, the whole business is childish, especially with the hype and the overemphasis, and you feel like an idiot when you walk out of the locker room and some kid says, "Autograph, mister?" and you start to sign and another kid says, "Aw, he's only a writer." That actually happened to me once. After that, whenever they asked me to sign, I'd put down, "Red Smith." At least they were getting the best.

Dulcy and I often chewed over these old potatoes, how I'd been dragooned into the "toy department," as she called sports, and how I'd learned to respect the players, because they were real, no fakes, phonies or pretenders allowed: *there's* the charm of sports.

It's like some guy wrote in *Sports Pictorial.* He said he'd once talked to JFK and kept his cool, but Nate Archibald made his knees tremble, because "any American can grow up to become President, but who can grow up to be Nate Archibald except Nate Archibald?" Only Justin Fell could grow up to be Justin Fell, and only Sweet Basil McBride could become Sweet Basil McBride, and so on down the line, all the way to Tyrone "Maraschino" Mays, our twelfth man, unique in his own way, even if he was only a Wasp. You can't fake it in sport; that's what I like.

After 12 years of marriage, Dulcy had begun to get the point. At least she could accept my "prolonged boyhood" or whatever it was. But she was still dubious about fans. "How sad!" she said one night after a sellout against the Knicks. "All those people living vicariously. Watching others, instead of doing something themselves."

I hoped she wasn't about to crank up the old "toy department" analogy. "What should they be doing?"

"Anything. Knitting. Gardening. Making love. Collecting stamps.

Anything but sitting around watching others."

"Everybody can't ride in the chariots, Dulcimer. Somebody has to be in the stands."

"Somebody has to be in the stands?"

"Certainly."

"Why?"

Sometimes my wife can reduce me to a sputter and a dab of grease. "Listen, honey," I said, "fifty million Americans love basketball. Basketball's a jam session, free and wild and open."

She just tilted her perfect nose and said, "Well, fifty million Americans can't be right." I suppose it made sense to her.

"Hey, Sam, you gettin' much?"

"Huh?" I said. I looked up from my courtside reverie and saw Pasty Pasticcino moving across the gym floor like a lopsided bowling ball.

"I said, 'How's your hammer hanging?' "

"It's hanging," I said, pulling myself back to the present. "That's the trouble."

"Come on in, I'll fix you up," the Wasps's trainer said, and I followed him into the training room. I stepped around the hydrocollator and the whirlpool and the two open-air toilets and into the treatment room with its cots and its rows of pills and medicaments, everything from aspirin to morphine, plus enough brand-name products to stock a new league: Q-D-A quick drying adherent, Release tape remover, Cramer Atomic Rubdown Liniment, Cold-spray, Tuf-skin, Germatan, Skin-lube, you name it. You say you jammed your finger and can't get your ring off? Pasty will nip it with his guaranteed Hoffritz ring cutter made of hardened Swedish steel. Feel a little down in the mouth? Have a "gobie," one of Pasty's green-and-orange "diet" pills, especially useful after parties or on long road trips. The old hands haven't toughened up yet? Pasty will spray them with Nu-skin, giving you the hide of a crocodile while your own skin hardens underneath. You say you can't get it up?

"You really can't get it up?" Pasty was asking me. He made a clucking sound with his mouth. "Terrible waste of a gorgeous wife."

"Just a figure of speech, Pasty," I said quickly. "No problem."

"Oh." He sounded sorry that I wasn't suffering from advanced impotence, as though I were trying to deny another challenge to his pharmacopoeia.

"Pasty," I said as he busied himself pulling jerseys and shorts and warm-ups out of the dryer and stuffing towels into the heat packs, "what's with the big guy?"

"Whattaya mean?"

"I mean, what's his story? Like who is he, anyway? What's his background?"

"Non parlo Italiano."

"Christ, we're about to start exhibition games and he's still falling all over himself. Why's he still around even?"

"He's not falling all over himself, he's falling all over the whole fucking team, and the coaches, and the press agent, and if you got to know the truth, the trainer, too." Pasty picked up a limp jockstrap left over from the day before and dropped it in a hamper. "Slobs," he said. "Think I'm their fucking slave."

"Is Buttsy gonna hang onto the kid?"

"Well, if he does, two things are gonna happen. Number one, we're gonna be laughed out of the league. Number two, we're gonna go bankrupt from buying tape."

"He's beginning to look like the mummy's tomb," I said, jumping up on the training table.

"He pisses the other guys off. I've never seen them dish out so much punishment to a rookie. See this?" He held up a new roll of adhesive and a box of Stockinettes, the cheesecloth foundations worn under ankle wraps. "He uses this shit like it's free."

"Well, it is, isn't it?"

"To him, maybe, but it comes outta my training budget. You know how much of this stuff he used the first week? Thirty-one bucks! And that's not counting the Ace bandages and the Orthoplast knee pads and everything else. Fucking kid, he wears everything but an iron lung."

"Why've they been breaking his chops?"

"It's his height, man," Pasty said. "That's all he's got, and they resent it. Unfair competition or something. They take it out by pounding him. His ankles are so fucked up, he's gotta have special wraps, twice a day, before each practice. A basket weave on his left foot, anchored at the top, five strips down the side and five strips up the ankle, just so, and a Louisiana heel lock on the other foot, and about nine fucking yards of tape around that thigh bruise, and who knows what all. The guy's driving me apeshit."

"A little like the cap, eh?" Sweet Basil McBride, the Wasps's captain, was our team hypochondriac, always beefing.

"Yeh, but Massy's really hurt. I keep telling Coach: 'The kid may be eight feet tall, but he's no athlete.' Maybe he's a fucking musician, I don't know. But he can't lean over the water fountain without pulling a—a—back muscle."

Pasticcino seldom used medical terms for parts of the anatomy. That protruding bone in your ankle? Pasty called it "the protruder muscle." In our trainer's lexicon, you had several "knotty muscles" and several "smooth muscles" in your arm, as well as some "squiggly muscles" going up to the shoulder. He must be leveling about the extent of Massy's injuries, because he preferred to blame everything on malingering. That way he couldn't be held responsible for a cure. "It's all in your mind," he said to Jones Jones one day when Jones came limping off the court. "You're faking it."

"Yeh, sure, man, I got me a sprained ankle of the mind," Jones Jones said disgustedly, sticking his swollen leg into the freezer.

"Play hurt!" Pasty offered. That was the extent of the treatment.

For all his complaining about overwork, Pasticcino actually did very little taping. Most of the Wasps would tape themselves rather than wait. Pasty'd sit in the middle of the locker room on a stool, smoking a cigar and pontificating on various subjects, while six or seven players were backed against the wall waiting. Then the team doctor would walk in and the trainer would scurry around like a pudgy angel of mercy. "This man needs a vertical wrap on his quadriceps," the medic would say, and Pasty would reply, "Yeh, I think you're right, doc." As soon as the doctor left, he'd pull down the anatomy chart and hunt up the quadriceps. He also liked to rush on the court with a little black satchel whenever anybody got hurt in a game. Only a few of us insiders knew that the bag was empty. Pasty would kneel next to the stricken player and snap open his bag and pretend to be rooting around for some tool of the healing profession, a scalpel or a pulmotor or something, and then he'd help the player to the dressing room and telephone for instructions. One night he ran out and opened his black bag and a white rat scurried out. We never did find out who did it, though I suspected the team's stand-up comedian, Jones Jones.

"Pasty, c'mon now, what's the story on Massy's private life?"

The trainer turned a dial on the ultrasonic machine. "Fucking thing," he said. "All I can get is static. You'd think we could at least bring in Philadelphia."

"Nobody seems to know much except that he's tall."

"What else is there to know? He's eight foot two, he's got the motor skills of a crippled yak, and he's hard on tape."

"What about his family?"

Pasticcino turned to the diathermy machine. "What's to know?" he said.

"Why'd he leave New Orleans? Why'd he come back to basketball?"

"What's the difference? He's not gonna make the club anyway."

I grabbed a stick of spearmint from the open box on the table. "Don't be too sure," I said. "Haven't you noticed the way Buttsy fusses over the kid in practice, all moony-eyed like he was another Kareem or something?"

"Yeh? Well, I don't know nothin'."

I heard a noise at the door, and Red Green came bursting through at his customary pace of 75 miles an hour, not waiting to see if anybody was leaning against the door, just blasting in as though he owned the joint. "Hey, dawlin', what it *is*?" he said, giving me a fast slap-shake. "What's happenin'?" he said to Pasty.

"How come you don't call *me* darling?" the trainer asked.

"Hey, Patsy, you 'member that headache stuff you gimme yesterday?" Red said, mispronouncing the trainer's nickname as usual. "That shit gimme a better headache than I already had. Listen, man, whose side you on, me or the headache?"

"Try some of this tonight," Pasty said, flipping a sample of Empirin-3 across the room. "If that don't work, you'll have to get a fix."

"Okay, dawlin'," Red said. "Won't be the first."

It probably wouldn't. Conrad "Red" Green was a black and therefore brown, except for rusty steel-wool hair and big gray protruding eyes that made him look like a Buddha on a diet. At 23, he was 6–6, 205, a natural forward, not the greatest sticker in the world, but a promising rebounder and defensive specialist. "My black DeBusschere," Coach called him, and kidded that "Red can't put a pea in the ocean."

The basis of the Red Green technique of defense was the quick finger in the opponent's eye, followed by the energetic elbow. When the ref would call a foul, Red acted deeply aggrieved. He said, "Who, me?" so often that it became his nickname on the road, and the Washington

Bullets actually listed him in their programs as "Who Me Green."

In the heat of action, Red referred to himself in the third person. He'd tell the referee: "Mr. Green don't think too much of these calls. . . ." "Mr. Green say that last foul was jive boolshit. . . ." One night he used the magic 12-letter word on Referee Jerry Rachlin, and Rachlin stuck his face up against Red's and snapped, "Tell Mr. Green I never had sex with my mother! Tell Mr. Green I don't accept that word he used! Tell Mr. Green he's out of the game!"

"Who, me?" Red said, pointing a long middle finger at his own bony chest.

Nobody liked to see Red leave, because he was a player who made things happen, careening around the court like a moose in heat, banging into walls, into the stands, into the uprights, often assisted by his two close friends, Benny and Dexxie. One night he got caught in traffic on a fast break, and he jumped up on the press table and cakewalked 20 feet across typewriters and tape recorders and microphones and then jumped back on the court. He had two speeds, fast and faster, and even when the Wasps were their customary 25 or 30 points behind, he played pure kamikaze. You'd hear the loud squeak of skin against maple, and there'd be Red, water-skiing on his knees, sliding along as if he played for the Montreal Canadiens. He held the Wasps's rebounding record, 29 in one game, set in his rookie year. With ten seconds left, Red had grabbed the ball off the defensive boards, and the PA announcer said, "Ladies and gentlemen, Conrad Green has tied the team rebounding record!" Red slapped the ball up against the backboard and caught it again, and the voice boomed out, "With that rebound, ladies and gentlemen, Conrad Green *breaks* the team record!"

"Don't eat too many of them things," Pasticcino was telling him. "Those Empirin-3s are great, but you don't want to mix them with other stuff."

Red nodded. He didn't require a lecture on drugs, you could be sure of that. In high school he'd lived by himself in the back of a junked bus on a Kansas City dump. The joke was that you couldn't visit Red unless you had the exact change, but I didn't find it particularly funny, because I'd had some long talks with him and I knew that he'd barely seen food till he hit the training table at KU, and the first time they served him roast beef he was sick all night. In Red's high school, the teachers didn't teach, they provided custodial care till one by one the students went to the reformatory or drifted away. The guidance counselor sold Jones.

"He sold who?" I asked Red when he told me the story.

"*Jones,* dawlin'. Oh, you po' whiteys, you so backward! Jones is heroyne, baby, *h-e-r-o-i-n,* heroyne."

"He sold heroin to schoolkids?"

"No, man, not just to schoolkids. He sold it to anybody that axed him, dawlin'! He wasn't prejudice!"

Red told me about a high school teammate who usually dragged into the gym late for practice and almost never bothered to attend school. "Come over here, chump," the high school coach said one day. "Where you was last night?"

"Stickin' up a gas station," the kid said.

"Well, you better start gettin' yo' sleep, hear?" the coach said.

Pasticcino was laying out the uniforms, and I started to ask Red Green what he knew about Broussard Massy's private life, but he already had his self-contained radio pulled down over his ears. Red was never without those big black earphones that poured out a constant stream of soul and hard rock. He sat in front of his locker lacing up his shoes, his pipestem legs moving in spasms to the beat. I wondered if he realized he was the white racist's cliché, sitting there exhibiting his characteristic rhythm. Probably not. Red was uncomplicated. I remembered the day I'd asked him why they called him Red instead of Conrad. "Aw, Conrad too long, dawlin'," he'd explained.

By now the other players were crowding into the locker room, stopping by to conduct their business with Pasty: paying debts, complaining about the interest (5 percent per week), borrowing a few dollars more, giving the trainer numbers to pass to the runner, griping about their wraps and their jockstraps. I wondered what it was like on winning teams. Was the whirlpool ever at the right setting? Were the hot towels ever hot enough? Did the pills ever accomplish what pills were supposed to accomplish? Did the Louisiana heel lock really lock Louisiana heels?

Not in this dressing room. The Wasps griped endlessly. Only Red Green seemed to float above it all, huddled in the corner of the room listening to his music. Massy was stolid and silent in front of his locker, strapping on knee pads that looked like pillows.

When all the athletes had arrived, I took an informal count: seventeen players. Three of them were white: Massy, Sutter Manno and Billy Ricketts. Five players still had to be cut, and by rights all three whites should have been dropped already. No, I take that back. Sutter Manno might be a little dense, as Nick Storen was always pointing out in the *Item,* but he was still a solid ball handler, and he fitted into Buttsy's system. Billy Ricketts, an ass-kisser from Purdue, belonged on the next plane out, but he'd lasted this long in camp by sucking up to Darius Guile, another Indianan. Bru Massy was by far our worst player, white or black, but I knew how the coach felt: Nobody eight feet two inches tall could be all bad, although the kid seemed to be trying to prove him wrong.

I watched the big man as he slowly unpeeled the neat stack of freshly laundered clothes that Pasticcino provided each player: two pairs of plum-and-white pants, two reversible T-shirts with plum on one side and white on the other, a half dozen pairs of sweat socks, a half dozen jockstraps and three pairs of canal boats. I knew better than to go over and strike up a conversation. I'd tried the day before, and it was like lighting a match in a wind tunnel.

"How you feeling, kid?"

"Fine, sir." He didn't look up when he answered.

"Sleeping okay now?"

"Better."

"Any visitors?"

No answer.

"How do you like the team so far?"

"Just fine, thanks."

"Learning our plays?"

"Fixin' to."

One by one all the men on the beat had given up trying to pry any news out of the kid. Pennsylvania Morgan of the *Off the Pigs News* was the last to quit. He just said, "Okay, kid, if that's the way you feel about it, up your ass!"

"I'm truly sorry, sir," Massy said, and kept right on lacing his treads.

"Aw, piss off!" Morgan said, and stomped away in his Earth Shoes. I never could understand why the *Off the Pigs News* covered the Wasps in the first place. What did the counterculture care about pro sports? I figured he'd keep on covering as long as we were losers, but in our first winning season Pa. would expose the team as capitalist warmongers.

"Okay, men, let's take and pep it up!" I turned toward the locker-room door and beheld the smiling face of Coach Francis X. "Buttsy" Rafferty, the overhead neon bouncing off his pink skull, his mouth a crooked slash. "Come on, gather up!" he snapped. "Move it, Green! Shag ass, Massy! Let's go, Basil! A little chatter here."

"Aw *right!*" the eager Billy Ricketts shouted. "Let's hear it, gang!"

Buttsy looked straight at the Purdue kid and said, "Siddown!" and right away I knew who the next cut would be. That would leave two whiteys, Manno and Massy.

"Basically what's the slogan for this season?" the coach asked.

"Play tall!" two or three players mumbled from their sideline seats, ashamed to be involved in such rah-rah silliness.

"What?" Buttsy said.

"Play tall!" This time three or four others joined in.

"I can't hear you!" Buttsy hollered.

"Play tall!" the players shouted, a mixed choir augmented by yours truly, the impartial scribe, and Pasty Pasticcino, the healer.

"More like it," the Butts said. "Pay attention. Next week we hit the bricks. Now what have we learned?" He looked in the general direction of Red Green. *"What have we learned?* Goddamn it, Green, take off those fucking earphones!" Somebody nudged Red, and he took the fucking earphones off and blinked like a Kodiak bear coming out of hibernation.

"What was you sayin', dawlin'?" Red asked.

"What have we learned so far?"

"Play tall?" Red said.

"Right! Meaning?" Nobody seemed to know. "I'll tell you what it means," Buttsy shouted. "Basically it means play like big men, big in body, big in heart. Means think of your teammates. Pass off! Set picks! It means don't be niggardly!"

The silence of the tomb. Black eyes rolled toward the ceiling. Red

Green reached for his earphones and snapped them back over his ears, as though to avoid the deluge. Abdul Rahman Buzruz frowned all over his shaven head and said softly, "S'cuse me?"

Jones Jones muttered, "Lay it on, Buz!"

Buzruz, our player rep and specialist in racial matters, rose to his 6–3 height and stroked his corrugated head. "S'cuse me, Coach, I wonder if you'd mind repeating what you just said."

"Said don't be niggardly out there, play tall, play together, play——"

"Now hold it right there, man," Abdul said disgustedly. "How come you talk shit?"

"What'd I say?" Buttsy asked, screwing up his eyes.

"Don't expect me to repeat no racist jive," Buz said.

"Hey, lighten up, Buz!" Justin Fell said, jumping to his feet. "Coach said 'niggardly.' Nothing wrong with 'niggardly.' " Our intellectual guard and black philosopher and holder of a master's degree from the University of Pennsylvania plopped back down, as though he had settled the whole delicate problem.

"Nothin' wrong wid dat?" Jones Jones put in, piercing Fell with a look of disbelief. "Whoo-ee! Nothin' wrong wid dat, dude says. The most worst word in black history, but it don't bother him. I tol' you he was passin'."

"Hey, look, you guys," Buttsy spoke up. "Niggardly just means stingy, selfish."

"Hold it, suckah!" Buzruz said, spacing out his words for emphasis. "That's the whole hassle with you whiteys. Right from jump street, man, when you want to say something negative, you just give it a color, man, and the color always the same."

Justin Fell repeated, "It's all right, Buz, it's *all right!*"

"I know them words," Buzruz insisted, "and they all disgusting. Nigger, nigra, nigro, niggerly, one the same as the other. Me, I say we take a walk."

"Taking a walk" was the Wasps's oldest grievance procedure, based on our owner's pretense that a professional sports team could solve personnel problems democratically. If any Wasp felt personally aggrieved, he had the right to call for a vote, and if two-thirds of the players agreed, the team would quit practicing till the front office straightened the problem out. The device had been utilized twice in the club's history, both times after blacks had been cut in favor of inferior whites, and both times our management had moved in and broken the strike within a few hours. Our owner liked the strike-vote idea, but only if management ended up getting its way. In pro sports, that's called democracy.

Jones Jones said, "Second the motion!" and somebody else hollered, "Aye!" I looked over at Buttsy. His pate had turned crimson, and my heart went out to the poor blunderer. All he wanted was peace and harmony and a few wins. Every season he lost 15, 20 pounds off his scarecrow frame, worrying about the players, nursing them through their personal crises and dreary performances. His family was always on the verge of leaving for Tahiti, his adolescent children scorned him and his profession, and he didn't have the faintest understanding of racial subleties. Back in his home town of South Youngstown, Ohio, the polocks had looked down on the hunkies, the hunkies hated the ukes, the ukes detested the wops, and they all scorned the niggers. Now here was Francis X. "Buttsy" Rafferty, a graduate of the hard-hat school of race relations and diplomacy, trying to handle a team that was 80 percent black and turning darker year by year. The poor man just couldn't get it through his head that he lived in sensitive times. "Sutter, you must be the dumbest living white man," he told Manno one day in front of the whole squad. And a few days later he cracked, "That's damn white of you, Buzruz." When the Seattle SuperSonics all-black club won the playoffs, who else but Francis X. Rafferty would appear on national TV and tell the Seattle coach, himself a black, "Buddy, you did it in spades"?

"Vote, vote!" Jones Jones was exclaiming.

"Any comment?" Buzruz asked quickly, as though hoping there'd be none and the motion would pass and the players could go down the road for a beer and a joint.

Bru Massy raised his big arm like the Statue of Liberty and stood there batting his dark cow eyes and rubbing the back of his neck. I hadn't expected comment on such a silly issue, least of all from the Colossus of Rhodes himself. "Could I say something?" he mumbled.

"Free country," Abdul snorted.

"Niggardly—that's no more a racist word than—uh—dandelion— or—well, uh—nightingale." A slow flush spread across the big man's chalky face. "But it does have a bad sound to it," he went on, picking his words slowly. He looked over at Buttsy, slack-jawed for a change. "And the bad sound's our own fault, us whites," the kid said. "Well

41

—uh—ummmm—that's all I have to say, I guess."

Buttsy waved his arms and said in a croaky voice, "Fellas, don't vote! Don't do this to me! Men, we got practicing to do. Now take and listen here. I was outa line. I apologize. I'm sorry. Never shoulda used that word. It was dumb, dumb! Hey, listen, Buz, you know how I feel. I love all you guys!"

"All *who* guys?" Abdul asked.

"All you—all you Wasps," the coach whined. For emphasis he threw his arm around Buz's bony shoulders. Our player rep wriggled away. "A li'l ol' fashioned respect'll do jes' fine," he said coolly. "Okay, I accept your apology."

Billy Ricketts jumped up to the fifth row of seats and hollered, "Let's hear it for two big men!" A few of the players applauded lightly while Buttsy and Buzruz bowed as though they had just finished singing the "Love Duet" from Toscanini on the stage of the Paris Opera.

Then Francis X. Rafferty daubed at his eyes. I swear, the man cried at juggling acts, he cried at the circus; comedies and magic shows depressed him. He'd bawl during games and sometimes have to be taken to the training room.

"Men," the Butts said, "I'm so proud of you I can't express myself. Basically I'm touched, I'm overwhelmed." He stopped to catch a sob in his handkerchief. "Men," he said, "you may be black on the outside, but——"

"Buttsy!" I said to myself.

"*—But you're black all the way through!*"

Captain Basil McBride looked at Buz, and Buz looked at Jones Jones, and Abdul Buzruz spoke with dignity. "Coach Rafferty," he said, "on behalf of the brothers, we thank you for that high praise." Buttsy was radiant.

I looked at Massy. He was plucking at the tape that covered his right thigh from knee to crotch. Sweet Basil turned and gave him a slap-shake and said, "Baby, you all *right!*" Maybe the hazing was over.

· · ·

9

Dulcy drove the 35 miles out from town to spend another weekend with me, and on Saturday she watched both workouts even though there was an unwritten rule about women being banned from practice sessions because they were bad luck and the team would sink in the Bermuda Triangle. She'd never seen Broussard Massy in his shorts before, and she couldn't get over it.

"Honey, his legs are like ski poles!" she said. "Hairy ski poles!"

By the time you distributed 245 pounds over eight feet two inches, you didn't have much excess—his proportions were about the same as a six-footer of 165—and Coach couldn't seem to put weight on the kid. He wouldn't eat meat or fish or anything derived from killing animals. The first morning at the training table, Pasty had asked him what religion made him so picky. Massy said we all had to die, but it hurt him to think we'd hit dumb animals over the head in a slaughterhouse or slash their throats or hang them by their feet. He said meat made him feel ashamed.

Pasty tried to get a rise by asking the kid if he'd ever been to a cauliflower plant and seen what they do to cauliflower on the assembly line—slash and core and stuff it into boxes and then flash-freeze it hard as marble.

"Many's the night back in Danbury I sat up in a cold sweat listening to them poor cauliflowers scream," Pasty said, but Massy just looked at his congealing bacon. I guess he figured he'd already exposed too much of himself.

Well, as I keep saying, he was weird enough to be a Wasp. Buzruz wouldn't eat shrimp or lobster or any of the other shellfish delicacies; he called them "swine of the sea," said when you ate them you were eating recycled garbage. He didn't eat swine of the land either, or a whole inventory of other foods. Jones Jones had a fierce allergy to peanuts and horses. His eyes would puff up, his skin would erupt into welts, and he'd have trouble breathing. And Red Green would crawl a mile through broken Pepsi bottles for a taste of junk food. When steak was served at the training table, Red would moan and say, "Aw, not that shit agin!"

"It's so sad," Dulcy said at camp as we watched Massy doing his calisthenics. "I can't stand to watch."

"You should have seen him a month ago," I said. "He couldn't even do whirligigs."

In the scrimmages, Massy was still tripping over his own Pumas, and letting himself get boxed out by a bunch of midgets, but at least he wasn't getting assaulted anymore. As to whether he was learning how to play the game of professional basketball, even his best friend would have answered no. He had a bush-league habit of standing back and admiring his shot as it floated toward the basket. "Goddamn it, son!" Coach screamed. "You're not a fan! When the ball goes up, you got two seconds to get inside your man. You ever hear of checking out?"

Massy hung his head.

"Son, if you don't check your man in this league, they'll take and break your neck." The scrimmage went on, and Justin Fell put up a shot, and Massy stood back with his index finger bisecting his lips and studied the trajectory. Coach Francis X. Rafferty blew his whistle and patiently repeated his instructions. "Now concentrate, son, concentrate!" he wound up.

Pretty soon the Butts was on the big man about "banana" cuts. "Move straight!" the coach ordered. "Stop running all them fucking parenthesises." He gave the kid the advanced course in the setting of picks and screens. "Use your ass, *your ass!*" he sputtered, spinning Massy around by the shorts. "You keep setting up frontwards, you won't have a tooth left in your mouth. Won't have a *mouth!* Take and set wide. Big guy like you, you could screen like a truck. And when you see somebody settin' a pick, holler 'Pick right! Pick left!' You don't have to be a deaf mute out there, son."

The team lined up for the Sergeant jump and reaction test, usually won easily by Edwin "King" Crowder, our regular center, 6–11 and 220 surly pounds out of St. Joe's in Philadelphia. In the Sergeant test, you stand sideways to the wall, feet together, arm as high up as you can reach, and mark the spot. Then on a signal you squat and jump as high as you can, and mark again. Three jumps and you average it out. King had hit 44½ inches of pure jump the week before, and nobody had come within two inches of him. Massy was way down the list at 35, and Pete Tyles of the *Herald* cracked that spring would be a little late this year.

When they finished measuring this time, King had dropped back to 44, and Massy was up to 39 flat. Pasty called out the figures, and I thought I saw the big man smile a little, but I might have been imagining. "Hey, did the kid smile?" I asked Dulcy.

"No," she said. "What's he got to smile about, the poor thing? I was looking at his legs when he jumped. Why, they're like a colt's—and those great big shoes at the bottom."

After a while, she asked, "Does the coach have to be so cruel?"

"Cruel? What do you mean, cruel?"

"Just listen."

Buttsy was roaring his head off, but Buttsy always roared in practice. "See the ball, Jones. See it, *see it*! C'mon now, a little hustle. Sutter, get your head out. Goddamn it, Basil, pick up! *Pick up out there*! No open shots!"

Every time Massy came running past, bobbing like an eight-foot skeleton on a string, Coach screamed something special at him. "Hustle! Left, left! You're trailing the play again. For Chrissakes, son, low post, *low post!* Oh, Jesus. . . ."

Once he blew the whistle and said, "Broussard, where'd you learn to dribble?"

Massy muttered something.

"Well, please, son, I'm begging you, poor old coach is on his knees pleading. *Don't dribble!* You're not a bipper, understand? Time you put the ball down and get it back, you could recite the Washington Monument. Oh, Lord. . . ." He began to look teary.

Then it was time for three-on-three scrimmaging. "Manno! Fell! Crowder!" Buttsy hollered. "Turn those shirts inside out." He beckoned to Massy and two other scrubs to take the ball out of bounds. The second Massy caught a pass he began to dribble toward the basket, and King Crowder slapped the ball across the end line. Buttsy's cheeks puffed out like a tree frog's as he blew the whistle.

"Son, come here!" The kid walked over in his patented hangdog slouch, ducking his head down near the coach's level. "From now on, you got a one-bip maximum. One! Then you pass or shoot or something —anything but dribble. Son, handling just ain't your specialty."

Massy inbounded, and Sutter Manno intercepted. A quick pitch to Justin Fell and the plums had scored. Then the first-string guards, Fell and Manno, put on a handling exhibition against their backup men, while Massy and King Crowder ground against each other's shoulder blades in the pivot, with Massy finally giving way.

"Is it always this physical?" Dulcy asked.

"Used to be worse," I said. "They all picked on Massy. Now it's just King Crowder. Worried about his job, I guess. Fat chance he'll lose it."

Coach was foaming at the mouth. "Get mad, Massy!"

Crowder's plums ran off six straight hoops, and then I saw King whisper in Massy's ear, and the big kid reared back against Crowder's shoulder and spun him hard. While our veteran center crashed to the floor, Massy took a pass and slam-dunked, rattling the backboard.

Then Sutter Manno inbounded, but Massy tipped the ball away, and a few seconds later he started one of those big rolling skyhooks, the kind Kareem Abdul-Jabbar perfected. Crowder bogarted him tight, and Massy flipped the ball from his outstretched right hand back over his own head to his outstretched left hand, about eight feet away, and converted the right-handed skyhook into a perfect left-handed push shot. I might have believed the move if Earl Monroe had made it, except "The Pearl" wouldn't have lost his balance and fallen afterward.

"Hey, what chew call that?" Basil the old master shouted from the sidelines. "That look like the Honeydew-drop with Butterscotch Float!"

"Yeh!" Jones Jones hollered. "And a swan dive at the end!"

"Way to go, kid!" Coach called out, and everybody whooped and cheered. Everybody except Edwin "King" Crowder. And Dulcy.

"Oh, I think it's just *heathen*!" she said. "When he falls down, they all clap?"

Coach told everybody to take five, and I slipped over to Crowder and asked what he'd whispered to the kid.

"Aw, nothin', Sam," the big pivotman said between deep gulps of air. He looked upset.

"I won't print it," I said. "I just want to know."

"I said, 'Hey, fairy, you shoulda stuck to your fuckin' piano.' "

"That's all?"

"That's all. Turkey sure touchy!"

Coach stood on the side of the court, jawing with the team captain. "See what I mean?" Buttsy was saying as I came huffing over. "Boy's a player."

"Could be," Sweet Basil replied.

After the practice was over I phoned in my story, 300 words. Dulcy and I were leaving the gym when we spotted Massy leaning against the orange-brick wall, his bag at his feet. I waved, and he waved back with his index finger, and on an impulse I strode over and said, "Waiting for somebody?"

"Yes, sir. King Crowder. Said he'd give me a lift."

I knew that Crowder had left at least 20 minutes earlier, and there was nobody inside except Pete Tyles and Pasty Pasticcino. Well, it was none of my business. Crowder intended to hold onto his job; maybe the kid would get lost on his way back to the dorm.

"Don't wait too long," I said, not knowing what else to say.

"Yes, sir." Massy smiled. "And sir?"

"Yeh?"

"You and the missus, y'all have a nice day, hear?"

I wondered what had worked this wondrous change, from weirdball loner to friendly extrovert. Slouched against the wall smiling at us, he looked almost contented. Maybe he'd come to terms with the acid man, made some kind of deal to relieve the pressure. But I couldn't believe it. There was a flinty integrity about Massy, or was it just mulishness? Either way, I couldn't see him making deals. The kid did things one way.

Walking back toward Dulcy, I decided to take advantage of the mood swing and blurt out my questions. I stopped and called "Bru!" but he had slipped around the corner.

"Never stays in one place very long, does he?" Dulcy observed.

"He has reason," I said.

Dulcy nodded. "You haven't said anything to anybody?" she asked.

"Course not. It's the kid's secret, honey. If he wants to spill, it's up to him. Remember what the man said?"

"Something about don't talk or I'll get you and Leon and Mike?"

"Right. If I talk, the prowler'll think Massy talked to me. He'll come back. And it's the kid he'll be after, not me."

"Stay quiet then, Sam," Dulcy said, tugging me closer to her side as we walked.

"Don't worry," I said. "I'm made of stone."

•   •   •

10

With the club pared to 14 players and two cuts left, we boarded the Wasps's chartered bus for our opening exhibition game, against the Atlanta Hawks in Wheeling, West Virginia. Usually we flew, but sometimes Darius Guile liked to cut corners, and he piled us into the Greyhound charter that the players liked because there was enough room for most of them to stretch across two rows of seats and snooze. It was a six-hour haul, and I heard all the typical snatches of conversation:

"Cain't sleep in that fuckin' trainin' camp, man," said a rookie.

"How the fuck you s'pose to sleep?" said another. "No sireens, no loud music, rto Puerto Ricans dancing in the street."

"Man, it ain't natural around there!"

"I'm a great friend of Jabbar's," Sweet Basil McBride said.

"Aw, you ain't so great!" Jones Jones cracked.

Red Green's alto voice piped up from the back, telling one of his favorite stories of brash youth. I hadn't heard it more than twenty times. "He say to me, 'Hey, give up the ball, Jack, I'm the shooter 'round here.' I say, 'Hey, dawlin', get outa my face! You on a no-cut contrac' and I'm fightin' fo' my life.' I say, 'You already got yo' million, and I'm still tryin' to make the club, and you want me to give up the ball?' I say, 'Hey, suckuh, back off, y'unnastan'?' I say, 'That enough signifyin' for now, you hear what I'm sayin'?' I say, 'You quit lightin' me up or yo' ass is grass, you follow my meanin'?' Man, that dude shut down fast!" In Red's stories, Red always had the best lines, sometimes the only lines, and he loved to find a rookie and go through his whole repertoire.

Back in the last row of seats, Pasty Pasticcino began working on Jones Jones's feet. Like some of the other black players, Jones had overlapping toes and compressed joints from being forced to wear shoes that were too small as a child, but he also had an extra problem of his own: the big toe on his left foot had been gnawed to the bone by a rat,

48

and the tissue was susceptible to infection. Jones and the trainer would sit opposite each other while Pasty kneaded and massaged the scarred toe, then sprayed it with antiseptic. Jones would crack wise as though he wasn't in pain, but everybody knew he was. There were limits to how long he could play—six, seven minutes at a stretch—and then he'd limp back to the bench to grind his teeth. Some said he was the best sub in the game, a black John Havlicek, but that was five or six years ago. He'd come to the team at 20, from his sophomore year at New Mexico State, and I'd always wondered how Darius Guile managed to sign him before his class graduated, a violation of NBA rules. "We got him as a hardship case, that's all," Guile said when I pressed him. "His father had a bad medical problem."

"Heart?"

"No. Indigestion."

"Cleared up the day you signed Jones?"

"Miraculous cure."

I rested my head on the back of the seat and listened to the whirr of the bus's tires on the wet highway. Rivers of dirty water from the last cloudburst flowed on both sides of the road, and the sky was pewter. I tried dozing off, but there was too much jabbering, so I yanked out a favorite book and started to read. Justin Fell came down the aisle and flopped alongside me. "What're you reading today, Sammy?" he said. "Xaviera's latest? Or 'The Best of the *Blade-Mirror*?' "

"No," I said in a fake huff. "It's *Dubliners.*"

"Great book, man!" Justin said, grabbing it out of my hand. "Which story you like best? 'The Dead'? 'Ivy Day in the Committee Room'?"

"I love that ending: 'Mr. Crosby said that it was a very nice piece of writing,' " I recited.

" 'Mr. *Crofton,* ' " Justin corrected. " 'A very *fine* piece of writing.' "

"Yeh, right," I said sheepishly. When Justin Fell corrected you, there was no point in arguing.

"How's your book coming along?" I asked. The Wasps's resident egghead had been working on a sociological study of pro basketball ever since he'd come out of the University of Pennsylvania five years before with a 3.9 average and about 50 offers to teach English, which he'd turned down for a paltry $100,000 a year from the Wasps.

"Slow," Justin said in his deep vibrato. "Slow but unsure."

"What are you gonna call it?"

49

"Don't know yet, Sam. How's *The Nigger Game?*"

"It'd play in Peoria. And where we're headed right now."

"Good old Wheeling. My grandmother's from there."

"No kidding?" I said. "I never would have associated you with hillbilly country."

"Yeh, well, the Fells didn't know their place, you dig?"

The truth was, nobody could ever put a tag on Justin Attucks Fell. He moved smoothly between worlds, black and white, hip and unhip, jock and brains. He'd been brought up in Inwood, which used to be a nicer part of town. Now it's junk-ridden, like the rest of Manhattan above 125th. Along the line, his preacher father and his teacher mother had managed to give him enough love and pride in himself so he could function above the level of color and race.

He looked like an African nobleman, a mahogany prince with just enough Arabian in the bloodline to give him a thin nose and bushy eyebrows and heavy-lidded dark eyes. He carried 200 pounds on a sinuous 6-4 frame, and he had the economical moves of a black leopard stalking prey. His specialty was sophisticated motion; he was always cutting little arcs and setting picks and slipping backdoor. He played nine-tenths of the game in his head, and a good thing, too, because he didn't have the natural skills of players like Oscar Robertson or Walt Frazier or Jerry West.

Justin still spent hours in his hotel room flipping anything he could find into anything he could find—matches into saucers, paper clips into bottles, bits of rolled-up paper into wastebaskets, always trying to improve his shooting touch. He told me how he used to sensitize his fingertips with sandpaper when he was a kid trying to make the Inwood team, and throw Ping-Pong balls into bottles when he couldn't get out to the schoolyard. He'd take his little brother over to 155th and Eighth Avenue, the playground where they hold the Rucker tournament now, and the brother would hold up a broom to block Justin's shots. They'd work out for three or four hours and then go home and hit the books for three or four more. If the Reverend Fell's kids didn't make it one way, they'd make it another. Justin had made it both. There were all kinds of offers waiting for him when he quit basketball.

"You heard the news?" he asked.

"What news?"

"I got me a roommate."

"Sure, I know," I said. "You and Red Green."

"Nope. Not this year. Me and Broussard Massy."

"You and Massy?" I said, trying to comprehend. "How are the six of you gonna fit in the motel room?"

"We'll manage."

Jones Jones, his toe therapy completed, came wobbling up the aisle as we rounded a bend. "Hey, brothuh man," he said to Justin. "How yo' Johnson?"

"Mah Johnson cool!" our black intellectual boomed out. "How *yo'* Johnson?"

"Which? Mah road Johnson or mah home Johnson?"

They laughed at their inside joke, and then Jones said, "I might could have the flux. Basil, he got the flux. His head hot."

"Well, stay cool, dig?" Justin said. They slapped palms twice and Jones Jones moved slowly toward the front of the bus, favoring his left foot.

"Translation, please," I said. Justin was my link to the third world. He could speak about six tongues: blacktalk, city white, Ivy League English and two or three foreign languages. The dominant speech in pro basketball—ghetto blacktalk—was easy for him. Most NBA stars were city blacks, guys who had practiced their moves seven nights a week, the finest players the game had ever known, and they brought their own vocabulary to the game, their own *lingua negra*. You'd hear a man like Justin Fell, IQ 150, talking to the other blacks, screeching out lines like, "He be burnin', man! Whoo-*ee!* Jack, his ass is up!" Then he'd walk over to me and speak the white vernacular with dignity and poise.

Blacktalk took some getting used to, but by now I had mastered certain of the phrases. A "Johnson" could be anything, as in "He stuck his Johnson right in my face." "Hey, man, you take care of your own Johnson, hear?"

"What particular Johnson were you and Jones talking about?" I asked Justin.

"His girlfriends. His road Johnson or his home Johnson, see?"

"Well, his home Johnson's his wife, right?"

"Not necessarily."

As for the "flux," I knew that could be anything from a headache to the bubonic plague, and everybody knew what "stay cool" meant, so I didn't require any further translation. It wasn't like the night some of the black players took me to Small's Paradise in Harlem and put on a regular sideshow, spouting cryptic phrases that might as well have been Sanskrit. I'd asked what they called their strange tongue.

"Ain't got a name," Jones Jones said, " 'cept among ourse'fs."

"What's the name among yourselves?" I asked.

"Cain't say," Jones said, backing away in mock horror.

"Oh, you talk shit, Jones!" Red Green said. "Listen, dawlin', we call it niggertalk."

I said, "You call it——"

"Don't say it!" Abdul Buzruz warned. "We the onliest ones can say it."

I said, "So my first lesson is——"

"First lesson is call it niggertalk and you get one upside the haid!" Jones said sternly.

As our bus inched through a hilly coal town, dirty raindrops began to dot the windows. I asked Justin how he felt about his new roommate.

"I must've talked to him for an hour," he said. "Remember Mailer's expression: white Negro? I think it might apply to Massy. He's kind of an outcast."

"You talked to him for an hour? Hey, that's a new club record."

"Well, I did most of the talking. Trying to draw him out, you know? But he only told me a few things."

"About his family? About New Orleans and where he came from before that?"

"No, nothing like that. If you mention his childhood, a screen drops over his face."

"He say anything personal?"

"Hey, man, I'm not trying to find out anything personal!" There was a note of impatience in Justin's voice. "That's your job, Sam. I'm trying to make friends with a roommate, get along with my fellow worker." He softened his tone. "He's just another Wasp to me."

"Sure. Just another eight-foot center."

"Well, that's the dominant fact, sure. He's the nursery-rhyme gentle giant, isn't he?"

"Except when he tangles ass with Crowder," I said. "What's getting into King? The other day he tells the kid he'll give him a ride back to the dorm. Then he takes off and leaves him standing there."

"What do you expect King to do, kiss him and say, 'Welcome to my job'?"

"Massy has about as much chance of taking Crowder's job as Buttsy has of teaching English," I said, keeping my voice down.

"Don't be too sure," Justin said. "I've been noticing. Massy's got more than just height, Sam. He's coming on."

"Slowly."

"Well, yeh. But it's mostly a personality problem. He'll get over it. How about the way he stood up for the brothers at practice? He's wiggling out, Sam. And when he's all the way out—man, that dude gone fly!" I appreciated his sly reversion to blacktalk.

I told Justin how Dulcy had noticed that Massy flinched whenever he was introduced to somebody. Instead of putting out his hand, he'd raise his right index finger up alongside his face and give a little waggle, like saying, "Hi!" but also avoiding the usual handshake. I thought maybe the kid was afraid to grab your hand, for fear he'd hurt you, and Dulcy said it certainly showed some deep-rooted phobia about loss of control or physical contact or maybe both. Dulcy had studied things like that in college, while I'd been learning to drink.

Justin heard me out, and said, "Well, as I've always said, your wife's got the brains in the family." Then he went into a long song and dance about the psychology of being tall, how most supertall men have a "height neurosis," a "white Negro" attitude, and they come on all shy and gentle, because they're trying to convince you that they won't hurt you, and at the same time trying to keep you from hurting them, "because physical freaks get hurt every day," Justin said. "They get hurt by every stare, every whisper behind their backs. You think they outgrow it? Never!"

The bus lurched out of the coal town and sped down the blacktop, running along a swollen creek, and an ugly picture surfaced from low down in my head. I'm eight years old again, and I'm crouched behind a porch rail with my buddy Lefty Ortiz, and we're peeping at a deformed lady as she struggles along the sidewalk, a bag of groceries in her arms and a great big glob of—what? fat? bone? jelly?—on her back, and her feet splayed out from the strain. Just as she gets in front of the house, I give Lefty a nudge, and we both holler as loud as we can in our pipsqueak sopranos:

"Hunchback!"

". . . So he gives you body language that says, 'Come on over here, I won't hurt you,' " Justin was saying.

53

"Who?" I said, blinking sharply.

"The prototypical giant. Our Massy, every Massy. It's Frankenstein and the blind violinist all over again."

I remembered making the Frankenstein connection before, but the kid was no monster, he was good looking, clean cut, not in the least frightening, except that his size seemed to produce certain trickle-currents in the brain, made the heart palpitate and the viscera tighten and ancient prejudices bubble up through the brainpan. If Lefty Ortiz were still around to offer moral support, would I hide behind a bush and scream "Giant"? Maybe Massy was aware of these strange vestigial feelings, maybe one part of him understood how people reacted to him. Maybe that's why he stayed in his own orbit, dressing quickly after each workout and hurrying away. It didn't help that King Crowder was so hostile, but I had the feeling that Massy would keep to himself anyway.

"So they have to project recessiveness," Professor Justin was saying. "Who could tolerate the giants otherwise? Look at Wilt—he refused to fake it, and he wound up hated."

"Yeh," I said. "What was it Wilt did when some fan asked him how's the weather up there?"

Justin laughed. "He said, 'It's raining,' and spit on the guy. But Wilt says it never happened."

"I like the way Big Fritz Ostedtler handled it at Wisconsin. Somebody'd come up to him and say, 'Hey, big fella, is it raining up there?' and Fritz'd pull out his schwantz and say, 'I can't hear you. Speak through this tube!'"

The bus bucked through the outskirts of Wheeling in a driving rain, and I picked out the words: Black Bros. Funerals. It was a sign, but I hoped it wasn't a sign.

11

Late in the evening we checked into the Lignite Inn Motel, an elderly desk clerk presiding. "Here's yeh keys," he told me after he adjusted his teeth. "You'll fand ass water and pop machines down the hole by the stairwell."

When Justin and Massy stepped up, the old boy made a slow study of Justin's complexion and then swept his rheumy eyes up and down the white-on-white colonnade that was Massy. "Gol-*lee!*" he said, doing a perfect Gomer Pyle impression, "Ah di'nt know the circus were in town." He chuckled, and Justin said coldly, "The keys, please?"

"Okay, boy."

I halfway expected Justin to take issue with the word "boy," but I guess he considered the source. You didn't get this racist guff in major-league cities anymore, but in the exhibition season you ran into people who still thought of integrated sports teams as a menace to their personal futures, like textbooks that discussed—you should excuse the expression—evolution.

After a quick hamburger in the motel coffee shop, I sat at my portable and began to compose. Game stories came easily, especially after you'd done maybe 1000 of them and knew the jargon, but pregame dope stories required a little thought, and that's just how much I'd given this one, what with brooding about Massy and the problems of giantism and the difference between a road Johnson and a home Johnson. I typed: *The Wasps were ready for the Atlanta Hawks in today's exhibition opener in the miasmic environs of Wheeling, W. Va.*

I reread my words and found them pale, except for that "miasmic environs" bit. I rolled another piece of copy paper into the typewriter and wrote: *The Wasps were set to open the eight-game exhibition season today in the miasmic. . . .*

I yanked the paper out and slipped in a new piece. *Way down yonder in the murky miasma of Wheeling, W. Va., the Wasps were ready for the Atlanta Hawks and today's exhibition opener. The bell tolled at 1 P.M., and the Wasps hoped it tolled for them.*

That would never get by sports editor Tex Pecos. I could just see him snorting once or twice and then flipping the copy to a rewrite man. "Here," he'd say, "take the ladies' literary shit out of this."

Well, he'd always advised us to "get the fucking in the lead." Maybe something simpler. *The time is 1 P.M., the place is Wheeling, W. Va., and the Wasps and the Hawks were the fucking opponents as this year's exhibition season got underway. . . .*

Jeez, I was getting punchy, and I hadn't even started. But what could I say that hadn't been said in 25 or 30 stories during training? How many ways could I write that the team had high hopes and Buttsy predicted they'd take and have a banner year? The only new ingredient was Massy, communicative as Mount Rushmore.

"Pretty thin stuff," Mr. Pecos had told me on my last trip to the office. "That sure is one dull ballclub—or else you're one dull sportswriter." He showed me our basketball scrapbook from the morgue, and the lukewarm junk leaped out:

WASPS HONE FOR OPENER
RAFFERTY SAYS WASPS SHARP
BUTTSY SAYS CAN DO

It was pedestrian; I wondered why I'd written it, and also what I would put in my overnighter. For a second I thought of calling the office and asking Pecos if he could assign somebody to interview the wives or the home Johnsons or maybe do a think piece on the beloved owner Abraham Lincoln Gross. But I just couldn't stand to hear our sports editor's voice after the long day on the bus. He always started the same way: "Are there any news?" He was under the impression that "news" was plural because it ended in *s*. If you wrote a line like "Sports is big business," you could count on Tex Pecos to change it to "Sports are big business" every time. There was a temptation to mock him, but only one guy ever did it to his face, and he was fired. He'd called in one day and Pecos had said, "Are there any news?" and the guy answered, "Not a new!"

I thought of leading my overnighter with a lively quote, but that presented problems, too. Pecos had a tendency to homogenize quotes, convert them all into middle-class white dialect. Once I quoted Basil McBride word for word: "Tonight we gone whomp 'em and stomp 'em! We be wheelin' and dealin' and squealin'!" Pecos saw the copy and gave me a loud lesson in journalism. "What are you trying to do, Forrester?" he whined. "We don't use Uncle Remus around here."

"That's not Uncle Remus," I said. "That's exactly what Basil said."

"Do you know what you're doing?" he said, taking off his rimless glasses and shaking them at me. "You're trying to make colored players sound dumb. You're trying to make it look like they don't know English."

56

"Certainly they know English!" I said, heating up a little "They've been to college. But sometimes they like to talk their own language. They call it—uh—blacktalk."

"Well, we use English in the *Blade-Mirror*. Try it. You'll like it." In the background, a couple of his toadies snickered. By the time Pecos finished with my copy, it came out:

> *"We feel we have a very good opportunity tonight," asserted Wasps's Captain Basil J. McBride. "Hopefully, I believe we're a match for our opponents."*

Later I discussed the problem over Scotch with Simon Keister, sports editor emeritus and 64-year-old office swinger and boozer and seducer of newly hired copygirls, a grizzled veteran who still called typewriters "mills" and scissors "shears." "No use fighting it, kid," Si said. He always called me "kid," even after I turned 36. "Guys like Pecos, they're stamped out with cookie cutters. Their first rule is never do anything original."

I said, "Si, sometimes I wish I'd been around when Grantland Rice was writing about the Four Horsemen and Ring Lardner was writing lines like ' "Shut up," his father explained,' and——"

"No, you don't, kid," the old man interrupted. "Those guys were as rare as tits on a bull. The rest of the sportswriters were nowheres near as good as today." He told me about interviewing Babe Ruth, and how the Babe had let loose a good-natured stream of cuss words and then begun answering every question with the same playful phrase.

"How do you feel about the season so far, Mr. Ruth?"

"Pussy good."

"What do you think of the Yankees' chances?"

"Oh, pussy good, pussy good."

"How's the pitching this time around, Babe?"

"Pussy good. Yes, sir, pussy good!"

"I went back to my office with nothing in my notepad except 'pussy good,' " Si said, laughing at the memory. "But I had to turn in a story or lose my job, so I just invented some quotes about how much the Babe was enjoying the season and he felt good about the Yankees's chances but the pitchers were still ahead of the hitters. Two nights later I ran into the Babe at a bar and he said, 'Koster, I sure enjoyed your story.

You know somethin', Costa, them quotes was me. Yes sir, Keester, you caught my style pussy good.' "

"Now, Sam," Simon Keister said after a long pull at his drink, "go and look up some old issues. Half the time you'll find Babe Ruth sounding like Henry James. Even in Grantland Rice's copy."

I put Si out of my mind and slipped a new piece of paper in my battered Olivetti *Lettera* and banged out the overnighter. For some reason it came as easy as ice cream, all those terrific phrases about how sharp the Wasps had been looking, moving well off the ball, penetrating to the basket and hitting the open man, and how Red Green had the hot hand, and the newcomer Massy showed a lot of moxie and he'd be heard from before the season was over, and blah blah blah. Pecos would love it. He could read it without moving his lips.

After I'd dictated long distance, I sat back to watch a late movie, and the phone rang. "Hey, teach," the voice said. "It's me, Basil."

"I know. Who else calls me teach?"

"You still up? Can I come over? Got sumpin' to show you."

"I thought you were all fluxed up."

"Naw. It cleared up soon's I got out the bus."

When Basil McBride first came into the league, the ABA and the NBA had been at the height of their feud, and he wound up with a fancy contract with stock options and a retirement fund and a half-dozen other emoluments that converted him from a barely literate junior college dropout into a barely literate millionaire. He hadn't been quite ready. His background was rural Florida, humping citrus crates in searing heat. He came out of a badly fractured household and six or eight foster homes and an all-black school system that trained him to read comic books, and he brought with him an ingrained awe of the white massa. "Used to be a steep embankment on the Seaboard Line," Sweet Basil told me one night, "and us black kids would climb up top and do flips, frontways and back, flat out, while the white kids stood there and giggled."

"Why'd you do a fool thing like that?"

"Showin' off for whitey, that's all! At home we always talked about how good black was, but underneath we knew which was the boss color. The white kids, we thought their shit don't stink."

That conversation was five, six seasons ago. Since then Basil McBride had gone through a lifetime of reeducation and reconditioning, and he was no longer the southern black who referred to the beach as "the wave place" and the saloon as "the bar place" because his vocabulary had been so neglected.

"Hey, babe," he said as he strolled into my motel room, light on his feet as always. "Got some papers I want to show you."

"Is that what you were working on in the bus?" Basil tutored ghetto kids from the settlement house, and sometimes he showed me their exercises and assignments, and sometimes I helped with a finer point or two.

"Yeh. Been grading."

"And every kid passed, right?"

"Right!" Basil said, balancing his elongated frame on the edge of a chair. "You know me, teach. I wouldn't let a kid flunk, 'cause these nigger punks, man, you flunk 'em and they go out and stick up a bank behind that! Ain't that what whitey says?"

"What're you working on now?"

"Vocabulary building. Verbs, nouns, what's a adjective, what's a adverb, stuff like that. Kid name Jimmy Watts, he's got a big problem. Says things like, 'Don't do that no more, *right now!*' All he knows is 'right now' is strong, ya know?"

"Because he used to hear his mother say, 'Get over here *right now.*' "

"Say, you're learning, teach!" He smiled his original "Sweet Basil" smile. "Look at this," he said. "I brought you some poetry exercises." Basil was trying to acquaint his students with poetry and at the same time stimulate their imaginations, so he'd feed them a line or two and ask them to improvise an ending. He handed me a paper:

How do I love thee?
Let me count the ways.
1 2 3 4. . . .

"How 'bout *that?*" Basil said. I looked at the next paper:

Whose woods these are I think I know.
His name Joe.

And:

> *Thy lips, thine eyes, thy very breath*
> *Lend nurture to my heart*
> *And give me paws.*

"You like that one?" Basil asked. "Remind me of a kid we had in junior college. Came on stage and said, 'Out, out, damn spot! *Split!*' "

"How's your worrying coming along?" I asked. Basil was the most anxious member of the squad. After a perfect pass, he'd say, "Hey, was that ball okay? Did I lay it in right, man?" Before a game he'd sit around shaking his head and say, "You think we can win it? Teach, I just hope we don't look too bad!" When we flew, he pulled a stocking cap over his face and tried to convince himself he was in the grand salon of the Orient Express. He never used expressions like, "When we get to Philly." With the captain, it was always, "*If* we get to Philly." Out on the streets, he kept his radar tuned for muggers. "Who's gonna mug a guy six foot seven?" I'd say, and Basil would answer, "Some dude with a two-inch blade."

After a while, I'd learned to understand his anxiety, even to accept it as realistic. All those blank faces out on the court, running around in their short shorts with numbers on their backs—they look so smooth, weaving down the floor, flowing back and forth in waves, making soft jumpers from 20 feet out, but deep inside some of them are torn in half, some are dying of terror. I'd see them before a big game, old pros and raw rooks, throwing up in the training room.

Maybe basketball was just "the silly business of throwing an inflated bag through a hoop," but to get to the pros, you had to learn to play it better than 50 million other guys and you had to *stay* better or somebody else moved into your place and back you went to the citrus grove, humping 200-pound crates and catching pellagra in the off-season. The stakes were high, the motivation was strong, and when you fell, you fell a long way. I remembered Elvin Hayes's mother down in Rayville, Louisiana, talking about the Big E: "He put up a bucket with a hole in the bottom, right on a beautiful water elm I had in the back of the house, and he threw a rubber ball into that bucket and stomped around that tree and dried the ground out till he killed it. Killed my beautiful water elm! Then he hung the bucket on the side the house and kept right on throwing the ball into it. Eleven hours a day. *Eleven!*"

Kids like Elvin Hayes and Sweet Basil McBride didn't have fancy asphalt courts, they didn't even have basketballs. "We'd put a rock in a sock," Basil once told me, "and we'd pretend to dribble it. We'd say, 'Bop bop' for dribble. Two bops and you had to stop or pass or shoot. We'd hold that sock by its end and shake it up and down, holler 'bop bop,' and throw it in a trash basket. We'd play H-O-R-S-E till the streetlights went on, and then play some more under the light." *Bop bop.* He told me he still said it now and then during a game.

"Hey, teach," Basil was asking me, "did you write your story yet?"

I nodded.

"What'd you say? Anything about me?"

"Yeh, I wrote that you're the captain, and the team hopes to coalesce around you and take all the marbles."

"Hey, man, lighten up! You causing too much pressure on me already."

"You can handle it, Basil," I said.

"I don't know, man." He shook his head gloomily and looked at the genuine imitation linoleum floor of the motel room. "We got no offense, never did have."

"You must have read Nick Storen in the *Item* the other day."

"Well, he's right, Sam. Coach teaches defense. Everything's D, D, D. Maybe that's okay, but once in a while you got to put the ball in the hoop, am I right or wrong? I mean you can bip the shit out of the ball, but they're not giving up points for that."

"What do you think of Massy?" I asked idly.

Sweet Basil got up and poured himself a half finger of Scotch, a half violation of training rules. "Man, that dude could rip the league apart!" he exclaimed. "They'd have to make up a new game for him, let him go out and play against his own self."

"Why doesn't he play better?" I asked, bestowing a small amount of J & B on myself, so my guest wouldn't have to drink alone.

"No desire, man, that's all. Sometimes I wish that cat woulda been down in Florida with me, bouncing a sock and saying bop bop. A little malnutrition, man, that's great for the desire."

"Yeh," I said, "if you survive it."

"What kinda raising did that Massy have?" Basil asked. "I mean, rich poor or what?"

"All I know is he played a lot of piano," I said.

"Shee-it!"

Basil left around midnight, kind of abruptly, but I understood when I looked at the dresser and saw with doubled vision that the Scotch bottle had emptied itself. Ten years in the league, and at last the captain was learning the cure for anxiety. I told you he had grown.

12

The exhibition game was in the afternoon, in a drafty National Guard armory, and there were about 4000 spectators lined up along the side-lines and packed into rickety stands set up on pipes. A few of the locals wore hard hats and emitted loud yells, and before the teams even took the floor for warm-ups, you could see the flasks being passed about. Francis X. Rafferty walked every inch of the court, as was his custom, checking for dead spots.

"The southwest corner won't take a bounce," he reported. "It's like the floor's laid over ice." Like all good coaches, Buttsy was in constant pursuit of an edge.

The Wasps dressed in a boiler room and hung their clothes on nails, but for a change nobody complained. "All right, men," Coach said when they'd finished loosening up, "take and form a circle. Now men, pertaining to exhibition games you can play to win or you can play to learn. Now the front office wants us to play to win, from the standpoint of ticket sales. Well, I say, learn something out there, too! Play to win, and learn, too. See the difference?" The players nodded vigorously. If they could follow this syntax, they were one up on me. Buttsy continued in his usual Sanskrit: "It don't count in the final standings, because, men, basically I feel good about us. Every one of you boys are a year older, a year more experienced. We got two good guards, two good forwards, we got a veteran center in King Crowder and we got another boy behind him could be a star some day. Now men"—he stopped and rubbed at his eyes—"I think we can go this year. You know I'm with you!" He wiped his eyes again. "And I know that whatever you do today"—sniff, sniff—"you won't take and blacken the name—I mean, I know you won't bring—now let's go out there and play tall!"

Everybody except Abdul Buzruz cheered, and then damned if we didn't run the Hawks raggedy-ass. Not that it should have been a complete surprise, considering the dynamics of preseason basketball. As Basil had said the night before, Buttsy emphasizes defense, and any team that stresses D in the training season is bound to get off fast, for the simple reason that the other clubs don't have their complex offenses worked out yet, and an obstreperous defense can make them look silly. Later the sneaker would be on the other foot. Our own offense wasn't spectacular, but it was as good now as it would ever be, all run 'n' gun, the full-throttle undisciplined style that the blacks had brought in from the schoolyards, and it was too tough for the Hawks, trying out rookies and tripping over their socks. After a wide-open first half, it was 66–51 Wasps, and when King Crowder won the jump to open the second half, it looked like a laugher.

The fans had been sitting on their hands, and I began to get the impression that most of them thought they had paid their way into the Roller Derby and wished they could get their money back, but now they opened up good and loud, cussing both sides impartially, yelling all those negatives that you hear so often in lopsided games. "C'mon you quitters, put out!" "We didn't pay to see no practice!" The Hawks had opened the second half with three white players (the only three whites on the squad and all of them nonstarters), and when Jones Jones stole the ball from one of them, a big man in coveralls cupped his hands and foghorned down at the Atlanta bench, "Put your best in there! Yer niggers kin whup their niggers!"

As the gap widened, I remembered the old formula for the quota system: You can play three blacks at home, four on the road and five if you're behind. Pretty soon the Hawks were playing five, but at the end of the third quarter, the Wasps led 91–68.

"Hey, where's your big freak?" somebody hollered. "Bring out the giant!" The crowd took up the chant, "Gi-*ant*! Gi-*ant*!" "Hey, Coach," a beefy man in a baseball cap shouted, "put in your goon!" Everybody roared.

With two minutes left, Coach tapped number 29, and the big kid slouched across the court the way he always did, as though his head might bump the rafters, and the fans let loose. I realized that a lot of them had come just to see the game's first eight-footer, and now they were having mixed emotions. At first I thought they were cheering, and then I thought they were booing. Finally I realized they were laughing, some nervously, some uproariously, lifting their children high in the air, and pointing and gesturing and chirping back and forth among themselves.

Against a press, Justin Fell inbounded the ball to Sutter Manno, our handler, and Sutter brought the ball upcourt with that quick jerky style of his, stopping and starting, changing from a high tight dribble to a low rapid-fire Meadowlark Lemon special, teasing the ball out toward his man and them pulling it back, faking left and moving right, faking right and moving left, faking right and going *right*. He still had the best stutter dribble in the division.

Whoosh!—Sutter fired a bonecrusher pass at Massy, and the next thing I knew the ball had bounced six rows into the seats and the kid was slumped to his knees holding his face. The ref blew the clock down, and Nick Storen of the *Item* turned to me at the press table and said:

"I see Dumbo Manno's found a new partner for his act."

"I wouldn't be too critical," I said defensively. "That was a real Wilson Special."

"Wilson Special" or "Wilsonburger" is what the players call a pass that's too hot to handle, because it has a tendency to leave the brand name imprinted on your face.

"Nothing wrong with that ball," said Pete Tyles of the *Herald*. "Massy never even looked up."

Out on the court, the big man shook his head a couple of times as though to confirm that he was alive, but Buttsy took him out, and the Wasps held on for the win, 111–96.

In my story, I concentrated on the result, the "new Wasps" off and winning, already 1–0 on the season and leading the grapefruit league at least for a day. I studied the stats; four players were in double figures and Justin Fell had racked up 12 assists and King Crowder had grabbed 16 rebounds. A team victory, to use the cliché. I used the cliché.

For my kicker, I wrote: "King Crowder may be feeling the pressure of the eight-foot rookie Broussard Massy on his neck, but for this game at least, the king was chairman of the boards." I'd read that phrase not more than 40 times, used it myself maybe 20, but the number of variations on a basketball game are finite, after all, and anyway I knew it would please our sports editor. He went along with the theory that clichés evoke instant recognition in the reader.

"That's all she wrote?" the dictationist asked after I'd read my 500 words into a terrible connection.

I told her to tell Pecos I'd call back if I turned up another new.

I ran into Storen and Tyles in the luxurious lobby of the Lignite, standing under one of the genuine imitation Louis D'or chandeliers with their brilliant clusters of three 40-watt bulbs.

"You guys filed yet?" I said, and they both nodded. "What'd you write?" I asked.

I knew Pete wouldn't tell me—he worked hard, he considered every story the biggest deal since Watergate, and he lived in mortal dread that I'd steal one of his exclusives, something like "The *Herald* learned from reliable sources tonight that Basil McBride has hemorrhoids." When we were covering games on the road, Pete was always nudging me and saying, "Watch that guy over there. He's on the Erie." "On the Erie" meant keeping your ears open, trying to steal another reporter's material. To hear Pete tell it, the whole world was on the Erie for his stuff, and Solzhenitsyn had used some of it in *The Gulag Archipelago*.

Nick Storen was not as reluctant to discuss his works. "What do you *think* I wrote?" he said, pulling out a carbon and scanning it lovingly. " 'The Wasps lucked out against the Hawks because the defense is still ahead of the offense, and eight-footer Bru Massy made his NBA debut by tripping over his shoelaces.' "

"That was kind," I said.

Storen flipped a butt at the ashtray, bouncing it off the baseboard. Judging by the brown flecks, he wasn't the first to miss. Ignoring my zinger he asked, "What good is he on the deck?"

The way the conversation was going, I'd have to agree with him, and if I agreed with the *Item*'s man about anything, Dulcy would never speak to me again. "You guys eaten yet?" I asked.

"Just finished," Pete said. "Some of the animals are still in there."

I wandered into the coffee shop and found Justin Fell and Red Green sitting in front of an array of used food at a round table in the corner. "Hey, dawlin', what it is?" Red called out, and beckoned me to join the feast.

"You been writing the inside story?" Justin asked.

"How's Massy?" I asked.

"He'll be okay," Fell said. "A little depressed is all."

I heard a couple of sharp intakes of breath from an adjoining table and turned to see two teen-age girls staring toward the door, their eyes popping, and in strolled Pasty Pasticcino ahead of Bru Massy, like a zookeeper walking his giraffe. Pasty headed toward our table, but I noticed that the kid lagged behind, as though uncertain of his welcome.

Pasty called out, "Come on, man. A brew for Bru! Do you good."

We scrunched around the table and made room, and a waitress about 16 years old handed out menus. "Why don't you sit down?" she said to Massy.

"He is sitting down," Justin said quickly. The waitress gulped and put her hand over her mouth. "Right back!" she squealed, and dashed away.

"Hey, we got some partying laid out," Justin said, and nudged Red.

"Be seein' you dawlin's later," Red said, extending himself to his full 6–6. "We gone wheel in Wheeling."

"Don't wait up, roomie," Justin said to Massy, and the big man nodded. "Does your face hurt?"

"Only if you look at it," Pasty put in. I wondered why he didn't let the kid answer for himself, but Massy just sat there shaking his head slowly, as though he didn't really want to discuss the matter, or any other matter, either.

I stared as Red and Justin walked out of the coffee shop, Red doing his limp-walk as usual, and Justin a couple of paces behind. I remembered something Basil had said to Justin one day: "Hey, man, with all that black-black skin, you almost look like one of the brothers. Till you walk. Hey, man, you got that white ramrod up your ass!" It wasn't meant nastily. Everybody liked Justin.

Pasty and Massy and I ate in silence and then the three of us left the coffee shop while necks craned and eyes popped. In the lobby, I couldn't resist asking Massy if he was hurting and he grunted something that sounded like "okay."

"How'd it happen?" I blurted out. "Did you take your eye off the ball?"

I thought he said something, but then he shook his shoulders and began walking through the lobby toward his room, head lowered as usual.

"What'd he tell you about getting hit?" I asked Pasty.

"You won't print it?" he said, as we eased ourselves into a couple of plastic-backed easy chairs in front of a black-and-white TV showing ghosts and snow.

"Christ, Pasty, I can't keep not printing things," I said. "That's the way the whole season's been so far. Either I don't find out anything about the kid, or I pick up some little tidbit that I can't print."

"You surer'n hell can't print this tidbit," he said. "Coach'd kill me."

"Okay, *okay!*" I said. "But sooner or later this off-the-record crap's got to stop."

Pasty lit a panatela and took a long puff. He loved to pause for dramatic emphasis. "Kid said he was"—puff, puff—"said he was scared shitless when Coach"—puff, puff—"when Coach sent him in."

I waved my hands to clear the smoke away, found the trainer in the same place and asked, "That all?"

"Said he shouldn't of come back to the fucking game, he'd never make it, the crowd scared him and shit like that."

"But why'd he miss the ball?"

"Said he saw something. He just froze, and the next thing he knew the ball hit him."

"Did he say what he saw?"

"Nope."

"You ask him?"

"Over 'n' over. Kept saying it was just—something."

"Kid's weird," I said.

Pasty tilted his head back and laughed. "Oh, Christ, Sam, you're a real quick study. Massy's been with us a month, and already you discovered he's weird!"

I went back to my room and called the sports desk on a hot line that's kept open for late-breaking stories, and the first thing I heard was old reliable Tex Pecos asking me, "Are there any news?" I told him I wanted to slip down to Louisiana and work up some background on the first eight-foot basketball player in history, then rejoin the club in Erie, Pennsylvania, for the game against Chicago two nights later. Pecos said it would be a waste of time and money, Massy was a cinch to be cut. He loved to pass "inside" information to his beatmen, as though he had sources we didn't.

"Rafferty's only got one cut left," I explained patiently, "and if he drops Massy he's down to his last white player, Sutter Manno, and 11 blacks. I don't think the front office'd go for that. They screamed bloody murder when he cut Billy Ricketts."

"I understand that, Forrester," Pecos said in his smug tone, like somebody getting the $1.50 cream shine, "but the fact remains that he's incompetent. You've said so yourself."

"Mr. Pecos," I said, "it really doesn't matter what you or I think of Massy as a player. Buttsy Rafferty's bound and determined he's gonna have the first eight-footer in the game, and not only that, he says the kid's gonna take us to the playoffs, if not this year, then next. We'll have to cover him sooner or later, Mr. Pecos."

"Didn't we already?" He sounded as though he might be softening.

"All we said was that he played in junior high and then quit for the piano. But nobody's ever found out why. It's a good question. If you watch the kid, you can tell he's not enjoying himself. So why bother to play at all? Mr. Pecos, there's something here someplace." I was tempted to unload the story of the prowler, to cinch my case, but I knew he'd blab it all over town and risk Massy's life. So instead I said, "Take my word, Mr. Pecos. I got a feeling."

"I got a feeling, too, Forrester. I got a feeling you're craving oysters Rockefeller, and all it's gonna cost us is about three hundred bucks expense money."

"You know me better'n that," I said.

"I do? Aren't you the same Sam Forrester that just *had* to go to the NBA meetings in San Juan and then spent a week on the beach eating stone crabs?"

"Mr. Pecos, I don't even have my bathing suit with me."

"Yeh, but you got your mouth."

After another ten minutes of wheedling and begging, I won the point. In the morning, I was on a six o'clock flight to New Orleans via Memphis.

•   •   •

13

I ducked into a booth at Moisant Airport and called Hap Gladstone, sports editor of a television station and one of the wisest heads in the South. We'd been together at the Medill School. "Hey, you ol' moffid-eye!" Hap said when I told him where I was. "What blew you into town, podna? How's Dulcy? How's the frozen wastelands of the North?" I made a mental note to ask him what a moffid-eye was, when I wasn't in such a hurry.

"Hap," I said, "remember Broussard Massy?"

"Big Massy?" he said. "We all heard of Massy around here. Say, what's happenin' with Massy? You're the second call I've had about him in two days. Guy named Nick Storen wanted a fill-in. You know him?"

"He's the opposition. What'd you tell him?"

"You know me, pal. We're all in this business together. I gave him the whole *histoire.*" How those native Orleanians loved to show off their French! I told Hap to tell *me* the whole *histoire,* so I'd at least be even with my competitor.

"Not much to tell," Gladstone said. "Why don't you hop a cab and we'll have a few ersters at Galatoire's?"

"Hap, I don't have time. I got about twenty-four hours to piece this whole thing together and be back up in Erie, P-A."

"Right, right, gotcha. Well, the kid was seven foot tall in junior high school, practically a one-man basketball team." I pushed the phone up against my ear with my shoulder and began taking notes. "Not only was he big, but he was graceful, he was strong, he had moves. It was like you were watching a young Jabbar in the body of a young Chamberlain."

"That's hard to believe, Hap. He's a complete klutz now. Are you telling me what you saw yourself or what somebody told you?"

"Hey, Sammy, would I bullshit you, pal? C'mon, you been travelin' too hard. I'm telling you what ol' Hap saw, with his own eyes, eight, nine times. I used to go downtown and watch junior high games just to see Broussard in action. The kids couldn't watch their own games, the joint was so full of adults. Scouts from the pros were there, and the kid's old man—he was a cajun, a head case—he'd be smoking these thick Havanas the scouts all gave him, and they'd line up to take him to Pascal's Manale for barbecued shrimp and then down to Pat O'Brien's for hurricanes till all hours of the morning. Funny thing, when I first met Mike Massy, he didn't have a tooth in his head, like a lot of those cajun folks over there. Not much calcium in their diet, ya know, Sam?"

I said I'd take his word for it.

"Then when the excitement started about Broussard, his father showed up with full uppers and lowers. I'm not sure, I think somebody said it was Utah in the ABA paid for 'em. Then he got himself a whole new wardrobe, right out of Hart, Schaffner and Marx, five or six suits, two hundred dollars, three hundred dollars apiece, mohair, sharkskin, double-knit jobs. Sharp, man, sharp!" Hap pronounced it "shawp."

"Who paid?"

"The Warriors. Or was it the 76ers? Then one day Mr. Massy came into our newsroom to tell how his kid'd just broken the school rebounding record or something like that, and the ol' man was wearing a pinstripe chrome-blue outfit with a lavender shirt and a dark purple tie, I think it was, genuine silk, A. Sulka, ya know? And on his feet he's got—you ready for this? He's got white socks and Hushpuppies!"

Hap waited while I clucked appreciatively.

"So I said to him, I said, 'Mr. Massy, why don't you do something for your feet, *copain?*' He comes back in a few days with coal-black alligator shoes and I saw him at a game a few nights later with tan alligator shoes and from then on that's all he ever wore. They musta shot up every fuckin' 'gator between here and S'reveport for his shoes."

"Who bought 'em?"

"The shoes? I heard it was Houston. No, maybe that was the deal with the Cavaliers. No, the Cavaliers bought him the Corvette he totaled down near Paradis. Man, for a while those scouts woulda bought the old man the Taj Mahal with the Great Pyramid for a chaser, he only asked for it. The mob was suckin' up, too, least that's what I heard from some of my contacts out on Tulane." "Out on Tulane" was the police department.

"The mob?" I said, perking up.

"A few bad-ass guys from the boogalie country, down around La-fayette, Lake Charles, over into East Texas."

My tired brain tried to figure out what some cajun hoodlums could gain from the father of a kid in junior high. I asked Hap, "Was there much betting on those games?"

My old friend laughed. "Oh, sure, millions!" he said. "Those junior high kids, they'd bet bubble-gum cards, arm patches, all kinds of valu-ables. I see you haven't lost your big imagination, Sam."

"Well, why the hell were hoodlums sniffing around the old man?"

"Everybody loves a winner, Sammy, you know that. Why's the mob lick Frank Sinatra's ass? Gangsters got heroes, too. Only they didn't wine and dine the kid, he was too young. It was the father, night after night. Broussard'd be getting his beauty sleep and the old man's out making points off his son."

"What grade was that?"

"Eighth, ninth."

"And the boy was *graceful?*" I still couldn't believe it.

"I'll tell you how graceful he was, Sammy. One night I saw him in a CYO game, and he was trying to get a shot off, and this eighteen-year-old punk from Metairie was really playing him tight, jabbing his fingers at Massy's eyes and shoving him out of position and doing all kinds of kinky things. The refs always let them get away with murder on Big Massy. I guess they thought they were equalizing for his height, giving the normal-size players a fair chance."

"Human nature," I said brilliantly.

"Right. So anyway, Massy fakes toward the hoop, with the Metairie kid all over him, and then he kinda leans backward, like he's gonna start a fadeaway hook from the right, and the Metairie kid jumps on his right hand, so Massy flips the ball to his left hand and then makes a soft jumper from sixteen feet."

"Hey, I saw him do something like that in practice!" I said. "I thought it was an accident."

"Sammy, Bru Massy had more moves than any tall kid I ever saw. He had more moves than tall *black* kids. He could shake and fake with any center around. You say he's a klutz now—hey, cousin, that's hard to believe."

"Well, lately he's been playing back to form, a little anyway. But he looked silly at Wheeling yesterday."

"Yeh, Storen told me. I used an item about it on the morning news."

71

"I hear he quit basketball in high school," I said, eager to finish up the narrative.

"That's right, but the story gets futzed up right about there. The kid dropped outa sight, I mean right off the face of the fuckin' earth. Then he turned up at Benjamin Franklin. The high IQ school? You know, the kinda place they'd rather square the circle than win a game? From then on, no more roundball. No more CYO, no more schoolyard, no more nothin'. Broke his father's heart, that's what I heard. You used to see the old man screaming and hollering at the refs in that cajun accent of his, protecting his kid, hollering about favoritism, challenging the officials to fights after the game. You've known fathers like that."

Not more than two or three thousand.

"They all went home. The psychiatrist that the Knicks sent down, the physiotherapist that came over from Atlanta to help on his growing pains, all the scouts, the coaches, the hoodlums too, they just evaporated, and the next thing I knew Massy was graduating high school and enrolling at Des Rocher to study piano, and from that day on he never explained nothin' to nobody, just turned away and kept on walkin'."

"Well, for Chrissakes, Hap, why didn't you guys just get the story out of the parents?"

"What parents? The mother died giving birth. Broussard was her only kid. Father's legal name was Michel Freret Massy, if I remember right. Some boogalie name." "Boogalie" is to cajun as nigger is to negro, but Gladstone didn't mean anything derogatory, being part cajun himself on his mother's side.

"What was the father's explanation?"

"Nothing. He disappeared, too."

"Disappeared?"

"Yeh. From the day the kid quit playing, nobody ever saw the old man at Pascal's or Tujague's or Pat O'Brien's or any of the places he used to hang out. He just took off. When I heard that Massy was trying out for the Wasps, I sent one of our men to find old Michel, but he came up empty. So I put in a person-to-person call to the kid himself, up at your training camp, but he wouldn't accept the call."

"Yeh. Next to him, Venus de Milo has logorrhea."

"Has *what*?"

"Logorrhea. That's diarrhea of the mouth."

"You always were great on those two-bit words, Sam. We don't use 'em in TV, ya know. We're on the KISS system: 'Keep It Simple, Stupid.' "

I thought of filling in my old friend on the weird events of training camp; maybe he could suggest a reason why somebody had threatened Massy's life and slung acid around to reinforce the point. "Hap?" I said. "Back in camp—" I interrupted myself abruptly. Gladstone was one of the slickest journalists I'd known, but he also had the true reporter's instinct: to tell stories, and to anyone who'd listen, whether it was Nick Storen or Sam Forrester or a guy shucking oysters behind the marble countertop on Bienville. I figured the incident of the night prowler was Massy's secret, not mine.

"What you said, cuz?" Hap's voice cut in.

"Oh, nothing, Hap. Back in camp the kid was a little strange, that's all." I asked him who Leon was in the kid's life, and he said it beat him.

I thanked Hap for his help, but I really hadn't learned much, and besides it would all be in Storen's column in the *Item* anyway, along with a suggestion that the big man get a job as a clown with Barnum & Bailey, or ship out to Africa and join the Watusis, some gracious suggestion like that. One thing about Storen, you could count on him to be consistent. They used to say that Ring Lardner was driven by negative impulses, that he saw nothing but pain and evil in the human condition, but he was Louisa May Alcott next to my competition.

14

I bought a cup of coffee at the airport snack bar, where a man could think. What next? If Hap Gladstone couldn't locate the kid's father, with all the resources of WWX, "The Deep Voice of the Deep Delta," how could a Yankee outlander expect to turn him up? Then I remembered a line from an old clipping I'd read a month before, something to the effect that Massy had studied piano under Miss Agnes somebody. I doubled back to the phone booth and let my fingers do the walking. Under "Music Instruction," I found it:

Concert Pianist-Coach   Students of All Ages
Beginning—Advanced—Professional

I jumped into a cab and tapped my foot all the way to the corner of Chartres and Governor Nicholls in the French Quarter. A little brass sign led me "Two flights up, turn left." On a filigreed-iron balcony I heard the painful sound of a beginner trying to run the scales. I opened a heavy door and sat in an anteroom on an ancient settee underneath framed oval paintings of some 18th-Century longhairs. The titles said Bach, Beethoven, Mozart, but they all looked like Benjamin Franklin to me.

After a few minutes a lilting soprano voice said, "That was ve'y nice, *ve'y* nice, Jonathan. Now just a li'l more work on our scales and next week we'll try again." The door opened and a glowering kid about six years old appeared, followed by a 50-year-old Blanche du Bois out of *A Streetcar Named Desire*. She said, "Why, we have a visituh!"

I introduced myself and stated my mission, and Miss Agnes Richardson's fading green eyes opened wide at the mention of Broussard Massy. She shooed little Jonathan out the door and sat down and began cooling herself with a paper fan that seemed to jump right out of her modest decolletage. "Oh, mah!" she said. "Oh, mah word! Broussard Massy! Ah declare! Broussard Massy!"

"Yes, ma'am," I said. "That's who I came to ask about." I felt like old Jack Webb on "Dragnet."

"Well, it's all just so sad? It surely is."

"Yes, ma'am. Well, anything at all'll be welcome."

She clapped her ringless hands together and let out a little whoop. "Ah can sum up Bru Massy in one sentence for you?" she said. She had the southern belle's habit of ending every other phrase on a question mark. "Ready?"

I pulled out my pencil.

She took a deep breath and said, "Broussard Massy could play the entire third piano sonata of Beethoven—got that?—the *entire* third— when he was ten years old."

I waited, but she just stood there beaming. "Yes, ma'am," I said.

"That speaks *volumes!*" Miss Agnes Richardson said, sensing it didn't to me. "Do you know how many other students Ah had that could play the third when they were ten? No one. *Personne?*" She

74

paused. "None!" she went on, making sure the dumb sportswriter got the point.

For just a split second, I had a mad urge to say, "Yeh, but could he bip? Could he stick?" But I didn't think the lady would understand, so I just said, "I hear he was good at basketball, too."

The piano teacher pursed her lips and shook her head sharply from side to side. "Oh, don't mention that damned game!" she said, and looked ashamed. "Ah'm so sorry, Mr. Forrester, Ah forgot mahself for a second? But Ah just hate, detest and abhor that awful game, what it did to Broussard."

"Didn't he want to play?"

"Only the piano. Basketball was his father's idea. Mr. Massy kept preachin' about the boy's destiny. A little child's destiny? Till it was enough to make you sick? He said God put Bru on earth to be a great basketball player, and Ah said God didn't give that child a two-octave span so he could run around bouncin' a ball in beach clothes."

"That was well put," I said, encouraging her.

"Well, Mr. Massy didn't seem to think so. He jes' interfered and interfered when Broussard was comin' here, and then the child had that breakdown—"

I must have shown my surprise, because Miss Richardson put her hand over her mouth and said, "Ah shouldn't have told you that. You won't put it in your newspaper, will you, Mr. Forrester?" She laid a gentle hand on my arm and tilted her head coyly, and I thought, Jesus Christ, the whole world's engaged in a conspiracy to keep me from ever writing another word in the *B-M* about the most fascinating eight-foot news story in town. I would go to my grave as the ranking authority on Broussard Massy, and every line of it virginal and unprinted.

"Ma'am," I said, "I can't promise you that, but I try not to hurt people."

She backed away a step or two and tucked a stray gray hair into her chignon. "Ah have a feelin' about you, Mr. Forrester. What'd you say your first name was? *Say-em*? Ah have a feelin' about you, Say-em. Ah think you have Broussard's interests at heart. Or you wouldn't be here?" She led me out of the anteroom and into her studio. Warm rays of sun slanted through a skylight, and a fat tabbycat preened like a bored cancan dancer on the arm of a worn settee.

"You'll excuse me while Ah get coffee?" She came back in a few minutes with a steaming pot of chicory coffee, the old Louisiana kind

75

that dissolves spoons and cups, and I sipped away and even asked for a second helping just as though my mouth wasn't about to fall off. Anything to maintain the mood—that's what they taught me in journalism school. Miss Agnes Richardson talked on and on, and I filled about ten sheets of copy paper with notes.

Bru Massy's people, she told me, had come from a little town called Marcilly, southwest of New Orleans, near where the original Acadians had landed and become known as cajuns, before they'd become known as boogalies. At birth, Massy weighed 14 pounds. His mother died in the midwife's arms, and the father, Michel "Mike" Massy, was heartbroken.

"Broussard had kin in Marcilly," the piano teacher told me as she leaned over to freshen up the witches' brew. "And Michel put the boy with his brother—Leo, I think it was—while he took off to make a livin' on the towboats and oyster luggers."

I was familiar enough with French to know that Leon, pronounced in the French style, sounds almost exactly like Leo. Now I knew who the man with the acid must have been talking about: Bru, his father Mike and his uncle Leon. But I couldn't imagine what they'd done to deserve such special attention.

"The father came back every couple of months to see the child," Miss Richardson continued, "and then he'd leave again. That was Broussard's whole childhood, a long succession of hello kisses and goodbye hugs, and how was a li'l bitty fella supposed to understand that? He told me his daddy used to remind him, 'For every goodbye there's a hello,' and then pick up his seabag and disappear for a year."

By the time Bru was five years old, the teacher went on, Michel Massy "jes' seemed to lose interest in his son, or else he was plain tired, like so many of the folks over in the cajun country." The family put him with an aunt in New Orleans and she enrolled little Broussard in piano lessons, "but he wasn't really little Broussard anymore," Miss Richardson said, laughing lightly at the reminiscence. "At six, he stood a full head over his classmates, and they used to make him play with the older boys, claimed he was really eight or ten. He didn't have athletic skills, but oh mah!—he played piano like Paderewski, that li'l dickens! Ah declare, he was ready for the concert stage by the time he was ten, and then his daddy popped up, working in a warehouse on Tchoupitoulas Street, and there was a family blowup about Broussard, and his daddy took an apartment in the Quarter and moved the boy in with him. The child was never the same after that, Say-em. He wasn't practicin'—the piano was at his auntie's place, and his father wouldn't let him go over there, and Ah would jes' beg and beg, 'Mr. Massy, *suh,* you've got to get this boy a piano, it's a *see-in* not to let him play!' And ol' Michel, he'd look at me with these bloodshot eyes. Always looked like he'd been up for days? And he'd say, 'No, Ah don't have to buy him no piano, Miss Rich'son. Look at the built on that boy!' He'd say, 'That *garçon* six foot tall! Ain't a piano he needs.' "

Agnes Richardson fluttered her pale hands in front of her finely sculptured face. "What could Ah do?" she said pathetically. "What could Ah say? He *was* the child's father. He had the lawful right. Why, Mr. Forrester—Say-em—Ah jes' cried and cried about it? And Ah didn't see Broussard for ages?"

"Well, what was going on?" I asked.

"Ah only know what Ah heard later from his auntie. Camille Schex-nayder? She said the boy jes' grew like a pecan tree, and his father pushed him and pushed him. First he tried to make him into a baseball pitcher, but they couldn't find anybody his age that could handle his throws? His *pitchings,* that's it! Then Ah saw the boy walkin' into the CYO down the street, and he was carryin' a basketball and a jump rope. 'Why, Broussard Massy,' Ah said, 'what you doin' with those things?' He said, 'Mah daddy give 'em to me, Ma'am. I'm gonna be a basketball player.' He didn't look too happy, but Ah didn't want to intrude, so Ah said, 'Isn't that nass! Well, Ah hope you won't forget your piano?' He said, 'Miss Rich'son, mah daddy says Ah'm gonna be a pro, a staw.' Honestly, Say-em, Ah jes' felt like cryin'? The boy stood a foot taller than Ah was? Why, he stood maybe *two* feet taller, but he still had his little-boy curly locks and his little-boy smile, and he said, 'Miz Rich'son, ma'am, Ah can touch the ree-im.' "

I smiled. "Touch the rim? How old was he then?"

"Oh, eleven or twelve, right in there somewhere. Ah didn't know what he meant, but he looked pleased with himself, and Ah said somethin' like how good it was to be able to touch the ree-im when you're still a child, and he said, 'Yes'm.' He said, 'One day Ah jes' jumped up and touched it in a game, and Ah was so surprised Ah jes' kept touchin' it over and over again, and mah papa come runnin' over and shook mah hand, and the coach stopped the game.' "

"Well, that's quite an accomplishment, Miss Richardson, touching the rim at twelve," I said, when it appeared that the teacher had run out of memories.

"Ah don't even like to talk about it, Say-em," she said. "It's all so painful? Then one of mah li'l girl pupils came in for a lesson, and she said, 'Miz Rich'son, have you heard? Broussard can *dunk*!' Ah said, 'Do tell!' "

I sat some seconds in awe. Dunking at 12. Then I pulled myself together. "Did you say something about a breakdown?"

"Well, Ah'm no expert on that part of the story," she said, resuming her seat across the dollhouse piano studio and arranging her print skirt around her ankles. "By that time he was seven feet tall and playin' basketball five or six nights a week, and then one of my students, he said, 'Oh, Miz Rich'son, they say Broussard's in the hospital!' Ah heard later it was Holy Spirit Clinic over on the Gulf Coast, and they only take the insane." She pronounced it *in*-sane.

Fueled by caffeine, I was overtaken by a scene from the future, one of my uncontrollable subliminal scenarios:

The Wasps have just blown the last game of the playoffs on a missed lay-up by star center Bru Massy. As the crowd streams out, the big man picks up the press table and heaves it across the court, felling a referee. He rips down the backboards at both ends and slings them into the crowd, killing eight or ten, and then tears down the walls and rips up the floor. The walls of the Helix begin to sag, and Pasty Pasticcino runs out and sticks a big horse needle into the kid, and he flops into an oversize stretcher carried by two burly attendants. "Okay, you fucking psycho!" the medic says, "it's back to Holy Spirit for you. You moffid-eye, you're in sane!"

"How long was he in the hospital?" I heard myself asking when I came out of my instant coma.

"A few weeks? Long enough to calm down? Then in the fall he enrolled in Benjamin Franklin and Ah hardly saw the child again. Somebody said he was workin' with another piano teacher uptown— Ah don't really know. Ah was *so* pleased later when Ah heard he was goin' to Des Rocher—that's our pride and joy, finest music school in the state. But no matter how many recitals Ah went to, he was never on the program. Ah don't know for sure, but somebody said he lost his technique. Left it over at Holy Spirit."

"Or under the boards," I said.

A bell tinkled, and I heard the anteroom door open and close. "Oh, mah goodness?" Miss Richardson said. "There's mah one o'clock?" I thanked her warmly and stepped out into the punishing midday sun, and after a half block I was sweating New Orleans chicory.

15

I never could understand how Orleanians stood up under the summer heat and humidity, but then they dressed for it—you'd see cabdrivers wearing sandals, old black women under thin parasols, cute young things parading up St. Charles Avenue in thin little outfits that must have weighed an ounce and a half counting the underwear. If any.

I slipped into the cool comfort of the Desporte Pharmacy and made a quick call to Hap Gladstone to get the name of Massy's junior high school coach. "His name is Wolbrett, Yancey Wolbrett," Hap said, sounding as though his mouth was full of soft-shelled crabs, "and you can find him at the end of Canal Street."

"What's out there?" I asked.

"The cemetery. Hey, why don't you come over here for a minute, cuz? I'll send out for another po' boy."

The cemetery? I never thought of junior high school coaches dying.

"He's not the only one at a dead end," I said. "I'm not getting a thing I can use."

"Join the club, man! That Massy family's the original stonewall, Jackson. I mean, shit, man, I *live* here, and I don't know that much about them."

"Teammates," I mumbled.

"Pardon?"

"What about his teammates on the junior high club?"

"Let's see," Hap said, still chewing away. "Billy Reed, that was one

79

of the forwards. Herman Dreshinski, he was a guard." He hesitated. "Can't remember the others."

"Any idea where they live?"

"Not the slightest. Been six, eight years now, Sam."

I thanked Hap for taking time out from his noontime gorgy and leafed through the tattered phone book. Reed, William. . . . No entry. There were about 16 other Reeds and Reids and two Rieds, but none named William or Bill.

I looked under Dreshinski, Herman.

Nothing.

I tried Drashinski, Drashinsky, Dreshinsky. Zilch.

I was about to close the book and head for the library, to look through back issues of the city directory, when my eye caught a line in boldface:

DREZINSKI HAULING

I dialed the number and said brusquely, "Herman there?"

"Big or li'l?" a delicate female voice inquired.

"Om—uh—little."

"Out on a job. Due back, though. Whom shall I say is calling?"

"Tell him it's Alphonse," I said, selecting a fine old New Orleans name. "Nothing important."

The Drezinski warehouse was on Rampart Street, a few doors down from an oyster bar, and I busied myself with two dozen raw, served straight up on the shell with horseradish and red sauce. Around four o'clock a truck bucked to a stop in front of the Drezinski warehouse doors and two men climbed out—a pipsqueak driver, backcourt size, and a burly helper of about 250, maybe 6–2. I threw some money on the bar and ran outside and said, "Herman?"

"He's Herman," the little guy said.

"I'm Sam Forrester," I said, shaking hands with the big man and maintaining the old eye contact. "Used to watch you play basketball. Grew a little, didn't you?"

Herman Drezinski glowered at me for an instant, then snapped in perfect Orleanian: "Whatchew want?"

"Nothing special Herm," I said nervously, running my words together. "I was just passin' by thought I'd drop in see how you're comin' along how's the old teammates Bru Massy and all ya know what I mean?"

"You're not from here," Herman Drezinski said coldly.

"Well, I—"

"You never saw me play no games, did ya." It wasn't a question. That's one of my liabilities as a streetman. I can't fake; can't impersonate. The minute I open my mouth, people know my life history. Other guys on the *Blade-Mirror* can call on the family of a murder victim and snap, "I'm Hansen from the coroner's office, just wanted to clear up a few loose ends," but whenever I try it, they scream, "You're a reporter!" and throw me out.

Herman Drezinski had "made" me instantly. So I did what I'd done dozens of times. I came clean. I told him exactly who I was and what I was after. I threw myself on the mercy of the backcourt.

"Well, shit, man, why dint'cha say so, cousin?" Drezinski said, a smile breaking across his broad face. "Come on inside, man. My uncle's a reporter. Alex Buras on the *Picayune*? I wanted to be one myself. But the family movin' business and all, ya know?"

We went into a small locker room, and Herman excused himself and returned with two steaming cups of chicory coffee. My lucky day! My esophagus was gone and my upper lip was paralyzed, but I sipped away bravely. "Good!" I said.

"You don't have to drink it you don't want to," young Herman said as he studied my face.

"Thanks," I said, putting the cup down with a clatter. In some ways he reminded me of Dulcy.

We sat in that little room for the next hour, and it's a good thing Herman was the owner's son. It turned out he hero-worshiped Broussard Massy. "I loved Bru, Mr. Forrester, and I'm not half as queer as a dollar bill." According to Herman, Massy had been "the whole Milton Durel Junior High team, I mean all we did was feed him and he'd pop the ball in and we beat everybody's ass. He coulda played pro ball right out of junior high."

"Well, why didn't he?" I asked gently.

Herman Drezinski, Jr., brought me a Dr. Pepper from a machine and then began a tale of father-love and ambition and "lack of balance, that's what it was, Mr. Forrester——"

"Call me Sam."

"Call me Harry. Lack of balance, that's what it was, Sam. Six, eight hours a day on the basketball court with his father pushing him. It got out of control. Somebody had to get it in the neck. And somebody did."

He painted a picture of the young Broussard Massy in the Milton Durel JHS gym, lights glittering off his braces, his black mane streaming behind him as he ran and passed and shot and dribbled like a tall Pete Maravich, every local kid's idol.

"Oh, my god, Mr. Forrester, the scouts came pouring into town like it was carnival day! Every place he went, Broussard had a scout on both arms and a whole pack of 'em after his daddy. And it never turned that boy's head. He stayed just as calm, just as fri'ndly? He'd see me on the street, he'd say, 'Hey, Harry, where you at?' He'd say, 'Hey, what's happenin', man?' Me, I was shorter then, had terminal acne, barely made the basketball team anyway. Massy didn't care. He liked ya, he liked ya, that's it, man."

One day on the court, Harry Drezinski got an indication of how things were going. Massy had been practicing free throws for over an hour under the eyes of his father. The coach, Yancy Wolbrett, the one who now resided at the end of Canal Street, came over and exchanged a few words with Massy's father. "You got to give him a break!" Harry heard the coach say. "Mike, he'll just get fed up, the boy."

Harry heard Mr. Massy say, "Let me worry about that, Y. W.," and Mr. Wolbrett had walked away, shaking his head slowly.

"Then there was the piano teacher," Harry went on. "Forget her name. Rich'son? That's it. Miss Rich'son. She come to the gym one day and she was screamin', 'Broussard! *Broussard*! You change clothes this minute! You got a piano lesson!' And Mr. Massy, he was down at the end watching, along with a couple scouts, and he tore-ass down that sideline and he sticks his nose in that piano teacher's face and he says, 'Woman, you interferin'! Get your ass outa here!' I can't imitate him, he had a thick boogalie accent, but he said, 'You let my boy alone now, goddamn you!' and he asked for Mr. Wolbrett to throw her out the gym."

Young Harry made clucking noises with his lips. "Then what happened?" I asked, drawing on my final reserves of soothing carbonated prune juice.

"What happened? Why, she was thrown out, that's what happened! Mr. Massy, he always got his way. She poked him in the face with her umbrella and kicked the coach in the shins and by mistake she kneed some other guy in the nuts. I think it was the scout from the 76ers and the coach from LSU finally took holt of her and carried her out."

In Drezinski's version of the story, Agnes Richardson had died hard. "Couple weeks later she sent out a tape recording of Broussard playing some moffid-eye piano piece, and damned if she don't get him a five-hundred-dollar prize and a year's tuition, and you know what ol' man Massy done told her? Told her to stuff it! Bru told me she said, 'Why, my lands, Mr. Massy, any child'd give his right arm for a scholarship like this. Why, it's worth two, three thousand dollars!' And Mr. Massy, he just said, 'Lady, that's hog-leavins next to what we're gonna do, me and my son.' Well, she said she'd never be back, called him all kinds of names aren't in the dictionary. Bru told me."

I wondered why Miss Agnes Richardson had left out these details, but people tend to smooth off the rough edges of their stories, especially about themselves. I guessed she'd rather not think of herself as a woman who'd leave a man clutching his crotch, even by mistake, and use naughty language. But I kind of admired her for it.

"When was this?" I asked, after the young mover had fallen silent.

"Eighth grade," he answered. "I know, 'cause that's the last year that Bru was right."

"Right?"

Drezinski hesitated. "Yeh, well, you know what I mean. The next year he kinda lost his touch. Started complaining about a charley horse, then it was his knee, then it was tendonitis, one thing after another. His father took him to a clinic, but they couldn't find anything wrong, said it was just growing pains. Bru and his old man kept going over to the cajun country to get shots for it."

"How'd his father react to the injuries?"

"Bawled him out. Front of everybody, man. One day Bru slipped on a drive, and ol' Mike screamed at him, 'Get up, get up! *Faker!*' I found Bru sitting in front of his locker after everybody else'd dressed, and I tried to talk to him, but he just sat there."

Harry looked at his watch and said, "Holy Jesus, it's five thirty. Wife'll kill me." He got up stiffly.

"Can we talk later?" I asked. "You've been so helpful and all."

"Talk later?" Drezinski said, opening the door to the warehouse. "That's it, Mr. Forrester. The whole story."

"But what happened?"

Harry stepped out into a cavernous room and looked around his walls. "Oh, he—he just—" He held out his hands, palms up, and turned away.

"What about Uncle Leon?" I asked, but he didn't seem to hear.

I felt embarrassed. I should have demanded the whole nervous breakdown story, but I'd already heard it from the piano teacher, and young Drezinski's expression was all the confirmation anybody could ask. Massy had suffered a mental collapse in the eighth grade, no doubt about it.

I had the story I'd come for.

Now how in the hell was I supposed to print it? I could see the headline:

WASP ROOKIE EXPOSED

AS MENTAL PATIENT

No, they wouldn't be that stupid, not even on the *Blade-Mirror*.

Or would they?

It never paid to overestimate the fairness of our editors. They were capable of ruining Broussard Massy or anybody else in return for a headline that would sell a few extra copies. A head like this would be a big hit on the streets:

WASP ROOKIE MASSY

SUFFERED BREAKDOWN

AS CHILD

Coach Promises to 'Keep Eye on'

Problem Player with History

of Nervous Disorder

Dulcy'd kill me if I wrote it. Worse, she'd probably *leave* me.

I couldn't do it. Not to Massy, not to anybody. Pecos always said I lacked the killer instinct.

After I'd worked out the tedious arrangements of traveling from New Orleans to Pittsburgh by plane and connecting with a midnight bus for Erie, I put in a call to the paper. Pecos wasn't there, but I told Charley Christensen, assistant sports editor, that I'd picked up some information "but it's kind of dull, you know? A bunch of jockstrap stuff," I told him. "Maybe we should sit on it till the kid gets famous, ha-ha."

"Well, get your ass back to the team and file when you can," Charley said. "I know how that tall-man bullshit works out. Everybody keeps asking the kid if it's raining up there and gets him all fucked up and then he discovers basketball and lives happily ever after. That about the size of it?"

"Charley," I said, diving for the opening, "you been around so long you know what's gonna happen before it happens."

"Yeh," he said matter-of-factly. "That's why I'm on the desk and you're out breaking your ass."

"Absolutely," I said. "Say, what'd Storen have in his column this morning?"

"Buncha shit about Massy used to have the moves of Jabbar in the body of Chamberlain, but that was when he was twelve, and now he has the moves of Moms Mabley in the body of King Kong."

"Nice touch Nick has."

"Then he went on about how the fucking scouts and the fucking psychiatrists and sociologists and everybody else ran down to New Orleans to see the kid when he was in junior high school, but then it all just kind of fizzled out."

"Did he say why?"

"He just gave the impression that the kid was an asshole, a big jack-off, one of those clumsy freaks. I mean, Jesus Christ, the fucking kid, he can't find his fucking way across the fucking street, am I right?"

"Well, I wouldn't put it quite that way," I said. Sometimes I wondered about assistant sports editor Charley Christensen. Was his vocabulary limited or was he just naturally foul or what? "Well, okay, Charley," I said. "I gotta catch a fucking plane to fucking Pittsburgh."

"Okay, Sam," he said. "Watch your ass!" He wasn't bright enough to know I was imitating him. I wondered why he seemed to feel that every other word had to be a showstopper. Dulcy's theory was that reporters are always messing around the edges of life; we deal with murders but we don't solve them; we're close to cops, but we're not cops; we pal around with pols, but we don't run for office; and we're close to jocks, but we don't even get to suit up. What we really are is left-outs, grown-up kids standing on the sidelines looking at our feet while the teams are being chosen, *and we don't get picked.* So we end up watching, and seething inside. And talking foul to feel involved. Like *big* boys.

I used to talk that way myself, fuck yes! But lately Dulcy the social

worker had been getting on my case. Not that she was shocked personally, but she was afraid if we ever had kids they'd grow up talking like
stevedores, or like newspapermen, which may be worse. "You ought to
watch your mouth," she warned one morning, but I kept right on
salting and peppering my language the way everybody else did down
at the *B-M*.

"After all," I said, "they're only words."

"I guess you're right," Dulcy said.

A few nights after that conversation, we'd entertained the Bradburys,
an older couple that still played the Goren system, and after they made
four spades doubled and redoubled, Dulcy pushed her chair back and
said in a flat monotone, "Sam, didn't you see my fucking signal?"

"Huh?" I said.

"I signaled you with the club ten, Sam. What kind of dumb fuckie
are you anyway?"

"Dumb what?"

"Fuckie. Is that wrong?"

The Bradburys turned the color of fresh snow, and I guess I looked
pretty wan myself. "What're you trying to prove, Dulcimer?" I said
loudly. "You're swearing a blue streak and you don't even know the
words."

"Oh? Should it be fucker? What do you think, Esther?"

"Dulcy's trying to tell me something, folks," I said. "She's——"

"Honey, they're only *words*! You said so yourself." She shuffled the
deck, a smug look on her face.

"Deal!" I snapped, but Walt Bradbury said it was time they were
toddling off.

"Well, bye-bye," Dulcy said at the door. "*So* glad you could drop
over. Watch that first step! It's a pissant."

"*Pisser!*" I whispered behind her.

"It's a pisser!" Dulcy called out.

After that experience, I tried to watch my vulgarity, but there still
were times when I sounded like Charley Christensen and the rest of the
foul-mouth brigade.

The incoming plane was two hours late, which meant I'd miss my
Erie connection in Pittsburgh.

Poo-poo.

16

The exhibition season (or the preseason, as the league insists on calling it) lasted less than two weeks, eight games in all, played in smaller cities where the facilities were like the armory in Wheeling. In Erie the fans sat so close to the court that the players had to back into them to take the ball out, and a guy blasted a Freon horn right in Sweet Basil McBride's ear and deafened him for the night. Not that it mattered. The Bulls played their racehorse game, and they had us down 22–8 by the nine-minute mark. We'd started Basil and Red Green in front, Justin Fell and Sutter Manno at guard and King Crowder in the middle, our strongest alignment, but the Bulls were slicing off screens and ripping through picks as though it was the seventh game of the playoffs, and at the half it was 64–42 and downright embarrassing.

I guess Buttsy figured he had to make some kind of dramatic move, so he opened the second half with Abdul Buzruz and Jones Jones at forwards and Massy replacing King Crowder at center. "Adjust your dials, folks," Nick Storen called down the press table, "it's the Buttsy Rafferty comedy hour, starring Broussard Massy as the lovable clown."

"Is it garbage time already?" Pete Tyles asked. Garbage time is when the outcome of a game is already decided, and the players can fire away to fatten their statistics.

Massy won the tap over the Bulls's 6–10 center and moved down to the low post just the way Butts had drilled him. Jones Jones set a beautiful 225-pound pick and Justin Fell rolled off it for two points. I looked at Massy and he was loping back on defense, and I crossed my fingers that he wouldn't fall down.

The Bulls went into a tight weave just outside the circle, and Massy slid smoothly between their center and the basket and blocked the first shot that went up against him, batting it halfway up the court while the crowd shouted its pleasure with the same "oohs" and "ahhs" that accompany the dancing bear when he does the gavotte.

The ball went to Sutter Manno and he passed off to Fell on a give-and-go. Justin faked out the Bulls's guard and flipped back to Sutter for an easy two.

The teams played evenly for three minutes on the clock, and then Manno cut loose with one of his facebreakers from the end line, a perfect outlet pass to Jones Jones, and after two quick passes big Massy was alone under the Bulls's basket for a nice easy dunk that your sister could have made, provided your sister was 8–2. The kid hurried back on defense, and I nudged Storen and said, "Did you get the time?"

"Four oh six," Nick said.

"His first two points," I said. Under my breath, I muttered, "But not his last."

"Don't bet on it," old rabbit ears said.

Up yours, Nick! I said in my head. Let's see if he could overhear that.

The Bulls took a time-out and got their act together, and we lost 132–119, typical playground-type basketball, but Massy had nothing to be ashamed of. He'd played almost the whole second half, scored 11, blocked three shots and rebounded six. I expected to find a self-satisfied kid in the drafty dressing room, but all I saw was 245 pounds of lump in front of his locker. "Hey, Bru!" I said. "Congratulations! You looked good, man!"

"Thanks," he said, and padded into the shower on clogs that looked like skateboards.

Pasty saw my puzzlement and interrupted his regular postgame chore of packing Jones Jones's bad foot in ice. "Don't bother the big man," he said. "He's hurting."

"Muscle?"

"No. Didn't you see those red marks on his thighs?"

"I don't go around studying athletes' thighs, Pasty. We've only been on the road three days."

"They got him with a fucking hatpin and at least two cigarettes. Maybe a cigar, too."

"You're kidding!"

"Just good, clean fun," Pasty said disgustedly.

"Anybody else get stuck?"

"I don't think so. You know fans. They always pick the prime target."

An old newspaper clipping leaped into my mind, something about a pair of ostriches and a baby rhino being clubbed to death at the Philadelphia Zoo. The cops caught a wolf pack of teen-age kids, and the head wolf explained, "We was just havin' a fun time." What could you expect from a kid who used "fun" as an adjective?

Buttsy ordered a scrimmage the next day in Hagerstown, Maryland, where we were scheduled to play the Washington Bullets. "I'm not down in the mouth," he said as he lined the men up against the wall of the local high school's gym. "You down in the mouth?"

Four or five guys made loud replies, "No, suh!" "Uh-*uh*!" "We *up* in the mouth!" But most of them, including Massy, just stood there.

"Basically it's up to you," Buttsy said, spinning a basketball on his index finger the way he always did when he addressed the team. "D'ya want to be the engine or the caboose? You wanna suck hind tit?" He was gathering steam. "Steak or hamburger?"

"Look at Massy," Storen whispered. "He already missed two out of three." I couldn't understand Nick's attitude toward the kid. Massy was 8–2 and Storen was 5–6. Massy had a full head of curly black hair and Storen was bald. Massy had sharp ascetic features and Storen's face looked like a snowman's. But Storen was a stunted bald snowman long before Bru Massy came along. Why resent the kid?

"We'll be workin' out every chance we get before the opener," the Butts was saying. A groan went up from the players. "*I know it, I know it!*" Coach went on. "Pertaining to practice, I feel the same as you guys. But just remember: When you're not working, the other guy is. And when you bump heads, he'll bust your ass."

For an hour and a half he had the Wasps running up and down the court like a herd of mule deer. "See the ball!" he kept screaming. "*See it, goddamn it!*"

He'd grab somebody like Sutter Manno and go into a heavy lecture: "Give up the ball! *Give up the ball!* They don't give points for dribbling. Jesus Christ, we're not the fucking Globetrotters." Some of the players looked as though they were sorry they weren't.

In the second scrimmage, three on three, Massy took the ball at the high post and began twisting his arms from side to side, looking for the open man. He hardly ever put the ball down anymore, and his passing was sharpening up, although he still had a tendency to throw curves on long balls. Buttsy and Justin Fell had shown him how to release the ball the way a pitcher releases a slider, with a little counterclockwise twist of the wrist, to take off the natural curve.

"Hold it, *hold it!*" Coach hollered, and walked out and grabbed the ball away from the big man. "Stick out your hand, son, flat against mine." Massy's palm covered Buttsy's whole hand, fingers and all. "Now can't you see that?" the coach implored. "Hand's fourteen inches from little finger to thumb, Broussard. Remember when we measured?" Massy nodded.

"Well, why'n the fuck you holding the ball with two hands?" He turned away. "How many times can I keep telling you guys the same things?" He shook his head pitifully. "Now from the standpoint of holding the ball, son—"

"Use one hand," Massy interjected.

"*Right!*" Buttsy said, as though the kid had solved a cube-root problem in his head. "Now you're using your natural smarts." He stood on his tiptoes and slapped Massy on the back. "What happens you hold the ball with two hands?"

"Overcontrol it," Massy said like a school boy.

"*Right again!*" Coach said. "Got to establish full control one-handed. Now some players can never do this, which they can't learn or they don't have the basic equipment. But you, kid—why, you're— you're——"

"A freak," Storen muttered.

"—You're *gifted,*" Buttsy finished, as King Crowder glowered at the two of them from a corner. "Just don't seem to know it. Now take and use what you got, or else you're just jacking off."

Massy nodded. Nick said, "Jacking off, I think he'd get more out of it."

The team didn't click in Hagerstown, but Bru Massy had the best game of his short pro career. Coach benched the slumping Crowder in the middle of the second quarter, and Massy played almost 30 minutes. He wound up with 14 points, most of them dunks; plus 11 rebounds, three assists and four blocks. When I filed for the three-star, I used a great phrase if I do say so myself. I compared the Massy situation to the old line about imperial China: "Let China sleep. When she awakens, the world will be sorry." Well, maybe I didn't get it exactly right, but it sure seemed to fit the kid, standing around the basket and batting away those Washington shots like they were tsetse flies, and giving the Bullets something extra to think about whenever they went up to shoot.

The only sour note was King Crowder, huffing and strutting around the dressing room, kicking his locker and threatening to quit the club. He grabbed Buttsy while most of the other players were in the shower.

"Look, Coach, there's only one way for me to get in shape and that's to *play,*" he said. "If I can't play here, goddamn it, trade me someplace I can."

"Weren't you my center last year and the year before?" Rafferty said calmly. "Didn't you start every game?"

"Yeh," King said begrudgingly. "Last year."

"Well, this year, too. Massy's gotta beat *you* out, son, not the other way around."

Maybe King saw the shape of the future, long before the rest of us. He warned Justin Fell that if Massy crowded him, there'd be trouble. Edwin "King" Crowder was the soul support of a mother and 11 siblings; he didn't intend to move them back to the ghetto.

After I filed, Tex Pecos got me on the phone and said, "What's this crap about Massy and China?"

"Well, the kid's been kind of suppressed so far, but now he's wheelin'——"

"Listen, leave out the literary fluff," Pecos's reedy voice came back. "You prove the old saying. 'A bit of learning is a dangerous thing.' Shakespeare."

Yeh, I said to myself, *a little learning is a dangerous thing:* Alexander Pope. I subbed for the literary fluff and polished off a half-pint of Scotch. I learned early that whisky is one of your essential tools for dealing with editors.

The Wasps finished the exhibition season at .500, a nice honest percentage, and everybody except Nick Storen was beginning to entertain mild hopes for the season. Preseason sales were up, with almost 4000 season tickets sold, leaving another 15,000 seats available for each game. I breezed into the house on the day the road trip ended and hollered, "Hey, Dulcy, honey, this may be the year."

"The *year*?" she repeated, looking at me as though I was retarded. "You've been gone twelve days and eleven nights and you come into my house yelling about the year? Honey, this is the *night!*" She dragged me by the wrist, not that it took a lot of dragging, with Dulcy wearing her sexy Austrian blouse tucked in at the waist and out at the bust—"same dirndl thing!" she always called it—and her green eyes glowing like somebody was welding in there.

"Well, what's up?" she said after I'd flang off my clothes and gained the upper hand.

"Nothing much," I said modestly.

By careful control I managed to last about four seconds, but the night was young, and we hadn't even left the living-room rug. I leaned back against the couch and sighed, and Dulcy said, "Have you been eating a lot of rabbit?" and I said, "My, my, you really been sharpening your act."

"What else was there to do? The Bradburys don't come over anymore, and all our other friends were out on the road with you."

"Maybe the neighborhood's heard about your vocabulary."

"My vocabulary? What about my vocabulary?" She leaned over and brushed her lips across my shoulder.

"Your foul language."

"Foul language? What fuckie had the nerve to say that? Any pricker that says I use foul language, I'll kick him right in the filberts!"

"The *filberts*?"

"Should it be the cashews?"

"The nuts. Is that what you're groping for?"

"No," she said, "*this* is what I'm groping for."

17

We woke up with a bang, and by nine o'clock we were considering the possibility of spending the entire day between the sheets, sending out for food. The phone rang.

"Ignore it!" Dulcy instructed, but I had already picked it up, and before I could get the phone to my ear I heard the excited voice of Darius Guile saying, "Sam! *Sam!*"

"Yes! *Yes!*" I answered.

"It's me. Guile."

"I know," I said wearily. "Who the hell else would interrupt me when I—when I just got back from a long trip."

"Say, listen, pal," he said, which was a bad sign, because "pal" meant that he wanted something. "Can you get down here right away? Mr. Gross has called a meeting, and he wants the beatmen."

"Hey, come on, D. G.," I said. "I been on the road for two weeks. Gimme a break!"

"Nine fifteen. In Mr. Gross's office." He hung up.

I don't know how to explain the process by which a professional sports organization chips away at your independence until one day you discover that you're not only working for your editor, you've also got nine straw bosses in the club offices. After ten years of covering the same team, you'd think I'd have earned certain privileges, but instead the Wasps practically owned me. It hadn't always been that way. When the Christmas presents came around, I used to return them. I refused to eat in the press lounge, where the team set up a fancy spread before every game. I never asked for free tickets, and when the club pressed them on me I pressed them back.

Then one night I got to the Helix late, on an empty stomach, and I accepted a Monte Cristo sandwich from the PR man, Jack Carbon. Pretty soon I was scarfing down the free meals like everybody else, but I still thought I was independent. Then one Christmas the present from the front office was a black-and-gold portable Sony with a five-inch screen, a miniature masterpiece, and I couldn't bear to return it. What the hell, you couldn't buy Sam Forrester for a $300 TV. Could you?

Then some of the regulars got involved in a gangbang on the road, and the stadium lizard who arranged the soirée went to the police and screamed statutory rape. Darius Guile and Jack Carbon had to phone all over the state to wake up politicians and fix the case. "You won't use anything, will you, Sam?" the press agent asked. "Nick and Pete Tyles already agreed." Now what? If I went ahead and spread the most fascinating sports story of the season all over the paper, I'd lose every source on the team and maybe fifty or sixty jocks around the league. If I ran the story, I'd be a hero for a day, but in whose eyes? Tex Pecos, king of the bromide, Charley Christensen, old septic mouth, and a bunch of fans who read with their lips. Meanwhile I'd wreck about five marriages and destroy a lot of dreams.

"No, Jack," I said, "I won't run anything."

That's how you're compromised, an inch at a time. After that, the front office can always call the sports editor and tell him how you made a deal, and then you're out of a job, and there are already thousands of sportswriters on the bricks and more thousands coming out of the J-schools every year, happy to start below guild scale. So you accept the Christmas presents and the free meals and the tickets, and you keep your mouth shut, and you try to draw the line somewhere. Myself, I drew it two places: I wouldn't write those phony puff jobs for the Helix program: "Basil McBride is off and running on his finest year yet. . . ." "Red Green is everybody's favorite, and this year he bids fair to reach the heights of his profession." You could write those exercises in about ten minutes flat, but they always reminded me of Truman Capote's description of a book he didn't like: "That isn't writing, that's typing." Teams pay $200 or $300 apiece for those puffs, and if you think it's just another way to buy the press, you're right, and every sportswriter in the business knows it.

I also drew the line at getting involved in contract negotiations. The front office liked to use its hired guns to shoot down holdouts. Nick Storen would write: "Justin Fell hasn't reported to camp, and Coach Buttsy Rafferty has reshuffled the lineup around a promising newcomer named Jack Scovil." Each succeeding day of Justin's holdout, Jack Scovil would draw higher and higher praise, until finally it looked as though the team had never needed Justin Fell in the first place and Jack Scovil was a cinch All-Pro.

As soon as Justin yielded to the pressure and signed, the stalking horse Scovil would be shipped back to the Eastern League, and all through the season the fans would ride Justin. Who needed this greedy ingrate? The team could always send for that great kid Scovil, ain't that right? Never shoulda let him go. Storen was a master at that kind of squeeze.

Everybody except Mr. Gross was in position by the time I arrived. They were seated around the 20-foot polished-oak round table in the Wasps's boardroom, the sanctum sanctorum where all the great decisions were made. It was a bigger boardroom than U.S. Steel's, with mahogany furniture and carpeting two inches thick and rosewood paneling on the walls and blow-up pictures of great Wasp players of the past (strictly speaking, there were no great Wasp players of the past, so they just used pictures of good Wasp players, or average Wasp players, and a few who were poor but memorable).

As I took my seat in front of my gold-plated ashtray and carafe of hot Colombian coffee and silver ice-water pitcher with monogrammed water glass from Steuben, I looked around the table at the well fed, all of them serenely convinced that the most important matter in the world was whether the Wasps got off to a good start. I always venerated the foot soldiers of sport and I suffered when they suffered, but some of these pompous movers and shakers bored me sideways and I suppressed a yawn. Just then Mr. Gross entered from the heavy sculptured door to his office, and the team personnel jumped up and started competing to see who could kiss his broad backside with the most sincerity and feeling.

"Please!" Abraham Lincoln Gross said, smiling on the dogs at his feet. "Sit, sit." Like most members of the front office, he was fat, with wattles descending from his chin and lumps of overweight protruding from beneath his sunken eyes like bits of cold Crisco. The legend was that he had started his business career with the Hagenbeck and Wallace circus, being fired twice daily from a cannon, but the act was discontinued when he doubled his weight and they couldn't locate another man of his caliber.

For all his bombast, Abraham Gross was no simple study. He prated about his own perspicacity, but you couldn't count on anything he said, because he was always altering his legend. With a name like Abraham Gross and a nose that curved out and down like the beak on an elephant seal, he was a natural target for every anti-Semite around the league, but he was a Welsh Episcopalian by birth and had changed his name from Cowsell or Cowshell or something similar. "I figured I'd get more respect in the business world if they thought I was Jewish," he liked to explain. I wondered how much was true and how much was Gross deception.

Our managing owner was nobody's idiot, that was clear from the day he took over. He listed himself in *Who's Who* as a "philanthropist," and his first sporting deal was with the city for rental of the $90 million Helix. He wound up getting the place for one dollar a year. "They wanted a million two," the philanthropist bragged on television, "but I Christianed them down."

As soon as he took over, the new owner redid some of the Helix decor at the behest of the internationally renowned designer and decorator and former Las Vegas showgirl, Mrs. Abraham Lincoln Gross. That's how the Helix became the only sports arena on earth with a hanging scoreboard in the shape and colors of a Tiffany lampshade. You could blind yourself looking at our scoreboard. But there was no denying the esthetic appeal, and at a modest $125,000 cost, too. The city council had been proud to put up the money.

You'd never guess from his wallful of citations and trophies for everything from good sportsmanship to civic achievement, but the old

95

man was heartily disliked by his players and roundly detested by agents and player reps. He was the kind of owner who was always in court, exploiting the fact that the U.S. judicial system tilts toward the rich. His fondest boast to the Wasps was repeated at the opening of every training camp: "Men, if you don't like being a Wasp, if there's anything Mr. Guile or myself are doing to offend you, *if for any reason whatsoever* you wish to leave this ballclub—forget it! You're ours, boys. Relax and enjoy it."

He was just as tactful to us hired whores that covered the team for the local press. We could write anything we wanted about Gross Abraham so long as it was complimentary. Once a writer named Harcourt had slipped in a phrase to the effect that Gross was "pressuring" Basil McBride to sign his contract, and Harcourt was canned.

Some NBA owners liked to sit high above the floor in "skyboxes" staffed by servants and stocked with bars, instant replay TVs, telephones and Western Union printers bringing in the scores of distant games. But Abraham Gross, man of the people, sat directly behind the Wasps—in a 16-seat box separated from the ordinary folk by a blue velvet rope and four guards, plus Wasps's security chief Pat Rhoades, a former city detective. There he would shout instructions to the bench. "I don't get annoyed," Coach Rafferty insisted. "The old man has good sense, pertaining to basketball."

I overheard a few of Mr. Gross's orders. Once the Wasps were losing by a basket, and Sweet Basil went up to the line with three to make two. *"Rafferty!"* Mr. Gross cried out. "For God's sake, impress the boy. *Make all three!"*

"Gentlemen," Mr. Gross told us tarnished knights of the round table, "certain people have been bad-mouthing our club." I tried to think of someone who *wasn't* bad-mouthing the Wasps. "Mr. Guile and I have worked up an approach that we think will silence the critics." I couldn't guess what his new approach was, but I was dead certain Abraham Gross did not intend to shell out money. His dollar-a-year lease would be up in a year, and the councilmen were primed to raise the rent. Maybe to two dollars. I wondered what the old pirate had up the sleeve of his white-on-white shirt. "Our press director will outline the new operation," he said, and oozed back into his chair.

"Thanks, A. G.!" Jack Carbon said, popping straight up like a hand puppet in a children's play. Mr. Press Agent was now upon us, speaking in his clangorous public voice, accenting every other word like a newly hired announcer at a 500-watt radio station. "You know, boys, I thought the boss had gone bananas when he outlined his idea, but—*ha ha——*" He turned and laughed in the monarch's direction to make it plain he was only kidding. "—But after I heard the whole plan I knew it was a stroke of *genius!*"

The last stroke of genius had been the removal of all water taps in the Helix. This being a free country, Mr. Gross had given the fans a free choice: soft drinks at 75 cents or beer at one dollar. At the next game a woman fainted and had to be revived with Dr. Swett's root beer, and when she came to, the hawker collected six bits.

"Boys," Jack Carbon said, flashing his Ipana smile, "we're getting an assistant coach!"

I looked at Abraham Gross, squeegeed into his chair. He was smiling like an oil Arab.

"Is Red Auerbach coming out of retirement?" Nick Storen piped up. "You activated Eddie Gottlieb?"

Jack Carbon smiled indulgently, looked slyly at Abraham Gross and said, "The new assistant will be. . . ."

Dramatic hesitation.

"The fans!"

I wish I could say that pandemonium reigned at that historic instant, but actually it didn't even drizzle. Nick and Pete and I just looked dumb. Pennsylvania Morgan kept right on dozing—the *Off the Pigs News* published when it was in the mood, and Pa. often nodded out during morning press conferences. Lucious Johnson of the *Afro-ite* was the only reporter alert enough to respond. "Huh?" Lucious said. "What kinda jive you puttin' down?"

"We'll bring 'em right into the action!" Jack Carbon proclaimed. He pulled down a wall chart and began a detailed explanation. Each arriving fan would be handed a punch card bearing the names of the twelve Wasp players. He would make his selections and stick the card into a wall slot inside the Helix. Ten minutes before the tip-off, a computer would spew out the names of the starting five. If the fans wanted to make a substitution during the game, they had only to chant the player's name, and Coach Rafferty would make the switch. The new man would remain in the game till the fans decided otherwise. In case of hesitation over whether to put in player A or player B, the coach would hold his hand over each man's head to see who drew louder applause.

I banged my ear with my open palm to see if I was getting the wrong station. I turned to look at Nick and Pete and Lucious, and all three of them sat mute. "Right on, baby," Pa. mumbled drowsily. "Power to the people!"

"Power to my dick," Nick said out loud. "You can't run a professional basketball team that way."

Abraham Gross's open hand came up and passed several times back and forth in front of his face, an Episcopal priest with a Jewish name offering Catholic absolution. "Don't you see the beauty of it, boys?" he said in his most oleaginous tone. "The fans are always saying we don't know how to run the team. Let them run it!"

"Listen," Nick said. "Can the fans make trades?"

"No," Carbon said. "Of course not."

"Can the fans buy new players?" I asked.

"No," Mr. Gross said. "But they can reshuffle the old ones."

"That's suppose to win games?" Lucious Johnson asked.

Abraham Gross built a stubby A-frame with his pudgy fingers and smiled over the roofline at the representative of the *Afro-ite*. "It'll win something more important than games," said our managing owner. "It'll win friends. It'll generate—er, uh—it'll produce—"

"*Money*?" I blurted out.

King Faisal smiled.

We were scheduled to open the regular season three days later, and Pete Tyles became the first to inform the fans of their new duties. The early afternoon edition of the *Herald* replated under the head

FANS TO HANDLE WASPS'S LINEUP

The line must have been written by the same copyreader who produced the famous Navy Day banner

ADMIRAL'S WIFE TO HOLD SAILORS BALLS

By 3 P.M. lines had started to form outside the Helix, and by 6 they stretched halfway around the block. General Manager Darius Guile put on extra clerks, but they couldn't keep up with demand. Our season tickets sold for $150 to $400 a copy, and there were plenty of takers. After Nick Storen and I gave the "assistant coach" system more ink in the next morning's editions of the *Item* and the *Blade-Mirror,* the crowds formed again, and this time there was trouble. Word went up and down the line that the opener against the New York Knicks was sold out and nothing was available except season tickets. "That settles it!" a man in a pinstripe suit said. "We'll just take a season box then." But a round little guy in a hard hat said he'd be fucked if he'd let that fucker Abraham Gross fuck him, and he'd get into the opening game somefuckinghow, and fuck the Wasps in the ass! A superfan wearing a plum-and-white jacket with WASPS on the back took a poke at the hard hat, and the brawl was on. The 24th Precinct came galloping over like a regiment of cossacks, but order wasn't restored till the fire department cleared the sidewalks.

"Kenny," I said to the team's play-by-play radio announcer as we watched the scene from an upstairs window of the Helix, "it looks like we tailed a tiger."

I could tell by his expression that I'd made a stupid remark. Like most sportscasters, Ken Hohlar was nonverbal. "What?" he said. "The circus isn't here till December." Once Pete Tyles had invited Kenny to "come over and break bread with us," and the voice of the W-A-S-P radio network had answered with his customary effervescence, "Will do! Should we eat first?" He was also the club's Mrs. Malaprop. He'd come out with remarks like, " 'Balls,' said the king, 'if I had 'em I'd be queen.' " His favorite expression was, "Anything can happen and usually does," which he used at least twice a game.

Now we were peeping out a slit in the curtains three floors above the sidewalk. The police led a couple of brawlers toward a paddy wagon, and just before they were tossed inside the door like rag dolls, one of them turned and spat on a cop's shoe. "Disgusting!" Hohlar hollered, shaking his head. "Punks like that oughta be shot, for their own good."

"See you, Ken," I said.

"Right," he said. "Will do." He loved to say "Will do" and "No way." His repartee swung between those two extremes.

Back home there was a scribbled message from Dulcy. "Bru Massy called. Very excited. Said he heard from Richardson. Said tell you this kind prying could be disastrous. Who Richardson?"

So dainty Agnes Richardson, the sweet piano teacher who kneed grown men, had dropped a note to her old student. I wondered what she'd said. Probably nothing too harsh—she'd formed a nice impression of me, or at least I'd worked hard at it.

I was trying to be tolerant about the kid's ways, but he wasn't making it any easier. I looked at the note again. "Disastrous." What kind of silly excess was that? The nuclear plant that wiped out Allentown, Pennsylvania, sure, that was disastrous. But not some basketball player getting put off his game by a nosy reporter. Well, when you're 8–2, I guess you have a different perspective. I'd try not to risk disaster again.

II
the middle

1

Looking backward with periscopic expertise, I can see that the whole season might have been different if the Knicks had beaten us in the opener, but they were playing without their star center, Orion Halliday, and they sorely missed his steadying effect, as well as sorely missing about six crip shots in the first half and finally blowing the game on a hat trick in the last few seconds. In hockey or soccer, a hat trick is an accomplishment, three goals in one game by a single player, but in basketball it means you stepped to the free-throw line with three to make two and blew them all. Credit this particular hat trick to the Knickerbockers's forward Bill "Pepsi" Kohler, if you're scoring.

Massy played about three minutes of the last quarter; the new "assistant coach" insisted on it, and Buttsy had no choice but to put him in, even though the original intention had been to wait eight or ten games until the kid felt more at home around the league. Massy jumped up as though snake-struck and ran out and covered the wrong man, but a few minutes later he blocked a shot and led a fast break, so his maiden appearance in a regular game came under the heading of that old Bronx expression: "Vouldn't help, vouldn't hoit." Buttsy sat him back down as quickly as possible, but this didn't keep King Crowder from steaming. "You don't bench the King," he kept insisting, but the crowd had benched him anyway.

"Smooth as a charm!" Press Agent Jack Carbon yelled in the dressing room after the game. "Can our fans pick 'em!"

101

The New York writers were clustered around Bru Massy, sitting there in his size-50 jockstrap, giving them a sample of what he'd been giving the rest of us all summer—grunts, "yehs" and "maybes," and staring fascinatedly at the floor, as though a Fellini movie was being shown down there.

I walked into the areaway as General Manager Darius Guile was being interviewed by Reggie Auchincloss of *Sports Pictorial.* "To be sure, to be sure," Auchincloss was saying in his Hotchkiss accent, "but shouldn't you develop a patterned game rather than—oh, what *is* it called?—burn on burn?"

"We play what it takes to win," Guile said. "You saw the results tonight. A perfectly coordinated team, well directed by the coach, well selected by the fans."

"Oh, to be sure, to be sure," Auchincloss said. "Chroist, so far you're fab, simply *marvy.*"

Sean St. Lawrence of *The New Yorker* asked how one could be certain that the spectators would continue to make the correct decisions, especially since one knew that the fans so very seldom got anything right, even including the correct color of shirt, "those of your fans who take the trouble to wear one."

"Ask me that question when the season's over," Guile said. "After we win the playoffs."

I rushed away to grab a quote or two from Buttsy, leaning back behind his simple wooden desk and sucking on a long stogie in his customary postgame ritual, answering the questions of the faithful Wasp reporters. "I agree with you, Nick," Coach was saying. "It was uncanny. The fans got a lot more sense than we give 'em credit for."

"But Buttsy, not *that* much sense!" Storen said heatedly. "Jesus, they started exactly the same team you'd have started. They put Jones Jones in just about the time you'd have put him in, and they yanked him exactly seven minutes later when his feet started to hurt, and they put Sutter back on the wood as soon as he drew the fourth foul. The only mistake they made was Massy, and we lucked out on that one."

"Basically, your average fan's got sense," Buttsy said.

"Basically your average fan's an asshole," Storen insisted.

"Basically go fuck yourself," Coach said, but he kept on smiling.

"The people're beautiful," Pennsylvania Morgan observed. "Everybody else, *fuck 'em!*"

"This all jive bullshit!" Lucious Johnson announced. "No crowd of fans'll make the right decisions."

"Well, they did it!" Coach said, rapping the desk top for emphasis. "And they'll keep on doing it. Should of started this system years ago. Crowd's there, why not use them? Why, teams like the Knicks been using them for years. Know what they call the crowd in New York?"

"The sixth man." I said.

"Sure, the sixth man," Buttsy said, "from the standpoint that the crowd gets behind the ball club and jacks 'em up. Why, I was scouting the Knicks one night when they were losing by eighteen points to Milwaukee and they took and scored the last twenty points of the game behind that crowd."

"The last nineteen," I said. It was a famous game, and it had inspired the lovable New York crowd to sing, "Goodbye, Lewie, goodbye, Lewie," to a good and decent man. I didn't have a whole lot of affection for "the sixth man" after that performance.

"Buttsy, I smell something," Nick Storen said.

"Yeh, well, my grandmother always use to say, 'Dog smells its own dirt first.' "

You could see the coach was in a euphoric mood. It was like the night down in Wheeling when we won the opening game of the exhibition season, and the Wasps were in hog heaven with a 1.000 record. I figured somebody'd better remind Buttsy of a remark Linda Lovelace had made a few years ago: "One swallow doth not a summer make." But I knew it would just go over his scalp.

After I filed my game story, plus a running score and a sidebar on the new computer system, I walked over to Gabinetto's Bar & Grill, three blocks down and two blocks over, the favorite watering hole of the Wasps, newspaper reporters and other evildoers.

"Plenty room! Plenty room!" Mario said as I walked in the door. Mario would holler "Plenty room" even if the walls were bulging, but tonight the place was almost empty, except for the usual intimate group from the *B-M* and the *Item,* drinking to celebrate the fact that both papers had been put to bed and they didn't have to use the word "allegedly" for another 16 hours. "Christ is allegedly risen, hallelujah."

"Hey, howsa you hangin'?" Mario said. The proprietor was a short white-haired man from Parma, and he knew about 100 words of English. His cook sprinkled paprika on everything, including the spumoni, and the thyme was always out of joint. But the drinks were strong and the place had plain white tablecloths and a stand-up bar with cigarette scars in the dark wood and a battered brass rail to prop a weary foot on. The waiters were homey, too, most of them in the U.S. illegally, living under Mario's protection, and they went about their duties nervously, afraid they'd be fired and deported any instant. One day an aging waiter tripped and dumped a bowl of steaming minestrone in Pete Tyles's lap, and before Pete could say a word the old guy snapped, " 'Atsa *you* faults!" Pete was okay after a few skin grafts, but there were lots of nights when he had to tell his wife that he had a sick headache.

I ordered a quick shot for rejuvenation and then a Scotch and water for social sipping, and after a few minutes Lucious Johnson and Nick Storen walked in with Jack Carbon. They were still arguing about the Wasps's "assistant coach," but I'd heard enough for one night.

"Come on now, Sam, you settle it," Jack called out after they'd ordered. "Does the gimmick work or doesn't it?"

"It works, it works," I said impatiently. "Anything you say, Jack."

"Bullshit!" Nick said to the press agent. "Eight to five you assholes didn't even use the computer. You just faked it and played the guys you wanted."

"Oh, we did, did we?" said Jack Carbon, master of the devastating response. "Well, just try *printing* your opinion, and see what happens!"

"What'll happen?" Nick said, turning his bald head toward Jack's greased one.

I thought the Wasps's press officer would say that the team would sue for libel, or he'd personally punch Nick in the mouth, but Jack backed off and said, "I'll confiscate your key to the cundrum machine," and laughed uproariously at his own lack of joke. If he meant the prophylactic machine in the press toilet, it had been empty for months.

"Drinks all around!" Jack Carbon said, flaunting his expense account, just as the outer door opened and several Wasps strolled in.

"Hey, *drinks all 'round*!" Red Green called from the vestibule. "Hey, that's cool! Make mine a double Scotch." He turned to the other newcomers. "What'll you dudes have a double?"

"Brandy alexander," Jones Jones said imperiously, adjusting a single gold earring.

Red laughed. "Won't get no brandy alexander in here, dawlin'. Mario don't serve dessert."

Jones changed his order to bourbon. Abdul Buzruz said he'd like a plain soda, and Mario shook his head impatiently and said, "Costa same. One-a buck."

Abdul's bulbous lower lip jutted out, and he said evenly, "Hey, fool, we been through this a hundred times. You serve the drinks, we'll take care of the dust."

"Dost?" Mario repeated.

"The cash," I translated.

After the drinks had been set up, Nick Storen turned to Jones Jones and said, "Well, Archibald, how's it going?" Instantly I knew there'd be trouble. Nobody called Jones Archibald, even though he was legally Archibald Preston Jones, Jr., of New Mexico State, once a fine all-purpose player, but slowing down because of his feet.

"Hey, chump, don't call me Archibald!" Jones said fast.

Jones Jones was usually the happiest player on the team, but he had one idiosyncrasy. The instant that Jones had found out he'd made the team, seven years back, he'd spelled it out. "Dig, you dudes, I don't want no nickname. I want to be the first Jones that isn't called Puddin-head, Too-tall, Jamboree or Jubilee. Don't call me Basketball Jones and don't call me Hambone Jones. My name's Jones, just simple fuckin' Jones. It *fit.*"

"Nice to meet you, Simple," one of the players said, and another threw in, "Simple Fuckin' Jones. Yeh, that do have a nice ring to it."

But Jones was serious, for once in his life, and from that day he insisted on his preferred name, which was why I usually referred to him as Jones Jones, or Jones[2].

"What's the matter with 'Archibald'?" Nick Storen said at the bar. "That's your name, isn't it? You ashamed of what your parents named you?"

"Hey, dawlin'," Red Green interrupted, "lighten up now. We jes' come in here for a li'l libation. Dig?"

But when the foul mood was upon him, Nick had to keep blundering forward, like a tank with no reverse. "I'm getting tired of calling you Jones," he said. "Let's try a nickname on you. How about 'Feets'?"

"C'mon, man," Red Green implored. "Stop playin' the fool."

"Look, I axed you a long time ago," Jones Jones said, fighting through Red's pick and jutting his jaw at Storen's. "I said I don't want *no* fuckin' nickname. Jones, that's it! Not Feets, not Goose, not Satch, not Stretch, not Old Folks. Can you dig it, honkie?" Nick shut up, at least for the moment.

I hated to see anybody aggravate Jones Jones, on or off the court, because his value to the team went far beyond his play. Jones kept the players loose, he helped to brighten the long road trips when the Wasps would be losing game after game. He did silly routines about his early life in Mississippi. He'd say, "My daddy picked cotton from dawn to dark. I says, 'Daddy, I cain't cotton to dat!' He say, 'Son, all mah life Ah been a hard-workin' cotton farmer.' I says, 'Daddy, where you find all this hard-workin' cotton?' And Daddy, he say, *chung!* He gimme a whack! Ain't nobody beat my daddy in a debate. *Chung!* How you beat that logic?"

Jones was a member of the Xerox school of elocution. If a line was funny, he felt it was twice as funny if repeated, and three times as funny once more. He'd say, "You know how I test my quickness? I switch off the light and jump under the covers before the room dark."

"That's quick," somebody would say.

"Before the room dark!" Jones would say.

"Whoo-*ee!*"

"*Before the room dark!*"

Once Jones had been our fashion plate, featured on the cover of *Sports Pictorial* and other publications, but that was before his bonus money dribbled away. In a league where style consists of letting your sweat socks droop around your ankles, Jones had been a beacon of chic. He wore red-dyed mink jackets, fuchsia suede cavalier hats, coal-black patent leather boots with six-inch stacked soles and heels, wraparound goggles of a violet hue. He showed up at practice in peau de soie tank-top underwear and moleskin shirts, unbuttoned to the navel. "Hey, babe," he said to me one day, "you ever stop to think how many moles died to make this thing?" He bought a $3000 sealskin coat, floor length, and Sweet Basil McBride told me a sea lion at Ocean-rama tried to fuck him.

When the militant Abdul Buzruz, née Ernie Robinson, came to the club, there was a heavy confrontation. I heard about it from Justin Fell, my contact with the Third World. Abdul asked Jones Jones what he'd done for his struggling brothers lately, and Jones went into a long explanation about setting an example, "showing the brothers what a po' kid from the ghet-to can accomplish, if he try."

"You figure that's cool?" Abdul said. "Running around like a jive-ass nigger? Snapping your fingers and saying, 'Be cool, be cool'? Don't you know the bloods are laughing at you, man? And the grays too?"

Jones didn't comment.

"Hasn't anybody hipped you, fool?" Buzruz pressed on. "You either cool or you not, dig? You can't *try* to be cool, Jack. Trying to be cool is *uncool,* dig?" Abdul said everyone was down on Jones in the projects and the mosques; the word was that he was a selfish nigger.

Within three weeks, Jones had sold his $36,000 pimpmobile with the herring scales and started showing up in jeans and sweatshirts. "Ain't *no* jive turkey gone call *me* uncool!" he said as he headed for a fur auction to unload his precious sealskin and a mink.

From that day on, Jones Jones was his old relaxed slaphappy self again, not trying to prove anything, just enjoying life. On the court, he'd watch a player skid along the floor, and he'd crisscross his hands in front of his knees and holler, "Safe!" He'd kiss the ball before shooting a free throw, and go to the wrong bench, and join the other club's huddle. The crowd loved it. When the referee called a foul on him, Jones would bow sharply and snap his heels together and give a Nazi salute, and flip the ball to the ref behind his back, or over his head, but he never drew a technical. Court jesters have special privileges.

"Good game, boys!" Jack Carbon said as we sipped our drinks at Gabinetto's.

"Oh, thank you, white massa!" Jones Jones said, bowing and showing his gleaming teeth. "Kin Ah fuck yo' sistuh?"

Nick Storen pulled a package of dried shrimp off a cardboard placard and slid it down the bar toward Buzruz. "Here," he said. "Have a snack!"

"Unclean!" Buz said, stepping backward.

"What's unclean about shrimp?" Storen said, pretending to be puzzled. "Perfectly good food. Better'n that candied yams and sowbelly shit you people eat."

"Hey, I don't eat no candied yams and sowbelly," Buzruz said. "I eat the diet of my faith."

Storen wiped a drip of Scotch off his chin. "Sure, you do. Pigs' ears. Possum trots and hog wallers."

"God is one, *Ahad,*" Buzruz intoned. He drained his glass of soda and left without another word.

"See what you done, dawlin'?" Red Green said, sounding upset.

"Hey, Mario, bring us a round!" I said by way of apology to the black players. "You dudes were really cookin' tonight."

"About time they did something right," Storen said, and I felt like poking him in the mouth. But Red Green reached across and tapped Nick on the sternum with a big spatulate finger. "Hey, dawlin' "—*tap tap tap*—"what's all this signifyin' tonight?"—*tap tap tap*, a little harder. "You havin' the ministration monthlies or sumpin'?" His finger began to sound like a hot run by Philly Joe Jones.

"Now dig, mothafucka!" Red said after he finally stopped his drum roll and looked down at Nick from his 6–6 perch. "We had 'bout enough of this boolshit, you foilow my meanin'? Now you git yo' fuckin' Johnson together, sucker, else you and me gone humbug right here!"

Storen said, "Fuck you!" and walked out intact.

"Poor Nick," I said to nobody in particular. "Something comes over him. He's like that guy in Li'l Abner that travels around with his own cloud. Joe Bftsplk? Every once in a while things go black."

"Things go *what*?" Red Green said, and I realized my mistake and turned to protect myself in the clinches, but Red and Jones were laughing at me. "Hey, you whitey honkie suckah, you!" Jones said, grinning and showing the diamond star on his incisor. "You was so scairt you didn't know whether to shit or shuffle!" He gave me a friendly whack between the shoulder blades.

"You better get outa my face, dawlin'," I said, "or I'll give you a shot upside the haid! We be wheelin' and dealin' and squealin'!"

Jack Carbon bought another round and everybody went home.

In six or eight hours.

2

We left the next morning for a game with Boston on Saturday night, then to Atlanta for a Tuesday game, to New Orleans for a Thursday game and another at Houston on Saturday afternoon. We lost every game and weren't even in the contest except at Atlanta, where the score was 78–all at the end of three periods and then our aging players just flaked out and died, unable to run with the Hawks's bruising young studs like Bear Brakhage and Anders Peterson. Massy sat on the bench the whole trip, not that his presence would have mattered, because the team was going horseshit. Pete Tyles asked Coach why he didn't give the kid some exposure during garbage time, but Buttsy just said he had to bring Massy along an inch at a time. "If I took and put him in now," Buttsy explained, "he'd probably stink up the joint and it'd break his spirit."

"How's he gonna get experience?" I asked.

"Basically you got to give him special handling," the coach said. "He's not like your average rook, you know, from the standpoint that he's got no place to run after the game. One of the other guys make a mistake, they just pull their cap over their head and go hide. But Massy's one of a kind."

After our fourth straight loss, Jack Carbon said only half-jokingly, "I think I know what the trouble is. We're on the road, and our fans aren't picking the team." But by the time we got back to the Helix for a game against Phoenix, the computer stunt had been banned. A TRAVESTY OF THE GAME, the commissioner had wired the front office. A PUBLIC RELATIONS STUNT IN THE WORST TRADITIONS OF MADISON AVENUE. Gross Abraham wasn't disturbed. He'd sold 13,000 season tickets, 6000 above normal, and the Helix was SRO for the next eight games.

The fans were irate. Telegrams poured in, and several hundred people demanded their money back, with predictable results. Darius Guile issued a public statement that there would be no refunds, but "the Wasps have planned so many special events that the new season bids fair to become the most exciting in team history."

One of the gala events was "beer night," when the first 5000 fans into the Helix were treated to free bottles of Maguire lager. The brewery had put up the beer as a promotion, and Guile thought he was getting a free ride, but the incidental expenses were high. After the Wasps eked out the win in the final minute on a desperation turnaround jumper by Justin Fell, the fans poured on the floor and tore down the backboards and ripped up seats for souvenirs. Guile and Gross decided against another beer night. Instead, a press release announced that the next big promo would be "Sutter Manno Night, when Wasp fans will show their appreciation for the gritty little guard who has given so many wonderful years to the Wasps."

"Why a Sutter Manno night?" I asked the general manager.

"Well, he's been around longer than any other player except Basil," Guile said.

"Then why not Basil?"

"Mr. Gross doesn't want our first player night to be for a black. We'll work up to it."

"*Work up to it*? You got a team made up of ten blacks and two whites and you're gonna work up to the blacks?"

"Black fans don't buy tickets."

"Maybe this is one reason why," I said. "Chrissakes, somebody's always giving Sutter a night." Hans Christian Andersen "Sutter" Manno was the son of a Finnish father and a Swedish mother, but the Italian-Americans had taken him to their *bonza*. "Don't let on you're not a wop," Guile had instructed him years back. At halftimes, Sicilian and Neapolitan societies would present him with salamis, and on the road he'd be named "Italian-American Basketball Player of the Week" and win plaques edged in red, white and green. Two or three times a year he'd have to make quick trips away from the team, to St. Louis for an honorary degree from a barber college, up to Providence, Rhode Island, for the Sons of Italy, out to San Pedro to help bless a tuna boat.

Sutter didn't care one way or the other. If the front office told him to go, he'd go. He was a sleepy-eyed fellow off the court. The first time he saw the Helix, as a farm boy fresh out of Brigham Young University, he said, "Boy, this place'd sure hold some hay!" But otherwise he was about as talkative as Massy. He accepted his awards and went on his way: a robot obeying his programmers. If Coach told him to press, Manno would stay within an inch of his man till death do them part. If Butts had told him to lie down in the middle of the court and whistle the "Bell Song" from *Lakme,* he'd have tried. Once in a scrimmage Buttsy hollered, "All right, move it! *Balls out this time!*" and Sutter began fiddling with his jock. "No, no!" Coach called out. "That's just an expression. Jesus, Sutter, put 'em back! Looks like two navy beans in a knapsack!"

On the court, he was renowned for his bogarting tactics and his facebreaking passes, like the one that caught Massy in the face at Wheeling, West Virginia. When Manno was 22 years old and a rookie, he'd played such aggressive defense and picked off so many enemy passes that Sweet Basil was moved to comment, "That dude can look west and watch the sun come up!" For a few years he was the man who engineered our attack—our "devout Roman catalyst," as Pete Tyles once described him—even though his shooting was below average, and he really didn't have an outside chance. Now Sutter was 29 and his best days were over. He started games, but seldom finished. His pace would sag by the end of the third period.

"Sutter Manno Night" was a hot ticket, with 19,000 fans crammed into the Helix up to the skyboxes. Every Italian in the state was there, and at halftime the assistant consul general gave Sutter an envelope containing a round-trip ticket to Fisherman's Wharf in San Francisco, all expenses paid. Our front office presented Manno with a new pair of Adidas sneakers and a gold-plated tie tack, and his cheek was brushed lightly by the moustache of Signorina Annabella Ritirata, "Miss Pizza with Everything Hold the Anchovies." The Wasps lost the game, to Detroit, but at the gate the evening was an artistic triumph.

When the Seattle SuperSonics came to town, we were 3–11 on the season and Buttsy Rafferty called the squad together for a morning practice at the Helix. Work crews had just finished laying a floor over the ice left from a hockey game, and wisps of fog hovered over the clammy maple as the team shivered through calisthenics. Red Green had splashed his hands with beagle oil, the aromatic hot sauce that trainers use on racehorses, and Sweet Basil McBride wore his wool stocking cap. "Men, I got a new play," Buttsy said in his best conspiratorial manner. "Now listen close." It was an out-of-bounds play for the final seconds, and it was schoolyard simple: Massy breaks for the basket, takes a high lob and dunks.

"You call that a play?" Nick Storen asked Coach as we sat on the sidelines and watched one player after another practice the lofted pass. "Every team has a routine like that."

"Don't you think I know it?" Buttsy said.

"Then why all this rehearsing?"

"I got to do something, don't I? Massy's beginning to look like a player. But I can't just take and put King Crowder on the wood, can I?"

"This your way of slipping the kid in?"

Buttsy patted Nick on the back. "A few more years covering this game," he said, "you'll know your ass from the free-throw circle."

"King'll never sit still for this," Pete Tyles put in. "A play just for Massy?"

"Fuck Crowder," the Butts said. "Never seen a red-ass like him in my life. Cries like a baby every time I look at the kid."

The team rehearsed the "play" 20 or 30 times in a row and Massy began to look smoother at catching the ball and dunking it. When it worked, the move was pretty to watch, with the ball sailing in a rainbow arc like an old-fashioned two-hand set shot, and just before it reached the backboard the kid's 8-2 form would intercept maybe 13 or 14 feet off the floor and stuff it on the way down. "Now who the fuck's gonna stop *that* move?" Coach called out. For once, Massy looked interested.

The Wasps got the ball that night with 30 seconds left and Seattle ahead 109–106, and Coach called time and sent Massy in for the lob play under the basket. Justin Fell laid the ball right on the kid's fingernails and Massy scored.

The Sonics went into a stall, but Jones Jones slapped the ball off their guard's shoulder and we had another chance for an inbounds play with six seconds left and Seattle ahead 109–108. This time it was Jones who threw the high lob, and this time the Sonics were ready. Their seven-foot center went up with Massy, and the kid used his extra height and grabbed the ball, but it squirted out of his hands as he started to dunk and he fell heavily, holding his stomach. The ref hollered, "I got seventeen on the elbows!" He pointed to the Seattle center and handed the ball to Bru.

We needed one to tie, two to win, and the kid fired those balls up there as nonchalantly as a schoolboy practicing in his back yard. The first shot traveled on a slight arc and went in without touching the rim, tying the game at 109, and as soon as the ref bumped the ball back, Massy swished the second shot through and the game was over. The crowd erupted, and the big man walked off the floor, gently pushing fans aside. He headed for the dressing room, grinning like a circus clown.

Watching him in his first tiny moment of triumph, my mind went back to the night of the prowler, and the kid's strange reaction, as though something was threatening him but he didn't dare admit it.

Sitting there at the press table getting ready to rap out my game story, I couldn't even form the prowler's silhouette in my mind. He seemed distant and vague. Winning does that. Wipes out unhappy memories.

For a night or two.

•   •   •

Buttsy Rafferty opened the room to the press in a few minutes, as he usually did. Some prima-donna coaches keep it closed for 20, 30 minutes, or won't open at all, but Butts knew we had our job to do and some of us had deadlines. I went straight toward Massy's locker, but I gave up when I saw the other reporters homing in like a shoal of porpoises. I stopped at Buttsy's postgame press conference in time to hear him say, "A routine play, boys. When you got somebody eight foot tall, you might as well use them."

By the time I'd filed my running score and game story and stats via the interoffice teletype, it was nearly midnight, and I figured I'd drop over to Gabinetto's and see what kind of trouble Nick Storen was brewing up. There was a drizzle, and the city lights glowed like out-of-focus fireflies as I headed across the gleaming concrete plaza of the Helix. Something caught my eye under the plastic canopy by the will-call window, and as I stepped closer something caught my ear, too. It was Roxanne the flutist blowing her nightly gig. She was a wisp of a young woman, with long hair that hung below her waist and a body that wasn't much wider than her flute and big oval brown eyes like one of those paintings that everybody used to buy. I knew what her hand-lettered sign said:

Sonatas and Fantasias
by
ROXANNE

I'd already written a feature on her and the other musicians who picked up change outside the Helix. Their stories were all the same—working their way through music school, taking the old joke seriously: "How do I get to Carnegie Hall?" *"Practice, mother, practice!"* I don't know about her mother but Roxanne had every intention of playing at Carnegie Hall, and since she had to practice six hours a day anyway, she figured she might as well go public and supplement her income. That's what she meant by "fantasias"—they were her standard fingering exercises, but who among the throngs spilling out of the Helix could tell a fingering exercise from Dizzy Gillespie anyway? On a good night, she would pick up five or six dollars, a little more if the home team won, but this was the first time I'd ever seen her tootling in the rain an hour after the game.

Then I spotted the reason. Bru Massy was huddled against a pillar of the building, almost out of sight, tapping the biggest foot in sport to some busy piece of fingering that reminded me of "The Flight of the Bumblebee." I walked up like an old friend and said, "Hey, Bru," and he smiled pleasantly and politely shushed me with an acre of palm. The two of us stood there against the wall until Roxanne unwound a couple of riffs for her ender. Massy clapped both hands against his straight-cut jeans; I figured he didn't want to draw a crowd.

"Hi, Roxanne," I spoke up. "I see you're working late."

Massy was still smiling like somebody who'd reached for a weed and come up with a Perigord truffle. "That was sure pretty, Miss Roxanne," he said in that sepulchral tone of his. "Telemann, wasn't it?"

"Third sonata," Roxy squeaked in her ultra-soprano, a voice to match her instrument, and when Massy said, "Excuse me?" she cupped her hands and called up at him. "Third sonata!"

"That's okay," the kid said, looking embarrassed. "I hear you okay." Then he dropped back a step or two and just stood there.

I asked Roxanne how she'd made out tonight, and she said, "Well, not too good, considering the Wasps won. Four eighty-five—till him." She nodded toward Massy, and her glance caught him around the belt buckle. I peeked into her opened flute case and saw a handful of silver and a twenty-dollar bill. "Mr. Massy's a musician himself," I said boldly.

"Used to be," Massy's voice floated down on us, softer than I'd ever heard it, and I'd heard it plenty soft, ranging almost to the inaudible.

"Would you like to hear something else?" Roxanne asked. I guess she figured she owed him something for his money, although she must have been out here playing for him alone for the better part of an hour.

"Sure would."

"Anything special?"

Massy tilted his head and was silent. Then he said, "Were any of

Mozart's piano works ever transposed for flute?"

"I can improvise." The girl rapped the silver tube against the palm of her hand and began a tune that sounded like the track from the Swedish movie *Elvira Madigan*. I still had my regular postgame headache, caused by crowd noise and tension, and I'm afraid I winced a couple of times on the high notes. I looked at Massy, standing behind me, and his eyes were half-closed, but they opened wide when Roxanne tapped her foot and swung into a speedy passage, with her fingers moving so quickly they seemed to blur, and her cheek muscles rippling across her face as she attacked the notes.

Then the tempo slowed, and she finished on a long trailing upswept note that just sort of hung in the wet air and died away. When she dropped the flute to her side, I looked around toward Massy and he was gone. "What?" I said.

Roxanne pointed her instrument at the far corner of the Helix. Without even stopping to say good night or throw two bits into her case, I grabbed my Olivetti and gave chase.

I guess the kid didn't think he'd be followed, because he slowed down as soon as he turned the corner behind the Helix, and by the time I came puffing around the bend I almost ran past him, standing there in the darkness. "Massy!" I said. "Hey, Bru! Where you runnin', man?"

He didn't say anything, but he didn't reach out and crush my bones, either—a good sign. I set down my portable and my briefcase full of stats and bios and sandwich ends and cracked, "Hell of a night to be running relay races."

I looked at his head, two feet up there in the shadows. No reaction.

"I mean, if you really want to run, we could go over to the athletic club and turn some laps. Only this time you carry the typewriter."

"I'm sorry, Mr. Forrester," he said, and once again that voice caught me unawares, coming down from Mount Olympus. I could imagine him dubbing the voice of God in a movie. "A funny feeling came over me," he said. "I don't know how to explain it."

"Listen, Bru," I said emphatically, "you don't have to explain a thing."

He nodded—gratefully, I suppose.

"Going home?" I asked after another silence. "I'll walk you."

"Yes, sir. Back to the hotel." I knew he'd taken a single room in the old Helix Excelsior, formerly the Excelsior Arms and before that the

Drummers Plaza, across the street from the stadium. He politely picked up my typewriter as we headed down the street, and said something that got lost in the stratosphere.

I was taking almost two steps to every one of his, and still it seemed I was holding him back. We reached the hotel in about as long as it takes a Lancia to do the 440, and he handed me my typewriter and did that funny little flip of the index finger that he always used when he met people or said goodbye. Then he disappeared inside the lobby. I'd barely started to hail a cab when he was shambling back out on the sidewalk, looking slightly upset. "Mr. Forrester!" he called out. "Sir, I just wanted to explain why I ran off like that? At the Mozart?"

"Sure, Bru, whatever you say." I held my breath. I was willing to bet this would be the first explanation he'd ever volunteered to a Wasp writer. Good, bad or mediocre, it was a breakthrough.

"I was too moved by the music," he said simply.

"Well, sure, it was beautiful. Marvelous talent that girl has."

"Yes, sir. Touching. Choked me up sumpin' awful."

We stood there like Gargantua and the flower girl for a few more seconds, but he didn't seem disposed to elaborate on his Gettysburg Address, so I figured I'd act like a reporter for a change.

"How about the game?" I said. "Jeez, those inbounds plays sure worked for us."

He paused, the way he always did before speaking. "I feel good about that," he said. "I really accept basketball, Mr. Forrester. Sometimes I think it's an okay game."

Stop the presses! *Broussard Massy says basketball is acceptable.* We'll sell a million extra on the street.

"But it doesn't reach me the way some other things do," he continued without prodding. "Like music. Music reaches you too, Mr. Forrester. I know. I glanced at you while she was playing." So he'd been studying me while I'd been studying him? "When she sustained that last note, the diminuendo? Didn't you just feel that you'd known Mozart personally all your life?"

"Oh, absolutely," I lied. "But wasn't that *Elvira Madigan*?"

"No, sir, that was Mozart." Too bad I didn't write the music column, I'd have had a clean scoop: "Roxanne Garfein played Mozart at the Helix last night before the biggest audience in town."

After another silence, I summoned up my bravado and said, "You know, Bru, we should talk once in a while. Do us both good. There's

116

things I can help you with. Whattaya say? How about a drink?" It never occurred to me that there was any other way to have a midnight talk. You go to a bar, you drink, you talk. Doesn't everyone?

"Well, sir, I don't drink," Massy said in his slow cadence. "I try to respect my body. But I was fixin' to take a walk."

I checked my typewriter and briefcase in the hotel and we started out in the drizzle. The first thing I noticed was that the kid stopped traffic, even at midnight. Drivers jammed on their brakes, busses slowed down, taxis pulled to the curb and then leaped away when Massy turned toward them. I was surprised that the kid didn't seem to be annoyed about the invasion of his privacy; it must be normal for him. And then it hit me what a perfect target he made on the uncluttered street. My God, a man who could slip undetected into my room in training camp could certainly track an 8–2 giant on a dark street at midnight.

"You take this walk often?" I asked.

"Just about every night we're not on the road."

Whatever this habit told me about Bru Massy, it told me something about the acid man: he couldn't possibly be on the case at the moment. And Massy knew it. Maybe Bru wasn't considered a target anymore.

I was tempted to come right out and ask. As we walked, I rehearsed a speech to myself. "Goddamn it, Bru, what's it all about? I've got an explanation coming to me, man! I'm the one that gorilla scared witless on your behalf!" But Massy had me trained by now. You took him on his terms, or you didn't take him at all. And the terms had never changed since that opening press conference in camp: Nothing personal. Never. At no time. N-O. Simple enough when you got used to it.

By now I was used to it.

Which may have made me a lousy newspaperman, but at least I was walking with him, getting to know him, however slightly. That's more than Pete Tyles could say, more than Nick Storen had accomplished.

Sometimes the race is to the inept.

•　•　•

4

If I thought the kid intended to keep up a folksy conversation, I was mistaken. He responded to my lame comments with little "mmms," "um-*hmms*" and "rights." There was no outpouring of reminiscence, no commentary on being basketball's first eight-footer, no intense discussion of his future on the Wasps. I contented myself with pretending that five miles per hour was a normal pace, and studied the people who were making a spectacle of us. It was like walking a pet kangaroo. Several teen-agers flattened against a wall when we came striding past, and all I could hear was "wow!" and "far out!" On a dim side street, two women turned abruptly and scurried off in the other direction.

"We headed anyplace special?" I asked after we'd walked five or six blocks west. His reply blew into a second-story window, so I just kept on trucking. After another two blocks, we turned into a side street and stopped at a place that proclaimed itself to be Sol's 24-hour Health Store.

"A little refreshment?" Bru said, and we made our way among wooden barrels of beans and grains that lined the entrance hall.

"Hey, whattaya say there, Bruiser?" a middle-aged man with a cherubic face said from behind the counter. Several customers sipped beverages and gawked at us.

"Da usual?" the man asked.

Massy nodded. One thing about him, he didn't play favorites. Here in a place where he was evidently a regular, he still barely spoke.

"What about da friend deh?"

"I think I'll have a hot fudge sundae," I said.

The counterman looked shocked, so I laughed as though I'd been joking, and asked what he recommended, and he listed about six weird concoctions ending with "eucalyptus tea and fireweed honey." I said, "Yeh, that sounds good. I always liked eucalyptus tea. Water chaser."

Massy took a seat at the end of the counter, where there was more stretching room, and in a few minutes the cherubic man brought him a mug of carrot juice and me a steaming pot of Vick's Vaporub. I started to say I didn't have a cold, but thought better of it. No point in wrecking the vibes. I took a sip—the drowning man goes under for the first time—and was surprised to find the drink palatable, if not in the same class as J & B on the rocks.

I waited for Massy to start talking. It was a long wait. He just sat there drinking his carrot juice like a dowager princess at high tea, and not until he was finished did he offer any conversation, and then it started with two words:

"That girl?"

"Huh?" I said.

"The girl with the flute?"

"What about her?"

He hesitated. "Oh, nothing," he said.

He didn't continue in that loquacious vein, so I just said, "She's been around for two seasons now. Name's Garfein. Roxanne."

"Nice name," Massy intoned.

"I wrote all about her in the *B-M*," I said, "before you got here. When the Arabs invaded Israel last year, Roxanne got a nose job. To make her nose look more Jewish. She said Moses didn't mind looking Jewish, why should she?"

Massy turned his head slowly and peered down at me. He looked mildly interested, so I plowed ahead.

"I wrote how she's working her way through music school by practicing in public, and she expects to study in Europe on a grant. Had a cute lead on the story."

"Lead?"

"That's the starting graf—paragraph. The lead's what you lead with, see? I wrote—let's see—'Roxanne Garfein the flutist does weekly concert engagements at the Helix. Some day she hopes they'll let her play inside.'"

"I like that."

"Well, I liked it, too, till the editors changed it."

"Changed it? Do they change what you write?"

"Try and stop 'em! They changed it to 'Someday she hopes they'll let her play inside, hopefully.' I won the publisher's prize contest for best lead of the month. A five-dollar purchase order at Kresge's."

"Talented," he said. "Purely talented."

"Well, my wife thinks so," I said modestly.

Massy looked startled. "Oh, excuse me, Mr. Forrester," he said. "I meant Roxanne Goldfein. I was fixin' to ask you—"

"Garfein."

"Garfein. I was fixin' to ask you to tell me more about her? If you don't think I'm being too personal?" He sounded like Miss Agnes Richardson, making everything interrogative.

"Well, she's in her third year of music school. Miss Klang's, out in the university section?" I was beginning to sound southern myself. I'd noticed it before: unconsciously imitating my interviewees. You got more news that way, but you also began to lose touch with yourself. "She plays flute and clarinet and I think some saxophone," I went on. "Oh, yeh, a little piccolo, too, but I understand all flutists can play piccolo." Massy didn't respond, so I babbled on. "Jeez, I think she even plays oboe," I said. "Remember what Danny Kaye called the oboe? 'An ill wind that no one blows good?'"

I heard a rumbling sound like a subway passing underneath and then I looked up and realized that Broussard Massy was laughing, a huge, jolly laugh that shook the walls and rattled my eardrums, and for an instant I visualized another lead in the *B-M*: *"I'm fixin' to shake this goddamn town down," Broussard Massy laughed, and the town fell down.*

He kept up for the longest time, till everybody in the place was staring at us or laughing with him, and then he cupped his hand over his mouth and said in a subdued voice, "Who said that?"

"I told you! Danny Kaye. In a song. 'Anatole of Paris,' I think it was."

"Who's Danny Kaye?"

It wasn't easy to communicate with a generation that had to ask a question like that. I explained and Bru said he remembered seeing Kaye in a movie, and then out of nowhere he said, "Is that safe?"

"Is what safe?"

"Playing flute outdoors at night?"

"It's safe for her. That skinny little thing—she's tough as a boot. Roxanne's a city broad."

Massy frowned down at me, and I could see he wasn't crazy about my choice of words. "I mean she's—a cityperson," I stammered. "She's been around. She'll be okay." He smiled again.

We walked back to the hotel in tentative camaraderie. He still hadn't mentioned my visit to Miss Richardson, and I entertained the hope that he didn't intend to. I went inside the lobby and claimed my typewriter and briefcase and said, "Well, Bru, sure been nice getting to know you."

"Yes, sir, same to you, Mr. Forrester."

"Name's Sam."

"Aw, sir, I couldn't call you that."

"Go ahead. Try!" I couldn't resist the crack: "I won't hurt you."

He laughed his earthquake special again, and stuck out his hand to shake, another first, and a seedy old man with a junk pack on his back and a heavy cane walked into the lobby. "Hey," he cackled, "how tall're you?"

"Six-one," I said. "Maybe six-two in my shoes."

"Not you," the old man said disgustedly. "The big boy."

Bru looked around the lobby, and I blurted out, "He's eight-two, something like that," anything to get the old fart away and finish the night on a pleasant note.

"That right?" he said, standing almost on Bru's instep, stretching his leathery neck like a sea turtle.

Massy nodded. The man began poking the metal tip of his cane into the kid's stomach, and caterwauling at the top of his lungs, "Yer no eight foot two! Yer not even eight foot. Goddamn liar! Why're you lyin' like that?" Bru pulled back just as the bellman grabbed the old man and muscled him toward the street.

"Don't hurt him!" Massy shouted. When the bellman returned, he said that old Mr. Willis came in every night and got thrown out every night, and was slightly—the bellman twirled his finger around an ear.

"Poor soul," Massy said, and turned toward the staircase. "I sure hope we didn't upset him." He waggled his index finger and took the steps four at a time.

When I got home, Dulcy was waiting up. "Well," she said, "who was she? Blonde, brunette or redhead?"

"Brunette," I said. "Black curls, ivory skin and a low sexy voice. Statuesque, too."

I told her what had happened, and she kept smiling till I came to the part about calling Roxanne Garfein "a city broad," and how Bru had seemed to bridle at that description.

"Is that the way you think of me, too?" Dulcy asked. "A city broad?"

"No, honey," I said. "You're from L. A. You're a country broad."

She threw a pillow, and then I told her about the peculiar scene in the lobby, and her face clouded over, and she said, "Oh, I just think

121

that's awful." She thought about it. "I wonder how often things like that happen to him. Every day, I'll bet."

"Probably."

"Sam, did we ever discuss the purple wildebeest?"

"Huh?" I figured she was getting dopey, or I was. We were floating on our water-bed with the lights out.

"The purple wildebeest."

"No," I said grumpily. "We've discussed the maroon aardvark and the cerise armadillo, but the purple wildebeest—no, I don't think so."

"The purple wildebeest is a well-known behavioral concept," Dulcy said, propping herself up on an elbow and sending out a small wave. "But then it didn't happen on a basketball court, so you wouldn't care."

I held my tongue and waited. Wild horses couldn't keep Dulcy from expressing one of her favorite social theories, or anybody else's. "They did this experiment in Africa," she said. "They separated a wildebeest from the herd, sprayed him purple and sent him back."

"I never saw a purple wildebeest," I parroted. "I never hope to see one."

"The other wildebeests stomped him to death."

"Why?" I said. "It was his own herd, wasn't it?"

"Yes, but now he was *different,* don't you see? Wildebeests don't try to figure out whether strangers are wildebeests or lions or what—they don't have time. It just registers on them that the other animal's different. So they fight or they run. That's their genetic protection from danger. Some claim that human beings have the same instinct."

"Don't say," I murmured, turning on my side.

"It would explain race prejudice, Sam. Distrust of people with accents. Looking down on bearded kids—" *And humpbacks,* I thought.

"I guess you figure it explains an old man poking his cane at Bru Massy," I said, swallowing a yawn.

"Sure," Dulcy said. "The old man's too senile to know how to hide his deep feelings, like the rest of us. So he—what's that awful expression you always use?—he lets it all hang out. But he's really expressing what everybody feels"—she snapped on the light—"on one level or the other"—she looked at the clock, which said 2 A.M.—"but we're socially programmed to conceal it"—she snapped off the light—"even from ourselves."

"A purple wildebeest," I mused, feeling overeducated and tired.

"Well, if a purple wildebeest had to come into the league, he signed with the right zoo."

"Be nice to him, Sam," Dulcy whispered, sliding her gentle fingers across my back. "His life can't be easy." Slowly I began to doze in the soft tide rips. The Wasps and I would be leaving for the coast at noon.

The curtain was rising on my first Technicolor dream starring a nude Princess Anne and a male wildebeest in pajamas when I felt a kiss on my stomach. "It's only me," Dulcimer said after I jerked convulsively, sending a wave across the bed and making us bob up and down like corks.

I mumbled, still half-asleep, "I'm bushed."

"Do you have a sick headache, like Pete Tyles?"

"How do you know about Pete Tyles?"

"Oh, we wives talk, compare notes, sizes, things like that."

"You *do?*" I sat straight up. Dulcy grabbed me by the shoulders and shook me like a terrier with a rat and rolled over on top of me, and I found myself suffocating in fresh-scrubbed blonde hair and the mysterious sandalwood aroma of the east while she giggled like a madwoman and yanked at my buttons. *La Dulcy Vita*! Surf's up!

"Help!" I shouted. "I submit, I submit! Please, Mrs. Rapist, do not abuse my body!"

So *that* was the secret—eucalyptus tea with fireweed honey. I pass it along in a spirit of friendship.

5

When teams like the Knicks or the Celts travel, brass bands and civic delegations turn out at the airport, but the Wasps didn't seem to inspire that kind of loyalty. All we had was Freddie Verhegen and Pipper Martin and a few stadium lizards, basketball groupies and lovers of the downtrodden. Verhegen was a jelly-bellied musician who billed himself as "the world's premier Wasps's fan" and hadn't missed a home game in the ten years of the franchise. He dressed entirely in plum and white, even to his underwear, and he'd show up at the airport with a loud-speaker system and play the Wasps's anthem composed by none other than Freddie Verhegen, his orchestra and his jelly belly. In the earliest years of the franchise, Fred and his Merry Men would appear in person to play the anthem live and unrehearsed, but airport authorities had put the nix on that practice. Altogether the Wasps made about 20 departures a year, and Freddie's music was driving customers to Amtrak. Now we had to settle for the loudspeakers; Freddie would set them up at the gate, and we'd walk through a curtain of inspiring chorale:

> *The Wasps!*
> *I kid you not.*
> *Always there to sting.*
> *Ready every night to win.*
> *The Wasps!*
> *They never let us down.*
> *So do not you let them down.*
> *The W-a-a-a-a-sps!*

Once Dulcy asked Fred if the song was copyrighted. "God forbid," she told him, "that anybody should try to steal the lyrics."

"Don't worry," he said. "I got it fully protected." We breathed a sigh of relief. Anyone with the courage to rhyme "Wasps" with "not" and "sting" with "win" deserved his reward.

The other regular at the airport was Pipper Martin, clerk and receptionist and token black from the team's office downtown. Pip always had a few last-minute business arrangements to make with the players —sign a voucher, exchange tickets—so she was a familiar sight at our takeoffs. Besides, Pipper was usually romantically involved with one player or another, and I never could figure out why somebody didn't just go ahead and marry her. She had brown eyes flecked with gold, a little upturned nose, and the kind of supple figure that made you want to grab her and spin her around a few times. Pipper was into "vines," as she'd explained to me one day, and we never knew what she would wear next. "Hey, did you peep out the Pip yet?" Sweet Basil McBride said to Red Green and me in the waiting area.

"She ain't wearing the bra again?" Red asked.

"She ain't wearing the blouse!" Basil said.

Just then Pipper came up in harem pants and five-inch soles and a loose halter that covered her nipples but not a whole lot else. "Hey, you really frontin' today, baby!" Jones Jones called out, and Red Green said, "Sho' look fly, dawlin'. What you got in mind on my body?"

Pip answered by walking straight up to Justin Fell and kissing him on the lips. "Oh, you like the pipe and slippers type, huh?" Sweet Basil said. Justin was always being kidded about being the staid old man of the team at 26.

I didn't see Massy when we boarded, but just before the pilot began running up the engines the kid came hunching through the cabin door and took his seat in the first row, where there was room for his legs. We were flying first class this trip—NBA rules specified first class for all flights over an hour, or else Guile would have shipped us baggage —but nobody looked forward to the flight. Your typical pro basketball team flies something like 70,000 miles a season and the playoffs add another 20,000.

They say you get accustomed to it. Sutter Manno was always sound asleep from the time the plane left the ramp till the stewardess came on the air to "welcome" us to a city she was reaching simultaneously with the rest of us, a practice that always puzzled me. Coach Francis X. "Buttsy" Rafferty was another cool passenger, playing cutthroat cribbage every inch of the way with Jack Carbon. The rest of us ranged from slightly uneasy to downright terrified. Sweet Basil flew with his wool hat pulled over his face, and Red Green and Jones Jones sucked up every liquid available and then partook of extra potions secreted in their Adidas flying bags.

Sometimes I got the feeling that I lived entirely in airplanes during the basketball season, and my occasional visits to home and Dulcy were just fantasy interludes. One Christmas season we flew 7000 miles in nine days, and that's not the league record. Once the Knicks covered 7000 miles in four nights: New York to L. A. to Portland to Phoenix to New York, and the Lakers claim they broke that record the next week.

Maybe an hour before we were to land at Seattle–Tacoma Airport, Justin Fell extricated himself from a panting stewardess and plopped down in the seat next to mine. "Looks like old Sheik Fell rides again," I said.

"Not me," Justin said. "That white stuff stunts your growth."

"Did you make a date for later?"

"She's trying to set something up for the whole club, big party

125

tonight. Did you notice her glancing over my shoulder at Massy? He's what she's really interested in. She tried to hit on him when we first took off, but he just rolled over and turned up his earphones."

"You mean to tell me she'd prefer Massy to a lusty black buck like you? Doesn't she know you guys've got the biggest——"

Justin raised his fists. "Hold off, honkie fool!" he said. "Or I light up yo' ass!" We played these little games all the time. It helped pass the time.

I asked how he was getting along with the new roommate, and he said, "No problems. He's a roomie, just like any other. It's better than rooming with Red Green and helping him come down from his pills every night. Four o'clock in the morning, sitting on the toilet reading *Sports Pictorial,* eyes bugged out like a tree frog's."

"Massy's normal, eh?"

"Well, I haven't made a clinical analysis of his behavior," our black Ivy Leaguer said, "but I'd say, yeh, he's normal. Whatever normal means." He paused. "Prays a lot, though."

"Prays?"

"Yeh. Kneels alongside his bed after we turn the lights out and talks to God out loud. Refreshing."

"What's he pray?"

"Come on, now, Sam, isn't that kind of personal?"

"It can't be too personal if he does it in front of you. You two aren't all that tight, are you?"

Justin hesitated. "Yeh, I see what you mean," he said. "No, he doesn't get very personal when he prays. Let's see—last night he asked God to forgive him for sending the check late."

"What's that mean?"

"Don't ask me. Sends God a check, I guess. Help the old boy out."

"What's he ask for?"

Justin gave me a sly look and said, "Hey, you're the foxy dude, aren't you? You getting ready to do Massy for *The New Yorker*?"

"Oh, sure," I said. "*The New Yorker*'s been running my stuff for years. They change the by-line. Sometimes they call me E. B. White, sometimes S. J. Perelman. Last week they ran a piece of mine on economics. Signed it 'John Kenneth Galbraith.'"

Justin smiled. "The other night," he said, "I had to put my hand over my mouth to keep from cracking up. Massy prays, 'God, I know this is silly, but could I have some help with my dribble?' Then he says,

126

'And it wouldn't hurt if You'd make me mad, too? Just a little bit annoyed?' "

"Well," I said. "It wouldn't."

"Of course it wouldn't!" Justin said, laughing. "But what's he expect from God? Miracles?"

6

We checked into Seattle's famous Hotel Ripon (which we called the Hotel Rip-off, because it lived on its past reputation at future prices) and the players split off to do what players do on winter afternoons in Seattle—go to porn flicks, bitch about the rain and tell stories. You might wonder why they don't go to first-run movies, and the answer is that by the time the season is a month old, every player in the NBA has seen every first-run movie that's around, some of them three and four times, but the pornies seem to flow in an endless spasm. To me, it was a case of when you've seen one you've seen 'em all. I mean, how many different ways can a la-la be inserted into a lu-lu, to quote the old joke? It was a dull pastime, watching pornies, but slightly better than crossword puzzles or self-abuse.

Seattle is blue-collar, and the citizens unload their fears and frustrations at the Sonics's games. One of their favorite techniques is to give beer facials. That's on days when nothing riles them up. On rowdy occasions, they're more likely to hand out knuckle sandwiches and other choice delicacies. Even the women will break your chops; I remember the night a grandmother type decked a referee with a right cross. Nick Storen said she was a diesel dyke, but Ken Hohlar said it didn't matter what she drove, she was still a tough cookie.

The teams hadn't even taken the court before the racket started, whistles and cowbells and sirens and firecrackers and a dozen other kinds of noisemakers that some clubs make you check at the door. We were one team the Sonics could usually murder, especially at home, and the fans knew it, and they were building up steam for the slaughter.

When the Wasps appeared in their plum-and-white warm-ups, a fog-horn voice boomed toward Massy, "Hey, play us a concert, pansy!" Someone in the upper tier called down, "Take off the stilts, freak!"

The kid missed a shot by a foot and the crowd hooted some more, and then he fired an air ball from about 20 feet out and there was another cry of glee. Two burly young studs in Hawaiian sportshirts ran on the court with a placard that said BAN THE MONSTER! followed by a pair of younger specimens bearing a sign that said BASKETBALL. FOR MEN OR ANIMALS? on one side and BASKETBALL OR RINGLING BROS.? on the other.

"What's this about?" I asked Jack Carbon. "Massy's played on the road before, and nobody ever stooped this low."

"Seattle's mad," the press agent said, and slipped me a dog-eared column from one of the local newspapers. The head was

SONICS LOSE TO BIG MAN

The story was about our earlier home game when Massy had scored the winning points in the last seconds. "Everybody in town's pissed," Jack said. "They don't think it's fair for Massy to score that way. There's already been complaints to the league office in New York."

Pete Tyles said there'd been another loud story on the same subject in an afternoon paper, and somebody named Loy Corney had editorialized on TV that the rules should be changed to keep centers 20 feet away from the boards during the last two minutes of each period. "That's ridiculous!" I exploded. "That's a rule aimed at one player. They can't be serious."

"They are," Pete said. "I had lunch with a broadcaster. He thinks Massy ought to be banned outright. Says he's making a spectacle out of the game. Guy's *furious!*"

The Sonics broke fast and you could see they were still smarting about losing to us back at the Helix. You don't encounter many full-court presses in the opening minutes of a pro game, but that's how they started, good old-fashioned pressure basketball as she's taught by Johnny Wooden. Normally, a press didn't bother us much. Justin Fell could always work the ball across the line in the allotted ten seconds, and so could Sutter Manno, our main handler, and between the two of them they'd usually shake something out for our forwards.

I was seated next to Ken Hohlar at the press table, and all through the game I could hear his mellifluous voice. "McBride has the ball, he fakes, he dips, he drives on Cox, he *scores!* Ladies and gentlemen, the most unique shot I've ever seen! He literally faked Cox out of his shorts! Yes, sir, McBride has the hot hand tonight! The momentum is going our way!" At that point, the Wasps were behind 29–16 and Sweet Basil's "hot hand" had produced a total of five points. And things got worse.

With the Sonics running away, I tried to concentrate on my score-keeping, but there was no tuning out the drone two seats away. "The Sonics enjoy a comfortable lead," Kenny was saying. "But don't go 'way, folks! You know how our Wasps can come back!" We did? "The Sonics are putting in the rookie Don Coulbourn. He played collegiately at Hofstra." How else can you play at Hofstra? I wondered how Hohlar held onto his job, and the answer was: barely. He'd almost been fired last year when the Japanese national gymnastics team came to town and Kenny introduced the first event by saying, "It's fall, and there's a little nip in the air." Still, it was better than what he'd said when the black pole-vaulter cleared the bar at 18 feet.

The Seattle game wasn't over till the start of the second half, and I kept my "running" listlessly. After a while I became aware of another grating voice, this one from directly behind our bench. "Put the freak in! Let's see Big Stoop in action!" By now the score was 68–40, and the local fans were as bored as I was. All through the third quarter the same sportsman kept up his barrage: "Hey, *hey,* the circus is in town! He walks, he talks, he crawls on his belly like a *rep*-tile!" I glanced sideways at Massy, but he didn't seem to be reacting. That was his specialty, not reacting. He'd had years of practice.

But Buttsy Rafferty was no silent sufferer. I could tell by the scarlet hue of his ear tips that he was approaching the flash point. Watch out, Seattle! When Francis X. Rafferty reached his limit, he would cry or rip up his jacket or beat his fists on the floor. If you pushed him far enough, he might even faint.

"Hey, tallboy!" the loud fan shouted. "I hear there's no furniture in your top story!" The crowd hooted with delight, and the entertainer, a wizened little man in a soiled jump suit, began prancing up and down the aisle behind the Wasps's bench, sometimes dipping close and giving Massy the goat's horns with two fingers.

"Get lost, creep!" Pasty Pasticcino hollered. "We got a game to play."

"I paid my way in," the fan responded. He put up the horns again.

"*Guard!*" Buttsy exploded, waving his arms. "Get this turd outta here!"

The intruder, anesthetized by the stadium's fermented liquids, kept on shouting as a pair of guards frog-walked him toward an exit. The fans shook their fists at the cops and made threats. I thought I'd die of embarrassment when Buttsy faced the crowd and thumbed his nose. Then he cupped his hands and hollered, "All you Seattle faggots come around after the game! I'll let you watch the kid undress!"

A woman hurled a beer.

"You too, lady!" Coach cried. "I'll let you touch his nuts!"

The fans stuck till the end. I guess they thought Butts might put Massy in for the tip-in play, but tip-in plays aren't designed to overcome 35-point leads. Garbage time lasted the whole fourth quarter, but Massy stayed on the bench. I think Coach knew what he was doing.

On the plane to Phoenix, I interrupted his cribbage game with Jack Carbon long enough for a short interview. "What about Massy?" I asked. "You can't keep him on the roster just for tip-ins."

Buttsy steered me to a pair of empty seats. "Listen," he said, "between you and I and the tailgate, that kid's gonna make it. Did you ever stop to think, it's a good thing we're bringing him along slow, from the standpoint that look at the heat already? And he's not doing a thing except take an out-of-bounds pass once in a blue moon."

I couldn't follow his reasoning.

"Look, I'm watching the kid all the time," Buttsy babbled on. "When he first came up, he was tight as a drum, couldn't stick, couldn't handle, couldn't nothin'. Now basically he still can't shoot and he still can't bip, but his court sense is better, his mobility's picking up, and I'm positive: the kid's a player. But bide your time, bide your time! Like I told him: 'Kid, when the season's half over and the rest of the guys begin to drag ass, you'll still be eight foot two!' "

I began to look around for an interpreter.

"But imagine if he'd been playing from the beginning," Buttsy went on. "Why, he wouldn't even be playing!"

"What's that mean in English?" I asked politely.

"They'd have thought of something," Coach said darkly.

" 'They?' "

"The powers that be. The fans. The teams. The league, somefucking-body. They'd of thought of a way to get ridda him. Why, there's already been complaints to the commissioner, and what'd the boy do? Scored a few points. Big deal! You heard the chatter in Seattle. How much can the kid handle?"

"Plenty," I said. "He's been taking static all his life."

"Yeh? Well, he ain't played at Phoenix yet. He ain't played at New Orleans."

"Does that mean you're thinking of playing him tomorrow night?"

"Pertaining to tomorrow night," Buttsy said, getting up and heading back toward his card game, "let me just say without fear of distinction, we'll see about tomorrow night when tomorrow night comes around. And you may quote me."

"It's a pleasure," I said. He got up to leave and I grabbed his arm and said, "Hey, look, Butts, I need an angle." I was desperate. It was my turn to ghost our sports editor's weekly column, "East of the Pecos," and I didn't have idea one. "Are you gonna play Massy or not?"

"Put it like this," Buttsy said, a frantic look in his eyes. "He's gotta play sometime, right? If there's garbage time down in Phoenix—well, who knows?"

I thanked him for this firm commitment.

7

Phoenix is still the Wild West. Tacos and enchiladas are sold in Vets Memorial Coliseum and the fans wear five-gallon hats and hand-tooled boots with blue leather curlicues and sometimes carry six-guns and automatics and .44 magnums that can take out a wall. Phoenix isn't the world's most sophisticated city, and sometimes shots ring out when an opponent lines up for a free throw, but usually they're just blanks and the game proceeds. Somehow Phoenix didn't strike me as the ideal place to play Broussard Massy.

But Coach Francis X. Rafferty heard other voices. Garbage time lasted four or five minutes, with the Suns ahead by almost 30 points, and Massy played. Well, Massy appeared, anyway. For the first couple of minutes nobody gave him a smell of the ball, and he just pranced up and down the court and flapped his arms like a sandhill crane. Then another garbage-time specialist, Tyrone "Maraschino" Mays, took pity and fed the kid a pass, and Massy let it skid out of bounds while the crowd gave out cattle-drive whoops and rodeo yells.

On his next chance for glory, the kid violated Buttsy's one-dribble rule and lost the ball against his foot. But then he blocked a Phoenix shot, grabbed the rebound and fired a perfect outlet pass to Abdul Buzruz. I looked over at the bench to see Buttsy standing up screaming, "Way to go, son!" as though it was the last ten seconds of a big game. I figured if you could become a pro by alternating two bonehead plays with one good one, maybe I'd suit up myself, but I had to admit the kid wasn't totally hopeless, maybe just three-quarters. I figured he could develop into a good schoolyard player, maybe, or a backup center in the Eastern League. The idea that he could become the NBA's first eight-foot regular seemed ludicrous.

Buttsy the patient one stuck to his method. In the game at L. A. two nights later, he played Massy for nearly half the final period, and the kid scored six points and only gave up a few more. At Golden State an angry King Crowder fouled out, and Massy played the whole last quarter in a game we might have won if Sutter Manno and Sweet Basil McBride hadn't run out of gas. In the locker room after the game, I heard Coach tell the kid, "Listen, son, don't let them insult you! Every time you get the ball they sag off. Don't let them get away with it! Start shooting!"

Two nights later Crowder got in foul trouble again, and this time Massy put up 11 shots and sank five, not a bad average considering how green he was. But he was sloppy on defense; he was basket-hanging and failing to get back to stop up the middle, the center's job in the Wasps's style of play. "He just can't concentrate on more than one thing," Pete Tyles said after the loss.

"He's a half-court player," Nick Storen said. "Everybody knows except Rafferty."

When we got back home a few days later, a fan wrote the *Item* that the Wasps could win every remaining game simply by exploiting Massy's height under the offensive boards. "Remember the first Seattle game when he took those two passes in the last minute?" the fan wrote. "Well, what's to stop the team from throwing him that same high lob the whole game long?" Storen pounced in his column:

*In order to have Broussard "The Goon" Massy continually take
that high lob under the basket, as you naively suggest, the Wasps
would have to play him full time, and in case you haven't noticed,
the big man gives up two points for every point he scores. Tip-ins
included. Some of you Wasp fanatics make the same mistake the
French made about DeGaulle—confusing bigness with greatness.
The rumor is that GM Darius Guile is working hard on a trade
—Massy and two free basketballs for a dead sparrow and a piece
of string. But he can't find a taker.*

After practice at the Helix that afternoon, Justin Fell and I went for
a short beer. "You read Storen today?" he asked.

"Every day," I said. "It's part of my penance as a sportswriter."

"Bru read it, too, right after the workout. He says the guy's right."

"Listen, Justin," I said, "Storen may be right and he may be wrong,
but your roomie's got to be fair to himself, too. He hasn't played
basketball since he was twelve, thirteen years old. And he's competing
with the best in the world. What can he expect?"

"I told him all that," Justin said as we nipped into Gabinetto's. "I
told him he had gifts. He said the only gift he had was his height and
it made him feel like Faust."

"*Faust?*"

"That's what he said." We stopped just inside the door of the saloon.

"Where's he now?" I asked.

"Said he was gonna buy a ticket back to New Orleans."

I grabbed his arm. "Massy's jumping?"

"Well, I don't take it seriously, but that's what he said. Told me he
didn't want to hold us down."

"C'mon!" I said, and we were out the door. The clerk at the Helix
Excelsior said Mr. Massy had just returned to his room, and I didn't
even wait for the creaky old elevator. I ran up the steps till I reached
the fourth floor and then banged against the kid's door. "Who is it?"
the hollow voice asked.

"It's me," I said. "Sam Forrester."

"Me, too," Justin announced, and the door opened on a scene of
chilling neatness and order. The bed had been stripped, the table and
chest of drawers were bare, except for a little vase of plastic roses, and
a single suitcase was by the door. The kid hadn't brought a whole lot
with him from Louisiana and he wouldn't be taking a whole lot back.

"What's this all about?" I said in a slightly hysterical voice. "What the fuck is going on?" Something made me wonder why I was reverting to my hard-boiled newspaperman patois, and I realized what it was: I was upset, and talking tough to conceal it. "I mean, what's happenin', Bru?" I said in a softer tone. I wondered why it mattered so much to me. Players come and go every year.

He sat on the stripped beds that the management had put together for him and stared back and forth at the two of us. It was that first press conference all over again. I asked the questions and he either ignored them or answered them in words of one syllable.

"Are you going home?"

"Yes, sir."

"Why?"

No answer.

"Aren't they playing you enough?"

"It's not that."

"Well, then, why quit?"

A shrug of the shoulders.

I guess Justin could see that this approach was producing nothing, so he sat on the bed next to the big man and said, "Hey, Rooms, c'mon now, man. Sam's our friend. At least tell him what you told me."

The kid gave me a searching look, as though trying to decide if I could be trusted with his innermost feelings, and I sat down and waited him out.

He started slowly and talked for maybe five minutes, never raising his voice, never seeming disturbed, just a reasonable man stating unpleasant facts. "So I added it all up," he said at the end, "and I realized that no good can come of this." I remembered Dulcy's using almost exactly the same words when she'd first seen the kid at training camp. "Most likely I'll drag the team down, and if I improve I'll just make everybody in the league resentful. I do seem to do that, Mr. Forrester. Make people resentful? Sure, I need the money, but I'll find a way."

"Bru, for Chrissakes," I said, "don't talk about dragging this team down. That's ridiculous. You couldn't drag this team down any more than you could resink the Titanic."

"I can drag them to a worse record than last year," Massy said, still speaking in that level voice of his, straight out of the Luray Caverns. "No, sir, Mr. Forrester. It's surely not fair. Everybody on the Wasps has played basketball for the last ten or twelve years, they've devoted their lives to the game. Basil's been playing since he was ten, and Sutter told me he made his first basket with a volleyball when he was six. That's twenty-two, twenty-three years ago."

"Yeh, but you played some, too," I said. "You look like a player."

Massy laughed, and the room shook. "I played with a bunch of schoolkids till the ninth grade, Mr. Forrester," he said, "and then I didn't pick up a basketball till this spring."

I thought of asking the big question: Why had he bothered to return to the game? But it seemed like poor timing, now that he was on his way home.

"All I'm good at is that tip-in play," he went on, "and that's just 'cause I'm taller than anybody else. The rest of the league says its unfair. Don't y'all agree? Mr. Storen says I'll never be a player. Don't y'all agree with that, too?"

"No, I don't!" I said, smacking my fist into my palm. "Nick Storen may never be a writer, but you'll be a player. Why, you're a player right now!"

"Absolutely," Justin said firmly.

"Coach is high on you," I added. "What's he gonna look like when you check out of here without warning? He's laid his job on the line for you, Bru."

The kid looked pensive, and I pressed on. "You know what Coach Rafferty told me? He said this team had one hope for the playoffs, and that hope was Broussard Massy. He said maybe we wouldn't make it, but he'd *never* give up on you, because you're like a son to him."

"No, sir, it's just that I'm eight foot two."

"No!" I said, shaking my fist. "That's *not* what he thinks!" I improvised madly. "He said you were stiff and out of practice and that was to be expected, but you know what he told me?"

I paused to think up my next line.

"He told me," I said in the strident voice of the panic stricken, "that he'd want you on the team if—if you were only—*if you were only a seven footer!*"

I halted again, to let the impact of my remark set in, and Massy stood up and ducked his head and it came over me what a different world this big man lived in—stooping over in his own room—and I felt a shock of compassion for this huge infant in his strange clothes. He was wearing his street outfit: size 28 Pumas, Big Man–brand pants in basic khaki, a gray button-down shirt with a button missing, and a plum-and-white tie with

W
A
S
P
S

in faded gold letters. I thought about Bill Bradley and how his New York teammates used to joke that he could walk through Central Park at midnight and not get mugged because he looked as though he'd already been mugged. Massy might have preferred to look more stylish, but as he explained it to me one day, "There's not much available to a man as tall as me. I have to take what I can find."

He opened his suitcase and rummaged through it, pulled out a hand-kerchief and blew his nose, and then sat back on the bed. He said, "What'll happen to Coach after I leave?"

"Oh," Justin said, "he'll probably——"

I interrupted. "What'll happen? He'll be out on his ass, that's what'll happen. And he'll be lucky if he gets another job in basketball."

"You're just saying that, Mr. Forrester," Massy said coolly. He stood up again. Once he got outside the room, we'd be finished. I scuttled around his bent form and stood in front of the door. "Listen, Bru, give us time!" I pleaded, screening him from his suitcase with my body.

For a second the kid looked annoyed, but then he smiled sympathetically. "Gee, Mr. Forrester, you're really shook about this, aren't you?" he said, peering down at me. "I wish you weren't so upset."

"Sure I'm upset!" I said. "I been with this team ten years. I don't want to see you go. I want you to have your shot."

"See what I've been telling you, Bru?" Justin put in, slapping his roomie on the ass. "People care. You matter, man!"

"I appreciate y'all," Massy said, gently prying the suitcase out of my hand and putting it back by the door. "I know you're my friends. I know y'all mean well." He paused and shook his shoulders like a water spaniel. "I—I—"

136

"Do me one favor, will you, Bru?" I asked. "Promise to wait right here?"

The kid nodded. "Well, sir, it doesn't matter where I wait," he said. "The plane doesn't leave for three hours."

I dashed across the street to the Wasps's office in the Helix. "Pipper!" I said to the front office's token, attired today in see-through pants. "Where's that fan letter file?"

"You need 'em right now? I'm awful busy, Sam."

"I need 'em—right now," I said, still trying to catch my breath. "I need 'em—an hour ago."

Pip left her desk and pulled a long drawer out of the wall. There were two letters in the Massy file. One was from a "Wilfred Massey" of Pascagoula, Mississippi, claiming to be a relative and asking for a loan of $25. The other was from a kid who said his hobby was collecting NBA autographs and he had every Wasp except Bru.

"Pipper," I said, "do you trust me?"

"What you got in mind, fool?" she said, arching her skinny back like a Siamese cat. "I don't go for that interracial stuff. But my roommate does."

"Listen," I barked, "this is no joke! You either trust me or you don't."

"Oh, Sam, everybody trusts *you.* "

"Then do exactly what I tell you. Get a pen and a couple of pencils. How many handwritings can you do?"

"What?"

"How many ways can you write? Typewriter and how else?"

"I can print regular, I can block-print, I can do script, and I can type. That's four."

"Okay, take some letters."

An hour later I was back at the Helix Excelsior. Massy and Justin were sitting on the bed talking earnestly, but the suitcase was still packed and waiting by the door. It was 90 minutes till plane time.

"Bru," I said, "I went over and got some of your mail. I know your mind's made up, but I just wish you'd look at a couple."

"Fan letters?" Massy said. "I don't get any."

"The team keeps a file. Look at this." I handed him a letter:

137

Dr. Mr. Masy—I am a shut-in six years old and living in La-fayette, La. and I would like a pitcher of you please. The other day I see you on national TV you look hansome. Lydia Harrison

And another:

Dear Brew: I know this is a impasition, but my mother says I can ask. This summer when the NBA is over can you and Justen Fell stay with us for awhile? My dad says he will not mind very much and you can have your own bed in my same room. Please bring a new basketball and your shoes. Please reply soon. Your bedrid-den fan, Marc Brown

After Massy read the second letter, he handed it back and sat on the bed shaking his head from side to side. "Kids," he said thoughtfully. "Look at this one," I said. "Came in this morning."

Dear Brussard Massy. I'm 9 years old and I love you so bad. Even to rite you seems to awe a girl. I have pierce ears and more than anything else in the world I would like a coppy of yourself. Thank you for your time. Gloria.

I handed over a few more and sat silently while Massy perused them. Justin said, "I'm in my fifth season and I don't get mail like that."

"They're nice," Massy admitted, and walked over and stared out the window, rubbing the upper bridge of his nose with his thumb and forefinger.

"Bru," I said, "are you gonna let these kids down?"

"Well, Mr. Forrester, I—I—I don't—"

"C'mon, rooms, unpack and stick around," Justin said.

I yanked at the brass clasps on the suitcase and the bag fell open and a clean pair of size 28 socks popped out. Massy leaned over and picked them up and flipped them from one big hand to the other. Then he opened a drawer and tossed them in.

•   •   •

8

I went back to the pressroom of the Helix and called Buttsy at home. After I told him about the near miss, there was a stony silence. "Butts!" I said. "*Buttsy!*"

"Excuse me, Sam," he said. "I near had a heart attack. Didn't you hear the phone drop?"

"Listen, Coach, faint later. Right now you're about two shakes away from losing that kid."

"I'm not gonna lose him, goddamn it!" The telephone began making the funny noise that it makes when you dial wrong, but it turned out to be the Butts, whining in my ear.

"Stop it, for Chrissakes. Stop bawling!" The sniveling tailed off. "You haven't lost him yet." I tried to sound calm.

"Everything's going wrong," the coach said. "First the front office, and now this. And Eleanor's leaving me."

"I thought she left you last Tuesday."

"She came back Wednesday."

"What's the matter with the front office?"

"Attendance."

"Attendance?" I was astounded. "The joint's packed. What's Gross want, standees?"

Buttsy blew his nose. "They want me to take and rehearse the team in a pregame show. Like the Trotters? Have somebody spin the ball behind his neck and somebody else put on a dribbling show and let his pants drop?"

"Isn't it bad enough the Trotters do all that yuck-yuck stuff?"

"Then he wants us to take and wear different colored shoes. Blue for forwards, white for the center, red for guards. Says it'll help us on court balance. I says sure it'll help us, Mr. Gross, as long as we don't look up."

"Old Abe's been on that red, white and blue kick ever since the ABA put in the tricolored ball."

"Yeh. Well, I still say, that ABA ball belongs on a seal's nose."

"Maybe you should ask Gross to bring back Theresa Twat," I suggested. "Theresa Twat" was the team's nickname for a mini-skirted cheerleader who'd gone out on the court between halves and turned 17 consecutive back flips while the crowd went wild, and then walked from one end of the Helix to the other on her hands and high-stepped off the court to waves of applause. Pete Tyles said the girl was so talented that her act would have been a success even if she'd remembered her underpants. An embarrassing oversight—or so we thought. Later Pennsylvania Morgan found out that she was a professional acrobatic stripper from Newark, New Jersey, and Gross had hired her to goose attendance.

Nick Storen asked him how he expected to increase attendance with an unadvertised strip act, and Gross Abraham told him to stick around till the next game. The Wasps had been drawing about 7000 average, a few more on games with the Celts and the Knicks, but the place was sold out for our next home appearance, against K.C.–Omaha, and attendance stayed well above the 10,000 mark for over a month. "Do you know how many extra tickets we sold because of that broad?" Darius Guile asked me. "We figured she was worth an average twenty-five hundred a game. Guys sitting and hoping. All because some ginch showed her wool. Mr. Gross knows people."

"Well, it was a terrific idea," Pete Tyles said, "and in perfect taste, too."

"Wait till you see our next promotion," the general manager said enthusiastically. "We almost used it against the Trail Blazers, but Gross chickened out."

"What's the next promotion?" I asked.

"A bottomless nun."

"A nun without underpants?" I yelped. "How would anybody know?"

"You haven't seen some of the new habits. The Sisters of Forbearance are wearing mini's this year."

"Mini's?" I said. "No kidding! What's Minnie wearing?"

Guile didn't get it. Nobody in our front office ever got a joke. A joke can't *get* a joke, that's the way I figure it.

The night after Massy almost jumped the club, he made his first official NBA start in front of an audience of 11,600 fans at the Helix. The biased historian would like to report that the young newcomer scored 50 points, grabbed 27 rebounds, contributed 21 assists and made 16 blocks. But the cold, hard stats showed otherwise. Massy looked inept from the opening tip, which he slapped to one of the Hawks's guards. He was seldom in position, he clogged up our own middle instead of the opponents', he got caught in the lane repeatedly and missed several dead mortal crips. Sitting on the bench, King Crowder looked sick at first, but as the game went on and Massy got worse, the King seemed to perk up.

When the teams came out for the second half with Atlanta leading 58–47, the kid was at center again, and the Wasps's fans booed. Standing back in his guard position, Justin Fell raised a fist and shook it at the crowd, and the boos grew louder. Massy tipped the ball to his roomie and went to the basket for a quick return pass and two points. He bounced back down the court like a large impala, boxed out the Hawks's seven-foot center Julius Johnson and took down a rebound. He spun free of Johnson's six arms and lobbed a floor-length outlet pass to Jones Jones for the bucket.

Atlanta missed a jump shot, and this time Massy led our fast break, taking a short pass at the top of the key and dropping the ball to McBride for an easy lay-in and the Wasps's sixth straight point. I watched Massy closely as he took his ten-foot strides back on defense; his chest was heaving, and his breath was coming in spurts, but he reached the lane in time to block a blue darter by Phil Sorotsky. The ball spurted to Sweet Basil and the Wasps worked the diamond two play to perfection, with Massy setting a wide screen and Basil ducking behind for his favorite soft jumper and two more points.

The Hawks called time, and Massy leaned over with his hands on his knees while a drop of sweat rolled down his nose. The crowd jumped up and applauded. King Crowder stared down at the floor. He didn't even fake a clap or two.

I knew Massy couldn't maintain the pace in his first starting assignment, and Buttsy knew it too, because a little while later he yanked the kid and put in King, and the clubs played fairly evenly till the last 40 seconds, when Buttsy called time with Atlanta ahead 118–116. With Massy back in, the Wasps put the ball in play at mid-court, and the old tip-in play, Justin Fell to Bru Massy, made it 118–all.

The Hawks worked the ball up court slowly, looking for the tie-breaking last shot, methodically working toward Julius Johnson just outside the lane. With eight seconds showing on the clock, one of the Hawks whipped the ball into Johnson and the big center soared upward in his patented "spiral staircase," twisting his body in midair, and just as he released the ball Massy slapped it off a Hawk and out of bounds.

"Red!" the referee hollered, meaning our ball. With five seconds left, Coach signaled the kid to move toward the basket for the tip-in play, and Atlanta stationed Johnson and a bogart forward on either side of him. When Justin lobbed the ball inbounds, the two powerful Hawks crunched together, and you could hear Massy's pained "ugh" as the ball slipped off his fingertips.

Sutter Manno grabbed the loose ball and passed back to Justin Fell, and with one second left Justin reared back and pitched the ball one-handed. We measured later and found that he had canned the shot from 45 feet out, or almost mid-court.

After the game, I chased Buttsy toward the locker room, leaving my typewriter and notes and briefcase and everything else at the press table. "Hey," I hollered. *"Hey!"* Delirious fans were grabbing at him as he chugged off the court. "What'd you tell Massy at the half?"

Buttsy's face was heliotrope, and the bright lights glittered in his wet eyes. "I told him——" he paused and gulped for air. "—I just said——" he shook his head.

"Chrissakes, Butts," I said, "spit it out! I got a deadline."

"—I told him, 'Kid, when you go down to the airport, you better get a ticket for the both of us.' "

9

Massy started again the next night against New York at the Helix, but history didn't repeat. The Knicks pressed him all night long, directed their attack straight at him to keep him in foul trouble, and when everybody in the place could see he was getting the blind staggers, they put two defensive-type forwards on him and crushed him in the pivot. "It's awful what they're doing to Bru Massy, ladies and gentlemen!"

the voice of Kenny Hohlar buzzed in my ear. "New York is literally destroying him!"

Coach took Massy out with five fouls and ten minutes to play, and somehow the Wasps were still in the game, trailing 78–76. New York had spent so much time and energy pounding on the big man that they'd let Justin Fell and Red Green rack up 42 points between them. All night long Sweet Basil McBride had fed the pair under the basket and in the backdoor, calling out "Was that pass okay?" "Should I've led you a little more?" Poor Captain Basil, three decades old and still insecure, but getting the job done anyway.

With two minutes to go and the game tied at 96, Massy looked rested and fit, although the upper part of his body was still reddened, and Buttsy sent him back in. King Crowder pulled a towel over his head and headed straight for the dressing room.

"Hey!" Buttsy hollered. The King never broke stride.

The Knicks had possession, but Sutter Manno made a steal and fed long down the court to the big man. Bru took his allotted single dribble and went high in the air to dunk, and at the top of his leap, a New York guard named Brock Faulkner slammed the kid's legs out from under him like a halfback dumping a blitzing linebacker and brought him down head first on the hard maple.

The referee signaled an undercut and two shots, while Massy lay in a heap of spindly arms and legs, all his own. For a second I thought he was dead, but then I saw his big foot vibrate convulsively, the way Ingemar Johansson's foot shook after Floyd Patterson knocked him cold. Pasty Pasticcino ran out with his black bag, followed by Buttsy in full uniform, and it took the two of them to roll the kid over on his back.

He was unconscious, you could see that from across the court. Pasty waved a wad of cotton under his nose, and the foot quivered again, and the kid's dark eyes fluttered open. Slowly he pulled himself up on one elbow and looked around, counting the house.

Pasty stuck his face up tight, and I knew he was demanding name, rank and serial number to see if Massy was in full control of his senses, and then the kid climbed ponderously to his feet and shook his head to signify that he was okay. The crowd gave him a nice round of applause for being alive.

He air-balled the first free throw and the score stayed tied. The ref lobbed the ball back and Massy shuffled his feet and fired on that flat trajectory of his, almost downward, and this time the ball wriggled through. Wasps 97, Knicks 96. One minute left.

New York brought the ball in and tried a set play for their center, but Massy plugged up the middle and the shot went wide, and then the Wasps came down with a play of their own and missed. With 23 seconds left, the Knicks lay back for the last shot. Massy climbed inside Orion Halliday's shorts. The New York center ran him into a pick but the kid sheared right through. With a second or two left, Brock Faulkner put up a desperation heave, a long rainbow shot that looked as though it would be both short and wide, and out of nowhere Massy leaped into the air, the wildest flight I'd ever seen him make, about five feet on the Sergeant jump and reaction test, and slapped the shot into the seats.

The referee signaled goaltending and the horn went off. Knicks 98; Wasps 97. What a way to lose!

When Massy realized what he'd done, he ran straight for the tunnel, and just as well, too, because the fans rushed out on the floor grousing. Buttsy's postgame press conference was a wake. Nick Storen kept asking snotty questions, and Pete Tyles put in a dig or two. The two-star deadline was pressing, so I didn't stick around long, but when I'd finished filing, I went back to the dressing room expecting to find it empty, and Rafferty and Massy were seated in the corner, still in their game clothes. I quickly ducked out, but I heard Buttsy holler, "Come on in, Sam. We're all friends."

"Hi, Bru," I said, and Massy gave me the old finger waggle.

"We were just hashing over the game," Coach said. "Pertaining to that goaltending call. I think we covered the ground, don't you, son?"

Massy nodded, and stared at his left foot.

"What'd you decide?" I asked.

"Well, no big deal," Butts said, forcing a smile. "I just told the athlete here, I said, 'Bru, in this whole fucking world, there's only ten things I'm sure of, and nine of 'em is you're gonna be a great player. Also you're gonna go out there and play like an asshole a hundred times before it happens, and maybe another hundred times *after* it happens,' and I said, 'Son,' I said, 'from the standpoint if you only have a little patience with yourself, it'll all work out.' Didn't I, kid?"

"Yes, sir," Massy said.

"And I told him I'd rather have an eager player blow a game than a lazy player win one, because basically in the long run my excited player's gonna win me plenty of more games before he's finished."

"Absolutely," I said, studying Massy to see how he was reacting to the pep talk. It would only take him a few minutes to repack his suitcase.

"Besides," Coach went on, "it wasn't even Broussard's fault here, it was the wop's. He told me the young man was fine after the undercut, but he wasn't fine at all. He barely knew who he was!" The Butts turned his head toward the training room, where an occasional sound could be heard. "Pasty!" he hollered. "Get your Eyetalian ass in here!"

A pale Pasty Pasticcino shuffled in with a gait like a whipped cur, his body language revealing the depths of his shame.

"Tell Sam what Massy said when you give him the smelling salts," the coach instructed.

The trainer mumbled something and turned away.

"*Tell him*, goddamn it!" Buttsy screamed. "Stand up for your mistakes! *What'd Massy answer when you asked him his name?*"

" 'Puddin' Tane,' " the trainer said, looking everywhere but at the three of us.

"And then what?" Buttsy insisted.

"He said, 'Ask me again and I'll tell you the same.' " Pasty hastened back to the training room.

"You better run, you dumb dago!" Coach hollered. "One more rock like that, and I'll take and send you back to the docks, yeh stupid greaseball, yeh!" Buttsy's Youngstown was showing.

Massy squirmed on the stool in front of his locker. "Coach," he said, "Pasty didn't blow the game, *I* did."

"Okay, son, have it your own way, but me and Sam here, we know better. You can't play pro basketball with scrambled brains. Now I just wanna know one thing. Pertaining to this long talk you and me had, what's the main point I've been making, I mean basically?"

"Have patience?"

"Right! Don't get down on yourself. You got to make up for eight years of not playing, son, and you gotta learn a whole new game. Why, you're ahead of schedule! Sure, you gimme a gray hair once in a while. What player don't?"

"Yes, sir, Coach," Massy said, and started making a deep gurgling noise in his throat. I hoped he wasn't crying—Buttsy was enough—and then I thought he might be suffering from some sort of digestive disorder or iron-deficiency anemia or maybe an attack of the flux, but then I realized he was laughing, and trying to hold it in.

"What's funny?" the coach asked.

"Oh, nothing," Massy said, shaking his head and covering his mouth with his big hand. "I was just thinking what the doctor told me when I was little."

"Your doctor?" I said, trying to draw him out.

"Yes, sir. Old Dr. A. Labas down in Marcilly, Louisiana. That's cajun country. Can't get much more cajun than Marcilly, Louisiana."

"What'd the doc say?" Buttsy insisted, but I gave him a look that said relax, let the kid talk. It wasn't often that Bru Massy reminisced about his childhood.

"Old Doc Labas, he said, *'Avec patience on peut enculer une mouche.'* "

"You wouldn't shit me, would you?" Coach said.

"Sounds good to me," I said, "but all I could understand was 'with patience.' "

"I'm sorry," Massy said, looking chagrined. "That's purely dumb of me. I still think everybody speaks French."

"What's it mean?" Buttsy said. " 'With patience——' "

" '—You can bugger a fly,' " Massy said, laughing again.

"Hey," the coach said excitedly, "that's good for you to remember, son! 'With patience you can bugger a fly!' By God, I'm gonna put that up on the bulletin board."

I hadn't seen Massy so amused since Danny Kaye's line about the oboe. He was doubled over to four foot one, and his chortlings bounced off the wall and brought Pasticcino scurrying back in with the black bag. "What's the trouble?" Pasty said as the big man tried to control himself.

"Down in Marcilly," Massy said, stopping to catch his breath, "when Doc Labas told me that expression, I was——" He held up one hand with the fingers extended. "—I was five! I must've repeated that line to every little girl in town!"

I waited for Massy to shower and dress, and the two of us headed down the street that led to the carrot juice and the lecithin cocktails, and who should be sitting at the counter of Sol's 24-hour Health Store but Roxy Garfein, outdoor flutist. Bru said, "Evenin', Miss Roxanne," and I said, "Hey, Roxy, big night, huh?"

She tapped the seats next to her, and we sat down with me in the middle. "Big night?" Roxanne repeated scornfully. "Three dollars! Any minute I expected somebody to reach in and take money *out*. What'd you guys do, anyway?"

Massy sat quietly, and I just said, "We lost," as though it was partially my own fault.

"Oh, I know you lost. What I mean is, *how'd* you lose? Did you just blow it?"

I gave her a stricken look, and rolled my eyes over in the corner of their sockets to indicate that a little mouse was listening. A big mouse.

"*He* blew it?" the flutist said.

"I got caught goaltending on the winning basket," Massy said quickly.

"Goaltending?" Roxanne said. "Well, if you goaltended the winning shot, what's the diff? I mean, you'd've lost anyway." I wondered where she'd learned so much about basketball, practicing her flute six hours a day, but then I remembered she had brothers.

"I didn't block the winning shot," Massy said matter of factly. "I blocked a ball that would've missed. So the ol' ref, he had to give the Knicks two points."

"Oh," Roxanne said, looking slightly disgusted. "Gee, wasn't that dumb." It was a flat statement. Roxanne had never been a diplomat.

"Well, uh, he wasn't himself," I said fast. "He was Puddin' Tane."

By the time I'd explained, Massy had consumed two large glasses of carrot juice and four protein bars, I'd eaten the first and last sprout sandwich of my life, and Roxanne had put away a mug of eucalyptus tea, despite my veiled warnings. It was 1 A.M., Dulcy standard time, and I got up to go home. "Excuse me, where's your ax?" Massy was saying.

"My ax?" I said. "What're you? Drunk on carrot juice?"

"He means my flute," Roxanne put in. "Ax is musician talk for your instrument." She reached down and picked up her battered brown leather case. "Never without my ax," she said.

"Gee, I'd have a job carrying *my* instrument," Massy said.

"Well," I said, "if anybody could, it's you."

"I used to play a little piano," Massy told Roxanne almost shyly. "But I retired."

"You *retired*?" Roxy said, and laughed in his face. "At what? At twenty-one? Well, can't blame an old crock like you." Massy laughed back, and I buttoned up my coat as a gentle hint, but by that time the arpeggios and the flatted fifths were flying back and forth and I had become a diminished chord. It took them about 30 seconds to establish that they venerated Haydn, were bored by hard rock, enjoyed Shostakovich but not his codas, admired Leonard Bernstein but not his station-wagon English, and agreed that Liberace should be sentenced to a life term listening to his own 28-second version of the "Minute Waltz." Cruel tongues!

"Listen, you guys," I said, reaching for the check. "I gotta be shoveling off——"

"Well, good night, Mr. Forrester," the kid said without making the slightest move toward getting up.

"See ya, Sam," Roxanne said. "Have a nice night."

I can take a hint. When I got outside, I looked through the crossed sheaves of wheat in the window and saw him placing another order. Well, who could blame a fellow for plying a girl with eucalyptus? Ogden Nash would have understood perfectly.

Candy is dandy
And liquor is quicker.
But eucalyptus
Really flipped us.

Almost as good as Freddie Verhegen.

10

In mid-January, halfway through the season, the Wasps's record stood at 15–26, almost identical with the previous year when we'd come up to the All-Star break with a record of 14–27. King Crowder had played every game at center the year before, so nobody could accuse Massy of making things worse than usual. The Atlantic Division stood like this:

	W	L	G.B.
Knicks	32	9	—
Celts	29	12	3
Braves	20	21	12
76ers	18	23	14
Wasps	15	26	17

It didn't look as though we had the slightest chance for second place and a playoff spot, but logic doesn't rule basketball, as *Sports Pictorial* is always saying. Coach pulled a surprise move by making our players stay in town over the All-Star break and go into two-a-day practices, an unheard of torture for a cellar team, or any other team for that matter. "Basically it's to shake 'em up a little," Buttsy the master psychologist told me on the Q. T. "Keep 'em from layin' down the way they usually do."

Abdul Rahman Buzruz presented the players' official complaint to the front office, but after a one-hour discussion Darius Guile sent him packing with a warning that "I'm not gonna be dictated to by a forward that's averaging nine points a game."

"Awright, awright, we'll play, we'll play," Abdul said, and started to leave.

"If you want me to, I'll get you a nice new collar," the general manager said.

"What that s'pose to mean?"

"For your dog in the manger act."

"That's antiblack!"

"It's antigrouch!"

At the gym, Coach lined up the players and began pacing in front of them. It was summer camp all over again. "Now men," he began, "basically we're gonna get back to basics. Do you want to be the engine or the caboose?"

Justin Fell and Bru Massy were sitting together at one end, and the way they hung on the coach's words, you'd have thought they were hearing the first pep talk of their careers. Sutter Manno looked sleepy, but Sutter always looked sleepy. Red Green, Jones Jones and Captain Basil McBride huddled together in the middle of the group, and their faces indicated that they would have preferred root-canal surgery. King Crowder looked positively surly, but he'd looked that way ever since Massy had started his first game.

149

"Cawch," Basil said, dragging himself up to his total of 79 inches, "we tol' you already, man. We answered all those questions in camp."

"What questions?" Buttsy inquired.

"The questions you askin', dawlin'," Red Green called out.

"Right on, Jack!" Jones Jones said. "We made it plain, Coach. Ain't no cabooses here. We the whole fuckin' engine."

"Nobody want to be a lame," Red Green went on. "Sure, we git a li'l flustrated once in a while, a li'l laxadaisical, but we been gittin' our Johnson together." There was loud assent from everyone but King Crowder, glowering at his fingernails.

Buttsy said he couldn't see where a record of 15 wins and 26 losses could be viewed as getting your Johnson together, and by God he was gonna work their hairy asses off and put them into the playoffs whether they liked it or not, basically. Then he reversed his field and said how much he loved each and every player personally and there was nothing he wouldn't do to get this fine bunch into the playoffs and pick up some extra paydays and some fat new contracts for next year, and working together they could still achieve this wonderful dream. He actually used that phrase, "wonderful dream," and then he turned his back and began to quiver.

"Okay, home boys, light up!" Sweet Basil called out, and the Wasps spun out of the seats like a skein of Japanese snake dancers, King Crowder trailing the play. Buttsy ran them through a new set of variations and then ordered a light scrimmage, and the play action became so intense that he had to blow his whistle and holler, "Hey, I said *light* scrimmage!"

A few minutes later, Justin Fell dumped Abdul Buzruz with a shoulder block and then Sutter bogarted Jones Jones into the first row of seats and Coach finally had to call off the scrimmage and order a relaxed game of H-O-R-S-E for decompression purposes.

"Nothing like a little emotion to inspire a team," he told me on the bench.

"You old crocodile!" I said.

Basil McBride won the H-O-R-S-E game with a 1949-vintage two-hand shot, and Pasty Pasticcino made a crack about the Siamese twins with the great four-hand set shot, and Coach blew the whistle. "Okay, Basil," he said, "now you think you're hot shit, right? Beat the whole club fair and square, huh? Okay, I'm gonna take and whip your ass. One shot for the money! Me, a fading old fart."

"For real dust?" Basil asked.

"For *money,*" Coach said. "Twenty bucks. How's that sound?"

"Sound like Charley Pride!" Basil said, smiling.

"Then make it forty."

"You got it, suckah!"

The players cheered and whistled as Coach rolled the ball from one shoulder to the other behind his neck. "Hey," Basil called out, "is that part of the shot?" In our style of H-O-R-S-E you had to match your opponent's move, including any advance la-la.

"Just getting the feel," Buttsy explained.

He stationed himself directly under the backboard, dribbled straight out to the free-throw line and flipped the ball 180 degrees backwards over his head without looking around.

Swish!

"Whoo-*ee!*" The players were flabbergasted. "Hey, right on, Coach!" "Hey, man, where you get that shot?" "WHOO-*EE!*"

A frowning Sweet Basil grabbed the ball and went through the same maneuver and missed the hoop by three feet. "Hey, Cawch," he whined. "You didn't say nothin' about no trick shots."

"Trick shot?" Buttsy said. "You ain't seen my trick shots yet!" He motioned the players toward the showers, and they ambled off the court talking in subdued tones and looking back over their shoulders.

"Buttsy," I said as we walked toward the training room together, "what won't you do for attention?"

"Nothing," he answered, "basically."

11

A behaviorist could write a library of books on the way teams suddenly start playing over their heads for no particular reason, or for some subtle reason that nobody can analyze. Look at the Philadelphia Whiz Kids, or that Giant club that overcame a 13-game lead in six weeks, or the USC football team that scored five touchdowns against Notre Dame in the third quarter.

Look at the Wasps.

We entertained the Philadelphia 76ers at home in our first game after the All-Star break and beat them 119–111. It was a team win all the way, with Massy and King Crowder alternating at center and Jones Jones coming off the bench like the supersub that he used to be, and our two sharpshooters, Justin Fell and Sweet Basil McBride, each scoring in the thirties.

Then we took the short flight out to Cleveland (economy class, because we'd be less than an hour in the air, and you should have seen our players trying to squeeze into those three-abreast seats) and surprised the runaway leaders of the Central Division by beating them in front of 19,000 fans in the Midwest Coliseum. This time Massy scored 16 points himself, mostly on dunks, and played more than half the game before the Cavaliers's center, Rufus Haynesberry, stomped him under the basket and sent him out with a severely bruised instep. Haynesberry had his own modus operandi, known around the league as "The Rufus of Haynesberry" rules, and anything was acceptable short of arson or rape. Stars have privileges.

"Team win! *Team win!*" Captain Basil exulted in the dressing room, and then the club went to Boston for another team win and down to Washington for still another. When we came back home for a Saturday night game against Buffalo, several dozen fans waited at the airport. Of course Freddie Verhegen and his accordion were there, along with 10 or 12 members of the Wasps's Hive. Everybody loves a winner.

Mrs. V. had baked a cake for every member of the team, that's a dozen in all, and it took a while to pass them out, and then Freddie presented a poem about this being the year of the Wasps. Most poets have shied away from the subject, because nothing rhymes with Wasp, but challenges never fazed Freddie Verhegen. He recited:

> This is the year of the Wasps
> The club which makes us gasp.
> A team that's supersharp and classy,
> Sweet Basil, Justin Fell and Massy.

Basil called out, "Beautiful! Beau-ti-*ful!*" and asked for a copy for the kids at the Settlement House. Abdul Buzruz wanted to know how come Freddie only mentioned 3 players out of 12, and Freddie explained apologetically that he'd been inspired to write the poem only that morning and hadn't had time to produce more than a single verse.

As we made the long walk toward the main lobby, Freddie and some musical members of the Hive violated airport regulations by serenading us with inspiring marches:

> *Oh, the monkey wrapped his tail around the flagpole*
> *To see his asshole. . . .*

Every once in a while a fan with a trombone would aim his instrument at some poor innocent traveler walking down the corridor and make a loud farting noise. It was in atrocious taste, but what's taste to a trombone?

Massy's instep responded to treatment, and Buttsy started him against the most physical center in the league, Buffalo's 6–11, 290-pound Willie "The Mountain" Danielson. By the time the game was two minutes old, every fan in the Helix knew the Braves's game plan: The Mountain would murder the green kid one-on-one, while the others played basketball.

The refs took their usual attitude; the old rule was "no harm, no foul," but for Danielson it was "no blood, no foul." Nobody wanted to inhibit a player who'd served two years for assault with a deadly weapon: his hands. The first time Massy moved across the lane, Willie did a hip-fling that sent the kid sliding under the backboard like a shuffleboard weight. "That's no foul?" Buttsy called out, tearing at the number 1 on his jersey.

The Braves poured back down the court on the turnover, but instead of looking for the ball, The Mountain went straight for Massy and began ass-pumping him toward the endline. When Bru held his ground, Danielson thumped him hard, and the ref's whistle blew the play dead. "I got number twenty-nine on the elbows!" he shouted, pointing at Massy. "Two shots!"

Buttsy started to run out on the floor, but Pasty Pasticcino held him back. "You got *my* man for two shots?" the coach protested. "That animal charges him halfway down the court, and you call a foul on us? *Jesus Christ get your head outta your ass ref!*"

The official gave him a threatening look, but it was too early for a technical. The Butts sat down and began a harangue that increased in volume and incomprehensibility every time the ref backed up near him.

"You can't play defense in this league. *Arrrgh!* Goddamn league! You *cannot* play defense in this league! Ooom-*ooom!* You just get driven back. What's Danielson, some kind of sacred cow or something? *Ummmm,* mother! How the hell can my man play defense if he just keeps assing him back? Huh? *Huh?* HUH? Tell me that, ya stiff ya! Hey, who's the most tiredest man after the game? *You,* ref!" I thought I saw the official's ears darken, and I held my breath. "Know why?" Coach droned on. "'Cause you gotta fuck a whole team every night!"

That drew the technical, which Buffalo converted, and the score was 13–6 for the Braves. Buttsy controlled himself for a while, but then Willie The Mountain smashed Massy again and this time the coach called time and everybody in the Helix could hear him shouting, "Goddamn it, son, get mad out there! Show some pride! That big jack-off's smearin' you!"

Massy took Sutter Manno's long facebreaker, making a spectacular leap to haul the ball down, and before his feet hit the floor the ref had called him for walking. "Walking?" Buttsy griped, jumping up. "Unbelievable! *Amazing!* Oh oh oh oh oh oh *oh!* You dumb polock! How can a man walk in the air? Show me how to do it! *Go ahead! Walk on air, you dumb polock! Arrrgh!* You called it, you oughta be able to do it!"

A few seconds later Justin Fell was tripped, but the ref didn't see it, and Buttsy hollered, "Hey, dummy, did ya swallow the whistle?" The ref energetically signaled "no foul," and Buttsy screamed, "No foul? Jesus, Mary and Joseph! Oh, I get it. *He knocked himself down!"* When the official came near the Wasps's bench, the coach cupped his hands and asked, "Hey, who's cleanin' the toilets while you're fuckin' up this game?" That drew the second technical, and Buttsy was dismissed from the premises. The zebra said it was for "continuous criticism," but I always thought it was for calling senior referee Nate Goldfarb a "dumb polock."

Coach pulled on his warm-ups and walked slowly toward the locker room, his knuckles swiveling into his eyes. As he passed Abraham Gross's box, he looked up mournfully, but the owner turned away, probably afraid that Buttsy would try to hit him for the automatic $100 fine. "Get 'em, boys!" our leader called out in a quavery voice as he ducked into the tunnel. The Braves made the T and their lead went to 24–11.

"Okay, Bru, cream that mother!" a voice squeaked from the second row of seats, where the players' wives usually sit. I thought it sounded familiar, and I turned to see Roxanne Garfein standing on her seat waving a Wasp pennant. Roxy was playing the Helix, indoors! My lead had come true. I thought I knew where she got her ticket.

The half ended with the Braves in control, 50–42, and a very battered Broussard Massy looked as though he had come down with a bad case of scarlet fever as he tottered off the court.

"Go, Bru, go!" Roxanne screamed as the club returned for the second half, and I saw him glance toward the stands, but he looked away quickly and busied himself drying his fingers on the bottom of his shoes. Basil McBride said something and patted him on the ass—it was "Coach" McBride now that Buttsy was gone—and the kid nodded, and then the ref blew the whistle for the jump.

Massy slapped the ball back to Justin Fell and raced downcourt to establish himself at the high post. The Mountain came right after him, nudging and elbowing and hacking at the kid's arms, but Bru slipped in the backdoor and canned an easy lay-up.

A few seconds later the Braves brought the ball down and Willie Danielson began one of his power plays, backing in and clearing the way with his muscular hips, finally taking a jump shot from six feet out. Massy timed his move perfectly and slammed the ball back twice as hard as it went up, and it caught The Mountain on the side of the head and made him blink. Then the kid did something I'd never seen him do. He hollered, "In your eye!" and bounded down the court.

He moved into the low post and fed Jones Jones for an easy ten-foot jumper, and the Buffalo lead dropped to 50–46. A few seconds later Massy blocked another shot while Captain Basil McBride shouted, "Facial! Fay-*shul*!"

Willie "The Mountain" Danielson did not earn his $140,000 a year salary by backing down, and he headed straight for Massy, and everybody in the Helix knew it was High Noon. The kid moved out to meet his man, and I distinctly saw Willie's elbow sink deep into Bru's solar plexus, but the ref was standing on the other side of the court wondering why Buttsy Rafferty had called him a polock, so no foul was called.

The ball went to Danielson, and for a second he dribbled in an angry quick tempo, and then with a whoosh he slammed into Massy. There was a crack like a couple of brontosauruses meeting, and both men went down, but Bru bounced back to his feet. The Braves's trainer rushed out and applied smelling salts to The Mountain. I don't know what Willie answered when he was asked his name, but it might have been

Puddin' Tane, because it took two players to cart him off the floor, and his legs were made of Silly Putty. As he passed the press table you could see that his eyes were focused somewhere above and beyond our Tiffany scoreboard, searching for geese.

With their flagship in drydock, the Braves sank fast. Massy controlled the boards and scored ten points in the second half and kept the opponents from scoring another ten or 15 with his blocks and interceptions, and the final score was 100–94 Wasps. That made five straight wins. I leafed through the team book and discovered that it was the longest winning streak in the history of the franchise. The copy desk put a masterful head on my piece:

WASPS STING TO NEW RECORD

My story mentioned the first Wasp team and its string of four straight wins ten years earlier, Buttsy Rafferty's only previous moment of glory. After brilliant editing by Tex Pecos, my final graf came out:

> "I can hardly stand the excitement," Coach Rafferty collapsed in the locker room. "I only hope we can maintain this high level of achievement."

It was definitely one of the finest quotes ever collapsed, wouldn't you collapse so yourself?

12

The team lost a tight Wednesday night game to the 76ers when Abdul's shot rolled out at the buzzer, but then we came home to the Helix and beat Golden State and the Rockets with Massy all over the court. He totaled 36 points in the two games and even made a skyhook like Kareem Abdul-Jabbar's and a long turnaround jumper from outside the circle, both firsts in his pro career. He was like a flower unfolding, an 8–2 hollyhock, and you never knew what he'd try next. In the second half of the game with Houston he took a pass in the corner and violated

Buttsy's one-dribble rule to drive all the way to the basket for a three-point play. "Hey, where'd you get that la-la?" Sweet Basil asked him, and Massy answered, "Eighth grade."

He even allowed himself to be interviewed by a TV-person. The exchange went like this:

CBS: Tell us a little something about your personal life, Bru.

MASSY: Yes, ma'am. Well, I'm into health foods, music. I like to read. (Pause) I'm a big walker.

CBS: You certainly are! (Laughter) *Om om,* what do you—*om om*—to what do you attribute your success so far?

M: Well, I haven't had a whole lot of success so far, ma'am, but—being eight feet tall hasn't hurt. (Laughter) And I've got a great coach. And fine teammates.

CBS: I've heard hints that there might be friction on the team——

M: Oh, no ma'am!

CBS: —Between you and the regular center, King Crowder. How do you feel about that?

M: About King?

CBS: Yes.

M: I think he's one of the best centers in the league. I'm lucky to play behind him.

Nobody in his right mind would call King Crowder "one of the best centers"—in fact he came close to being the dreariest, but before Massy he was all the Wasps had. And as for being "lucky to play behind him," well, Bru was now our starter; King was playing behind him. The kid just wanted to soothe the older man's hurt feelings. Crowder had been acting squirrelly lately and was begging to be traded. The problem was: Who could use him? He was playing out his string, and not very gracefully. If he'd just lighten up on the open resentment, he'd have a job for two or three more seasons with the Wasps, as backup pivot man. But nobody could get the message across to him. "Play me or trade me!" he kept insisting, as if those were the only available options. There was a third: Get waived out of the league and go home to the North Philly ghetto. It was all very sad, but it would have been a hell of a lot sadder to keep Massy on the bench.

The kid's first network interview had gone so smoothly that the laconic wonder of TV sportscasting lined him up for an appearance on his weekly show. The laconic wonder threw an arm around the kid and announced to ten million viewers, "Ladies and gentlemen, this is my good friend Broussard Massy of the Wasps. Tell me, Bru——"

"Excuse me, sir," Massy said politely. "Sir, I just met you a few minutes ago."

The rest of the interview sort of fizzled out. It was the first time I'd ever seen the laconic wonder speechless.

With Massy's exposure increasing along with his skills, he began receiving sacks of fan mail, and Pipper Martin and I were freed from the creative writing business. A kid wrote from Rock Lake, Wisconsin, "Myself and my brother Robert are one of your best fans." A boy in Sequim, Washington, invited Massy to dinner and listed the menu: "Meat, roast beef, chicken, cheese, baket potatoes, sammon, salad and Coke, but if you don't come we will be only having cold slaw." I helped him answer his mail, slipping in genuine autographed pictures of the big man and copies of next season's schedule and price list, per Darius Guile's instructions.

The schedule called for one of those backbreaking trips where you play four games in six nights and fly thousands and thousands of miles and land in fog on runways sheathed in ice. Now that the team was making a move, even if it was too little and too late (as Nick Storen kept writing), there was a lot of high-spirited jacking around at the airport, and close to 100 people saw us off. A few of the wives showed up—Evelyn Manno, Joan Jones Jones, Abdul's wife Ashram and their little son Fez, and Red Green's bride Emerald. I always felt a pang of discomfort when I saw Emerald Green because a year ago she'd been one of the Wasps's most active stadium lizards. Almost every man on the roster had enjoyed her favors, and so had Nick Storen, Lucious Johnson and Pennsylvania Morgan. Then one day Red told me he was dating a gorgeous blonde, and when it was Emerald who showed up to meet him at the players' exit, I blurted out, "Hey, man, you got a sure thing there," and gave him a congratulatory slap on the back.

"I hope so, dawlin'," Red said coldly, "'cause I dig this chick."

Basil McBride walked up. "What's happenin', man?" he asked.

"Got a date, dawlin'. Peep out the lady over there."

Sweet Basil slapped his thighs. "Whoo-ee!" he said. "You got a date with that mullion? Hey, man, you gotta wait in line for that leg!"

"Get outa my face!" Red said, and strode off. A week later they were married, and as far as any of us could tell the marriage was steady on course. Naturally, Red kept chasing foxes on the road, but that only proved he was a professional athlete. Jocks take special marriage vows. Where the ordinary wording goes "love, honor and obey till death do us part," the jockstrap ceremony adds "or until the club leaves the city limits."

Dulcy saw me off, and this gave her an opportunity to speak to her favorite new subject, Broussard Massy. "Nice to see you, ma'am," the kid said, as though he were greeting the Dame of Sark, and my Dulcimer, coolest of the cool, reached up and shook his hand daintily. "Happy here?" she asked.

"Yes, ma'am," he said. "Sure am."

"Just wondered," Dulcy said. It was time to board, and Massy walked onto the plane with his body bent over as usual. I started to kiss Dulcy goodbye, but she was staring after the disappearing mastodon.

"Got the itinerary, honey?" I asked.

Dulcy tossed her head like somebody trying to shake water out of an ear, and then she said, "What? Oh, yes, I've got it." She reached up and kissed me and I gave her a squeeze and hurried away. How I hated to leave her behind!

"What'd you say?" I called back.

"I said, 'I don't see how he can be happy!' " Dulcy hollered, and I waved and said, "Bye bye, earth mother," and stepped aboard.

That night turned out to be typical of the aggravating nights in the life of a team on the road. The Heydrich Plaza of Milwaukee, "Hotel of a Thousand Services," had rented our rooms to the overflow from a convention at the Schroeder, and we wound up on the top floor in cells, one per player.

At midnight I tried to go to sleep, but the air was still, and I was afraid I might drown in a sea of used breath. My narrow bed had been stuffed with mouse droppings and used transmissions, and a rock band was rehearsing on the rooftop gardens. The musicians had the grace to quit at 4 A.M., after running through "Light My Fire" 17 times.

Just before dawn, I managed to drift off, but I woke up with that claustrophobic feeling that comes when you can't figure out where you are and can't find the light switch and your subconscious mind is convinced you've been entombed, and when you finally find the light, your heart slams into your rib cage like a jackhammer.

I did a rough calculation in my disordered brain and reckoned that the air in the room was now about 98 percent carbon dioxide, so I stuck my shoe in the door for ventilation and went back to sleep. When the fire alarm went off, I jumped up and started pulling my shorts on. It clanged again, and I realized it was the telephone. "Hello?" I said.

A strident female voice sang out, "Good *murning,* Mr. Frost! It's nine o'clock and it's snowing *hurd* outside and the temperature's eighteen." The way she made her announcement, you'd have thought I'd won the state lottery.

I felt mean and grungy and I started to ask her to call me back if it began to snow hurd *inside,* but instead I stumbled naked across the room to shut the door. I'd forgotten that I was a guest in the Hotel of a Thousand Services. My shoe had been shined.

Downstairs at the pregame breakfast, I saw that I wasn't the only one who'd slept fitfully. Red Green dozed at his seat, his long brown fingers resting in his hotcakes. Pete Tyles poured half a pitcher of maple syrup into his coffee. Buttsy Rafferty was stone-faced, and even the usually exuberant Jones Jones was reduced to eating in silence, occasionally grumbling at his eggs as though they were aggravating him. And Massy——

"Where's Massy?" I said out loud.

"Massy?" Buttsy echoed.

"Didn't come down," Pasty said from the other end of the table. It was rare that a player failed to show. Wasp policy, as spelled out by Abraham Gross and Darius Guile, called for a nutritional breakfast at club expense. Anyone who didn't attend had to buy his own. Few players opted for private breakfast.

I poked at my eggs for a while and then got Massy's room number from the desk clerk. Nobody answered my knock, so I knocked harder. I figured the kid must be out shopping, or visiting an art institute or a museum—that's the sort of thing he did while the other players were at the pornies.

A voice came from inside the room: "Who's there?"

"Me. Sam."

"Sam Forrester?"

"Sam Forrester," I said. "Star sportswriter for the *Blade-Mirror.* Come on, open up! Whatsa matter with you?"

"Slip your press card under the door."

Huh? *Slip my press card under the door?*

"C'mon, Broussard," I said impatiently. "Quit jackin' around."

I heard the knob shake, followed by a scraping sound as though something was being pulled away from the door. It opened a crack, and I could see a sliver of the kid's face.

I pushed in and noticed that the blinds were drawn on the single window facing Lake Michigan. The room was the size of a broom closet. An overstuffed chair had been pulled alongside the door.

"What's happenin', man?" I said.

"Oh, nothing," Massy said. "How about you?" His voice sounded slightly higher pitched than usual. Travel strain?

"Missed you at breakfast."

"Yeh, well, I was feelin' poorly, little stomach upset. I'll be okay." He spoke jerkily. Odd for him.

"Didn't eat?"

"Maybe later."

I noticed a half-gallon milk bottle on the window ledge and a plastic bag with one or two leftover sunflower seeds inside. "You couldn't be too upset, you ate all that," I said.

"Oh, that was last night. Before I went to sleep."

I picked up the empty bottle. "Sure stayed nice and cool, here over the radiator," I said, conscious that I was pushing.

Massy didn't answer. He was sitting on the bed, his head in his hands, studying the floor.

"C'mon, kid, what's up?"

He turned toward me in the half-light, and he looked awful. He couldn't have slept much. His eyes were puffy, and his curly black hair stuck out like an unkempt Afro.

All at once I knew. I don't know how I knew, but I knew.

Things had been going too well for the kid. For some people, success just isn't in the cards. Maybe it's their karma, their fate, like Nick's. Or maybe it's something within themselves. They can't stand prosperity, or prosperity can't stand them, one or the other.

Massy had had company.

"Night visitors?" I asked softly.

The kid mumbled something.

"What?" I said.

He looked up as though he'd forgotten I was there. "I'm sorry, Mr. Forrester," he told me.

"Listen, goddamn it, you gotta say something!" I said. "Look, kid, we'll help you. The club'll protect you. They got people that don't do anything else."

"The club can't protect me!" Massy said excitedly, standing up and grabbing me by the arm. "Now let me alone. Please! *Let me alone!*"

I went back to my room in a lavender funk. My brain whirled with possibilities, and not one of them made sense. Somebody was putting heat on Massy, but why? And where had they been keeping themselves since training camp? Maybe it hadn't mattered so long as the kid was tripping over his own feet and catching passes with his face. Now that he was established as a player, had the man with the acid come back?

I dialed his room, and when I said, "Hey, Bru, it's me, Sam," he hung up.

One call to the league office in New York and the kid would have spent the rest of the season with an honor guard of plainclothesmen, whether he liked it or not. But something told me not to make the call. Massy would act like I was loopy, and I'd be out on a limb alone, and I had enough problems already.

I sat on my bed for an hour, trying to dope out why on earth somebody in danger would want to stay in danger.

Then I remembered the $500,000 life insurance policy.

It didn't pay off on suicide, no. But there'd never been a life insurance policy that didn't pay off on murder, and sometimes double.

I couldn't believe it. I went over the facts again. In my addled state, a weird idea kept intruding. The kid was trying to get himself knocked off for the insurance.

Self-induced murder. Another first.

The game started at two o'clock, and the Wasps played like the old-folks'-home jayvees. Twice Sutter Manno slid off the bench, half asleep. Sweet Basil McBride passed out to Ray Giobbe in the clear, a dandy play if Giobbe had been a Wasp. Jones Jones moved like a deepwater diver, and Massy reverted to his early form, tripping several times over the free-throw line. The only Wasp who played respectably was Red Green, but then Red never went on a road trip without the company of his medical staff, Dr. Benzedrine and Nurse Dexamyl.

"Well, we blew one, that's all," Coach said at the airport, yawning over his third cup of caffeine mit schnapps. "Basically we'll be okay."

He was right. We went to Houston and won 98–66, the fewest points the Rockets had scored since leaving San Diego, and a strangely inspired Massy racked up 14 blocks for a new Wasps's record. His shooting was still spotty—7 for 17 from the floor and 3 for 7 at the free-throw line—but as long as he kept constipating the middle on defense the Wasps were tough. I'd never seen him play so hard—maybe he was trying to send somebody a message.

The new pattern continued through three quick wins out West, with Massy windmilling those long arms of his and tying his men up and blocking shots like Ping-Pong balls. He also took a steady pounding, but he barely seemed to notice. Washington Rubell of the Warriors elbowed away at Massy's side for 40 minutes of action till I halfway expected to find a gushing hole there, and when I asked the kid in the locker room what he thought of Rubell's style, he just said, "Strong player, yes, sir." Then he dressed and slouched through the door.

Two nights later the Lakers went after him like a lynch mob, three of them fouling out in the effort, and again Massy didn't seem to be bothered. On the long plane ride home, I sat next to Justin Fell. "Say, how's your roomie feeling lately?" I said.

"Seems okay," Justin said. "Little withdrawn, yeh. He stays in the room playing cassettes. Incessantly."

"I thought you people loved music."

Justin ignored my racial jest. "How'd you feel if you had to listen to the same thing over and over and over again, till you felt like maybe a tape was implanted in your brain? Hey, babe, I mean six, seven hours at a stretch, one cassette after another."

"What do you mean, 'the same thing'?"

"Flute, baby. Flute in the evening, flute in the morning, flute when you're taking a shower, flute when you're trying to read or sleep. Sometimes I think I'm gonna turn into a fucking flute."

Justin seldom used the language of his peers, so I knew he must be disturbed. "Why don't you make him get a pair of earphones?" I asked solicitously.

"I did, but they wouldn't fit. His head's too big. So we compromised. He sits in the bathroom with the door shut and the water running and plays the thing on low. But I can still hear it. It's like I'm running the Colorado rapids, six hours a day, with a crew of flutists. I don't understand him, Sam. Why the flute?"

I knew why the flute, but I didn't say anything. Let the big man keep his own secrets. God knows he had enough of them.

163

13

Back in town, I made one of my infrequent visits to the *B-M* office, and Tex Pecos steered me into his cubicle. "Forrester," he said, "that kid Massy's hot copy right now. We want a feature piece on his life."

"Premature, T. P.," I said, thinking fast. "The kid's like a dormant volcano. Everything's quiet now, but any little shock could set him off. Why take the chance?"

"Because we're running a newspaper, not a basketball team!" old Pecos snapped, running around from behind his desk and sticking a finger in my face. "Round up everything you can find, from his birth certificate on up. *Everything!*"

I said nothing.

"Do you know anybody in New Orleans we could use as a stringer for maybe fifty dollars?"

"No," I said, "but there's somebody we could use free." Hap Gladstone has money from way back. He'd be offended if I offered him more.

"Sam, do you realize how little our readers know about this freak?"

"They know he's learning his trade. They know he could carry the Wasps to the playoffs. What more should they know?" I was thinking of my conversation with Agnes Richardson, and Massy's nervous breakdown, and the footloose father that nobody ever heard the kid mention, and the acid man. Let China sleep!

"Forrester, get the story!" Mr. Pecos said flatly. "I don't care what it costs."

"Mr. Pecos," I said, "if——"

"Just get the story! That's your primary responsibility right now, understand?"

"I don't cover games anymore?"

"Of course you cover games! Work on Massy in your spare time! What the hell do you think we're paying you twelve thousand dollars for? Get those news!"

I drove toward home and thought about the information I already had on Massy, and how little of it I'd shared with our readers, and how old Pecos might even be right for the first time in his life. The working journalist in me had been competing with the idolator, and the idolator was way ahead. I had ignored what I owed my employer, and what I owed the fans.

But what *did* I owe them? Sure, they were entitled to know that Massy was improving, that he made 14 stops against Houston, that the club with Massy had a shot at the playoffs. But were the fans entitled to know that the kid's father had almost wrecked him? Were they entitled to know the details of a young boy's nervous collapse? And the fact that his life was in danger?

No question about it, I was withholding information that the *Blade-Mirror* had sent me to New Orleans to get, but nobody'd ever seemed to care that I'd come home empty. But Massy was just an oddity in those preseason days, a sideshow in Pumas. Now he was blossoming into a star, and the situation had changed.

The more I thought about it, the more I realized I had to tell the story, bite the bullet, take my medicine, whatever the cliché was. If I didn't write it, then Nick Storen would, or Pete Tyles would, and I'd be beaten on my own story.

I reviewed my file on Massy, including the interview with Agnes Richardson, and started to write: "How tall is great?" I ripped that lead out and put a fresh piece of copy paper in the machine. "How high is up?" I added that one to the circular file. Another start: "When Broussard Massy was a boy, his father. . . ." But what did I really *know?* Only what a few people had told me. I didn't mind breaking the whole fascinating story of the kid's life and hard times, throwing the cat among the pigeons, as the French say, but it wasn't worth doing unless it was done right. I thought I knew a way. I dialed Roxanne Garfein.

"Oh, Mr. Forrester, I mean Sam!" she said, sounding happy to hear from me.

"I wondered if you'd help me on a story, Roxy," I said coming straight to the point.

"Anything at all. You're one of my favorites. Are you doing the street musicians again?"

"No, I'm doing Massy."

"Oh, *Bru.*" For a second, she was silent. Then she said, "Well, sure, anything I can do. Why not? You like him, don't you? I mean, you're sympathetic? I mean, you think he's a terrific human being, don't you?"

"Sure I do, Roxanne, or I wouldn't be writing the story. But you know Massy—he hates to talk about himself."

I swore her to secrecy and we made a date to meet after the game that night. When I went home and told Dulcy my plan, she told me I was an unethical fuckie and I should be disbarred from journalism. "What's that high and mighty slogan you're always quoting from Damon Runyon?" she griped at me. " 'An irresponsible reporter with a typewriter can do more harm than a drunken surgeon with a scalpel'? You still believe that, Sam?"

"Sure, I believe it," I said, "but I also believe a reporter's gotta get the story."

Dulcy flounced from the room in a long blonde huff, and I followed her till she slammed the bathroom door in my face. "Look, honey," I said through the keyhole. "I'm not gonna knock the kid down and beat him up. All I'm saying is there's a lot of unanswered questions, like why'd he quit piano and come up here in the first place? Where's his father? Harmless stuff like that."

"And the psychopaths that're after him?"

"I'm not touching that. Just the harmless stuff, honest."

Dulcy opened the door and appeared in alabaster splendor, the naked Maja of psychiatric social work. "Then you've got to respect his feelings," she said, briskly rubbing her face.

"I *do* respect them, honey. Look, I never printed a word about his personal life. Don't I get points for that?"

"A few," she said grudgingly.

"I'll tell you what's gonna happen. The second the good ol' boys down in Louisiana realize that Bru Massy's gonna be the hottest property in sports, why, somebody'll come out of the swamps and unload the whole story. In detail. Maybe it'll be his father. Maybe it'll be an uncle or a third cousin. And I'll end up with zilch."

"Good!" Dulcy said emphatically. "Then you can go back on cityside and we'll be happier."

"Dulcy," I said, "you romanticize the past, honey. I wasn't on cityside, I was on the women's page. Don't you remember? POTATOES TAKE THE LIMELIGHT?"

"Well, you were on your way, you'd have made it."

"But instead I went to the toy department."

"That's right. Fun and games. Kid stuff. *Sports.* Whatever you want to call it, Sam, it *is* the toy department."

The recent history of the United States flashed before my eyes like the old Movietone News: Lyndon Johnson showing his scar and lifting his beagles by the ears; Richard Milhous telephoning a pass play to George Allen; Wilbur Mills cavorting onstage with his strip dancer; Gerald Ford reading Dr. Seuss in bed; Watergate, the CIA . . .

"Honey," I said, "times have changed. It's *all* the toy department now."

I knew Roxanne Garfein wouldn't be ecstatic about the idea of tape-recording her conversations with Bru Massy, but I had hopes she'd do it if I flashed a little expense money under her nose. If Roxy had an obsession, it was her music. She'd have punched out a crippled old lady if it brought her any closer to Carnegie Hall.

Over soybean shakes at Sol's, I twisted her arm. "Well, I do owe you a favor," she said.

"I know it doesn't sound quite ethical," I said, "but we've both gotta realize this man could change basketball. This man matters."

It turned out that Roxy came from a long line of sports nuts, which was why she'd been so thrilled lately when she'd looked into her flute case and found box-seat tickets nestled among the quarters and halves. "Does Massy still listen to you play flute?" I asked.

"Almost every game. Stands back there against the pillar where nobody can see him, ya know? And he always drops something in the case when I'm concentrating, and then he asks if he can walk me home, and I make up some excuse."

"Why?"

"I wish I knew. I think I like him—I mean, he's nice to talk to, and he knows music. But walking down the street with him——" Roxanne shook her head, and her shiny hair rippled down her narrow back in sine waves.

"Sometimes I feel the same way," I said.

"It's not Bru, it's those creeps, the way they pull over and stare. Grosses me out! They act as though he's not human, and then I—*I* begin to feel freaked."

We drove to the *B-M* office and picked up the equipment—a well-worn Sony TC-55 and a stack of two-hour cassettes—and installed the rig in her loft, among the Renoir prints and the Picasso silkscreens and the music stands and the plastic Winged Victory of Samothrace and the stacks of paperbacks and sheet music. I left $20 in expense money on an orange crate end table.

Three days later we rendezvoused in the *B-M* lobby. Roxy seemed nervous as she handed everything over, and she left quickly without saying goodbye, just stuck her hand up the way Massy always did and waved and ran out into the soiled municipal snow. I raced upstairs and opened the first box. A $20 bill fell out. I snapped the cassette into place, and all I could hear was hiss. Then the birdlike voice of Roxanne Garfein came in high and clear:

> *Sam, I'm sorry. I know I agreed, and I meant well, but—I can't do it. See, a few days ago Massy was just another jock to me, ya know? I mean, how could I take him seriously? But I didn't really know him, Sam. Now we've had a few talks, and—well, it's different now. I know you have a job to do, but I hope you won't do it. Oh, Sam, can't you just—leave him alone?*

I sat in a kind of stuporous silence for a while and listened to the rest of the tape roll noiselessly on. *Can't you just—leave him alone?* I heard the voice over and over, like a penalty imposed on me for the crime of pushiness. Maybe Dulcy was right; maybe I was an unethical fuckie.

"Sure," I said to myself. "I'll leave him alone. I'll write the minimum, try to get away with it. And some day I'll get beat on my own story. You'll see. I'll be out on my ass, looking for work." Oh, well, the market needed bagboys.

14

With 30 games left, the Wasps slipped into third place behind the slumping Celtics, but second place and a shot at the playoffs were still a long reach.

	W	L	G.B.
Knicks	40	12	—
Celtics	32	20	8
Wasps	24	28	16

I called on Darius Guile in his mink-lined office and found him up to his shirtsleeves in requests for tickets. Clutching at straws, I believe it's called: The fans were desperate after ten years of what Red Green called "flustration." Guile grunted his displeasure.

"It could be worse," I said. "We could be back in last place again."

"No, it couldn't," the general manager griped. "They're driving me crazy, the sons of bitches."

"Hey, D. G.," I said, "that's a hell of a way to talk about the people that pay your salary."

"I'm not talking about those sons of bitches, I'm talking about the sons of bitches around the league." He pushed a telegram across his cluttered desk to me:

BOSTON CELTICS PROTEST DISTORTION OF EASTERN DIVISION BY UNDRAFTED PLAYER WHOSE ORIGINAL AVAILABILITY ILLEGALLY CONCEALED FROM REST OF LEAGUE BY WASPS MANAGEMENT

"What's this?" I asked. "Some idiot's idea of a joke?"

"Well, if you call the general manager of the Celtics some idiot, well, yes, it is."

"Pat McGrady sent this?"

"Yeh. To the commissioner."

"What'd the commissioner do?"

"Off the record?"

"I guess so," I said reluctantly, knowing that I wouldn't get the inside information any other way.

"He scheduled a secret meeting of all the complaining clubs. That's eleven different ones."

"Jesus!" I said, genuinely shocked. "When're they meeting?"

"Last night," Guile said, relighting his soggy cigar. "They don't think we know about it, but I got my sources. They went all around Robin Hood's barn. When they finally realized there was no way they could sit Massy down for the rest of the year, they started talking about raising the basket, widening the lanes, stuff like that. *In the middle of the goddamn season!*"

"Shows how scared they are."

"Fucking A," the general manager agreed. "My source told me the whole mess of 'em—eleven general managers, the commissioner, another six or eight flunkies from the NBA office—there was only one thing they agreed on all night. The kid's wrecking the game."

"Bullshit," I said.

"Yeh, well, tell them, don't tell me. Jocko Coryell of the Sonics? He said somebody ought to put out a contract on the kid."

"Not serious?" The acid man.

"Course not. But our jests—our jests—what's that quote?"

" 'Our jests reveal our intentions.' "

Guile nodded.

"Those guys sure hate to lose, don't they?" I said.

Guile pushed the cigar box across to me, secure in the knowledge that I detested them. I took six.

"Hey!" he said, knitting up his eyebrows. "I thought you hated cigars."

"My wife," I said quickly. "They're for my wife."

"Dulcy doesn't smoke, Sam! What kinda bullshit you handing me?"

"Her brother does."

The general manager retrieved the box hastily and stuffed it into a lower drawer of his desk.

"Those other teams—they've got no case, do they?" I asked.

"No, but they got power!" Guile said, slapping his open hand down on the desk top. "What's having a case got to do with anything? Did the National League have a case against Curt Flood? Did the NFL have a case when they dumped Joe Kapp? Did the Romans have a case against the Christians? They axed 'em, didn't they? It's not how much case you got, my boy, it's how much *cojones,* and the NBA owners got plenty."

I told the GM it had never been clear to me how the Wasps managed to sign Massy, with a couple of dozen other teams searching the country for star centers. "That's just it!" he said, grinding his pudgy left fist into his pudgy right palm. "He wasn't a star center when he showed up, Sam. He was a star klutz. Remember? Nobody else was interested. We were barely interested ourselves, till Buttsy saw something in him."

"You mean nobody wanted him, or you kept him in the closet?"

Guile tipped his head to one side and smiled sheepishly. "Well, it was kind of a fast shuffle, just between you and I. We called around the league and told everybody we had an eight-foot freak that couldn't hit the side of a barn and dribbled like Dame May Whitney, whatever that old broad's name was, and they took our word, all except a few scouts that came sniffing around and took one look at the kid on the court and died laughing."

I was still thinking about the Celtics's telegram when I strolled onto the empty court and spotted Kenny Hohlar stapling up his pregame banners, the ones that said FAVORITE SON KENNY HOHLAR and HELLO AMERICA FROM KENNY HOHLAR'S FANS and KENNY AND THE WASPS BOTH NO. 1. Tonight's game would be on national TV.

"Another spontaneous outpouring, eh, Ken?" I called hollowly across the floor.

"Oh, hi, Sam!" Hohlar hollered back. He was anything but embarrassed. He was a professional entertainer, doing his job. "Say, Sam," he said as we met at mid-court, "have you heard what I heard about the Knicks?"

"They're questioning Massy's eligibility?"

"Not that," Hohlar said. "I was talking to their color man this morning, picking up some advance color, you know? You understand?" Yeh, I understood. A color man was usually your best source of color. "He told me the Knicks were fed up with the controversy about Massy and they're gonna take care of him."

"Take care of him? What's that supposed to mean?"

"Search me," Ken said, grinning and holding up his arms as though to be searched.

"Sounds like an idle threat."

"Listen, Sam, Massy's no idol to those guys!"

Continuing my relentless search for the news behind the news (which I wouldn't print when I got it), I strolled up to the press room to see if anybody was around. I found it hard to credit Hohlar's story simply because I'd had long experience with him and his practice of rattling on about things he dimly understood. No doubt about it, the New York team must be steaming, with the lowly Wasps forcing them to play basketball instead of providing a breather on the schedule.

Some of the fans were just as upset. Now that the novelty of Massy's height had worn off and he'd begun to play more like a professional and less like a straight man for the Globetrotters, the vindictiveness had started. In Boston, a fan had released a box of snakes under the kid's feet and said, "Heah's ya bruddas!" An elderly woman in Philadelphia told him, "Go back to your cage!" Whenever Massy stepped into the lane at Buffalo, a claque of rooters began to count, "One! Two! Three!" at half-second intervals, and then they'd insult the officials for not calling the imaginary offenses. When the big man lined up at the free-throw line in Washington, containers of beer came swirling out of the stands at him, and one night in Chicago an open switchblade whizzed by his ear. Massy insisted later that he hadn't noticed a thing, like the see-no-evil monkey. "They're just fans," he said. "They get emotional."

He showed a lot of cool for a man with five months pro experience backed by an outstanding junior high career. The fans get emotional, absolutely, and the fans are deeply involved, but not every rookie understands how much. Look at the poor soul in Denver who wrote, "I have been a Broncos' fan since the Broncos were first organized, and I can't stand their fumbling anymore," and killed himself. Or the baseball nut who shot one man through the head and another in the stomach and explained, "They shouldn't of taunted me about the Dodgers." Or our own Wasp fan who stuck with the team for the first five years and then inhaled a bottleful of something, leaving behind a cassette of the Wasps's anthem and a message in a wracked voice: "We'll *never* make it. I tried to be patient. I've fouled out of life."

A fan can only endure so much indignity to his borrowed persona: the team. You'd see it in a boy nine or ten years old, sticking out his program at the players' exit and saying, "Autograph, Mr. Buzruz?" If Abdul ignored him, the kid would say something like, "You're all washed up anyway," and there'd be tears in his eyes. You'd see it in the poor fanatics who hid all day in the men's room so they could get into a night game without a ticket, or the rich socialites who waged custody fights over their season boxes, or willed them to their children like shares of diamond mines. "What do you think of the Wasps's chances?" the husband said to the wife in a *Blade-Mirror* cartoon, and the wife replied, "Oh, dear, let's not talk religion."

And when losers like the Wasps suddenly start to win—then you've got mass hysteria. Don't we all think of ourselves as losers? Don't we all live for the day when we'll suddenly rise up and *win?* If we can't do it ourselves, the home team offers a second chance. At the Helix, it was SRO.

With all three papers counting down for the playoffs, everybody in town became a Freddie Verhegen. When Massy took one of his infrequent walks, cars still slid over to the curb and people still stopped and gawked, but they cheered him, too, and rushed up to offer a handshake and wish him well and thank him for the season. Massy never shook back. He'd just wave his index finger in front of his face, smile slightly and walk faster. Maybe he figured he'd make a tougher target.

With kids, he'd mutter a few words and sign an autograph if they asked, but all the time he'd be looking around him, behind him, like a split end waiting to get blind-sided.

Or an oversize rabbit, waiting for the fox.

15

On a night when we were playing the Knicks at home, our fifty-third game of the season, the fans were lined up at the players' entrance two hours before the jump. I went down the line interviewing them, preparing a sidebar. "Why're you out here in the cold?" I asked a pigtailed girl of 11 or 12.

"See Massy," she said, giggling and hiding behind her scarf.

"Do you like Massy?"

Another giggle. I turned to the next standee, a man about 60, but somebody hollered, "Here he comes!" and the crowd streamed down the sidewalk. I saw Massy strolling toward the Helix with Roxanne Garfein on his arm, a faraway look on their faces. "Hey!" I called out as I pushed through the entourage. "Which way is it to Hamelin?"

"Pardon?" Massy said. If he recognized me, it was through a fog.

"He means the Pied Piper," Roxanne said, smiling. Massy leaned way over and gave her a quick squeeze at the players' entrance and ducked inside, and I showed my press pass and hurried after.

"Need this one, kid!" I said, but all he did was nod.

Inside the dressing room, Pasty Pasticcino was wrapping Basil McBride and repeating over and over: "I'm taping a winner. No doubt about it, I—am—taping—*a winner*! Hey, hold your fucking ankle steady!"

"You think we can do it?" Basil asked. "Man, I just don't know, Pasty. Say it again!" The inspiring captain! Sweet Basil McBride, wrapped in self-doubt and adhesive tape. "Say it one more time, man!" he begged.

"I am taping a winner! Winners only at this taping table. Do not approach if you're not a winner!"

"Yeh, I like the sound of that," Basil said. "Oh, man, if I could only believe!"

Off to one side, the distinguished coach Francis X. Rafferty was doctoring the game balls with a hand pump and a needle. League rules specified a pressure of 7½ to 8½ pounds, and the Wasps always tailored the pressure to the opponent. New York was a sharpshooting club, and a team like that preferred a soft ball, one that gave a little when it hit the rim. The Wasps were more of a jumping team; we liked the ball hard so it would spring off the backboard, except when we were playing an acrobatic club like New Orleans and preferred the softer ball ourselves. Coach always got to the Wilsons before the game and did the job with a pressure gauge and a hand pump. He also liked to replace the balls once in a while, throw in a brand-new one. An unroughened ball won't absorb moisture; sweat beads on the smooth leather and makes it hard to control. That's why new balls are never used in NBA games. Well, hardly ever. Sometimes Buttsy would slip one in to throw off a flashy bunch of handlers like Phoenix or L. A.

Two hours before game time, almost everybody was in the locker room, and the walls rattled with the high spirits of strong young jocks, loosening up, ragging one another. I love those times. Sutter dragged in, wiping sleep from his eyes, and somebody shouted, "Hey, where you been, fool?"

Sutter dropped his Adidas bag in front of his locker and yawned.

"I know where he was," another voice rang out. "Went down to buy a jockstrap, but the juniors was closed!"

There was loud laughter, and shouts of "Whoo-*ee!*" Somebody said, "What size you wear, baby? One and seven-eighths? Maybe you better get a size two, leave a li'l extra room!"

"Real class," Justin Fell said. "You guys've got real class."

Jones Jones sneaked over and gave him a goose, even though it wasn't Christmas. "Hey!" Justin yelped. "Honoré de Balzac!"

"You better get stompin', whitey!" Jones said to me, his eyes twinkling. "Don't want no sickly ghost faces around here."

The pregame revels were interrupted by the arrival of the last player.

"Evenin', dawlins," Conrad "Red" Green called out as he stood framed like a pruned maple in the door that led to the corridor. "No applause, please. That only embarrass me." He stepped into the warm room, and behind him came three overdressed gentlemen who looked about as comfortable as mice at a convention of owls. "Dawlins!" Red shouted, holding up his pinkish palms for order. "Also sportswriters and coaches! Please, *please,* quieten down! Meet Mr. Cotter, my agent. This Mr. Kuhn, my ghost writer. In the two-tone suede shoes, that's Mr. Shrake, my editor. They handlin' my book, *From Ghetto to Hero.*"

The three men produced nervous lip smiles and stared at the players. Then the voice of Abdul Rahman Buzruz sliced through the formalities with a crisp, "Bad luck, man!"

"Whuzzat, Buz?" Red called across the room.

"You countin' your chickens," Buzruz said. "You gone put the sign on all of us."

"Yeh," Jones Jones put in. "How you know you gonna *need* a agent and a editor and a ghost?"

"Bad *luck!*" Abdul repeated.

"Pay no 'tention!" Red said loudly to his business partners. "Dig, they just annoyed they didn't sign up with you dudes first."

The three visitors formed a police lineup against the wall, and Pasty looked away from Justin Fell's ankle and called out, "Red, are these gentlemen gonna be playing tonight? If they are, we better start taping. If they're not, they better move their ass."

"Jes' a few minutes," Red said, putting a restraining hand on the arm of Shrake, the editor, who looked about to flee. "They diggin' the atmosphere."

When Red disappeared behind the swinging doors of one of the private reading rooms for his customary pregame ritual, Cotter the agent lit up a cigar and offered one to Pasty, and Kuhn the ghost writer said to nobody in particular, "I think we're gonna play a great game tonight."

"*We're* gonna play a great game?" Pasty said. "Who's *we?* You got a fuckin' tapeworm?"

A few minutes later the editor asked where Red had gone, and Pasty said, "Oh, *we're* in the shithouse. *We're* takin' a dump." Sensitive to hostile climates, the three literary men slank away. When Red came out, Pasty read the riot act about strangers in the dressing room, and Red mumbled.

The film of our last Knicks's game started at seven o'clock, an hour before tip-off. Coach pointed out a few goofs and blunders, and when the lights came back up, Justin Fell said, "Don't worry, Coach, we know what we gotta do," and Captain Basil McBride shook his head dolefully and said, "Yeh, if only we can do it." Then the players washed their hands and rubbed the bottoms of their shoes for tackiness.

Outside, I saw Nick Storen at the press table, puttering with his tape recorder. Lucious Johnson and Pennsylvania Morgan were talking to Press Agent Jack Carbon, and the stands were already three-quarters full of the faithful. "Well," I said to Storen, "do we make the playoffs or not?" I already knew his answer—it had been in his column that morning— but I loved to prod the enemy.

"I'll clue you," Nick said, blowing smoke in my face. "The copy-desk's already written the head for my game story: THE BUBBLE BURSTS. Snappy, isn't it?"

"Snappier than usual," I said. "What'll you do if the Wasps win? Replate the obit page?"

Storen's problem was that he'd written himself into a corner. For the first half of the season he'd ridiculed the Wasps and their rookie center, and now he couldn't admit he'd been wrong. If the club made the playoffs, poor Nick would look like a total moron.

Well, I wasn't much better off. I still hadn't produced my epic feature on Massy, due in two days, and Tex Pecos was making noises. Maybe Nick and I could open a PR office. He could handle funeral parlors and blood sports.

I could keep the books.

16

The Helix crowd was in a frolicsome mood, taunting the refs by singing "Three Blind Mice" when they walked on the court. There were only two refs, as usual, but who said basketball fans could count? When Knicks's Coach Eddie Pfalz came out, a banner rolled down from the second balcony—PFUCK YOU, PFALZ—and across the way another sign appeared: UNTO YOU A SAVIOR IS BORN, AND HIS NAME IS BROUSSARD M.

Abraham Gross reigned in his 16-seat box, surrounded by nouveau riche admirers, including the mayor and three councilmen and a couple of construction magnates. All of them were equipped with pennants and that silly plastic wasp that you swing around your head on a string, and every time Mr. Gross stood up to whirl his toy, his group arose in slavish imitation and a lot of plastic wasps tangled. Win a few games, and people you never knew will come out of the woodwork and kiss your ass.

The ball game wasn't two seconds old before I was reminded of the remarks the New York color announcer had made to Ken Hohlar. On the jump, the Knicks's big Orion Halliday went up half-heartedly for the ball and then rammed an elbow into the part of Massy that was closest, which happened to be just south of the abdomen. I saw the kid wince, but he recovered fast and set up in the low post, and with ten seconds gone he took a high lob from Justin Fell and dunked it clean.

He turned and started those loping strides back on defense, but before he'd gone half the length of the court the Knicks's wiry guard Brock Faulkner stuck a foot between his legs. I waited for the whistle, but both refs were out of position. Maybe after a few minutes they'd loosen up and start calling fouls. The senior man was Link Randolph, famous for his vocabulary. When a player would curse him out, Link would say, "This is not a propitious moment for such characterizations, young man," and one night he told Coach to "desist from these silly innuendos."

The other ref was Hal Marbley, "the bull moose." Halfway up in the peanut gallery you could hear him slapping his hand behind his neck and skipping across the floor as he bellowed, "Charge! I got twenty-nine on the charge! No hoop, no hoop!" The Bull Moose's language was not quite as genteel as his partner's. I remembered a conversation between him and Buttsy after Red Green had been thrown out of a game. "Hey, ref, I heard the whole thing," Coach had protested. "All Red said was, 'Mr. Marbley, Mr. Green did *not* like that call.' "

"No, you got it wrong," Marbley said. "The fucker used the magic word."

"He didn't use any goddamn magic word," the Butts whined.

"He referred to me as Mr. Marbley *you muthafucka!* So I run the asshole!"

In tonight's game, the two veteran officials seemed oblivious to the fact that Broussard Massy was being ridiculously overplayed. Once he was submarined on a jump shot, and that's one of the dirtiest moves in the game, wiping a guy's legs out from under him when he's in the air. Marbley screamed, "Twenty-nine on the push!" and flipped the ball to a Knick.

Coach ran halfway down the sidelines to discuss the ref's genealogy, and the Bull Moose hit him with a T, so the Wasps wound up losing possession plus a point. A few minutes later Massy was trying to get back on defense and the same New York guard who'd banged into him earlier kept jumping into his path. "Give him room!" Justin Fell hollered, as much for the officials' benefit as anybody's, and Hal Marbley called out, "Let him go 'round!"

By the time the second period was half over, with the Knicks leading by three, Coach was fit for a wet pack. He'd ripped off his warm-up jacket and sat there in his regular jersey, number 1, slapping his hands to his face in astonishment. Once in a while he'd fall to his knees like a supplicant at Lourdes and badger the refs. With one T already, he was risking expulsion with his steady barrage of words and sound effects: "Charging! Walk! *Walk! Aaarrrk!* Three seconds, *Three Seconds. . . . Oooooh!* Aw, shit. . . ."

With New York on offense, two Knicks crowded into the lane and clawed at Massy, and Coach hollered, "They're building houses in the key! *Houses!*" Then he pointed to Orion Halliday, the one-man wrecking crew, and shouted, "Ref! The big guy's pushing. Ooh! Ooh! *Ooh! Watch him! He's shoving my man! Owwww!* Gimme a break, ref!" Then he fell back on the bench and covered his head with his hands.

Near the end of the half, the Wasps cut loose on a fast break, but big Halliday dropped back in time to shut down the middle. Red Green took a feed and put up a soft jumper, and the ball bounced into Bru Massy's hands in the middle of a melee of arms and legs in the lane, also known as "the butcher shop," "death alley" and "the boulevard of broken dreams." When the scrum was over Massy held the ball high above his head in one hand, and he dunked backwards to tie the game at 44.

The Knicks called time. The kid sank to one knee in the huddle, and

Pasty sprayed Chill on his shoulders and upper torso, where his white-on-white skin had turned to red-on-pink.

With time back in, New York tried a tricky set play, Brock Faulkner slipping backdoor and putting some la-la on Red Green for a reverse lay-up, but the ball rolled around the hoop and dropped out, and everybody at courtside could hear Red taunt the little guard: "Hey, dawlin', ain't the pea s'pose to go in the basket?"

Faulkner flipped the bird after they exchanged elbows in the corner, and I heard him holler, "Blackie, you couldn't hit a fly with a tennis racket!" and Red said, "No, snow whitey, but I can hit you!" and caught the Knick with a hard right jab to the chops, just as the half ended. Before the refs could jump in, the two men were rolling across the floor, kicking and gouging at each other. Red was making liberal use of the magic word, and Faulkner was threatening emasculation.

When peace was restored, Referees Marbley and Randolph held a brief conference at the officials' desk and announced that our man Green would have to vacate the premises for throwing the first punch. Red shuffled off the court with his skinny arms forming a V above his head, and the crowd praised his name.

In the box just behind the Wasps's bench, Abraham Gross and his claque of fair-weather fans appeared to be suffering galloping apoplexy. Mr. Gross ran up and down the narrow aisle, shaking his pennant like a saber and baiting the refs. He beckoned Darius Guile to the rail, and the next thing I knew a message was booming over the PA system:

> *Attention*, plee-*uz! We direct your attention to the box directly behind the Wasps's bench, where managing owner Mr. Abraham Lincoln Gross is telephoning his protest directly to Commissioner Deford.*

The fans roared their sanction, and the house lights dimmed as a solo spot picked up Gross, ostentatiously dialing on his gold telephone. He began speaking into the mouthpiece, gesticulating with his free hand and jerking his head emphatically.

"Hey, Sammy, who you bet he's calling?" Pete Tyles asked. "The weather lady or dial-a-prayer? What an act!"

"Sells tickets," Nick Storen said.

I filed my running score and checked the first-half stats after Jack

Carbon handed them out. Massy had four personals, the hatchetmen Halliday and Faulkner had one each. The team listings showed 14 for the Wasps, eight for the Knicks. The officiating stank.

The third quarter opened with Massy batting the tip to Sutter Manno, and Sutter did a solo snake dance to the basket for two points and the lead. The Knicks were methodical about coming back on offense—they looked as though they were setting up—but a jump shot missed off a Halliday screen and Massy fired the outlet halfway down the court to Jones Jones and our lead climbed to four.

Then the big man blocked two shots a few seconds apart, and the crowd jumped to its feet and the organist pumped out "Charge!" Sweet Basil grabbed the ball and engaged in a slick passing drill with Jones Jones till the last defender was faked out, and Massy wound up with a slam-dunk for a 62–56 lead.

One of the Knickerbocker guards brought the ball back up, and Bru slid over to cover his man, Orion Halliday. As he did, the big New York center sprinted for the basket to take a long lead pass. The kid leaped high for the interception, and Halliday undercut him and dumped him hard. As Hal Marbley ran over puffing on his whistle, his cheeks bulging, Brock Faulkner slammed into the fallen Massy knees first, and it sounded like a sack of ice cubes being crunched. The kid flipped over on his back and covered his face with his hand, and Pasty Pasticcino hurried out with his black bag.

Massy eased himself to his knees, and when the trainer gently pulled the big hand away, you could see the rich dark blood welling out of both nostrils. Pasty slapped a towel up against the kid's face and Massy lurched toward the dressing room like a newborn foal.

With our key man gone, Hal Marbley threw Faulkner out of the game. It made sense, but not as much sense as calling the fouls fairly from the beginning. Now a player was hurt. That's what happens when a game gets out of control.

I found it hard to concentrate, thinking about the kid's face and the Knicks's cheap shots and how long he might be sidelined and whether the Wasps's bubble had burst and a couple of dozen assorted mixed metaphors and dangling similes, and I was the most amazed person in the Helix when the gun went off and I looked down at my "running" to see that the aroused Wasps had won, even without Massy and Red Green, 121–119. That poor old worrier, Sweet Basil McBride, squeezing a final season out of his tired bones, had racked up 31 points behind feeds by Sutter Manno and Justin Fell, and almost every starter was in double figures.

I had about 20 minutes to file for the two-star, but I wanted to see how the kid was doing. "It's broken two ways," Pasty was telling Coach when I beat my way into the dressing room. "East and west."

Buttsy slipped the towel off Massy's pale face. The kid was goggle-eyed, slumped against the wall, and his nose looked like a truck had backed over it. Pasty had wiped away most of the blood, and I could see right away that the bridge had been flattened.

Justin Fell stood to one side, lightly patting his roommate on his bony shoulders. Abdul Buzruz looked as though he'd just sat through the last scene of *Hamlet,* and over in the corner Sweet Basil McBride was throwing up in the toilet.

"Oh, my god," Coach said. "We won! Poor kid! Oh, Jesus. *Poor kid!* That's the worst I ever seen. We won it! Oh, I bet that hurts! What a game!" He picked up a towel and covered his own face, and his shoulders shook.

I said, "Justin, what the hell happened out there?"

"How would I know?" Massy's roommate said, shaking his head angrily. "It's just your typical piling-on play, fifteen yards for a personal foul, happens every game. That *was* football we were playing, wasn't it?" You seldom heard bitterness from Justin Fell, Mr. Goody Sneakers personified. "Goddamn game!" he said, flinging his treads into his locker.

"Did you see it happen?" I asked.

"No, but I heard it." He looked up at me, and a vein throbbed in his temple. "I knew something wasn't right. It was Sam Peckinpah night, man. Everything was different."

"Like how?"

"Like hateful, ya know? Hal Marbley baited Massy all through the game. Didn't you notice?"

"No," I said.

"Kept challenging him, egging him on. One time he called a charging foul and Bru just stared. You know, the 'who me' look? Marbley followed him down the court saying things like 'One word and you're out, understand? I'll throw your ass right off the court!' He'd say, 'Come on, try me, *try me!*' And Bru wasn't saying a word!"

"That's not like the Bull Moose," I said.

"It's not like *any* NBA ref," Justin said. "But that's what I'm saying.

181

It was different tonight. The moon was out." As we talked, a ballboy distributed final stats. Sixty-five personals had been called, 41 against the Wasps.

The team doctor lit up Massy's eyes with a silver flashlight, and I wondered about the connection between a broken nose and the eyes, and then I took a closer look and saw that the skin around the upper half of the kid's face seemed to be blue and yellow and dark red and dirty brown. By the time they led him away, his skin had turned almost as dark as Justin's, and a whole lot puffier, and his eyes had closed to slits.

17

The next morning I might as well have been back in the Hotel of a Thousand Services. The first phone call was at 7:30 A.M. "Hey, Sam," Justin said. "Sorry to wake you, man. What time's visiting hours at St. Florence's?"

I started to blurt out something appropriate to the occasion, like "How the fuck would I know, I'm not even Catholic," but a bloody vision of Massy loomed in front of me with his index finger shaking slowly in front of his face.

"Don't know, Justin," I said. "Find out, will you? I'll go too."

I fell back on the pillow and Dulcy said sleepily, "Can I come, honey?" We'd sat up till 4:30 going over the whole story. Lucky Dulcy, she got all the news from the horse's mouth, and then she pored through it again in the morning paper. But every time my favorite social worker studied a set of facts she found something new. At first she'd decided that the Knicks had just been overstimulated by the competition. "That's why they're successful," she said. "They rise to the occasion." Then we went over the case again and she decided that Brock Faulkner must have nursed a grudge against Massy, maybe the typical short man's resentment of tall men, and finally she announced her conclusion: "Somebody wants him out for the year," Inspector Dulcy said darkly.

"Why?" I said. "He's the greatest thing ever happened to the game."

"Sure, in *this* town," Dulcy said. "But how about in New York? Philadelphia? How do they feel about him in Boston?"

I turned over and yawned. "I lie corrected," I said. "C'mon, honey, let's——" but I was unconscious in mid-sentence.

When Justin called back around 8 A.M., I had to tell Dulcy that she couldn't accompany us to the hospital because there'd be limited room for visitors and Justin and I had to be there for professional reasons. "Sure," Dulcy said in her piqued voice, "I understand. Well, it's my day off, so I'll just stay home and do the dishes and the floors, for professional reasons." She was still mumbling when the phone rang again and Sweet Basil McBride asked if I knew what time the hospital opened. Fifteen minutes later Justin phoned and said he was on his way, and ten minutes after that Roxanne Garfein called and screeched, "Oh my God I just heard what happened oh my God Mr. Forrester Sam what hospital is he at can I go with you I've gotta see him oh please Sam is he all right?"

I calmed the poor flutist down and told her Massy was expected to survive. The second I hung up I heard the horn on Justin's black BMW. "Bye, honey!" I called to Dulcy, but she switched the vacuum cleaner to high.

The kid was in a private room on the third floor of St. Florence's. Most of the upper half of his face was bandaged and the rest looked like a cross section of ripe olive. He was sipping a dishwater milkshake through a glass straw and batting his long dark eyelashes at three nurses when Justin and I walked in. One of the nurses told us, "Please don't make Mr. Massy talk too much. It hurts, you know." I had to smile at the image of Broussard Massy talking too much. Why, certainly, ma'am, we won't make the Sphinx say more than a few words.

"How's the nose?" I asked stupidly.

Florence Nightingale interposed. "It's a *very* bad break," she said. "Took three hours to get all the cartilage in place. He also has a depressed fracture of the cheekbone. I don't think we'll be playing any more basketball this year." She turned to Massy and smiled sweetly, "Will we?" she said, and the kid batted his eyelashes. Maybe they had some kind of semaphore system going.

"Hey, roomie, we won it!" Justin said, and the corners of the kid's mouth turned up about a half millimeter, and he raised one fist like a barbell. As soon as the nurses left, Jones Jones arrived with Sweet Basil, both of them carrying bouquets big enough for the Kentucky Derby, and before the doors had stopped swinging Red Green steamed in and spread "dawlins" all around, and within the next hour Buzruz and Sutter Manno arrived with gifts of frankincense and myrrh.

The place began to sound like the locker room at halftime, with everybody talking at once and Jones Jones giving Massy a rundown on the second half, especially the play where he ran Sonny Estes into a pick and knocked him on his honkie ass and screamed "Get down, fool!" and scored right over Faulkner and Halliday.

"Hey, you guys, be cool!" I said. "He's trying to talk." I leaned across the bed and stuck my ear right next to the kid's mouth and heard this voice from 10,000 leagues under the sea, saying slowly, "Perhaps you wonder why I've called you all together?"

"He said, 'Perhaps you wonder why I've called you all together,' " I repeated, and everybody roared at the sick man's sick joke.

"Hey, baby, all *right!*" Basil McBride said, touching his hands against Massy's, and Red Green said, "Dawlin', you *toooooo* much!"

Flushed with his success, Massy lay back on the bed, and Abdul Buzruz said, "Hey, babe, how long you in for?"

Massy shrugged.

"Well, lemme ax you: What chew need, brother?" Basil put in. "Can you dig a little light refreshment? Say Black Label on the rocks with a twist?"

"He cain't be drinking with women," Jones Jones said.

"I can get you some greens," Red Green said in a conspiratorial tone. "Good for what ails you, dawlin'."

"Sure," I said, "that's all he needs."

"Cain't never get too much of what's good, baby!" Red said, and Massy started to laugh and then shook his head as though in pain.

"Hey, don't make him laugh!" Justin Fell said. "It hurts."

Massy beckoned his road roomie over and whispered something. "What'd he say?" Sweet Basil called out.

"He said, 'It only hurts when I breathe.' "

"Well, restrain yo' breathin' then, baby," Jones Jones said. "Do what Dr. Justin tell you."

When the party was at its height, a heavily cologned attendant burst into the room and advised us that there were too many bodies in too small an area, and anyway visiting hours were over and we'd have to leave. "We got rules, you know," he announced.

"Oh, yeh?" Basil said. "Well, we got rules, too, and we stayin'."

Red Green jumped up and said to the newcomer, "Hey, dawlin', shake it on outa here, or we gone do our number two play right up yo' back."

"You are, are you?" the attendant said snappily, backing toward the door.

"Yeh, we is, is we!" Red said. "Now git yo' Johnson outta here!"

The attendant slipped through the swinging doors. "You'll hear about this!" he said from out in the hall.

"Dig, we already heard about it!" Red said. "Don't come back without a cannon." Five minutes later a security guard arrived and announced we could leave or be arrested. Massy made no noticeable objection. Maybe he was asleep.

I drove straight to the office and finished my long feature story on the big man, throwing in a lot of bromides about dedication and hard work and some cute lines about the choirboy becoming king and how the whole league was watching with trepidation and wonderment as Broussard Massy changed the game of basketball. I went along in that easy vein, big on style and small on content, a bucket of whipped cream, with just a few references to his early childhood in Louisiana, "the Acadian country made famous in Longfellow's *Evangeline,*" and no mention whatever of his piano playing and the threat hanging over him and the father who pushed him into a nervous breakdown. My ender wasn't too bad: "Now the big man lies in St. Florence's Hospital, his face a wreck, his future an eight-foot question mark. Will he return?"

I shoved the copy through the slot in Tex Pecos' door and went back to my desk. The sports editor came out five minutes later, looking like a man who smells a moose turd but can't quite locate it.

"This the whole thing?" he said, crinkling his nose.

"Kids's not very communicative," I said, trying to look as though I'd just climbed down the ladder after painting the Sistine Chapel. "Everything I know's in there."

"Sorry to hear that," Pecos said sourly. As I walked away, he said reluctantly, "Okay, we'll go with this. What the hell, he's out for the year."

• • •

18

That afternoon I took Dulcy to see the patient, on condition that she would politely split if any Wasps showed up. "You'll inhibit them, honey," I said, and she said, "What do they want to do? Hold hands?" Massy looked better. A little of the natural lack of color had returned to the upper part of his face, and he could talk aloud, although he sounded like Smoky the Bear from inside a hollow log. He acted pleased when Dulcy kissed him above the bandage, and he seemed to respond more to her than to his Boswell, Samuel Evan Forrester. He told us haltingly how Roxanne had spent an hour with him earlier and played flute solos till the attendant made her stop, and he pointed to his tape recorder and a new pair of oversized earphones and a stack of cassettes. Then he mentioned two other visitors: Darius Guile and Abraham Gross.

"What'd they want?" I asked suspiciously.

"They were nice," Smoky the Bear said painfully. "They told me—they're fixin'—work something out."

"Work what out?" Dulcy asked.

"So I—can play, ma'am."

"Oh, how *sweet!*" Dulcy said, slapping her hands together in front of her face. "They don't want you to miss anything. How *thoughtful!*"

It developed that Guile had called Johns Hopkins in Baltimore and asked for information on a special facial harness that Lloyd "The Carpenter" Barber had worn after a crushed nose, and Pasty Pasticcino was already fabricating one of aluminum strips and foam.

"They asked—if I wanted to play, and I said—I surely do, but I don't want—to hurt my nose anymore," Massy said. "Well, Mr. Gross gave me—his word on that."

"What's the doctor say?"

" 'No way,' " Massy said, a little louder. "Told me—go fishin'."

"Well, my goodness, Broussard," Dulcy said venomously, "you

don't suppose the doctor knows as much about medicine as the front office, do you?"

"I'll just—have to play it—by nose," he said, and we both laughed politely. "I owe this team—a lot."

"Yeh," I said, "and vice versa."

Dulcy started to speak, but I gave her a heavy glower and she subsided. It wasn't our place to intercede on behalf of human decency. The Gross giveth and the Gross taketh away. Counting the playoff rounds and the championship series, there could be two or three million dollars at stake. Dulcy and I were out of our depth.

The next night I slipped away from the scrimmage at the Helix and drove to St. Florence's to see how the kid was progressing. His earphones were on and his eyes were shut when I tiptoed into the room, and his giant hands were tracing arabesques in the sterilized air. "Hold it!" I said when he saw me and eased the phones off. "You're conducting—let's see—do that last little curlicue again—*ah ha I've got it!* You're conducting 'The Wildcat's Revenge,' by Claude Balls. Right?"

Massy laughed and winced. "I'm sorry," I said. "I'll try not to be so hilarious."

"Don't worry, Mr. Forrester," the kid said, his voice stronger than the day before. "I'm okay." Then he said, "Did you come for an interview?"

"Look, kid," I said gently, "I didn't come here for any special reason. I just thought you'd like company."

"Well, sir, that was pure friendly."

"That's one of the problems of being a newspaperman," I said. "Everybody thinks you're out to learn their darkest secrets. Matter of fact, I *was,* once." While the patient propped his head against a bolster, I began talking compulsively about my meeting with his old New Orleans teammate, Harry Drezinski. He seemed interested in how Harry had looked and what he'd said, but after a while he began to flash those dark eyes of his around the walls, as though he was looking for an exit, but I didn't catch the portent, and I kept rattling on about my trip to New Orleans and how Agnes Richardson's coffee had dissolved my fillings. When I started to tell him what the piano teacher and his old teammate had said about his father, the kid's face tightened into a plaster-of-paris mask around the bandages.

"I never used a word in the *B-M,*" I said quickly, "and I never intend to. I mean, you've got a right to your private life."

Then something came over me, maybe the last vestige of a journalist's professional curiosity, or maybe just plain nerviness, another occupational hazard. I figured this might be the closest personal conversation I'd ever have with Bru Massy, even though I was doing most of the talking myself, and I couldn't resist the temptation. "Bru, Miss Richardson told me about your dad," I said, "and how you quit basketball." I laughed lightly. "When you showed up in camp this summer, I took one look and I knew there were a million things you'd rather be doing, and I've always wondered—well, Bru. . . ." I studied his deep brown eyes, expressionless and emotionless, as I struggled for words. "What I mean is—Bru, can I ask you a personal question?" At last I'd learn what had brought him back to the game.

Massy ran a heavy hand through his black curls and sucked in a deep breath through his mouth. "No," he said, and shut his eyes.

19

When the big man and his aluminum-cantilevered facemask rejoined the Wasps after 20 days, we were in third place and playing at New Orleans, and the top three Atlantic Division teams stood like this:

	W	L	G.B.
Knicks	48	14	—
Celtics	38	23	9½
Wasps	31	30	16½

We had 21 games to play and seven to pick up to catch Boston for the second and last playoff spot, under the revised league rules. No wonder Gross and Guile wanted Massy back fast. Without him, we'd be lucky to hold third place. With Massy in good shape, we'd have a prayer for second. But was he even in mediocre condition? Some players come back off a major injury better than ever, and some collapse.

From the jump that night in New Orleans, the kid seemed distracted, letting his man lure him deep into the corners where height was of no advantage and forgetting to switch off and force the mismatch, but he managed to score 16 points and block eight shots before Buttsy took him out in the third quarter with the Jazz leading by seven. Coach patted him on the ass and told him he knew it was tough, playing with that engineering display across his face. Two strips of heavy tape splayed out over his cheeks in broad V's, and two more climbed up to his hairline. Somewhere under a mound of tape, an aluminum cup with rubber edges nestled against his reconstructed nose, and on top of all that he had to wear a football lineman's birdcage, taped around the back of his head. "He barely looks human," I commented to Nick Storen.

"So what's new?"

I should know better than to talk to the cynical bastard.

According to my running score, Jones Jones came off the bench and scored the last eight points to squeak out the win, 117–116, but that oversimplifies the story. Justin Fell had put so much pressure on the Jazz that their two best guards fouled out with nearly a period to go, and Red Green raced up and down the court with such abandon that I knew he must have had a long session with Dexxie and Bennie. By the time Jones came tearing off the bench, the Jazz had been reduced to a slow waltz.

We were staying at the Maison Gris-Gris, one of the authentic new luxury hotels in the French Quarter, and after I filed my running and my game story and stats I pushed through the swinging doors into the hotel's merry-go-round lounge. Buttsy and Pasty, the old roomies, were at the rotating bar, and when it rumbled around my way, I climbed aboard. "What time does this train get to Biloxi?" I said cheerily. They both grunted.

"Excuse me," I said. "Aren't you Francis X. Rafferty and Armando X. Pasticcino of the Wasps? Didn't you two gentlemen just win a basketball game tonight? Isn't this New Orleans? Aren't I. . . ."

"Dummy up!" Buttsy said disagreeably, and when I looked chagrined, he said, "Guile's been on the phone, crying his eyes out. Says the whole fucking league's protesting."

"So what?" I said.

"So we might have to put the kid on the wood," Coach said.

"What for?"

189

"To call off the dogs. Basically just to calm them down."

"Well," I said, getting tense myself, "basically we might as well pack up and go home for the winter. What've we got without Massy? He not only plays a steady game but he turns the other guys on. When did you see Justin Fell put on a performance like tonight?"

"Plenty times," Pasty said without conviction.

The Butts ordered another absinthe frappé. "Stuff rots your brain and makes you horny," he said, winking. As though on cue, a couple of flamboyant camp followers strolled over, but Pasty shooed them off. Another first. I didn't have the heart to tell Buttsy that genuine absinthe was illegal and his drink was imitation wormwood extract with all the aphrodisiac effect of Midol.

Nick Storen hopped aboard the carousel and took the seat next to mine. "What're you geniuses conspiring about?" he asked.

"Off the record," Coach said, "we might have to bench the big man."

"Oh?" Nick looked perturbed. Could Massy even be winning *him* over?

Then Pete Tyles arrived to complete our quorum and immediately began chattering about an AP report that Massy would be banned by edict of the commissioner.

"No comment," Buttsy said.

"No comment," Pasty echoed, trying to sound equally important, "goes for me, too."

"On what grounds?" I asked.

"That's the big question," Pete said. "I heard it's something about the way Guile signed him."

"Or maybe something about the way he's fucking up the game," Storen said.

"Well, I like Massy," Pete said, "but you can't deny his effect on basketball. Jesus Christ, he's not halfway up to his potential and he's made a cellar club competitive. Whattaya think'll happen next year? Who could compete with an experienced eight-foot player?"

"The Knicks?" I suggested. "The Celtics? The. . . ."

"Bullshit!" Pete said. "When Massy reaches his potential, he could handle the Knicks and the Celtics on the same night with four dwarfs for his teammates." Where had I heard *that* before? "You know I'm right, Sam."

Yeh, I knew he was probably right, but I didn't want to face reality.

The old ostrich trick was good enough for me, at least till the Wasps won it all. I mean, ten years is a long time.

Nick said, "Massy'll never be that dominant, but what about the other eight-footers coming along?"

Buttsy downed his aphrodisiac and ordered a double. "The league made a quiet survey," he said. "Guile told me about it. Checked down to the fourth grade, found ten or twenty potential eight-footers and a couple dozen possibles. There's even a nine-footer out in Arizona, but he's in a wheelchair, from the standpoint he can't support his own weight."

"Ten or twenty eight-foot *players*?" I asked.

"Maybe more," Pasty put in, "and plenty of seven-footers, but they're no threat to the game. I mean Wilt and Kareem and the rest of those guys didn't shut us down. . . ."

"No, but a healthy eight-footer will," Pete interrupted.

"I'll tell you something off the record," Buttsy said after a long sip. "At that secret meeting of the owners? The foghorn out at L. A. told the commissioner, 'Why don't every team in the league take and give the kid two hundred G's and tell him to go to the beach?' "

"Terrific!" Storen said.

"And when he goes to the beach, we go back to the cellar," I said.

"The game of basketball's a whole lot more important than one weird kid from Louisiana," Storen said, raising his voice. "But how the hell would you understand?"

"What is it with you and Massy?" I said. "You've had a hard-on for him from the beginning." I loosened my collar: The old fight-or-flee impulse was overtaking me, and I looked around for a place to flee.

"Nothing except he belongs in a cage," Storen said bitterly.

"I got an idea," said Buttsy the peacemaker. "Let's ask the league to call a meeting pertaining to"—he stood up and emitted a hundred-proof burp—" the problem of Massy."

"When?" Pete Tyles said, pulling out a pencil.

"The day after the playoffs," Buttsy cracked, and wheeled through the swinging doors toward the men's room.

Storen and I exchanged insults for another few minutes and then he dismounted from the bar and said, "Well, don't think it hasn't been fun proving you're stupid, Forrester, but it's midnight and I got to go to work."

"Sure, you do," Pete called after him. "Blonde or brunette?"

"Bald," Nick cracked as he walked toward the doors.

"Bald but sexy?" I called out. "Like your girlfriend in Houston?"

"No, skinny with big tits," Storen shot back, loud enough for everybody in the bar to hear. "Sort of like—your wife."

For a second I thought I'd misheard. I *hoped* I'd misheard. No remark was too tasteless for Nick Storen, but usually he managed to retain a semblance of control until he'd had four or five drinks, and tonight I'd only seen him take one.

"Excuse me," I said as forcefully as I knew how, climbing down from the carousel. "What did you say?" My heart was pounding. I'd always been a lover.

Repulsive little weasel Nick had never been known to back down; he had the courage of his own stupidity. "Look, sonny," he said, jutting his chin upward at my face, "you're outta line. You made a crack about some broad in Houston, I made a crack about some broad you're married to. We're even, so piss off!"

When he turned to push through the door, I grabbed him by the tail of his jacket.

Nick turned and swung a roundhouse punch that missed my cheek by the thickness of my Aqua-Velva, and the momentum toppled him off balance just as Buttsy came barreling back through the swinging door.

The heavy slab made a loud knock against Nick's head, and he slid to the floor. I straddled him like a hockey player and somebody grabbed my arm.

"Short fight," Pasty Pasticcino said, leaning over Storen and waving his hands in front of the fallen man's face.

My heart was pounding, and I realized that I had just taken part in my first fisticuffs since the fourth grade. And *won!*

"He'll be okay," Pasty said, cradling Storen's wobbly head.

"What happen?" Nick said fuzzily.

"What happened?" Pasty said, leaning over the prostrate warrior. "You lose, that's what happened."

Storen fingered the bump on his head as the trainer pulled him into a sitting position and called for some brandy.

"Don't fuck with Sam," Buttsy said. "Keeps in shape."

"Lucky punch," I said modestly. What the hell, winners should be gracious.

20

We weren't scheduled to fly to Kansas City till the next night, which gave everybody a free day in New Orleans, "The City that Care Forgot," with its 24-hour massage parlors and strip joints and colorful antebellum inns built in 1966. I left a wake-up call for 11 A.M., but it wasn't my year for sleeping. The phone woke me at 4 A.M. and a faraway voice said, "Mr. Forrester. Mr. Forrester! *Sir!*" Lately Massy had been sounding as though he was talking through a telephone even in normal conversation, but this time his voice had been routed around the world two or three times. "Mr. Forrester, *please!*" he repeated faintly.

"Whassa matter?" I was getting accustomed to calls at all hours of the night, but not from Broussard Massy.

"Sir, I need your help," and before I could say "Why me?" the kid added, "Can you get down to the lobby?"

"The lobby?" I muttered. "Where? I mean when?"

"Right now." He sounded panicky.

When I got downstairs in my charming evening outfit, a double-knit suit over a complete set of cotton pajamas, the kid was pacing near the main entrance while a jockey-sized bellman looked him up and down suspiciously. "Quick!" Massy said, steering me out the door. "It's about three blocks away."

"What's three blocks away?" I asked, running to keep up.

"The car rental place."

"Car rental place? Bru, you don't drive."

"No, sir, Mr. Forrester. But you do."

He jogged around a corner and almost sent a couple of woozy night owls sprawling. "Where are we going?" I said when I'd caught up.

"You were asking about my daddy?"

"Yeh?"

"He's dying."

Custom Car Leasing told us there was one rental left, a specialty car, and they didn't think we'd want it. "It's a Porsche 911S, fifty bucks a day, fifty cents a mile," the clerk said.

"We'll take it," Massy said quickly.

"I'm not sure you can fit in it," the clerk said, studying the oversize bandage on the kid's nose.

"We'll fit." Massy said. "Can we get a move on, please?"

We signed the papers and a garageman drove the beige car out to the street, where it sputtered and spat like an Irish time bomb. "Hates to go under a hundred," the garageman said fondly. "Can't *stand* idling." With the passenger's Recaro seat moved all the way to the rear and the seat back lowered as far as it would go, Massy managed to squeeze inside. I eased the Porsche into gear and let the clutch out slowly, and suddenly we were 50 yards down Iberville Street. "Hey, take it easy!" the kid said.

"Tell the car!" I said frantically. We bucked and pitched through the city streets while I learned the five-speed gearbox, and by the time we reached the Huey P. Long Bridge I had the beast under some semblance of control. The 911S made my Spitfire feel like a tricycle. How would I ever drive the poor little thing again?

"What's the matter with your dad?" I asked as we sped over the Mississippi and into the black night.

"You'll see," the kid said. "That's where we're going."

"Why me?" I said as we leveled out in a long, flat stretch. "I mean, don't get me wrong, Bru, I'm glad to help. But why not Justin or Pasty or somebody else?"

"You're involved," he said softly.

"In what?"

"Everything, Mr. Forrester. Me, my life, my family. It took me a long time to realize it. You've never written one bad word about me."

I resisted the temptation to tell him I was also on the edge of being fired. I didn't want to sound like a crybaby, and besides, I wanted to meet his father, preferably alive. I shoved down on the gas pedal, and for nearly two hours we pounded through towns like Boutte and Paradis, followed the meandering Bayou Lafourche into Napoleonville and Pain and then turned onto route 70 toward Marcilly.

Downshifting across a canal bridge, I spotted the red flash in my mirror and checked my speedometer. It said 98 miles per hour. I slowed and pulled over, and the red light came up behind and pulsated across our faces.

"Mornin', boys," the big trooper said with an admiring smile.

"Hi," I said, as though I was certainly glad to make his acquaintance. I held out my driver's license, but his glove just stayed locked in its grip on the side of the door. He was staring open-mouthed at my passenger.

"Bru!" the trooper said, and slapped his thigh with glee. "Broussard Massy! Hey, cuz, what chew doin' back?"

Massy peered across me and said, "You're—you're. . . ."

"Bubba Lafontaine? From Marcilly? Don'tcha 'member? Hey, what's the matter with your nose?"

"Broke it, Bubba," Massy said with a little less enthusiasm than the trooper. "How you anyway?"

The two childhood friends exchanged a few more sentences, and the trooper congratulated the kid on making the big time and asked in a conspiratorial tone: "Say, Bru, tell me one thing. What's it like playin' with all them niggers?"

"Bubba," Massy said in a flat voice, "we're in a bad hurry. My papa's sick at the clinic in Marcilly."

The trooper's mouth fell open, and he covered it with his gloved hand. "Well, follow me, podna!" he said, and ran back to his car.

As we tailgated the flashing light at a relaxed 90 miles an hour, Massy mused aloud. "They're my people, they're *good* people," he said, "but sometimes I don't understand them. Racists, rednecks, no-nothings, call 'em whatever you want, Mr. Forrester, but they're good people, too. That make sense?"

I tilted my head noncommittally. No, it didn't.

"Just when you think they're not worth a lick," Massy went on, "something'll happen and you'll need help real bad, and here they come runnin'. They rebuilt my *grandmère*'s house when it burnt down. They helped my daddy when nobody else could."

We drifted around a sharp bend and came into sight of Marcilly, not much more than a bayou and a crossroads and a few houses up on stilts, huddled at the edge of a dark lake that I could barely make out in the dawn. "A lot of folks have changed around here," Massy was saying. "A few haven't."

Bubba Lafontaine's patrol car slammed to a halt in a cloud of chalky dust in front of a white frame building. Over a lighted red cross in a front window, a sign said, "A. Labas, M.D."

I followed Massy inside, and a short bald-headed man with a stethoscope got up slowly from a tattered sofa where he'd apparently been dozing and asked the kid about his nose and hurried him down a dark hallway before I heard the answer. A few minutes later the old doctor came out and said, "He's coming around now. Awful thing, eh? That young man has a burden. It's as though he's the papa and the papa's the son."

I said, "Doctor, I'm Sam Forrester. Friend of Broussard's?"

He extended a flabby little hand and beckoned me to the sofa, and I asked for a fill-in.

"Well, I guess he's told you about Michel," he said wearily.

"Michel? Who's Michel? Oh, the father!"

"You say you're a friend?" He sounded suspicious.

"Doctor, I *am* a friend, but Bru doesn't talk about his family."

He shook his head knowingly and said, "A strange *ménage*, the Massys. Good people deep down, but strange. Maybe *un peu fou*, eh?"

"*Fou?*" I said, groping for my high school French. "You mean crazy?"

"Peculiar," the old doctor corrected.

"Look, doc, we rushed down here because Bru said his father was dying."

"Well, he *was*. But he's past the crisis now. Another close call, but we'll make it again."

"Again? This happens often?"

He got up wearily and motioned me to follow. We tiptoed down the hall and peered through a glass inset in a door. At first my eyes couldn't focus in the dim interior, but gradually the scene came clear.

Massy's long frame was stretched across a bed, hugging somebody. He let go and then leaned over and took a thin hand between both his own, and I could see the kid was fighting not to cry.

Now I got a look at Michel Massy, a sallow figure of a man, somewhere between 50 and 80. His body seemed to be the terminus of a network of wires and tubes leading out of a machine that looked like the panel of a supersonic airplane. Two green lights glowed softly, and another flickered at the approximate rate of a heartbeat. Now and then Broussard leaned over the bed and said something, but no one seemed to be answering.

Dr. Labas led me back to the waiting room and poured coffee and motioned me to sit by him on the worn old sofa. As the sun rose over the cajun village, he sketched in the story. It wasn't complicated.

After years of dissipation, Bru Massy's father had suffered a renal collapse eight months before. An artificial kidney machine was needed to keep him alive, through the process known as dialysis, "washing" the blood, but the going rate for treatment was about $2000 a month, and Mike Massy, freeloader and wanderer of the earth, had no savings.

"Michel came here to the clinic to die," the doctor said, inhaling a long sip of steaming coffee, "and we phoned all the Massys, the Labadieville ones and the Marcilly ones and the ones in Breaux Bridge and Pierre Part, and the next thing I knew his son Bru was guaranteeing the payment and a machine showed up, bought and paid for. He's been getting the treatments ever since."

"But it doesn't help him?"

"Help him? It *saves* him." The doctor shrugged his shoulders. "Mike Massy—well—he likes a drop now and then. Suicide! It's like you or me drinking turpentine."

"Did he drink last night?"

"He and his brother Leon, they went over to New Orleans to watch Broussard play. Afterwards Leon rushed him here and said Mike had been drinking heavy with a newspaper writer, and I put him on the machine. I was sure he was dying, and I told him. Around three-thirty he asked me to call his son at the Maison Gris-Gris in New Orleans." A cough came from a back room. "Excuse me," the doctor said.

He returned with Bru in a few minutes, and they were both smiling. "C'mon, Mr. Forrester," the kid said to me. "You wanted to meet the papa, didn't you?"

I didn't know the etiquette for greeting a man having his blood washed, so I just said, "Hi, Mr. Massy." His long bony arm lifted an inch or two and he slowly waggled an index finger at me.

"He shouldn't talk," Bru said, "but he's gonna be okay. Right, Doc?"

"Certainement," the doctor said, and Mike Massy smiled wanly from the bed. I couldn't see much of him, lying under the sheet and draped in spaghetti tubing, but I estimated the distance between his head and his feet to be around 6–4. His eyes seemed to be the same color as his son's, an intense brown, but his hair was gone except for a gray-white fringe. His skin was rough and grizzled, and his face was a map of a difficult life.

I felt like a ghoul, taking mental notes on the stricken man, so I just

197

turned to the kid and said, "Maybe we better leave him alone."

Out in the hall, Massy chuckled and said, "Mr. Forrester, you're *some* reporter!"

"Thanks," I said. Let him think I took it as a compliment.

21

For breakfast the doctor's housekeeper brought over five different kinds of crawfish: *étouffée*, bisque, crêpes, stuffed crawfish, crawfish salad. "You like dose?" the white-haired Creole said in her cajun accent, and I told her I could eat dose till *les vaches* came home. "You some *Français!*" she said, and patted me on the head, and Massy made obscene noises behind his facemask. A laugh, I guess.

"You slurp those crawfish pretty good yourself, buster," I said. "How many you got stored under your bandage?"

"No, sir," Massy said. "You don't have to slurp these. Our cajun crawfish, they jump right in your mouth and purely dissolve!"

"Make sure they don't purely jump up your nose. You got enough trouble."

"I spent a lot of time in this place. My daddy used to carry me over here for vitamin shots, when we lived in New Orleans."

"Carry you?"

"Yeh. In the car."

Vaguely I remembered somebody—Harry Drezinski?—telling me how the kid had been injected with vitamins.

"What for?" I asked. "Growing pains?"

Massy laughed. "Well, if they were for pain, they didn't work. I had awful growing pains, yes, sir. Used to lift me right off the bed, those pains."

"The vitamin shots didn't help?"

"Help? I swear, they did more harm than good, Mr. Forrester. A day or two after I'd get the shots, my legs'd feel like somebody was scraping me with track shoes. Then I'd start to feel better till the next shot, and they'd hurt all over again. Hated those shots!"

"Funny kind of vitamins," I said.

"Excuse me?"

"Oh, nothing."

Later in the morning, the doctor told us we could go in and "visit with" the father. "Hey, Brou-Brou," the old man said in a gravelly voice as he struggled to lift up his head. "You got da nose, eh?" I smelled alcohol, but it might have been medicinal.

"Lie back, Papa." The kid gently touched his father's skinny chest with his huge hand. "This is Mr. Forrester."

"How do," the father said weakly, and I told him it was a real *plaisir.*

"Oh, *merci bien,*" Mike Massy said, smiling feebly as though he was honored by my attempt at French.

Bru said quickly, "How long can we talk?"

"Just don't get him overexcited," the old doctor said.

I realized that *père et fils* might have a lot to discuss, so I excused myself and took a long walk around the shell streets of Marcilly, and when I came back an hour later Dr. Labas was climbing into an old sedan. "I'm taking Broussard for a quick visit with the cousins," he said. "Will you sit with Mike?"

I went inside just as Bru came out, and the father was asleep again, snoring, with all the tubes disconnected. I eased my tired bones into a worn chair and tried to interest myself in the *Journal of the American Medical Association,* which could use a few bright leads. After a while, the patient began to babble in French and English and wriggle around, slowly at first but becoming more energetic until I thought it would be best to wake him up.

"Eh?" he said. *"Qu'est-ce que. . . ."*

"It's just me, Mr. Massy," I said. "Bru's friend Sam."

"I was having da dream," he said. "Dat nice new blood, he make dreams, eh?" He produced a dry gargling sound deep in his throat.

"What were you dreaming?"

"Sacre Nom, what do I always dream? You just saw him, Mister, what I dream."

"Broussard?"

"Ah *oui!* Brou-Brou. *L'enfant.* Dat was us: Massy and son."

I sensed that Michel Massy was tiring himself again, and with no one else in the clinic I wouldn't know how to handle complications, so I told him to lie back. After two or three minutes he began to mumble again, this time almost entirely in English, as though he didn't want to risk being misunderstood. "You are da frien' of my son?" he said. "Den you know what happen to him, *non?*"

"Er—uh—I think so."

"*Petit* Brou," he went on. "You know how many school was interest in my boy? Purely two hundred, t'ree hundred! In da sevent' grade! Pro team, too. *Beaucoup* scout, eh? Come 'round, make friend, you *comprenez,* mister?"

I told him I *comprends.*

For 10 or 15 minutes the poor man rambled on about his son's childhood and their great expectations. He told me how a coach had given Broussard a jock strap in the fifth grade, because he was a six-footer by then, and the boy had thought it was a nose guard and tried it over his face. He told me how Bru had been taunted by teen-agers who thought he must be five years older and couldn't understand why he wasn't skilled at their games and sports. "Den I take him to Doc Labas, and he give vitamin shots for to make him big."

"What kind?" I asked.

"Oh, da best! Come in from Europe and all like dat."

"You don't remember the names?" I was curious to know what vitamins caused so much pain.

"All I know is da shot, dey hurt like hell. Poor kid, scream his head off. But dey make him *big!*"

"I noticed," I said, turning my head so the sick man wouldn't see my face. Lots of professional teams fed their athletes vitamins to flesh them out, but I'd never heard of massive doses administered to make an abnormally tall person even taller—and a child at that.

"You must have wanted a basketball player bad," I said.

"I'm sorry," Mike Massy said, lifting his head to look at me. Apparently he had caught my disapproval. "It was wrong, mister. Let him grow *naturellement,* eh?"

"Yeh."

Then I found myself leaning over the sickbed saying, "Mr. Massy, I think somebody might be trying to hurt your son, maybe even kill him. I don't know who or why. Do you?" I didn't plan to say anything like that. Maybe Tex Pecos was working through me.

Mike Massy's head flopped back on the pillow, and he closed his eyes. He put his bony hands over his face and dug his knuckles so deeply into his eyesockets that I was afraid he'd hurt himself. I felt like a sadist.

"I'm sorry, Mr. Massy," I said when it was plain he wouldn't answer. *Comme fils, comme père.* . . . "I'm sorry I said that. It's probably just my imagination."

He opened his eyes and looked at me and slowly shook his head. "No," he whispered, "it's not."

A car drove up, and the outer door to the clinic slammed. A tear slid down Mike Massy's long cajun nose and disappeared in his two-day stubble. "Please, Forrestair, no more," he implored me in a quavery voice. "I didn't mean no horm." He poked at his eyes with the sheet.

A few seconds later Broussard slipped into the room. Mike had ducked nearly under the covers. "You okay, papa?" the kid said. "What's the matter?"

"Not'ing, son, not'ing at all," the thin voice said. He reached out and Bru took his hand, and I got out fast.

22

On the drive back to New Orleans to catch the team plane, theories reeled through my overheated brain like fruit on a slot machine, and I told myself that if I didn't chase this story to the end, I should just get out of the newspaper business and take up welding. Besides, I liked Massy. He was weird, sure. He *resisted* being liked. But he deserved a friend and I appointed myself.

I saw him out of the corner of my eye, stretched backward like a 17th-Century miscreant on the rack with his seat back flat and his head resting in the rear-window well. "Comfy?" I said. "Can I get you a drink? A magazine?"

When he didn't answer, I realized that he'd hardly spoken since we left Marcilly, and I wondered if his father had mentioned our private conversation. "Er—uh—did your dad say anything after I left?" I asked.

"Say anything?"

"Oh, you know, anything special."

"Papa's a funny guy. Last thing he said was—he told me in French —'Son, step carefully. Be on guard.' Can you imagine? Just like I'm still a child?"

"Well, it's not bad advice," I said, relieved.

I tried to pick up the thread of my thoughts, but now Massy had begun to babble away. I guess he was giddy from lack of sleep, and also relieved that the old man had weathered another crisis. "See that bayou?" he said excitedly. "That's Bayou Laguerre. Used to catch sac-a-lait there. Means bag of milk? I think y'all call 'em bream up north." He pronounced it "brim."

"Yeh," I said. I was trying to imagine what kind of a moral degenerate would inflict painful vitamin shots on his own son, for the sole purpose of creating a jock. And where did the acid man fit in, if he fitted in at all?

"Maybe you call them crappies," my passenger rambled on.

The old man was in danger himself. *Wise up, kid, or you and Mike and Leon, you're all dead.* Father and son and uncle, the endangered trinity. It was as clear as *Finnegans Wake.*

I had exhausted my patience with these close-mouthed bayou people, carrying their secrets to the grave.

"Bru," I said, raising my voice to cover my nervousness, "what the fuck is going on?"

"Crappies?" he said slowly. "Greenish white fish, kinda bony?"

"Goddamn it, kid," I snapped, "listen to me! Your own father says somebody's gunning for you. Now what's happening?"

"You shouldn't've talked to papa about that," Massy said in the voice of a betrayed man. "I thought I asked you, Mr. Forrester." He shut his eyes and didn't say a word the rest of the trip. Well, it was my own fault. I knew his pattern.

Justin Fell met us at the airport. I left the two roommates jawing away, found Jack Carbon and told him to hold my hotel room in Kansas City, I'd arrive on a later plane.

"What's up?" our press agent said.

"Personal," I said. I was learning from Massy.

This time I flogged the Porsche to Marcilly in 91 minutes flat. It was late afternoon when I pushed through the front door of the clinic into —hot, sticky silence.

"Hello?" I called out.

A lukewarm half-pot of coffee rested on an electric ring behind the receptionist's desk. The switch was off. "Anybody home?" I called. I walked down the corridor to Michel Massy's sickroom. It was empty, and the bed was unmade. Tubes and wires hung slack from the dialysis machine, and the red and green lights were off. Washday must be over. I returned to the anteroom. The wall thermometer read 88 degrees. There were still no signs of activity. I wondered why the door was left unlocked, but I realized that a country clinic must be left open, even on Sunday. Barring emergencies, no one would disturb me.

I locked the main door from the inside, so that visitors would have to ring the bell and give me fair warning, and then I began looking for the files. They were in a back room, lining the walls. Under "M," I found:

MASSY, ARMAND
MASSY, BEATRICE
MASSY, CHLOE
MASSY, FRANCOISE
MASSY, GEORGE
MASSY, LEON

and about two dozen other Massys, none named Broussard. The kid had been treated here. It made no sense for his file to be missing.

Then I discovered why.

MASSY, BROUSSARD lay open on a table. Dr. Labas must have pulled it after I left. But why did he want to study the kid's records? The father was the patient now, not the son.

Bru's file was thick with correspondence from people with funny titles like Klaxon and Kleagle. I read a short note from an M.D. in Memphis, describing a drug "that is said to have been successful in Switzerland—derived from goat glands. May be effective in adding height."

Another letter, marked "for your eyes only," was from the head of a drug company in Alabama. It read, "Our research proceeds with all due haste, but in the meantime the best hope seems to lie with steroids and growth hormones. We suggest you gradually increase dosages till growth stabilizes as close to 1.5 cm. per month as possible."

The words jumped off the page at me. *Steroids and growth hormones.*

For years cattlemen had fed them to steers, to increase weight. Some said they also increased cancer. That hadn't kept a few professional football teams from using anabolic steroids on their own beef cattle, mainly linemen. I'd never heard of such drugs being used to increase height, but then I'd never heard of injecting schoolkids with massive vitamin shots, either.

Massive vitamin shots, my eyeball! That had to be a cover story, to fool Bru and his father. Labas had used the kid as a guinea pig. He'd shot him up with—who knew what? I read another letter, but I couldn't understand phrases like "mutagenization of cells" and "genetic dynamism" and one beaut that I jotted down to get the spelling right— "deoxyribonucleic acid."

A lazy flow of Sunday traffic hummed outside the screened window of the old charlatan's office, but no other noises intruded on my research. I picked up a note signed by a Grand Kleagle. He urged Labas to "redouble your efforts, and we will do the same likewise." The return address, Indianapolis, puzzled me till I recalled that the Ku Klux Klan had been founded in Indiana.

A message from "Your Research Kommittee" told of "recent setbacks in the program but we remain undeterred in our efforts to return our great national sports back to the white man." Three failures were cited: "The lad in Vida, Ore., has grown to six foot eleven, but is now in stasis." A youth in Granville, Iowa, had responded to the treatment by developing arms "nearly 4 foot long, but he shows signs of cortical deterioration," and "the promising case in Arkadelphia died of an embolism at 7'4"." The report ended with a scribbled P.S.: "Brother Labas, we count on you! God is with us. We will meet the nigger challenge!"

Other parts of the file showed that the Kommittee's financial base had been broad, and that the program dated back at least ten years, when it was kicked off with a secret million-dollar bequest from a Louisiana wholesale grocer. A report from a Klaxon in Baton Rouge listed contributions from Texas oilmen, northeastern industrialists, and a couple of millionaires with major investments in pro sports.

I winced at a letter from an NFL owner, now retired, whose team had ridden to financial success on the backs of underpaid black stars. "While I don't necessarily share all your ideas about race," the old hypocrite had written, "I am a businessman, and the simple truth is that whites won't support colored teams forever. A white superstar would be a wonderful boost for our attendance." At the bottom of the letter there was a notation: "Encl. Personal check, $1000."

A scrawled note from a plumbing contractor in Atlanta warned Labas that "the niggers are poluting all sports except Hocky, and Basketball is tops on their list. Here's $90. We must recover the sport for The White Race!" The note was signed, "Klaude K. Klark." The poor demented creature had probably gone to court to change his name. A man had to be krazy. . . .

The most recent material was four or five years old. There was a letter from an M.D. in Pass Christian, Mississippi, bemoaning the fact that "the growth research program is now moribund, and I wish to God we could find a way to revive it. What's happening in American sport is enough to make a white man gag."

So the program had been abandoned.

I wondered if it had produced any successes, and how many dead, and how many zombies.

The front door rattled. I quickly rearranged the papers, but I was still shuffling them when she came into the room.

It was the doctor's Creole housekeeper, the one who had brought our crawfish breakfast.

"Why, Mr.——"

"Forrester," I said, smiling innocently.

"Where you came from?" she asked in her soft cajun accent. "I t'ought you lef' to carry Broussard back to New Awlyuns."

"Yes, ma'am, I did. My briefcase—I left my briefcase. Thought it might be in here someplace."

"I declare dat's a shame," the old lady said, her black eyes flicking back and forth between me and the open file. "Well, me, I gotta straighten up aroun' here."

When she disappeared down the hall, I raced to the front door and took the steps two at a time and sent up spurts of hot dust as I flogged the little brown car away from the clinic. Bayou Lafourche gleamed dark and depthless on my left as I tore past the village limits, and on the shimmering open highway I pushed the car up to a steady 90, passing Sunday drivers in bunches.

For the second time that day, I spotted a red light in my mirror, maybe a half mile behind. I took my foot off the gas, being careful not to show my brake lights, and tried to act as though I hadn't been going faster than 55.

"No suh," a clean-shaven deputy sheriff insisted, "Ah gotta disagree with you, mister. Ah clocked you at eighty-five fo' sure."

"Ninety," I started to brag, and realized that the events of the long day had made me punchy. I was digging for my driver's license when an electronic beep came from the police car parked behind me. " 'Scuse," the deputy said, breaking into an ungraceful jog. "That's an all-points."

I watched him in my mirror. He started scribbling something, then backed out of the front seat and reached the Porsche in about three long strides.

"You're Samuel Forrester," he said breathlessly. A bead of fluid dripped off his nose. I hoped it was sweat.

"Why?" I felt a forlorn emptiness in my stomach.

"Never mind why." The pose of southern courtesy was gone. "Folly my car back to town."

"What's this about, officer?" I said in my most saccharine manner. "I've got a plane to catch. I'm a friend of Broussard Massy? *Om om* —and Bubba LaFontaine? Er uh—Dr. Labas in Marcilly?" The deputy didn't change expression as I rattled off my honor roll of impressive names. "I'm with the Wasps? The basketball team?"

"You gone get plenty chance to talk back in town," the deputy said, and turned toward his car.

Maybe I was overreacting, but I knew what I had to do, trip-hammer heartbeat or not. I had vivid memories of certain other Yankee meddlers who'd been stopped for routine questioning by redneck deputies and wound up under ten feet of concrete. How far would the local establishment go to keep the clinic's filthy secret? I didn't intend to find out.

The 200-horsepower engine turned over with a snap. I rammed the stick up into first gear and stood on the gas pedal. The little car jumped out like a goosed gazelle, skidded almost broadside in the highway, then straightened out and hunkered down. Before I picked up the red light in my mirror, I was almost a mile ahead.

The top speed of a Porsche 911S, as tuned and race-prepared by Custom Car Leasing in New Orleans, is 126 at 7200 revolutions per minute, take my word, and I held that speed for two or three minutes, long enough to get around a bend and out of sight of the deputy in his Detroit smog-belcher. I nipped off the highway at a shell crossroad and another few minutes of power-drifting and frantic shifting brought me out on a two-lane country blacktop, slightly mushy in the heat. I turned away from the sunset and drove at a normal speed in the general direction of New Orleans, through quivering waves of baked air.

A sign said I was three miles from Thibodaux when I spotted the roadblock. I could make out at least three police cars with their party hats spinning. Before the picture became any more distinct, I skidded off the road and steered the bucking Porsche into a grove of cottonwood trees. As I jumped out, a raccoon looked at me cross-eyed and scuttled off sideways, making me feel even more unwelcome.

I hoped Dulcy had made my last insurance payment. If the local constabulary was totally committed to catching me, it wouldn't take long to find the car, and if I fled into the surrounding cypress swamps like a runaway slave, hounds would rout me out in minutes, if the cottonmouths and alligators didn't get there first. Audacity wasn't my long suit, but neither was cement, and I realized what I had to do.

I peered through the brush toward the roadblock, about a mile down the highway, and nothing seemed changed. The cops must have thought I stopped for a picnic, or maybe they hadn't even noticed me. At that distance, the little brown Porsche wouldn't have been anywhere near as conspicuous to them as the roadblock had been to me. Besides, there was plenty of traffic, and from a distance I was just another driver.

When I saw that they hadn't "made" me, I walked boldly to the shoulder and stuck out a thumb. I took off my sports jacket, to look more like a good ol' boy, and discovered that the small of my back was a sump of sweat. It was rolling down my arms and dripping off my fingertips, and my soggy shorts had ridden up around my armpits and were threatening to make me a soprano again.

Three cars passed me up before I made out a police cruiser rocketing off the horizon from the other direction, roof light spinning. I dived back into the brush, and the car roared by at something around 100, *whoop whoop whoop,* his howler on full blast.

The next time I waved my thumb, an ancient Volkswagen van lurched to a stop. I wedged my sodden body into the curtained rear compartment among four or five semi-inert forms and quickly declined an offer of a toke. "There's a roadblock just ahead," I said. "You dudes better clean out fast."

"Hey, thanks, man," the driver said as he gulped and swallowed his roach.

"Right on, babe," a female voice said lazily from the rear. "What can we do for you, man?"

"You can slip me through that roadblock."

"What'd you *do,* man?"

"Do?" The elderly vehicle lurched forward. What *had* I done? Oh, yeh, breaking and entering. Exposing secrets. Snooping. "No big deal," I said matter-of-factly. "Sold a few lids is all, man."

"We'll handle it, man," the driver said with more assurance than I felt. "Just lay low and keep quiet."

As we slowed for the line of red lights I stretched out on the floor and three bodies of varying squishiness rolled on top of me. I could breathe, but barely. The driver had turned the heater on high to clear out the grass fumes, and I was catching a steady blast. Luckily I had my own air-conditioner—a beagle licked enthusiastically at my face.

We slowed and stopped.

Over the slurp of the dog's tongue, I heard a high-pitched masculine voice say, "Where y'all gwine?"

"Thibodaux," the driver replied.

"Seen a tan sportycar goin' like a sumbitch?"

"No, sir, man, we ain't."

"What's that funny smay-el?"

"Man, we're takin' our dog to the car wash."

"Well, move on out!"

The van lurched forward about six feet, shuddered, and stalled. "We'll get out and push," said one of the bodies atop my frame.

"No!" the driver said quickly. "Chrissakes stay down!" He battled the starter, and then there was silence. "Dead, man," he said.

"Trouble?" I recognized the voice that had questioned us.

"Battery's dead."

"Y'all wont a push?"

"Surely would appreciate it, yes sir."

Just as I began to pass out from anoxia, I felt a bumper nudge the VW gently, and we slid away in silence. The engine coughed and caught, then turned over smoothly, then died. After another shove from the cop, we were on our way, the engine wheezing and grinding and threatening to go out of business altogether. The driver tooted the horn, I guess to give thanks.

I propped myself up on one elbow and groped for my wallet. I had $77 of road money left. "Hey, far out!" I said. "How much you want to take me to the airport in New Orleans?"

"A lid?" a female voice called out.

"How's fifty bucks instead?" I offered.

"You got it, man," the driver said.

I didn't find out till after I'd paid that they came from New Orleans, and they were headed home.

23

When I checked into my room at the Muehlebach, I was so tired I barely knew whether it was day or night or I was in Kansas City or Marrakech. I started unlacing my shoes for a nap, and then I noticed a blinking red light on my phone. I dialed "0" and the message operator told me to call "Mr. Tex Pakers" as soon as I got in.

"Well, I'm in," I said. "How many times did he phone?"

"Let's see," the operator said. "We have six slips. Starting at eight this morning."

I waited while she placed the call. Good old Tex Pakers, he certainly kept life interesting. Here I'd thought I was going to have a boring half-hour siesta before the night game at the Kemper Memorial Arena, but instead I could look forward to an Aristotelian discourse from one of the great minds in journalism ha-ha. "That you, Forrester?" the penetrating voice came on the line.

"It's me," I said, still feeling light-headed from lack of sleep.

For the next several seconds, the sound that came out of the telephone consisted of intermingled screams, shrieks, hoots and cries. Insofar as the normal human ear could ascertain, Mr. Pecos was communicating some kind of information about the *Item*, Nick Storen, Bru Massy and a person called Michel Massy. *Michel Massy?* Then I remembered the kid's father, lying alongside the dialysis machine.

"Mr. Pecos," I said, "slow down. Take it from the top. *Please.* We have a bad connection."

"Listen, you incompetent asshole!" the voice screamed into my ear. *"You're fired! Get that?* F-I-R-D. *Fired!"* Then there was a click, and a refreshing silence. Sure, I got it. Why did he always have to mince words?

I sat on the side of the bed and tried to collect my thoughts. Being fired was an exhilarating experience; it went to my head like a sip of sparkling burgundy brew or a whiff of Dulcy's Le Dix. Dulcy! Did she know?

I put in a call home, and when I heard my wife's angelic voice, I felt thoroughly ashamed. "Honey, sweetheart," I said, "brace yourself, honey. I've got bad news."

Her voice came bright and lively over the long-distance wires. She sounded as though she had just picked the right envelope on "Let's Make a Deal." "Sam, I *heard*! You're fired! Honey, I could just hug you to death!"

"Dulcimer," I said, "could you help me with just one little thing, sweetheart? I mean, Pecos is blowing his top and you're gonna hire a hall to celebrate, but, honey, I'm confused. *Why am I fired?*"

"Hold on a sec," my wife said cheerily. "Maybe it has something to do with Nick Storen's story this morning? Marked 'The Item Corp., all rights reserved?' Headlined EXCLUSIVE: MASSY FATHER TELLS ALL?"

"Yeh," I said shakily, "that might be it."

Dulcy read aloud. Storen's piece started on page one, not page one of the sports section but page one of the whole *Item,* and it jumped to a four-column head in the sports section. The story was so long it took Dulcy five minutes to read. There was line after line from Mike Massy, poignant human-interest stuff about Broussard's childhood in the cajun country and growing up later in the French Quarter of New Orleans, spiced with down-home quotes that Storen must have embellished, because he suffered from a bad case of *tinnus aurus,* or tin ear, when it came to quoting people, and Michel Massy spoke cajun English, not the strange Ozark tongue used in Storen's piece. " 'Why, shor, I'd of married his mama,' " Dulcy read to me, " 'but she'd passed on by the time I come back from shrimpin'. Well, I accepted the li'l feller as my flesh and blood, and we stuck together for a year or two, but the times, they was tougher'n cow meat, and I finally had to turn him over to kinfolk. Then he started growin' like a Jimson weed, and graceful, too —gracefullest li'l ol' boy you ever seen—and when I noticed him a-sproutin' up, I figured this was a break for the Massys. My boy had a chance to *be* somebody. But he plumb quit on me. In junior high. I guess he done let us Massys down. But we all got another chance now, and mighty glad of it!' "

Dulcy paused for air, and I said sarcastically, "Pussy good! Pussy good!"

"Did you say. . . ."

"That'll kill the kid, just *kill* him."

"I thought so at first," Dulcy said comfortingly, "but now I'm not so sure. Sometimes it's good therapy to bring things out in the open."

"Read me Nick's ender, hon."

" 'Now old Mike Massy alternates between visits to the kidney machine in Martilly——' "

"That's Marcilly."

"Not in the *Item*. 'Between visits to the kidney machine in Martilly and trips to the library, where he follows his son's progress in the out-of-town newspapers.' "

"That's the end?"

"No, it winds up with another quote from the father. 'I keep on livin' for jes' one thing. To see my son a winner, jes' like I tol' him years ago. I want one Massy to make it afore I die. Now that ain't much to ask, is it?' "

I could imagine the scene in some dark joint in New Orleans the night before, with Storen urging drinks on the sick man, and the old cajun saying, "Now none of dis goin' in da paper, eh?" and Storen telling him not to worry. I knew how Nick operated: Get the story any way you can. You might mess up a few lives, but *get the story!* Too bad I hadn't hit him harder.

I told Dulcy I'd call back, and I phoned Jack Carbon. He told me that they'd already heard about Nick's piece and Massy seemed to be taking it surprisingly well—just about the way Dulcy had predicted, in fact. I said it didn't matter to me, I was fired.

"What?" he said. When I gave him the details, he said excitedly, "Doesn't Pecos realize this club's going all the way? Who's he gonna send out here to cover? A coupla guys named Joe? Goddamn, Sam, there's not a player on the club that'd talk to anybody from the *B-M* except you. Not now, anyway."

"Thanks, pal," I said, "but Pecos doesn't see it that way. He just said I was fired. F-I-R-D. Fired."

"Can't spell either?"

"He's a sports editor, isn't he?"

"I'll get Guile to ream his ass, and I'll get Gross, too, if I have to," the PR man said angrily.

Fifteen minutes later my telephone rang, and a tightly controlled Tex Pecos asked me how I was feeling. "Down," I said. "I went out to buy food stamps, but they're too expensive for the unemployed."

"Listen, Forrester," Pecos said in a syrupy voice. "I just talked to Abe Gross, and he asked me as a personal favor to give you another chance. Well, I think it's reasonable."

"Reasonable," I repeated like a mynah bird.

"Everybody gets scooped once in a while."

"Once in a while," I said, and slapped myself upside the haid to bump my needle into another groove. What was that word he'd used? *Scooped*? I hadn't heard a newspaperman say "scooped" since college.

"Here's what we've decided. You *were* scooped on the Massy story, will you admit that?"

I admitted that.

"You looked like a raw cub, am I right?"

I said he was right.

"I mean, this was the one story you should never have missed. Do I exaggerate?"

I said he didn't exaggerate.

"So here's our decision. You stick out the rest of the season with the team."

"And?"

"After that, we'll see," Pecos said, like a teacher indulging a favorite dunce. "We'll give it some thought. You know, Forrester, sometimes it pays to shift your beat men around. That way they don't stagnate."

I saw the point. "Sometimes reporters get closer to a team than they are to their office. That's a good time to move 'em to something else. Do you see the wisdom in that?"

"Oh, sure," I said, trying to sound agreeable.

"Forrester," the sports editor asked after a short pause, "what do you know about lacrosse?"

The Wasps won the game with K.C.–Omaha, but not before Massy was charged, hacked, bumped, elbowed, undercut and poleaxed by the Kings. Coach gave him a breather with two minutes left. Afterwards,

I caught him in the corner of the locker room. "They really stomped you," I said.

Massy kept on undressing. "Turn the other cheek," he said, smiling wanly. "That's what it says."

"How long can you keep turning it?"

"How long does Papa have to stay on the machine?" He touched my arm lightly and said, "Thanks for what you didn't write," and clattered toward the shower in his clogs.

For what I didn't write I could get a Pulitzer.

I walked into the coaching room and found Buttsy and Nick Storen studying a piece of plastic. Coach handed it to me and said, "Well, what do you think?"

"It's an *H*," I said, "the kind you stick on your mailbox."

"No shit!" Storen said. "Hey, Buttsy, it's an *H*! All this time we thought it was a lemon tree."

"Very funny," I said, glowering at the heavy-handed sarcasm. I considered taking him on again, but thought better of it. After what he did to Mike Massy in New Orleans, leave him to heaven.

"We *know* it's an *H*," Buttsy said. "The question is why would anybody take and mail it to Massy?"

"Maybe you ought to ask him," I suggested.

"I did," Storen said. "He just turned away."

"Gee," I said, "what an ungrateful punk he is! You'd think he'd be dying to help a dear friend like you."

Back at the hotel, I dialed Massy's room, and Justin answered. "What's this about an *H*?" I asked.

"Oh, nothing," Fell told me. "Somebody's idea of a joke, I guess. It was here when we checked in this morning."

"Looks like somebody's playing H-O-R-S-E by mail," I said.

"Bru's not in much of a mood to play."

"He there now?"

"No, he went to the lobby to call Roxanne."

"Call Roxanne? Does he do that often?"

"Only two, three times a night. Maybe once during the daytime."

"How's the flute music?"

"Omnipresent."

Trust Justin never to lose his style.

24

We arrived home three days later, after knocking off the Bulls, and I took a cab straight to the Wasps's office. "Pipper," I said, "let me see the latest fan mail for Massy." She handed over about 20 letters, and I leafed through till I found one that was oversize and stiff. I pulled out a plastic *0* and a note made up of words clipped from magazines:

OKAY CREEP YOU GOT H & O JUST WIN A FEW
MORE AND SEE WHAT HAPPENS

I put the letter aside and looked at some of the others. There were the usual requests for money from various deadbeats, human and organizational, and a few raves, and a Mailgram from New York City that said, "All I want out of life is a chance to spit on you, but the line's too long." I picked up the first note again. OKAY CREEP YOU GOT H & O. . . . Why would anybody go to the trouble of clipping all those letters out of magazines, like a Bonnie and Clyde ransom note from the Thirties? I counted up. Fifty letters, even. That's a lot of cutting and pasting.

On a hunch I called Pat Rhoades, the Wasps's director of security, and asked him to meet me in the Helix. A crew was starting to lay maple over ice, and I waited in Mr. Gross's plush box, surrounded by 18,999 empty seats.

Pat Rhoades and I went back ten years together, and I knew I could trust him. Like almost everybody else in the Wasps's front office, he was a corpulent rascal, but he wasn't sensitive about his weight like some of the others. Once I mentioned Pat in a feature story and it came out, "Also present was the Wasps's security chief, Fat Rhoades." That was back in my second year, not long after the S. Tuneros debacle, and I called and apologized and promised to run a correction. Pat just laughed it off, and laughed even louder when he saw the next morning's *B-M:*

214

In Thursday's editions we inadvertently referred to Wasps's Security Chief Pat Rhoades as Fat Rhoades. The Blade-Mirror *extends its apologies to the entire security farce.*

I heard a noise behind me and saw Pat clomping heavily down the long staircase that led from the skyboxes and the front office. "Hey, sports fans!" I called out. "Isn't that Fat Rhoades approaching?"

"Hey, isn't that Bones Forrester?" Pat called from the heights. "I can hear you down there, but where are you? Is that a man, or a praying mantis on the welfare?"

He dropped into the seat next to me and waved his fresh manicure at the empty arena. "What's the score?" he cracked. "Crowd seems kinda quiet."

I handed him the note to Massy and watched his face as he read it. "The usual horseshit," he said, slipping it into his inside pocket. "We'll be getting a lotta that now."

"Why?"

"*Why?* We're a factor now, Sam. Not much of a factor, but anything's an improvement."

"Yeh, I know what you mean. I hear rumors some of the gamblers are feeling ugly."

"Screaming bloody murder."

"We're upsetting their handicapping?"

"Well, sure. Look at it from their side. They pay big dough every year to handicap the leagues. That guy out in Vegas, why, shit, they must give him a half million a year alone, just to figure who's gonna finish where. So all the handbooks follow his predictions and then—*poof!*—along comes an eight-foot freak and turns the figures upside down."

"An eight-foot human being, Pat," I said gently.

"Yeh, yeh," he blurted out. "I didn't mean anything, Sam. Don't be such a fucking bleeding heart. I'm just a simple soul. I call 'em like I see 'em, and lemme tell you, pal, the front office may be doing hand-springs over this kid, but to me he's two hundred and forty-five pounds of migraine."

"What've we got, one chance in a hundred to make the playoffs?"

"Six to one against," Pat said. "That's what they're quoting. But the pressure's on, Sam. We're beating teams we shouldn't beat, night after night. We're bollixing up the whole apparatus. You know how much

215

it costs the gamblers if we finish second instead of fourth or fifth?"

"Not too much."

"Not too much, eh?" Pat blew a perfect smoke ring out across the puddled ice. "How's eight or ten mill sound?"

I was incredulous. "Who gave you those figures?"

"A little birdie, nosey. You know who gave 'em to me."

Sure, I did. Pat's figures and Pat's orange juice came fresh-squeezed every morning. He'd been a detective lieutenant assigned to vice till he'd made the mistake of working over a guy named Dal Nagro whose uncle was a judge. Pat was eased off the force, but he still had more pigeons than St. Francis of Assisi.

"Tell you something else," the security chief went on. "Know what happens to the bookies if we make the playoffs? Not *win* the playoffs, just get into 'em? They're fucked, that's what happens. They take the biggest bath since the Johnstown flood is what happens."

"Dream on," I said. "And I guess if we win the playoffs, City Hall'll fall down."

"Don't mention it. I can't even think about it. If we won the playoffs, why, stuff like that gag this morning would seem like fun."

"What gag?" I asked.

"You didn't hear?" Pat said, looking genuinely surprised. "I thought that's why you wanted to interview me. Why, somebody rang Buttsy Rafferty's doorbell at six this morning, and when he opened the door, a barrel of manure slopped into his hall."

"On that Oriental rug his wife loves?"

"On that Oriental rug Eleanor used to love."

"Can you guys handle the situation?" I asked.

"*Any* situation."

Pat wasn't just blowing smoke. No sport is policed like pro basketball. I remembered a night in the Seventies when Sweet Basil McBride's life had been threatened: Pat Rhoades and the league and the local law put 89 plainclothesmen in the Helix before the game started. Can you imagine 89 men being assigned on short notice to a rape or a murder? A week later the threat was repeated, and this time the FBI collared a terrified streetcar conductor. He said he had a big bet on the game, and he was just trying to put Basil off his form. The Wasps prosecuted, and the conductor did six months, first offense. That's called clout.

Pat got up and brushed ash from his vest. "People are pissed about this kid, Sam," he said. "Never seen anything like it. In a way, I can understand. I mean, he's so—so. . . ."

"Big?"

"No, that's not it. I can't explain it. He's just peculiar, ya know what I mean? He's so—different."

"Aren't we all?"

"Not that different," Pat said, and began climbing heavily upstairs toward his office. "Cripes, Sam, you gotta draw the line somewhere."

"Between what and what?"

"Between people and—aw, I don't know, Sam. Sometimes you're too heavy for me, pal."

I had a feeling I had just listened to *vox populi,* and the message was clear and direct. Different is okay, but 8–2—isn't that stretching things too far? Shouldn't that purple wildebeest watch his step? I mean, you gotta draw the line somewhere.

25

You can never tell how an athlete will react. Your typical jock, reading a piece that makes his father sound like a greedy southern cretin, would probably come out swinging, or file a million-dollar libel suit, or try to get some of his influential friends to get you fired.

But who ever said Bru Massy was your typical jock?

The first time Storen came up to him after the article, Massy acted as though nothing had happened. Maybe he was glad to have some of his secrets out in the open—maybe they were heavy on his brain.

Out on the court, he seemed to settle into a routine, which wouldn't be saying much for any other player. But when you're 8–2 and playing a steady game, you're already on a par with a Wilt Chamberlain and a half. Against Cleveland, he grabbed 17 rebounds and blocked eight shots, and the next afternoon he came back against the Bullets and improved his figures. Three nights later, with the nose mask off for the first time and the Hawks acting like they were trying to flatten his face all over again, he shot 16 points from the field and 14 more from the free-throw line for a personal high of 30, and as if that wasn't enough he blocked 15 shots, including one that slammed back into Artie Satterfield's eye and detached the retina. When the game was over and the Wasps had racked up their fifth straight win, the Atlanta crowd was on its feet screaming for Massy's hide, and security guards had to escort the Wasps to their dressing room. We rode to the hotel behind sirens.

Now we were down to ten games on the season, and the only sure thing was that the Knicks had one playoff slot locked and the other opening was between the Wasps and the Celts with maybe a 1–10 chance for Buffalo to squeak in. That made us a prime target, and every club tried to break our ax, which meant two men on Massy and all-out warfare against his corpus night after night.

The fans didn't want to be left out of the vendetta. In Portland, where the spectators are usually well behaved, the kid yelped with pain as he loped along the sideline, and everybody in the Memorial Coliseum could see the blood running down his thigh from a series of long scratches. After the game, the clean-up crew found a plastic glove with tacks set in the palm. For years NBA players had complained that Portland fans sit too close to the action.

In L. A., Massy smashed through their big center's pick and sent him limping off, and the game was halted for 30 minutes while janitors scooped up debris, including a live bullet and a penknife.

As always, the least hospitable place was Madison Square Garden, "the new Garden" as old-timers persist in calling it, home of the Knickerbockers and the Rangers and the brightest people and the stupidest animals in the world. Every team hates to play in the Garden, and it doesn't matter whether there's a hot race or you're just playing out your string. In New York, the customers even razz their own. Everybody knows the case of Howard Komives: the Knicks fans booed him when he made a turnover; they booed him when he double-dribbled; they booed him when he missed a free throw; and pretty soon they were booing him when he appeared on the court and also booing the coach for playing him. They ended up booing a highly talented professional right out of town. Power crazy, that's the New York fans. Intoxicated about being called "the sixth man" and chanting *"dee-*fense! *dee-*fense!" and singing wise-ass lyrics like "Goodbye, Lewie. . . ."

They were ready for us, and the NBA office knew it. Our last game at the Garden was scheduled for March 16, and there was talk about moving it to the Yale gym or out on Long Island. But after hasty conference calls, the high muckamucks decided that hard-core Knick fans would only take the move as a challenge.

Fifteen minutes before the teams were to take the Garden floor, a man who sounded as though he was talking through his scarf phoned the visitors' dressing room and told Jones Jones, "We're holding your wife and your daughters. Don't score over six."

Jones wanted to call the cops and the FBI and the 82d Airborne, but Buttsy told him to relax. "Basically that's old stuff around New York," Coach said. "Some ribbon clerk musta bet his paycheck on the Knicks. Call home and you'll find Joan and the girls sitting right in the living room, watching the game on TV." Jones made the call, and Buttsy was right.

"Shee-it," Basil McBride said, "somebody pulled that jive on me right here in the Christmas tournament! Said they'd chop up my mama and mail her to me. I didn't know what to do, I was jes' a kid. So I went out and scored thirty-nine."

The Wasps forgot the threats long enough to reel off five straight buckets on the division leaders and run the lead up to 22 points before Buttsy took pity and put in the scrubeenies, all the way down to Tyrone "Maraschino" Mays, our twelfth man. There's an old saying about games like this, to wit: When you don't need the breaks, you get 'em. In the second quarter, with the Wasps flying, Red Green threw a full-court pass and missed Sutter Manno by a good ten feet. The ball went in the basket. "Hey, dawlin'," Red squealed at his opponent, "you can't gimme that shot all night!" Massy scored 18 in the first half and presided over the boards at both ends before Buttsy sat him down and gave King Crowder a chance, the first time that King had played more than a few minutes in weeks.

After the game, Pete Tyles flailed happily at his typewriter, describing "the most impressive win of the year," but I tried to temper my favoritism with common sense. I reminded the urbane readers of the *Blade-Mirror* that the Knicks had a lock on first place and therefore played with a certain lack of motivation. But if the Wasps ever met them in the playoffs, I wrote, it was bound to be another story. Playoff basketball was a whole new mini-season, and nobody rolled over.

I was trying to think of an ender when a man and a boy strolled along

219

the empty corridor behind the press table, and from ten feet away I could tell the kid was bawling. I wondered what his poor father had failed to buy him—the fourth orange soda or the sixth hot dog?—but when they passed directly behind me I heard the kid say, "It's not fair, daddy. He's too *big*."

"They'll do something about it," the father said angrily. "If they don't, I will!" I looked around and saw an ordinary human being; he looked like an appliance salesman. Clark Kent, talking tough in front of his kid.

After filing I fell into the Wasps's traditional New York watering hole, Ho Ho's on 50th Street, and found Pasty Pasticcino's nose buried in a dish of moo goo gai pan up to the hairline. "What's happening?" I said.

"Nothing much," Pasty said, flailing away with his chopsticks, beating the food to death, occasionally managing to convey a few grains of rice to his mouth. "Oh, yeh, Massy got an *R*."

"In the mail at the hotel?"

"No, back at the office. Pipper called about it."

"Was there a message this time?"

"Yeh. Let's see. It said, 'Keep on digging your grave.'"

"'Keep on digging your grave'?"

"Something like that."

I wondered how the kid had reacted. "Did anybody tell Bru?"

"I doubt it," Pasty said, plucking a sprout off his turtleneck. "Clown stuff like that, who bothers?"

26

We beat Buffalo on March 19 and then prepared to meet the second-place Boston Celtics. Buttsy worked the team on each of the two off nights before the game on the twenty-second, and he was Vince Lombardi reincarnated. No more simpering and whimpering and pleading. "Goddamn it, Sutter!" he exploded. "Move the ball *out* of the corner, not *into* it!" He screamed at Basil for drifting on his jump shot. "Stomp your foot on that last step, make your last bip extra hard!" Coach said. "That'll give you stability. Christ, Basil, that's fundamental!"

"Right, Cawch," Captain Basil said humbly, and at the next opportunity he went into the air as straight and solid as a telephone pole and canned a swisher from 20 feet.

"More like it," the Butts grumped.

"Thanks, Cawch," Basil said as three of his students from the settlement house jumped up on the sidelines and cheered. Playoffs or not, everybody knew the captain was in his last season. It was nice he had his teaching to fall back on.

The only Wasp who seemed to be spared the tongue lashings was Massy, driving himself as hard as the coach was driving the others, showing up early at workouts and squeezing Roxanne goodbye at the door and then putting out like a donkey engine. At times he almost seemed to be overdoing it.

Once they were scrimmaging three-on-three, with Massy lined up against Crowder, when King made a slick move and ducked inside. The kid went over the top and dumped them both. As they scrambled up, Massy said, "Sorry, King," but Crowder just walked away.

Massy hurried over and stuck out his big hand. "C'mon, King," the kid said. "I said I 'uz sorry. Let's be friends."

Crowder looked at the outstretched hand as though it was a live rat. "Shake?" Massy pleaded. King leaned over the hand and spat.

A whistle pierced the air. "That's it, that's it!" Buttsy hollered. "Time for shit, shower'n shave, men. Back here tonight at eight."

In the locker room, Massy was quiet, and Crowder dressed and left quickly.

"What's eating King?" I asked Justin Fell, as if I didn't know.

"Some guys don't like to lose their jobs," he said.

"Yeh, but can't he be more gracious?"

"King? He didn't get here by being gracious."

Pasty strolled over and asked Justin, "What's with the roomie? I've never seen him move so good. He taking something?"

"All I know is what he told me after the Buffalo game the other night," Justin said. "Said it was the first game this year he didn't have leg pains."

"Took him the whole fucking season to get in shape," Pasty Pasticcino put in. "Your long-muscled centers don't shape up as fast as you little cracker-asses."

221

"What's the name of those long muscles, Pasty?" I said.

"Well, the lower ones are called the calf muscles and the upper ones are called the thigh muscles."

"What're the Latin names?" Justin asked.

"What's the use of giving you the Latin names?" Pasty snapped. "You wouldn't understand anyway."

"Try me," Justin said. "I was a Latin major."

Pasty gave him a frantic look. "You don't look like a Latin major to me."

"Not the right color?"

"I didn't mean that," Pasty said. He handed over his clipboard. "Here," he said, "write something in Latin."

Justin scribbled "*cogito ergo sum*" and handed it back.

"That's familiar," Pasty said, wrinkling up his nose. "I remember that from school. *Yeh!* 'I think, therefore I add.' "

"Amazing!" Justin said, and wrote "*caveat emptor.*"

"Shit, man, that's too easy," Pasty said. " 'Caviar for the emperor.' "

Justin said we were lucky to have such a scholar with the club.

After practice, I picked up Dulcy for dinner, but she refused to go to Gabinetto's on the grounds that its macho atmosphere was wrong for femalepersons. "I'm sick and tired of that waiter patting me on the backside and calling me 'hot mama,' " she said. "If you had any pride you'd say something to him."

"Well, I did, honey," I said as we drove toward another restaurant, "and he said he didn't mean a thing by it, he just thinks you're a helluva person. His exact words were—let's see—he said, 'The signora, atsa some nice ass!' "

Dulcy reached into her extra-heavy supply of smashing ripostes, and laid one on me. "Humph!" she said.

When we got back to the apartment after dinner, the phone was ringing and Tex Pecos was on the line. "Forrester!" he rasped. "Get down to the Helix Excelsior! There's a fire!"

He didn't have to tell me twice. "What is it?" Dulcy said as I dashed for the door.

"Fire!" I said.

"Oh, my God! Get the cat!"

I picked up the cat and ran for the door and then dropped the cat and said, "Not here! At the Excelsior!" I ran out to the car and started the engine, and just as I began backing our Spitfire out of its assigned parking space Dulcy ran up.

"The Excelsior?" she said as she jumped inside. "That's where Massy lives, isn't it?"

"I hope so," I said.

We could smell smoke a block from the old hotel, and a cop motioned us to the curb at the fireline. I flashed my press card and sprinted the last 50 yards, and then I saw the searchlights and the ladders and a swarm of rubber-coated hose jockeys bulldogging their equipment and cracking icicles off their helmets. High in the air above the Helix Excelsior a curl of dirty smoke hung in the searchlights, but I couldn't see a trace of flame. I looked for the white hat and spotted him sucking on a cigarette alongside a pumper. "Chief!" I said. "Where's the fire?"

"It's all interior," the chief said. "Third floor through the sixth was fully involved. But I think we got it."

"Anybody hurt?"

"Didn't lose a man."

"What about the residents?"

"Don't know for sure."

Dulcy ran up, slipping on the icy street, and I apologized for getting ahead of her. "Oh, Sam, is he all right?" she asked.

"Don't know for sure," I repeated. We stomped our feet and craned our necks for an hour, and then a captain reported to the white hat and the hose companies began to take up. Dulcy and I went inside the dampened lobby and found an elderly clerk in a soiled raincoat checking names against a list.

"Broussard Massy!" I said.

Without looking up, the clerk said, "The big guy on the fourth floor."

Dulcy asked, "Is he okay?"

"Haven't seen him," the old man said without emotion, continuing to look at his list. I ran for the stairwell. "Hey, you can't go up there!" he called out.

"I want to try his room."

"There's no room to try. The fire started in the room below Mr. Massy's. They're both gutted."

"Oh, Jesus!" I said, and Dulcy eased onto a faded divan and put her hand over her mouth.

I ran back to the desk clerk and grabbed him by the collar. "What happened?" I heard myself shouting. "Is he dead?"

"All I said was I haven't seen him," the clerk said with dignity. "Now take your hands off me or I'll have you arrested."

"You haven't seen him all night?"

"He went out around six." I looked at my Timex. It was 2 A.M. Where was Massy?

"Honey!" I said. "Let's go!"

We ran to the car and sped downtown and pulled up in front of the brick building where I had once interviewed Roxanne Garfein in her loft. "Wait here!" I told Dulcy, and took the rickety steps three at a time.

The door to Roxy's room was locked, and I stood outside, trying to catch my breath, and then I heard the soft sound of a flute, almost like a bird, tweetling around at the top of its register, followed by a deep bass laugh and a peal of girlish giggles.

I tiptoed down the staircase and squeezed the car door shut. "Massy's okay," I said.

"How do you know?" Dulcy asked as she slipped the Spit into gear.

"A little bird told me."

For a long time, everybody in the Wasps's front office talked about the kid's close shave. I'd gone to bed at dawn thinking it was just another case of a careless smoker in an old hotel, but instead it turned out to be just another case of arson. The fire lab identified a residue of sulphuric acid in the charred remains of the room under Massy's, and a flyer was out for a man who had signed the register as "Eugene Toeten" an hour before the first alarm. The night clerk told the marshals the man was about medium size and spoke with a slight accent, maybe southern, he couldn't be sure.

I figured I'd already made the man's acquaintance. Months ago, in training camp. I thought about calling a contact of mine, a deputy fire marshal, and laying the story out from the beginning, but there'd be a hell of a lot of explaining to do, especially why I hadn't spoken up before and why I'd never written a line. So I kept my mouth shut. Anyway, it wasn't my secret to reveal, it was Massy's. That was my pet rationalization, and I was stuck with it.

Pipper Martin said it certainly was lucky that the big man had been out on a stroll when the fire started, and I agreed that the basketball gods had been with us from the jump. When Massy arrived to pick up his check, everybody in the front office crowded around and congratulated him. The kid said thanks and quickly dropped the subject. Sly dog! I wondered how many nights he'd been practicing with Roxanne Garfein.

Well, they said it was good for the complexion, provided, of course, that you practiced to climax.

27

A lopsided win over Boston left both clubs with five games to play and the Celts hanging onto their playoff slot by a two-game edge. After another quick road trip, we'd cut their lead to one and a half games, and then K.C.–Omaha beat Boston and closed the gap to one. The 76ers pulled into town on April Fool's night, and Buttsy announced for the nineteenth straight game, "Men, basically we gotta win it."

"Cawch," Captain McBride piped up, "you don't have to tell us. So please, Cawch, *don't tell us!*"

"Right on, dawlin'," Red Green said. "We ready to humbug!"

"Goin' to the moon!" Jones Jones added, and there was a chorus of "right on" and "all *right!*" and even a restrained "hallelujah." I looked over in the corner to see who was silly enough to shout hallelujah in a locker room, and it was Sutter Manno.

The big man's game was off a little, but even on an off night he managed to clog up the middle like a diesel locomotive, and the 76ers were reduced to gunning from outside and giving up the ball two or three times per goal. The result was the Wasps's ninth straight win, 107–94. On top of that there was good news out of Boston: The Buffalo Braves, mathematically out of the race, had smitten the mighty Celtics at the Boston Garden, and now the Celts and the Wasps were tied for second. Boston had made the classical mistake—looking ahead to the game with us.

The town was like a ticking bomb on the final night of the regular season. The mayor and all the councilmen and several hundred other alleged dignitaries showed up at the Helix to see our Wasps nail down a playoff post for the first time in history, but somebody forgot to show the shooting script to the Celtics. Their 6–10 center, Paul Kneeland, outjumped Massy to open the game, which should give you an idea how psyched up they were, and before Buttsy could call time and deliver his inspirational Epistle to the Galatians, the Bostons had run up a 12–4 lead. As Ken Hohlar kept putting it succinctly, "There's no tomorrow, folks! It's all or nothing tonight! It's odd man out, and there's *no tomorrow* for the loser of this contest!" I think he was trying to say that there's no tomorrow.

"Patience!" Buttsy screamed impatiently in the huddle. "Patience, goddamn it! The way I told you! Basil, you got yourself mixed up with the Fourteenth Field Artillery. Work the ball inside for a shot! Sutter, stay more in the backcourt so we can start our movement. If you cut through when Justin has the ball, you take and kill our court balance. And Justin, when you're inside for Chrissakes don't come back out. Otherwise you run right into the play. Okay? *Okay!* The way we practiced! *Patience!* It'll come."

With time back in, Red Green made one of his double-jointed specials in the pike position and Massy blocked a Boston shot and threw a floor-length outlet pass to Basil for two more points, and the packed house screamed and waved banners while the organist played "Charge!" But then the Wasps's movement stopped as fast as it had started and the relentless Celtics pushed the score up to 38–24 by midway in the second quarter.

The Butts stalked the sidelines, cursing the officials and babbling to himself in a voice that carried into the fifth row: "Nobody listens. *Tsssssst!* Nobody gives a shit! *Ooooooh!* Nobody works. It's not a team game anymore. *Um um um!* My god, no! Nobody looks for the other guy. Nobody checks out. Well, I don't care. *Om-ah, om-ah, om-ah.* Well, if *they* don't care, *I* don't care."

The Bostons galloped down the court like a pack of wolves in full howl, and the Wasps chased after them, and pretty soon the coach called time and flung his jacket on the floor and hollered, "Hey, let me know the next time you're gonna do this! *Let me know!* I'm *entitled!* When you're gonna drag ass, when you're gonna give up—*tell me!* Um um um um. Then I'll relax and I'll understand it's everybody's night off. Manno! *Manno!* Let me see the bottom of your shoes. Where's the nails? Well, what the fuck is holdin' you down?"

This was the eighty-second game of a long season, and I knew what was holding us down. The Wasps had never had the talent to come this far, but they'd made it on guts and determination and Broussard Massy. The mystery was that our wagon hadn't broken down a long time before.

I looked at poor puffing Sutter, 29 years old and covering players six years younger and a step faster. I looked at the captain, pushing 31 and all worn out after the first quarter, forcing his shots because the game was a must and the Celts were sagging off on him inside, and still he couldn't hit. I looked at Massy. I remembered all the wise guys saying an eight-foot center could clean up the league with four anythings as teammates. But could he do it forever and ever? Wasn't the big man entitled to an off-night, too? He was being suckered into chasing his man to the corners, an old failing, taking them both out of the action. It was a fair exchange for Boston, neutralizing a center of 8–2 with one of 6–10, and Massy wasn't making the switch that would have taken him back to the boards where he was needed. I hoped the old grapefruit wasn't pressing on his larynx.

At halftime the lead stood at 56–42. I banged a note on my Olivetti: *"Avec patience on peut enculer une mouche"* and handed it to a ballboy. "Give this to Massy," I said.

All through the halftime, I presided over my typewriter in an indigo funk, wondering if this was how the season would end, a give-up game on the last night of the year and in front of the home fans to boot. I barely heard the usual report on the PA: "Your attention, please! Your attention, *plee*-uz! A lost child has been found. If you are their parents, please come pick them up. Thank you."

The cheerleaders leaped high in the air, higher than any of our players, making pretty V's with their legs, but hardly anybody watched, except for a few sickos still lusting for Theresa Twat. The vendors made their rounds methodically, some of the snap gone from their voices, and Ken Hohlar interviewed Abraham Gross and asked if he agreed that there was no tomorrow.

Massy won the jump to open the second half, and the teams played even for six or seven minutes. Then the kid grabbed a rebound and flipped the ball to Justin Fell and the Wasps moved down the floor on a tightly controlled 1-C play that ended in Red Green's unmolested two-pointer.

I could hear the Wasps as they came back. "Take mine, I got yours!" "Stay, dawlin', you all right." "Pick, *pick!*" Sutter flew through the air like a stripling of 28 and grabbed a Boston pass, and Sweet Basil screamed, "Up! Up!" and then it was Justin Fell dribbling at half-speed across the center line and saying, "Talk to me! Talk to me!" and Massy hollering, "You're alone, Rooms, you're alone!"

Justin threw his fine brown frame into overdrive and rammed his man into a solid Massy pick and drove the lane for two. After three periods, our big Tiffany scoreboard showed:

CELTS   87
WASPS   79

"That's patience!" Buttsy said as the Wasps knelt around him at the sideline. "Now take and play it my way for one more period! *My way!*"

"All the way, Cawch!" Sweet Basil called out, and the Wasps slapped hands and backsides and took their positions before the ref even blew the whistle.

Unfortunately it was the old pro Boston Celtics who came out to meet them, not the Little Sisters of the Poor, and the Celts also knew how to play with patience, especially with a lead. They kept letting the shot clock run down and waiting for high-percentage tries. When Massy tried to force switches, big Paul Kneeland just hung on him, throttling him in the corners and more than once stepping on his foot or grabbing his shorts to cut down on his jump-power. The refs didn't seem to mind.

With six minutes left, the Celts held an eight-point lead, but Jones Jones limped off the bench and the net result was two quick baskets. Boston's Kneeland hit on a short inside shot, and then a very tired Basil McBride got his Johnson together and hit from his sweet spot, 20 feet out on a slight angle, and the scoreboard read Celts 115, Wasps 111.

Boston called time, and Massy breathed hard and slumped to his kneepads. The upper half of his sweatband was dark with moisture. Buttsy spoke excitedly in the middle of the pack, but this time I couldn't hear over the din of the crowd. Three places away at the press table, Ken Hohlar held his hands over both ears and screamed into the mike that both clubs were letting it all hang out and don't go way, folks, we got a real donnybrook on our hands. "We're coming to you from the Helix, folks," he burbled, "where anything can happen and usually does."

For three more minutes of play, the teams fought back and forth, exchanging hoops, exchanging misses, exchanging blocks by Massy and Kneeland. The kid had a chance to bring us two points closer, but he blew a skyhook from six feet out. The crowd moaned, but Massy had never been renowned for his sticking, everybody should have known that. Somehow we had to use him to work the ball inside to surer-handed players like Justin Fell and Sweet Basil McBride. If we had to depend on Massy's hooks, the season was over.

With 42 seconds left and the Celts ahead 128–124, Buttsy called time again. Pete Tyles nudged me and pointed to the red-faced coach, scratching out a play on his oversized pad. "Now we're gonna be saved by the genius," Pete said. "The old hipper dipper, Manno to Justin to Massy, and we lose by two points." He sounded disconsolate. I looked down the row at Nick Storen, and his face was a bland mask. I figured he must be torn, wanting the Wasps to win so he could cover the playoffs, but also hoping we'd lose to support his sour predictions. Well, maybe he hadn't been completely wrong at that.

The Wasps took the ball out at mid-court, and one of the Boston forwards bogarted Justin Fell as he tried to find an open man, and then Justin reared back and lofted a high rainbow pass toward the basket and Massy sailed up and over the backboard and grabbed the ball and dropped it in. The most predictable play in our repertoire, and it worked! 128–126, 24 seconds left.

The Celts brought the ball down against a full-court press, with exactly enough time on the clock to go into a freeze and get into the playoffs by two points and send 19,000 fans grumbling out into the cold winter night.

Boston's handler Frank Cassidy dribbled carefully out near mid-court, with Justin Fell inside his shorts, and when the Celt passed off, Massy's long arm flashed over his head like a backstroker's and tipped the ball away. For a second it rolled free and then Sutter Manno pounced.

Massy was already halfway down the court and in the clear, and Sutter fired one of his cannon shots. I winced, but the big man caught the pass on his fingertips and started dribbling toward the basket like Walt Frazier, completely ignoring Coach's one-bip rule. The ball Yo-Yoed in front of his chest, five or six feet up and down, and by the time Paul Kneeland could get back and jolt him from one side while another player elbowed him from the other, Massy was corkscrewing into the air and slamming the ball through the cords like a slaughterer clubbing a steer.

I looked at the clock. Regulation time was over. The score was tied at 128, and Massy was down. The fans were dancing in the aisles and the organist pulled out every stop and the scoreboard operator let loose the firecrackers and sirens that were usually reserved for a win.

Pasty Pasticcino waddled out on the court with his black medical bag, but Massy was already on his hands and knees, shaking his head dazedly, and motioned the trainer back.

The big man stood up and the official shoved the ball into his midsection and motioned him toward the free-throw line, but several fans had started an impromptu conga line at center court, and then more followed, and the officials called time while the security men gave chase. It was 15 minutes before order could be restored.

Massy stepped up for the free throw, and I could imagine the scenario. He'd had far too much time to cool out, and he was only a 62 percent foul-shooter to begin with. He'd go up to the line and the house would fall deathly silent and he'd miss the shot by a half a mile. The fans would go "ohhhhh" in that low disappointed sigh, and the Wasps would blow the game in overtime to the cool assassins from Boston.

I was still refining my ode when Massy flipped the ball like a dart. It hit hard against the support that holds the rim, squirted three feet up in the air and then plopped straight through the cords as though it had a road map.

The Wasps were in the playoffs!

There *is* a tomorrow!

I leaned across my portable to protect it, and a horde of Visigoths and Franks poured out of the stands and over the press table. I must have stayed in a semifetal position for 15 minutes, shielding my notes and my work tools while plastic cups and programs and rolls of toilet paper cascaded down on my head like a sound-stage blizzard. Tons of hysterical fans were pouring past to grab the Wasps and squeeze the crap out of them.

An hour after the game the uproar still hadn't subsided, and I was forced to dictate my story from Jack Carbon's ringside telephone because there was no way to get through the mobs to the teletype upstairs. Tex Pecos listened in on an office extension as I dictated, occasionally suggesting a way to "hype up" the story, as he put it. At the end he said, "Well, Forrester, those are *some* news!" I thanked him for the unwavering faith he had shown in me and the team.

Around midnight, I folded my tent and headed for the locker room, but nobody was there except a clean-up detail knee-deep in champagne corks and soggy confetti and dyed rice. Up in the pressroom, Pete Tyles was just hanging up on the *L. A. Times,* one of his strings, and the two of us walked over to Gabinetto's for a nightcap. The crowd was three deep at the rail, but Mario led us back to the kitchen, where Buttsy and Pasty and a few of the players were passing around bottles of aromatic liquid.

When I lurched home at dawn, Dulcy told me to wait at the door —I think she was extinguishing the pilot light on the stove.

"You may come in now," she said. "Did you say you represented the distillery or was it Wry's goat farm?"

I told her to—*gulp!*—stand aside.

"I wish I could!" Dulcy said sarcastically, supporting me with one hand. She turned to the honor guard provided by the city. "Would you officers like coffee?"

"No, thanks, lady," a cop said. "Was this the package you was expecting? He says he's Sam Fucking Forrester."

"Sam Fucking Forrester," I repeated.

"Pardon our French," the other policeman said hastily.

"Yes, he's the one," Dulcy said, accepting her burden. "Thanks a bunch."

"Glad to be of service, lady. There's bodies all over town."

"Well, we Forresters always bury our own," a pair of Dulcys said as they steered my limp frame toward the sofa. I ordered some eucalyptus tea with fireweed honey, but the three Dulcys said I had to be kidding.

III
the end

1

I was being held in the dragon teeth of a leering pterodactyl and suddenly I was flung into the sky like a Frisbee and landed inside a Chinese gong that kept ringing and ringing till I realized the cruel phone was ringing cruelly. *"Ahhrakkkkk!"* I said into the wrong end. *"Didarakanockanew! Bftsplk!"* and hung up. It rang again a few seconds later, and I heard a familiar voice saying, "Sam. *Sam!"*

"Rockshan?" I said. "Zat you, Rockshan?"

"It's noon, Mr. Sportswriter, time you were up," my favorite flutist said. "I wanted to ask you something."

"Hmmmmm."

"There was a letter under my door this morning."

"Who from?" I said, swinging my feet around to the floor and reaching out with my hand to steady the walls.

"That's what I don't know."

"Well, read it."

"No, I don't mean that kind of letter. I mean a letter of the alphabet."

I shook my head to warn the spiders, but they were already routed by the news. "Wait," I said, and sucked in a deep breath of musty stale air, the leavings of my own befouled respiration. "Roxy," I said, "it's an *S*. Am I right? Black plastic on a gold background?"

"Oh, Sam, *you're* the one that sent it! Isn't that a silly game for a mature man? What's it supposed to mean anyway?"

"Roxy," I said, "somebody else sent it, honey. An *H* and an *O* and an *R* and now an *S*."

"Hors?"

"Well, you could say it that way, but it's also the first four letters of H-O-R-S-E. The basketball game?"

"That silly game my brothers play? If you miss a shot, it's a horse on you? Five letters and you lose?"

"Right."

"But what's that got to do with me?"

I started to say that somebody must have found out where Massy was hanging his hat, but I corrected myself in time. "I just don't know," I lied. "But our security man—Pat Rhoades?—he told me we'd have to expect a lot of crazy things if we got into the playoffs. Where'd you say you found it?"

"I went out, and there it was, right by the door. I haven't seen Bru since last night. We played a few duets to celebrate the win." She paused. "We're thinking of living together."

Ah, the younger generation! Simple forthright sentences, and none of the games people play. "Why not?" I said in my most lighthearted voice. "You're a nice musical couple. You belong together. You're like me and Dulcy. A marriage made in heaven. I mean—an affair made in heaven. I mean. . . ."

"I know what you mean, Sam. But you do approve, don't you?"

"Approve? I *applaud*! Why, I'll be glad to give the—*om uh*—I'll be glad to give the old lady away."

"Well, Sam, since you feel that way, I'll tell you the truth," Roxanne said with a sigh. "We're already living together. Bru's been staying here since the fire."

"Well, I'll be damned! I'd never have guessed. I thought you were waiting for a music scholarship or something like that?"

"Nobody said I had to wait alone."

An hour later my phone rang again, and this time Roxy didn't sound so cool. "Sam!" she said. "I just had a breather!"

"A breather?"

"A *breather*. Unreal! One of those creeps that call up and breathe at you. Only he said some words at the end. He said, 'Romans twelve one.' Sounds like the Bible, but I don't have one here."

Romans 12:1. That had to be either the Bible or an old score from the Coliseum: "It's halftime, ladies and gentlemen, and the Christians are taking a beating."

"Hold on, Roxy," I said, and lurched into the living room to look for Dulcy's old Bible, the one we opened every Christmas Eve. Romans turned out to be in the New Testament—surprise!—and 12:1 went: "I appeal to you therefore, brethren, by the mercies of God, to present your bodies as a living sacrifice, holy and acceptable to God, which is your spiritual worship." I flinched at the phrase "living sacrifice," and dragged my anxious bones back to the phone. "Sorry, Roxanne," I lied again, "I can't find our Bible. Dulcy must have taken it to work."

"To work?"

"Why don't you leave for a while, get some fresh air?" I blurted out. I didn't like the idea of her sitting alone in a firetrap loft while a bunch of acid-slinging psychopaths zeroed in on her and/or her roommate. "Where's Massy?" I asked. "The two of you could see a movie."

"He's down at the Helix."

"I'll be right over," I said. "Don't answer the door for anybody else."

"Where are you taking me, you dirty old man?" Roxanne said as we drove off. She smiled like a kid on the way to Baskin-Robbins.

"Anyplace but here," I said, gently propping up my flaming eyelids. I gave her a long song and dance about the pressures Massy could expect, and I added, "I don't like the way the H-O-R-S-E game's going."

Roxy told me I was acting positively paranoid, and if she and Massy weren't worried, why should I be worried? She said she'd had a phone chat with Pat Rhoades and he'd already explained the extremes to which unbalanced fans and bettors would go to disrupt a winning team. "It's all talk," Roxanne chirped in her sparrow voice. "Hot air."

"Not always," I said.

"Sam, you can't go through life in fear. That's what Broussard says, and he's absolutely right."

Nicely but firmly, she insisted that I drive her back to the loft; she said she still "owed" three hours of practice, and Bru would be along soon for lunch. I argued halfheartedly, but I finally gave in. The after-effects of one lousy bottle of Scotch had made me as skittery as a cockroach.

On the way back, I couldn't resist asking, "Roxy, are you kids in love? I mean, is this serious?" I felt like a nosy mother-in-law.

She turned and looked at me and pushed her hair back with her index fingers, like Veronica Lake in the old movies. Her tiny face was framed in brushed-bronze hair, and it gave her the look of a chipmunk peeking out of its burrow. A *pretty* chipmunk.

"Is this for publication?" she said after a deep look into my ravaged face.

"Roxy," I said incredulously, "are you kidding? Ever since I laid eyes on Bru Massy, *nothing's* been for publication. I got enough unpublished material to teach a course on the kid. I bet I know things *you* don't know about him."

"Well, I know one thing you don't know. You ask about love. I don't think Broussard knows what love is. I mean, I don't think he ever experienced it, ya know?"

"Not even as a kid?"

"Least of all as a kid. He lost his mother, his father treated him like sh—like. . . ."

"Like shit," I said, so she'd know I was nobody's prig, despite my advancing years.

"Right. A bitchy aunt took care of him. The closest thing he knew to love was a piano teacher in New Orleans. He says maybe she loved him like a son, but then he really had no way of judging."

"Is he in love with you, Roxy?"

Another pause, another rearrangement of the coiffure, another sidelong look. "He says he is."

"What about you?"

"I'm—I'm in love with my music, Sam. You know that."

I laughed, a little embarrassed at my nerve. "Didn't mean to pry, Roxy," I said.

"Okay. Bru says that's what he likes about you—you don't pry. How'd you ever get to be a reporter?"

The question was on everybody's lips.

• • •

2

The Eastern Conference semifinal series came under the heading of the Latin expression *nolo contendere*, which Pasty Pasticcino would probably define as "a good big man can beat a good little man anytime." The Washington Bullets's style was fancy set plays, with two busy guards feeding two slippery forwards slicing off their linebacker-type center. But every time they tried to run their patterns against the Wasps, they bounced off 245 pounds of Broussard Massy, blocking traffic like a jackknifed truck in the Lincoln Tunnel. We won the series four–zip and the closest game was a 126–110 screamer at the Capital Center the night Massy developed a charley horse, and still he blocked seven shots and pulled down 16 rebounds.

Whoever had been needling him through the mail didn't seem to care if we beat Washington or not, because the game stalled at H-O-R-S, but the Bullet fans provided plenty of psychological warfare. Before the second game, a live chicken was flung through the window of our dressing room. When the kid walked on the court before the games at the Capital Center, you could feel the resentment oozing down from the stands, and signs called him everything from the old standard "Big Stoop" to "The Jolly Green Giant's Bastard Son."

There was a short intermission before we were scheduled to play the other semifinal winners, the Knickerbockers, for the Eastern Championship, with the first two games in Madison Square Garden. The New York press and broadcasters used the time to inveigh against the big man.

The *Post* discussed "the obvious unfairness of a pack of losers reaching the championship series on the strength of a single asset: a bullish giant who uses his height for all it's worth."

The *Times* called the situation "not just a strategic puzzle confronting the Knicks, but a problem for the entire league. Broussard Massy personifies the cult of the behemoth. All by himself, he exposes the antiquated rules that permit a creature of abnormal physical endowments to outplay smaller and more skilled opponents. Pro basketball no longer tells us that the race is to the swift, or to the skilled. It is to the tall."

The *News* warned that the venerable sport of basketball was being turned into a circus sideshow—" $10 to see the geek"—and "if something isn't done about this particular Massy, the rest of the Massys in the nation's high schools and colleges will come along and finish the destruction he has started."

Professor Gilbert Ragan of Columbia sent a Shakespearean quote to all the letters columns:

> *O, it is excellent*
> *To have a giant's strength; but it is tyrannous*
> *To use it like a giant.*

New York fans needed no further prodding. Our chartered bus was stoned when we rolled into town for the opener, and a chip of broken glass sliced Jones Jones above the ear and sent him to the doctor for repairs.

The switchboard at our hotel, the Manhattan Ritz, stayed alight all night as cranks threatened to blow the place up or maim Massy or Buttsy or Abraham Gross or all three.

At 2 A.M. a gang of drunken ad men burst into the lobby screaming, "Where's the freak?" but a quick-thinking hotel engineer threw a switch on the main electrical panel, shutting down the elevators, and after a few half-hearted shouts of frustration, the mob fled toward Charley O's, hiccuping clichés.

Now that the local press had orchestrated a riot, the *New York Times* did a turnabout and ran a page-one editorial counseling good sportsmanship. *Sports Pictorial* hit the streets with a provocative think piece by Harry Whitehead, the magazine's Scotty Reston. It began:

> *Eldridge Cleaver said it first: "Violence is as American as apple pie." With the New York fans and the whole National Basketball Association frothing at the lips about the Wasps and their dominating center, and league officials donning bulletproof vests for this week's Eastern Championship opener, one cannot help but recall the Celtics-Rangers soccer game in Glasgow a few years back, when 66 fans were killed and another 145 injured. No,*

238

that's not a typographical error. 66 dead, 145 injured. *We would bite our tongue before dignifying rumors that a similar blood bath is shaping up for the Wasps-Knicks opener.*

Whitehead traced murder and mayhem at sports events back to antiquity. "Indeed, the original 'Donnybrook' was a town where such battles occurred with regularity," the jockstrap sage reported. "Village fought village and town fought town, and a good time was had by all who survived. It seems clear that 20th century man has not fully sublimated such murderous exercises into the organized activities we call sport."

Heah, heah!

Pete Tyles of the *Herald* dashed up and down the halls of the Manhattan Ritz showing the *Sports Pictorial* piece to anyone he could corner. "It comes to this," he told me and Pasty grimly. "If the Knicks win this series, it'll be our ass. But if the Wasps win, it'll be our ass."

"Fair's fair," Pasty said.

Buttsy Rafferty wanted to trot the team over to the Garden for a midafternoon work, just enough to break a sweat, but Knickerbocker officials begged him to stay away. "They said it'd be tough enough getting us through the crowd once, let alone twice," the coach reported. "All them crazy assholes're milling around outside."

At three o'clock on the afternoon of the opening game, a police captain phoned Abraham Gross in his penthouse suite at the Ritz and advised him to keep Massy inside; the police department was taking the threats seriously. I figured the game would be postponed for sure, but our owner calmly announced that "this is the hottest ticket in the history of basketball. Why, people are paying scalpers two hundred dollars a ticket!" He sounded disappointed that he couldn't scalp a few himself.

After the short press conference, I asked Big Management, "Did you hear about the cops? They're bringing in extra men from the Tactical Police Force."

"Yeh, we got the message," Guile said, looking pale.

"Nothing to worry about." Gross slapped me on the back and steered me toward the door of his suite. "Just normal high spirits."

"How're you gonna protect Massy?" I asked.

"Protect Massy?" Gross said, laughing. "Who has to protect a man eight feet tall?"

Pete Tyles said he'd talked to the 14th Precinct and the department was taking riot precautions. "They intend to surround the floor with cops," he said.

The smile disappeared from Gross's face. "Nothing doing!" he said. "How'll the fans in the box seats see through a wall of uniforms? I won't allow it! You got to treat fans right."

"Mr. Gross," I said, "Massy's been threatened. He's been getting weird letters through the mail, and you've read the papers——"

"Terrific!" the owner said, opening the door and easing us outside. "We've developed the biggest attraction in sports. Relax, boys! Enjoy yourselves! The Garden has the best security in the world."

I wanted to ask if it was better than the Texas Book Depository's. Better than the Hotel Ambassador's in Los Angeles? Better than. . . .

But I found myself looking at a closed door.

3

When our team took the court that night, every seat in the Garden was occupied and every spectator was on his feet screaming, and some of the remarks couldn't even have been printed in the *Off the Pigs News*. I wondered how Kenny Hohlar and his engineer were screening the choice words. It was like the time a soundman aimed a shotgun mike at a famous NFL quarterback and the salty old pro took that occasion to label his center an ignorant cunt-lapper, and this highly personal information went into 21 million homes. I looked down the press table, and Kenny was chattering away. I imagined he was telling the folks back home that the New York fans were literally raising the roof. This time he wasn't far off.

I watched Massy, warming up at the free-throw line, and tried to gauge how he was reacting. He didn't look any different. I guess when you're 8–2 you develop a certain imperturbability about the bawling pygmies around your feet. Pasty waddled out and reached up and patted him on the ass, and Massy smiled shyly and tossed up an air ball. The crowd jeered and hooted, but the kid just stepped into the crip line and dunked a couple, making the backboard rattle with his power.

He also won the tip-off, but that's about all the Wasps did right in the first half. New York came out kicking and gouging and butting, and the Wasps played intimidated. They'd expected a rowdy game to match the rowdy crowd, but not a tag-team wrestling match. At nine minutes, Orion Halliday, the Knicks's star center, dumped Massy under the basket and didn't draw a foul. A few seconds later the kid set up in the low post and the ref called a moving pick.

"A moving *pick!*" Buttsy screamed from the bench. "Hey, ref, you gotta *move* for a moving pick! *Aaaarrrgh!* My man never moved! Holy gee whiz, ref, that's awful!"

"*Holy gee whiz?*" I said into Pete Tyles's ear.

"The coaches were told they'd be bounced if they cursed," Pete explained. "Security's scared shitless."

"Then Buttsy's not gonna last," I said. "I guarantee it."

At 8:02, New York's guard Brock Faulkner slammed Abdul Buzruz all the way back into the upright behind the basket, and the official called it Knicks's ball. Buttsy yelped, "Holy cripes, ref! He like to killed my man! Gee whiz, dad blame it, ref! Holy galoshes!" As the official skipped by, Buttsy stage-whispered, "Your mother sucks dick," and drew the foul. Four minutes of playing time gone, and already our coach had been T'd, and the New York lead went to 7–2.

We took the ball out, but Basil McBride was late getting into the lane to take a feed from Red Green, and Orion Halliday intercepted and fired the ball the length of the court to the Knick's forward, "Pepsi" Kohler, for a dead mortal lay-up.

"Get your head outta your ass!" Coach hollered, but Basil didn't seem to hear. The captain was wandering around the court like a victim of locomotor ataxia. Toward the end of the half, with the Knickerbockers ahead 56–44, Buttsy replaced him with Jones Jones. McBride flung a towel the length of the bench and screamed, "Why'd you snatch me out?" Everybody in the Garden knew the answer. The caterwauling would have unnerved a giant sloth, let alone a jumpy type like Basil.

When a foul was called on Brock Faulkner for yanking on Red Green's shorts, the partisan audience began chanting:

Bull-SHIT!
Clap clap.
Bull-SHIT!
Clap clap.

The cheer wasn't new; I'd heard it a hundred times before, and so had anybody who'd ever watched the Knicks on TV. Local broadcasters had long since stopped apologizing for the New York fans. Naturally Ken Hohlar had to make a point of it. "We're sorry, folks," he said, holding a hand over one ear. "There's certain sounds we can't filter out here in Madison Square Garden, where anything can happen and usually does." The chant stopped when Buz was called for charging.

I looked down at Francis X. Rafferty, and he was turning into a gibbering apoplectic. Once he stood up and hollered, "Get back, Basil! Basil, goddamn it, where are you?"

"Right here, Cawch," Basil answered from the next seat.

Pete and I mingled with the Wasps as they streamed toward the dressing room for the half, and the first thing we overheard as we stood in the entrance hall was Buttsy screaming, "Basil, untie your shoe and tie it again!"

"What fo'?" Basil asked.

" 'Cause when you get back to Raintree, Florida," Buttsy raved, "I want you to be able to say you did one fucking thing right in Madison Square Garden!"

We heard a few embarrassed coughs, but no excuses and no wisecracks, and then the coach's voice came loud and clear: "All right, men, now where're we fucking up?"

"In New York?" Sutter Manno offered after a long silence.

"Shut up!" Coach said. "Now listen: you jack-offs think that's basketball being played out there, but it's not, it's fucking war. So basically we got to stick it to them. Massy, whatta you do when you got position on Halliday and he moves into you?" Evidently the kid didn't respond quickly enough, because Buttsy kept right on talking. *"Knock the shit outa him!* Got that?"

I couldn't hear the answer.

"Pertaining to the rest of the guys, get a little red-ass!" Buttsy ordered. "I don't mind losing, but I want these New York pussies to know they been in a basketball game. Basically I want muscle! I want contact!"

"But Cawch, what if we foul out?" Sweet Basil asked.

"McBride," Coach said sarcastically, "you fouled out before the jump."

He was still lashing the Wasps when a security man closed the door to the inner locker room, and Pete and I made our way back to the press table. Conn Smythe's advice to his Toronto Maple Leafs kept running through my mind: "If you can't beat 'em in the alley, you can't beat 'em on the ice." Maybe the same was true of basketball. Man for man, I thought we could handle the Knicks in a brawl, if that's the way they wanted it, but how do you handle 20,000 fans? Wouldn't that be the question?

Led by a red-eyed Basil McBride, the Wasps bounced out for the second half, whooping and yipping and smacking each other on the ass. But the Knicks were psyched up, too, responding to the roar that greeted their entrance, and for the whole third quarter the teams crashed and slammed into each other, and New York's lead swung between eight and 12 points.

Then Brock Faulkner, the dirty little guard who'd flattened Massy's nose earlier in the season, tried to repeat his samurai performance, but instead of hitting the kid with his elbow he caught Sweet Basil square in the mouth, and the captain came up spitting dental caps and blood and curses and tore across the floor toward his tormentor.

I jumped up for a better view, but all I could make out was the south end of Brock Faulkner scurrying into the stands, with the crowd parting in front of him and resealing its solid front, whereupon our frustrated captain punched the Knicks's trainer and kicked their assistant coach and then turned to challenge the whole line-up and the entire population of greater New York. "C'mon, muthafuckas!" Basil screamed, jerking spasmodically and twirling his fists in tightening circles in front of his face. "Le's duke! Le's humbug!"

Massy loped over and wrapped his long arms around his teammate, and a dozen cops rushed on the floor blowing their whistles. After ten minutes of bedlam Basil was ushered to the dressing room under guard, and the officials read the riot act to both teams, and the PA announcer begged the fans to settle down and stop throwing sharp objects. Dull objects apparently were acceptable. The court was slick with sweat and beer and blood, and it took the attendants 20 minutes to mop up. When the game continued, 11:30 of playing time remained, and the Knicks led 82–72.

At that exact point, number 29 took personal control. It was a Massy nobody had ever seen—at least this incarnation. He dunked and passed off, he set impenetrable picks and screens, he rebounded and blocked and raced up and down the court like the fastest awkward man you ever saw. When Orion Halliday gave him an elbow, the kid reached back and cocked a fist, something I'd never seen him do, then quickly opened it and brushed at his hair. The New York center flinched anyway. It seemed as though every time the Knickerbockers tried a shot or a pass, Massy's big hand was there to block it and start another fast break. He bossed the game like a cowboy foreman on a cattle drive.

With five minutes left to play, the kid's awesome slam-dunk tied the score, and by the time the clock had wound down to 30 seconds, the Wasps were ahead 106–98.

Jones Jones stepped to the line for a free throw, while the frustrated fans swirled toward the exit to the accompaniment of a low growl of discontent, multiplied by 20,000. I happened to glance at the officials' table, and a couple of security men were gesturing wildly to the PA announcer. One of them pointed at the ceiling, that vast bowl with dozens of apertures for air conditioning and lights and other equipment, and I followed his direction and saw that a single bank of lights in one of the dark interior rings had been turned on and pointed directly at the court. Then everybody heard the PA voice:

Guard to the lightwalk! Guard to the lightwalk, please! Code 5 Emergency! Security guard to the lightwalk! Hurry please!

Jones cradled the ball for the free throw, but one of the sideline officials ran out on the court and began pushing the players of both clubs.

"What's goin' on, dawlin'?" Red Green called out, but the official steered both teams under the basket. Five minutes later the faulty bank of lights flicked out and the game was wrapped up.

"Now I've seen it all," Nick Storen grumbled. "One fucking battery of lights flips on accidentally, and everybody goes apeshit."

"Yeh," I said. "They're sure as hell jumpy. Like me."

"They'll get jumpier," Pete Tyles put in. "I think I'll just sit here till the animals thin out."

After I'd filed for the two-star and conducted a couple of short interviews for the final, I ran into Pat Rhoades, walking by himself in the empty corridor. "Close call," our security chief said, rubbing his forehead.

"Close call?" I said. "I wouldn't call one-oh-nine to a hundred a close call."

"You mean you honestly don't know? You great newshawks didn't see what happened right in front of your eyes?"

He told me that one of the building custodians had happened to look up and spot the extra bank of lights shining down on the court. Luckily the man knew the Garden routine inside and out, and he realized that something was fishy up there.

"How could he tell?" I asked.

"Hold your pants on," Rhoades said. "The guy knew exactly what lights were used for basketball and what lights weren't. These lights belonged *off.* So he called for the guards."

"Pat, why would anybody turn lights *on?*"

"We don't know, but we will," Pat said. "But lemme tell you what we found up there on the catwalk, right behind the light mounts."

"What?"

"An Arisaka rifle, full load, steel jackets. And this."

He handed me a transparent envelope. I looked inside and saw a picture of Massy, one of the 8 x 10 glossies that the front office distributed by the thousands. There was a big black *X* across the forehead.

4

We had an open date before the second game of the series, and the hallways of the Manhattan Ritz buzzed with conjecture about the mad marksman. Only Massy seemed unperturbed. "If he was fixin' to kill me," the kid told me and Justin Fell and a few other players in his room, "he had plenty of chances. Don't y'all imagine it was just some kind of a stunt?"

"Sure," I said. "A stunt. With steel-jacketed bullets."

"Onliest thing I can't understand," said Red Green, "is why that dude turn on the lights? Don't he know that gives him up?"

"Well, the way Pat Rhoades reconstructs it," I said, "the guy figured that anybody looking up would have to stare right into the high beams, so he could fire without ever being identified——"

"—And then slip down the catwalk and mingle with the crowd," Justin finished for me.

Massy muttered something.

"What?" Justin asked.

"Nothing to sweat about," the big man said.

"Neither was Lee Harvey Oswald," his roommate said gloomily.

My mind flashed back to the $500,000 life insurance policy and the possibility that the kid might still be trying to get himself knocked off, which would explain his cavalier attitude. But it didn't add up. Once upon a time, the theory might have made a certain amount of sense, at least as much as any of my other zany theories about Massy's erratic behavior. But in those days he'd had no friends, no roots, no future except to make a spectacle of himself on the basketball floor, take the money and run.

But now he had Roxanne. People in love owned the world, didn't they? Just ask me and Dulcy. So why didn't the big man open up to Security? Why didn't he admit that a prowler had threatened him in Milwaukee? Why didn't he release me to tell about the first visit in training camp? Why didn't he *put somebody's ass in jail*?

I wondered who the hell he was protecting. Certainly not himself. I looked at him across the room. His earphones were on, and his foot was tapping away in rhythm. It seemed as though there must be a whole platoon of hit men running around with his name and description in their wallets, and here he was relaxing to music.

The New York newspapers were so full of Massy's dominating performance in the opening game that they hardly mentioned the incident on the lightwalk. The *Post* mentioned "a minor commotion" near the end of the game, and the *Times* ran a sidebar about a prankster who climbed out on a catwalk and turned on some lights.

The rest of the coverage was all Massy. You'd think that King Kong had returned to torment ten million citizens. The *Village Voice* printed the thoughts that seemed to be on everybody's mind in a piece called IS THIS WHAT DR. NAISMITH INTENDED? The story summed up all the boring old arguments about Massy's height and strength and how he'd come out of nowhere at the beginning of the year, without so much as a bidding war or a draft process, and how he should be suspended until the whole matter was straightened out. But at least the writer had enough class to introduce a little whimsical frankness; her ender was, "Broussard Massy should be banned or else traded to our Knicks."

The *News* ran a fire-eating column by Mark Irwine excoriating Massy for "almost knocking down" a ten-year-old boy who had waited outside the players' exit for an autograph till two hours after game time. "This lad will never return to a Knicks's game," Irwine wrote, "and thus the New York club must pay for the visiting giant's brutishness."

Jack Carbon spent the morning running from room to room trying to get the truth of the little-boy incident, but Massy couldn't help him. He said, "I'm awful sorry, Mr. Carbon, the police officers rushed us away so fast, I surely don't remember seeing anybody at all."

"Besides," Justin Fell added, "Bru was never rude to a kid in his life."

A smiling Abraham Gross burst into the room waving the *News*. "Did you see it?" he asked nobody in particular. "The column by Irwine? I tell you, the man's a bulldog! He'll be writing about that little kid for ten years!"

"What about the public apology?" Jack Carbon asked. "Do we give it or don't we?"

"Don't apologize!" the owner ordered. "Keep it brewing."

Carbon nodded.

"This is the kind of fuss the fans love," Gross Abraham continued. "Controversy! That's what they pay for, not basketball." He went away smiling.

Around noon the 14th Precinct called and advised Wasp players to stay in their rooms for the day. Packs of superheated young fans were sallying in and out of the lobby, screaming for the big man's scalp. The phones rang constantly, and by three in the afternoon, every Wasp phone had been shut off. The only way to communicate was to walk from room to room.

I called on the players one by one and found them itchy but undaunted, considering the circumstances. Basil McBride, our world-class worrier, spoke through a cracked lip and announced that any motherfucking New York Knick that laid one motherfucking finger on him tomorrow night would get his motherfucking nuts cracked, y'unnastan'? "I was nervous last night," Basil said. "I admit it. Meant too much to me, I guess, gettin' in the finals. Thought the Knicks were a bunch of redhots. But we really lit 'em up, didn't we?" His gap-toothed smile made him look like a hockey defenseman. "We stomped on 'em, Jack. Hey, the big man showed he can choke 'em off, didn't he?"

"How would you know?" I said. "You were in the locker room cooling down."

"Saw it on the TV. Shee-it, he whup that big turkey Halliday up, down and backways!"

"Looks like Massy's found himself," I said.

"Yeh, he's together now," Basil said, whistling through the gap where Brock Faulkner's elbow had caught him. "Look like we can relate around him."

Justin was standing at the window when I went back to his room, and Massy was still propped against the headboard of the bed wearing earphones and waving his bare toes around as though he was practicing to become the world's first one-footed conductor. His eyes were closed. "What's he listening to?" I whispered.

"Three guesses," Justin said, "as long as they're all flute."

The Wasps's resident philosopher stretched his 6–4 frame and yawned. "I was just looking toward Inwood, way uptown," he said with a touch of nostalgia in his voice. "See where the river comes out? That's it."

"That's what?"

"That's Inwood, where I was raised."

In the confusion of covering basketball under siege, I'd forgotten that Justin was a native New Yorker.

"Thought I'd wander up to the old grammar school after the series," he went on, still standing at the window and peering through a bilious yellow haze that hung outside like a poison mushroom. "Like to check the radiator, see if it's still there."

"Everybody gets that feeling sometimes, go back to the old alma mater, see the radiator," I said.

Justin laughed. "This one was practically a teammate. In the middle of the gym. We'd use it for picks. That was one of our plays: number two spinner off the radiator."

"No kidding?"

"No jive, Sam. There's kids in Inwood that still have scars. Tried to fight through the pick and the radiator wouldn't give." He laughed again. "You remember how much trouble I used to have shooting from the corners?" I nodded. "That was 'cause of that same gym. Had low beams in all four corners, and you either had to shoot a dart or dribble outside and set up again."

"After this playoff you can afford to buy the neighborhood a whole new school."

"Fun-*nee,*" Justin said, sitting back down. "I'll buy 'em a nice new radiator instead. A sponge-rubber one." He shook his head and made a clucking sound with his lips. "Tough to figure out what to do for all those UTB's."

"UTB's?"

"Used-to-be's. Playground heroes. They're mostly addicts now. Or dirt poor. Scramblin' and scufflin' to survive, you know? Some of those guys used to spot me the *H* and the *O* and the *R* and beat my ass. They had moves like mamba snakes. They used to deal on me and holler, 'Get down, fool!' Go right up over my block and stuff the ball and holler, 'In your eye!' Then the Puerto Ricans started getting in the game, and they'd holler *'En su ojo!'* Must have been two, three hundred kids in Inwood alone that could light me up."

"Move on *you?*"

"That's right, Sam. Fire my ass! They'd make me look like a lame."

"So why're they UTB's now?"

"Oh, all the usual reasons. Couldn't keep up in school, got on the hard stuff, mama shot papa, familiar stuff like that."

"The black condition," I said, quoting Dulcy.

"The *poor* condition's more like it," Justin said. "Kids up there, they never cared about anything except a full stomach and basketball. Basketball Jones, everyone of them. A way out, ya know?"

Massy eased the earphones off his head and said, "Hi, Mr. Forrester."

"Don't let us interrupt your music hour," I said.

"I'm fixin' to take a walk." He pulled himself up and ducked to avoid the ceiling.

"No walks!" Justin ordered.

"I mean just around the halls." The kid stretched and smiled. "Don't worry. If I see any vigilantes, I'll let out a whoop, and y'all can come save me."

"Be cool," Justin said, "and don't go near the lobby."

Massy bent over and walked through the portal. "Thanks for worrying," he said. "My brother's keeper."

"I'm not worrying about *you,* Candy-ass," Justin snapped. "Who're you to worry about?" Professional athletes would rather crawl through ground glass than admit affection. They mask it under gibes and insults, even Justin Fell.

With Massy gone, our Ivy Leaguer hugged himself as though a chill breeze had blown through the hotel room. "I can't shake a down feeling," Justin said. "I know it's irrational, but sometimes he makes me want to sit down and bawl. He'll look at me, kind of like a child? And I keep thinking of a line by Green I came across."

"What line by Green?"

" 'Fling but a stone, the giant dies,' " Justin quoted.

"Shouldn't that be, 'Fling but a stone, the giant dies, *dawlin*'?" I quipped.

"That's another Green. This one's Matthew. English poet."

I wondered how many other NBA players could quote such an obscure line. Maybe Bill Bradley. Tom Meschery. Jerry Lucas might have tossed it off, along with the St. Louis phone directory and the square-root table. But not many others. Not many sportswriters, either. It gave me a funny feeling, to be dumber than a jock.

"He scared me half to death last night," Justin said, flopping on his bed. "I woke up at four and he was gone. I called *everybody.* No Massy. Didn't I talk to you?"

"Four A.M.? No. Pete and I were just getting thrown out of Ho Ho's."

"Well, I was about to wake up Gross or Guile and have somebody get the police. I was sure the kid was lying in a gutter with a bunch of crazies using him for a dance floor, ya know? Then he walks in the room and starts unlacing his shoes. I says, 'Where you been?' He says, 'Oh, hi, Justin! I was at the chapel.' "

"Crazy!" I said.

"I told him! I said, 'Don't you know you're public enemy number one in New York?' He says, 'Not in church.' I says, 'Yeh, but first you gotta get *to* the church, man.' He says, 'There's one right around the corner. Athletes' Chapel, something like that. Five or six people inside.' I asked him what the other people did when he walked in. He says, 'I don't know. I knelt down and prayed, and when I got up they were gone.' "

"He still doesn't understand his effect on strangers."

"Well, he's into his own thing, you know, Sam? He's—I don't know —he's on another plane."

"Still prays every night?"

"Mostly for his mama."

"His mama? He never knew her."

"He prays for her soul. He says, 'Forgive me, mama, I hope you'll forgive me.' "

It hadn't occurred to me that a son might grieve for a lifetime over a mother who had died bearing him. There were so many handier guilts available.

"Doesn't he know it wasn't his fault?" I asked.

"Sure. But morbid feelings like that, Sam—they're not easy to get at, know what I mean?"

Massy came in as I went out, and I was glad to see him smiling.

5

The Ritz lobby was sprinkled with cops, and Buttsy Rafferty and Jones Jones stood behind a potted plant, plotting together like a couple of pickpockets. They looked contented, and why not, with one leg up on the Eastern Championship and the club healthy and intact for the second game.

Just seeing their sly faces made me feel more secure; they were the sheet I could pull up over my head. I said, "Hey, Butts, how's it going, from the standpoint of pertaining to life in the big city? I mean, whattaya say we take and see the sights?"

Coach gave me a funny look, but Jones said, "What sights did you have in mind?"

"I don't know," I said. "The Guggenheim? The Metropolitan?" A pair of Easter Island stone faces peered back at me. "Lincoln Center?" No reaction. "Ho Ho's? Jersey City?"

"Carbon mentioned something pertaining to cribbage," Buttsy said.

"I'm goin' to the flicks," Jones said. I knew what flicks he had in mind. *Down and Dirty. Airport Girls. Beaver Brigade.* They all featured snappy dialogue: "Do you smoke after intercourse?" "I don't know, I never looked."

"Make sure you bring a newspaper," I said.

"I switched to a popcorn box," Jones said.

Coach snorted. I smiled politely. Jones repeated the line twice, then exited smartly. The performance would have been more impressive if someone had been laughing.

"Well, how are you gentlemen of the press spending the day?" Buttsy asked. "Shopping for bulletproof vests?"

"Been interviewing some of your mules," I said. "Now I think I'll tour the subway system. You buy a token at Grand Central, head south, and by the same token you ride all the way to Brooklyn."

Buttsy scowled, his mind on serious matters. "A police captain phoned Guile this morning. Said we better get over to the Garden early tomorrow, before the mobs show up. Said pertaining to our safety he couldn't guarantee it, the whole fucking National Guard couldn't guarantee it."

Around suppertime a bellman handed me a message to call home right away. I raced downstairs to the same booth I'd used to phone in my story and when I heard Dulcy's voice I said, "Hey, honey, what's the matter?"

"Oh, Sam, *Sam,*" she whimpered. "I've been trying to get you."

"I'm okay, honey. Don't worry. What've you been reading? That scare piece by Storen? Dulcy, you know how fans are. A lot of noise and bluster." I wished I believed it.

"Sam, sit down," Dulcy said.

"I *am* sitting down. I'm in a phone booth in the lobby. The room phones are plugged."

"I know. I've been trying to get through for hours. Sam, a Dr. Labas called. He said you were the only one he knew up here, and nobody'd tell him where the team was staying. He got our home number from information."

"I never expected the old quack to call," I said. Maybe he'd decided that I hadn't found anything in his office after all, that the housekeeper had interrupted me before I'd gotten into the Massy file.

"Dead," Dulcy was saying.

"*What?*"

"Mr. Massy's dead."

I took a deep breath and closed my eyes hard. When I opened them I was still in the phone booth in the lobby of the Manhattan Ritz and Dulcy was still on the other end of the line. That meant Mike Massy was still dead. All I could think of was my first peep through the window of his sickroom in Marcilly, and the way the kid leaned over and embraced his father and clamped the old man's hand in his own.

Between gulps, Dulcy relayed the details as Labas had passed them to her. The day before the Knicks game, Michel had visited a bar across the bayou and knocked back a couple of boilermakers and another three or four drinks set up by some newfound friends who'd been excited to meet the TV hero's father. A *cousine* had found the old cajun sprawled outside the door of his 30-foot trailer when she'd arrived at noon the next day. Rigor mortis had come and gone.

Dulcy's voice was faint by the time she finished. "Aw, honey, don't feel bad," I said. "The man was awful sick, you know."

"Sam, I'm not feeling bad about Mr. Massy. I never *saw* Mr. Massy. I'm upset about that poor boy. Going back for the funeral and all, the death trauma. He's already disturbed."

I told her the poor boy would survive. We'd sit on the news till after the second game, maybe wait till the championship series was over, if we could keep it quiet that long.

"You will not!" Dulcy said emphatically. "Tell him now, Sam! His father's been dead for nearly two days. He deserves to know. You're supposed to be his friend!"

"Sweetheart," I said soothingly, wiping my moist brow with a moist palm, "you don't understand. Honey, he worshiped his father. If he finds out now——"

"How can you even *talk* like that?" Dulcy squealed in my ear. "Oh, Sam. . . ."

"Honey, stop crying! Pull yourself together."

"Tell him, Sam! The second you hang up!"

"Don't worry. I'll do the right thing. You can count on me."

"To do what?"

"To do the right thing!" I hedged.

"Why, you fuckie!" Dulcy shouted, and I held the phone away from my ear till the diatribe ended. My loving wife told me and our neighbors and anyone within a mile of her voice that she could be in New York in a few hours and if I didn't tell Massy about his father's death *right now* she'd damned well do it herself in the middle of the night and what would *that* do to the team's morale?

I promised to do my duty by God and country.

I paced the lobby for a while, trying to regain my composure, and then I stepped outside. The wet air was too cold for my shirtsleeves and sweater, but I didn't feel it. A few night people huddled under the canopy of the hotel, but they looked nonviolent. I walked along the downtown edge of the Garden and saw the huddled masses in parkas and blankets stretched in a double line waiting for the ticket office to open in the morning. On the Seventh Avenue side, a big orange-on-black sign announced

TWO THOUSAND STANDING ROOM
SEATS GO ON SALE AT 9 A.M.

For all my mental turmoil, I couldn't help wondering what a "standing room seat" was, or should the sign have said that two thousand "stands" would go on sale?

Pictures of Michel Massy flitted through my head as I walked. Lying alongside the dialysis machine, muttering "I didn't mean no horm." Sitting in Pascal's Manale, arm-deep in a bowl of barbecued shrimp, while scouts and Mafiosi ply him with alcohol. Standing under the basket, screaming instructions at an embarrassed kid.

After that I couldn't see anything in my mind but Bru Massy. His suffering was just beginning. The dead don't die, only the living.

At Ho Ho's I asked Wong for a double vodka. He'd been my favorite New York bartender ever since the night he passed me a card that said: I MAY BE WONG, BUT I THINK YOU'RE WONDERFUL. I knocked the drink back and said, "Gimme a refill, pal."

"Everything okay?" the bartender inquired solicitously.

"A death in the family," I said.

"Death in famree?" Wong said, and when I nodded he tossed his head back, showing a dozen gold crowns, and cackled uproariously. I smiled and thanked him for honoring the ancient oriental tradition. I was in Ho's the night Robert Kennedy was killed, and every waiter in the place had split his sides. In its old-world ancient way, the laughing tradition made sense—if you could bring yourself to observe it.

Fortified, I rushed back to the Ritz and rapped on Massy's door.

254

There was no answer, and I banged again. The kid opened the door and smiled down at me, the cord from his earphones draped across his shoulders and chest.

"Bru!" I said, shoving into the room. "Your father died!"

That's what I said.

All the way back I'd rehearsed the most delicate way to break the news—"Bru, there's some bad news from Louisiana. . . ." "Bru, this is gonna be tough, I know, but it had to happen sooner or later. . . ." "Bru, your papa. . . ." But instead I just gulped and hit him with the full shot: "Your father died." Period. Paragraph. Ashamed of my own clumsiness, I flopped down on his bed.

After a few seconds I felt the mattress sag next to me. Without thinking, I jumped up. The kid was sitting and blinking hard. "Bru, didn't you hear me?" I said. "Your father died last night."

"Yes, sir, I heard you, Sam," Massy answered. It was the first time he'd ever called me Sam. "I kind of been expecting it."

He walked over to the bureau and opened a drawer and pulled out a handkerchief. "Go on and cry, kid," I said. "You'll feel better." I was choked up myself, watching him folding and unfolding the handkerchief, tilting his head from one side to the other, the way a puppy does when he thinks he hears something in the distance. Then he sat down slowly and asked me in a firm voice, "Did he suffer?"

"He died in his sleep," I told him. It was only a small lie, and I'd do it again.

"I always worried how he'd go," Massy said. "Never *when*. Dr. Labas told me to get ready." He paused. "Papa made some mistakes, did you know that?"

"I heard a few things."

"He only got to the fourth grade. Knocked around. Went to jail once. But he—he believed in me, he surely did."

I said I knew.

"Never had much chance. Aunt Sissy always said he had too much of his own self invested in me. Does that add up, Mr. Forrester?" We were back on the old footing.

I shook my head an inch or two and managed a smile. For a few minutes he just stood there, the cord to his earphones dangling like a pigtail. "That was all he wanted—for me to be something."

"I guess he got his wish," I said, not knowing what else to say.

"I was never strong enough," the kid rambled on, as though I hadn't spoken. "I gave up. Papa didn't understand. He always thought I was puttin' on. When I came home from the sanitarium the doctors said no more basketball, and papa, he just said, 'Sure. Okay.' Then he took me to my auntie's and disappeared. Worked on towboats, roustabout, jobs like that, up and down the river. I used to go over to the French market and try to find him in the stalls, walk around the coffee warehouses, look into tall men's faces at Mardi Gras time. Then he showed up last year half-dead, said he was ready to go home."

He stood up and hunched around the room aimlessly.

"You did everything you could, Bru," I said. "More than most sons."

He sighed. "Papa's still gone."

He put his head in his hands. "Don't take it on yourself, kid," I said, reaching up and trying to pat him on the shoulder. "Fathers die. There's never been a son that could stop it."

I stayed with him for an hour in the hotel room while the neon tints of Manhattan glowed and flickered against the wall. Once in a while he'd look up and say something, and once in a while I could make it out. He seemed to be blaming himself for everything.

Then Justin came in, and the two of us baby-sat the kid for another couple of hours, and then Buttsy banged on the door and that's how we found out it was one o'clock in the morning.

"Don't bother bedchecking," I said softly, pushing the coach into the hall and squeezing the door shut behind us. "Bru's father died."

"Oh, Christ!" the Butts said, his mouth agape and his dishwater-blue eyes open wide. "Oh, the poor kid! Aw, for Chrissakes! Jeez, what a tough fucking break!"

The door to the room came open and Justin ducked out and said, "Hello, Coach."

"What about tomorrow night?" Buttsy asked nervously.

"He'll be all right," Justin said.

It was never in doubt.

.   .   .

256

6

Around eight the next morning, Jack Carbon called and told me that the mayor had declared a state of emergency for the area around Madison Square Garden. Mounted cops patrolled from 31st to 33d streets and from Seventh to Eighth, and the TPF was stationed in vans at every corner in the danger area. I phoned the Garden PR office and after 30 minutes of busy signals I learned that three fans had been injured in the early hours of the morning. They had been waiting in line when battles broke out over such important matters as Brock Faulkner's date of birth, Orion Halliday's lifetime free-throw percentage, and how to handle Bru Massy.

"Heavy pressure's building to postpone the game and replay it in a neutral arena," a commentator said on the CBS news. But on the "Today" show, a panel of New York sportswriters agreed that rules were rules and the game must be played in the Garden.

Barbara Walters put on her most innocent look and said, "But hawf the players might be killed!"

"People die every day, Barbara," said Mark Irwine of the *New York News.* "That's no reason to postpone a playoff game." Irwine said that part of our problem in America was disrespect for the past. "We should stick with tradition."

The Knicks's board of directors issued a statement decrying the police department's "massive intervention" and predicting that New York fans would "live up to the high standards of sportsmanship observed at the Garden for years." A beaming Abraham Gross appeared on camera to say, "The Wasps have waited a long time for this. An army couldn't keep us away!"

At noon, an announcement came down from the commissioner's office: "Irresponsible sources have suggested that certain players in the Eastern Conference Championship Series will be in danger if tonight's contest is played on schedule. The National Basketball Association

257

categorically disavows all such wild and exaggerated allegations. The game will be played as scheduled."

Good old Commissioner Deford, judicious to the end. A loaded Arisaka rifle was now considered "exaggerated allegations," and mobs rioting around the Garden and flinging bricks at the lower windows of our hotel were just fun-loving fans. The game's the thing. Bet your a$$!

At 4 P.M. the Garden security chief phoned Darius Guile and told him to escort the Wasps's party to the freight entrance of the hotel.

"What the fuck is this?" Nick Storen griped as we folded our poker table.

"I think we're gonna run the blockade," Pete Tyles said.

At the hotel loading dock, we were ushered into the back of a van marked "Penobscot Fish Co.," and a man in a neat new apron and a couple of workers in clean overalls tied a heavy tarp across the rear, concealing us from view.

"Cops," Guile said, pointing to the workers. "TPF."

The fish truck eased away with its lively catch. "Hey, baby, shouldn't we be iced down?" Jones Jones called out, but nobody laughed. We bumped along the streets until a low hum like surf began to reach our ears and somebody said, "Fans!"

"Dummy up!" one of the cops whispered. "We're outside the Garden."

I peeked through a rope-hole and saw acres of faces. It looked like New Year's Eve in Times Square, with people milling about like the survivors of a wrecked anthill. Over by the wall I caught a glimpse of two guys punching each other while the crowd made room. I tried to remember where I'd seen similar excesses: the Indianapolis Speedway grounds the night before the 500, a soccer field in Mexico City after the home team lost on a penalty kick, in Pittsburgh the night the Steelers won their first Super Bowl.

Our truck dropped into low gear and began to climb, and then it squeaked to a halt and the back was opened and we spilled onto the fourth floor of the Garden. "How we did that?" Red Green called out, and old veteran Basil McBride said, "Up the inside ramp, fool."

For want of anything else to do, the players dressed in their plum-and-white warm-ups and scrimmaged lightly. Massy slapped a short jumper back into King Crowder's face and turned away without apologizing. Well, allowances had to be made, and even King seemed to know it.

Just before the doors were opened to the public at 6:30, an hour before the tip-off, I circled the topmost walkway of the Garden. The stands below looked like an assembly area in a war zone. For the first time in my life, I saw ushers in helmets, being briefed at the 31st Street end. Uniformed cops stood three deep at every exit, and a couple hundred more were spaced about six feet apart around the entire court, flipping their nightsticks and facing the audience. Along the walls of the corridor to the dressing rooms, security guards were shoulder to shoulder.

As I passed an opening behind the skyboxes, I heard a snarl and peeked inside a service area to see a platoon of German shepherds straining at chain leashes. "Move along, bud!" a cop in a plastic facemask snapped at me, and when I said, "Press!" he shouted, "Listen, move along!" I started to flash my pass, but one of the animals bared its fangs, and I decided to leave. Police dogs can't read.

The first fans moved to their seats in a properly subdued manner, blinking at the show of force and acting humble. But as the arena began to fill, a drone started, low at first, then picking up like an approaching army. A group in an upper tier unveiled a sign about 4 feet high and 20 feet long:

TUESDAY APRIL 16: MASSY GETS HIS!

and another sign said:

ORION HALLIDAY, AX-MAN!

Two young men at a lower level circumnavigated the Garden bearing a placard:

WE'LL DO WHAT DAVID DID!

By thirty minutes before game time, all of the 19,694 seats were filled and standees had begun to pack in. The undertone that had started with the first arrivals was building to a roar, and a fight had already broken out. I hoped our faithful Wasp delegation was lying in the weeds quietly. More busloads had arrived in the afternoon and been warned by Pat Rhoades to "keep your mouths shut during the game. This is no normal situation." I was glad Dulcy was home, by her own choice. Standing behind the press table, I tried to spot Abraham Gross in the lower boxes. "Where's the owner?" I asked Jack Carbon.

"Some fan threw a tomato at him," the PR man explained. "In the can. He went up to a skybox."

When the Wasps took the floor, every spectator stood up and hooted, and a water-bag splatted near our bench. Eggs rained down on our players, and a squat man with a sumo wrestler's profile ran on the court and swung a muscle-bound right cross at Massy. The last I saw, the weightlifter was being escorted out, with one cop in front and another in back. The kid glowered. Apparently he was finding it harder to turn the other cheek.

You could barely hear the introductions over the cheers and catcalls, and Buttsy and Eddie Pfalz of the Knicks finally gave up and sent the teams out en masse. The house lights dimmed and twin spots played on an oversized American flag. I guess they played "The Star Spangled Banner," too, but you couldn't be sure in the noise.

Nobody heard the opening whistle, either, but the ref flipped the ball in the air and Massy scraped his shoulder blade against Orion Halliday's face and slapped the ball backward to Justin Fell. I was so excited I thought my heart would pop through my shirt. I could barely hold the pencil. "Nervous?" Pete Tyles hollered as the Wasps worked the ball up the court.

"Nope!" I said, but my voice cracked.

When I glanced at Pete, he was grinning sheepishly. "Don't be embarrassed," he said. "I think I peed my pants."

In this second game, the Knicks's roughhouse tactics came as no surprise, but the fans let out a whoop of joy just the same. Halliday followed Massy down the court and as the kid set up in the low post, the big Knick center slipped him a knee.

A few minutes later the bogart backcourt man, Brock Faulkner, caught Justin Fell sliding across the lane and threw a forearm smash that would have done credit to Mean Joe Greene. You could hear the grunts and groans as two-man wars were fought all over the court, but the refs seemed reluctant to call fouls. I think they sensed the mood of the fans. They wanted blood. Preferably ours.

With a minute and eight seconds gone, Sweet Basil McBride tucked behind a Massy screen and sent a soft 15-foot jumper through the cords, and lighted cigars and cigarettes showered from the stands like meteors. One of the refs crisscrossed his arms and blew the whistle, and attendants rushed out and broomed the floor clean.

The Knicks brought the ball out and tried to go backdoor, but Massy blocked "Pepsi" Kohler's lay-up, and after two quick passes Abdul Buzruz scored and the Wasps were ahead 4–zip. I looked up from my running score and saw Massy bend over and clutch his thigh, and again play was stopped. "What was it?" I hollered down the press table to Jack Carbon.

"I think a dart," the PR man called back. Pasty Pasticcino applied a Band-Aid, and the fans booed and shook their fists. I guess they were sorry the kid hadn't bled to death.

The Knicks broke into the scoring on a long one-hander by Orion Halliday after Massy had sealed the middle, but Sutter Manno brought the ball back to the circle, faked a drive and fed the big man for a clean dunk. 6–2 Wasps. A bottle crashed on the floor about a foot from where the kid loped back on defense, and the whistle blew, and the faithful clean-up crew jogged out again. I looked at my running score and wondered if I'd make the two-star deadline at 10:30. It had taken 15 minutes to finish the first two minutes of playing time.

The first period ended with the Wasps on top 32–19, and Massy in control of everything except the crowd. The fans were challenging the Wasps and threatening the officials and chanting "bull-*shit*" whenever the refs called a foul against a Knick, which was seldom enough.

You can tell the pattern of the whole game from my second-quarter running:

Time	Play	Wasps	Knicks
12:00	Halliday vs. B. Massy—Manno controls Massy's tap		
11:51	Foul vs. Massy		
11:19	Massy lays it in left from Fell	34	
11:10	Faulkner one-hander from right side		21
10:50	Massy blocks		
10:38	McBride jumper from top of key	36	
10:21	Foul vs. Kohler		
10:09	Massy dunks from Manno	38	
9:55	Massy intercepts, dunks unassisted	40	
9:31	Massy blocks Faulkner		
8:50	McBride spinning jumper from Fell	42	

8:34	Foul vs. Green	
8:28	Halliday jumper from behind key	23
8:18	Fell spinning one-hander from Massy	44
7:58	Massy blocks Kohler, dunks unassisted	46

That's four minutes and two seconds of playing time, and it took 22 minutes on my watch. Every time Massy made a move something flew out of the stands, and the court had to be cleared. Once it was a live lobster; award the guy points for originality anyway. Then it was a whole string of firecrackers, giving our bench a bad case of Saint Vitus's dance.

With the Wasps running away 119–97 and two minutes left in the game, I heard a chant above the general din and I nudged Pete and asked if he could make it out. Several rows of fans were rocking in unison in an upper tier, and as we watched, others joined in and the words were unmistakably echoing back and forth across the great well of the Garden. It sounded like films of Hitler addressing his followers in front of the Reichstag.

"Get him!" the crowd was screaming, and gradually the cry was improved and lengthened, Liverpool style, with one side answering the other:

GET HIM!

GET WHO?

BIG STOOP!

THAT'S WHO!

I looked at the kid. Maybe he heard and maybe he didn't. His face gleamed with sweat as he fought to keep Orion Halliday in his sights, and every now and then you could see both of the mighty centers grimace as they slammed together in the pivot. Tonight there'd been no apologies, no extended hands to help each other up, no quick slap-shakes or ass-pats to show that it was only a game. Halliday's cold behavior didn't surprise me. Massy's did.

With a few seconds left and the Wasps breezing, our guards were working against a Mixmaster press when Brock Faulkner elbowed Justin Fell in the belly. Our usually peaceful master of arts blinked twice and cocked a fist, but a Knick stepped off the bench and pinned his arms.

262

Faulkner threw two hard punches to the face, and Justin slithered to the maple like a dead eel. Bubbles of blood frothed up in the corner of his mouth. I heard myself shouting, "Hey, this isn't hockey!"

Then I looked upcourt and saw Bru Massy churning toward the action like a scalded hippopotamus.

Faulkner must have spotted him, too, because he jumped behind the Knicks's bench. Fair fights weren't his style.

Massy ran around the New York bench. Players scattered, but Brock Faulkner tripped over his own feet and Massy hoisted the little guard high over his head and dashed out on the court, eyes opened wide like a man out of control.

For a second I thought he was going to try a new human hammer-throw record or whirl the Knick senseless in an old-fashioned Bruno Sammartino airplane spin, but instead he lurched downcourt still holding his victim 11 or 12 feet in the air.

Then he dunked him head first through the Knicks's basket. The backboard dissolved into a hailstorm of glass pellets, and Faulkner wound up on the floor, wearing the rim for a necklace.

For the first time all night, the noise slackened as the fans tried to comprehend what they had seen, and then the booing began, not your ordinary Garden-variety booing but a shriller sound that meant that everybody was cutting loose, not just the malcontents. Mothers with children were on their feet booing. Dainty young maidens in party dresses were booing. Uniformed ushers and cops were booing. Garden officials in their skyboxes were booing. Everyone was giving the gut response to the oldest threat in folklore: the attack of the giant.

The noise compressed my eardrums, as on a deep dive, and just when I thought the din was so loud it couldn't possibly get louder, it got louder.

The police line held as the first angry fans left their seats. Under the basket, a subdued Massy reached out to help the fallen New York player, but Faulkner lay limp, his eyes staring in two different directions. Bru looked up at the crowd, a shocked expression on his pale face, and lifted his palms in apology.

Then he knelt alongside the wreck of the Knick and brushed his opponent's hair back gently. As he straddled the fallen player, a cop ran out and shoved him away with his club and beckoned to the Knick bench for first aid.

Massy stood up, his dark eyes searching frantically about him. I knew why he'd done it—the calmest person has his flash point—but I doubted if he knew why himself. Maybe later, when things calmed down. Now he was wiping tears from his face.

The fans shoved against the sagging police line, flicking their fists and their insults at the big man just out of range, wanting to draw blood, but not their own.

A teen-ager with long black hair and a Levi jacket slipped through the cops and kicked Massy in the ankle from behind.

A chic-looking woman in a leopard coat and wraparound goggles cracked a bottle on the side of his head.

Beer rained from the stands, spraying everyone at courtside. A couple of unopened cans hit close to the kid.

A cop raised his nightstick and waved it at the crowd. When he did, the police line bellied inward as the fans pushed toward the court.

Then the organist played "Charge!" and the line cracked like an eggshell.

I jumped up on the press table, ashamed for not running to help Massy, but also knowing that I was helpless.

I heard myself call "Massy!" as the kid disappeared behind a wall of flesh. Then I was dragged down myself, all in slow motion, floating to the floor and hitting painlessly. I lay there paralyzed by my own lack of will while battalions of shoes marched past my face: wingtips and Gucci loafers and suede tennis shoes and patent-leather pumps and Italian boots and mod shoes with platform soles, shuffling toward the carnage.

The crowd parted, like the curtains on a Greek play, and where Massy had stood a few seconds before, alive and whole, eight feet two inches of troubled human flesh, now there was nothing.

7

"Oh oh oh oh oh oh oh. . . ."

A sharp smell filled my nose and my head jerked sideways. I opened my eyes and found out who was making all the noise: It was me.

I gazed upward at an orange ceiling of acoustical tiles. A voice spoke from a worried ring of faces. "He's awake," it said. I recognized Pasty, and then I recognized the visitors' dressing room in Madison Square Garden.

"Huh?" I said. The back of my head was an anvil, and the blacksmith was hammering away.

"You got hurt," the trainer said. "Got a nice little cut in your scalp."

I reached back and touched a dab of raspberry jam. It tingled.

". . . Out cold," Pasty was telling somebody else. "Press table collapsed."

Suddenly I remembered the lynching of Broussard Massy.

"Massy!" I said. "Oh, Jesus, the poor kid!" I started to sit up.

"What?" I heard Buttsy say.

"Oh, my god, what a way to die," I cried, "Oh, Jesus, horrible——"

"Basically what's so horrible about Massy?" the coach said. He pointed across the room.

I turned my head painfully and saw the big man sitting in a corner, surrounded by reporters. The blacksmith dropped a cherry-red horseshoe on my wound, and I fell back heavily.

"You okay?" Pasty asked.

"Massy," I said drowsily. "I thought they killed him."

"Killed him?" Jack Carbon put in. "You dreamed it, pal. When you were unconscious. The cops got him out okay."

I must have dozed off again, because the next thing I knew they were loading me on a wheeled stretcher. "Hey," I protested, "Pasty! What——"

"Precautionary," the trainer said. "You'll be out in the morning."

"Wait!" I said, struggling to get up. An ambulance attendant shoved me down with his index finger.

"No, no!" I called out. "I gotta file! My notes! *Where's my notes?*"

"Tyles has your notes," Jack Carbon said patiently as they started to roll me away. "He's doing your game story."

"He's *what?*"

"Writing your game story. I already filed your running. Pennsylvania's doing your color story, and Lucious is covering the King Crowder business for you."

"The Crowder business?"

"You didn't hear?" the press agent said. "No, how the hell could you? Pat Rhoades nailed King on the threatening letters. H-O-R-S-E? Found a sliced-up magazine in his locker. Getting ready to send the *E*."

"Oh, Jeez," I said. Poor King, he'd just bought himself that one-way ticket back to the ghetto.

"Hey," I said, "do me a favor. Don't bother Dulcy. I'll be fine."

"Fine?" Pasty said.

"Fine," I repeated. "What she doesn't know won't hurt—*oooooh!*" The pain flashed again, and I stopped talking.

At the hospital, they X-rayed me and stethoscoped me and gave me a shot and the lights faded and died and the Wasps won the playoffs in four straight games.

I led the scoring myself.

There was no game scheduled for two days, and I racked up a good night's sleep in the hospital. The tests were negative, and I was back in the Manhattan Ritz by noon. I called Dulcy and talked to her for an hour, $31.80 on the expense account, and worth every dime.

At first she'd sounded upset, but then she found it funny. "Oh, honey, that's typical of you!" she said, cackling into the phone. "Really, Sam, you're so dramatic, you're so *dumb,* you sweet thing!"

Pasty and Buttsy must have visited my hotel room six times during the afternoon, poking at my head, changing the bandage and cracking smart. "What'd you think you were out there, a fucking diver duck?" Buttsy asked.

"Not my fault," I protested. "Didn't you say the table broke?"

"Yeh, but that don't mean you gotta do a one-and-a-half gainer to the floor. You coulda fell graceful, ya know?"

"Well, I wasn't planning on falling," I said. "I was watching Massy."

"Who wasn't?" Pasty said as he lifted the square bandage from my head. To my disappointment, it wasn't even bloody.

"Shit," Buttsy said, "I had worse cuts shaving."

There was still a large bump back there, and I cherished it. I thought of myself as a soldier, injured in battle, and napped for an hour on that comforting idea.

Around four o'clock, Massy tiptoed in, all sympathy and concern. To tell the truth, I wondered what had taken him so long; I'd expected him to be one of my first visitors. "Missed ya, kid," I said after he told me how sorry he was about my accident. "What's happening?"

He sat on the end of my bed and started to speak, but then he went over to the window and pulled the shade almost all the way down. I thought he looked a little pale in the face, but with the Massys it was hard to tell, so I said, "Anything wrong? You suspended or something?"

"Roxy phoned," the kid said. "Her fellowship came through."

"Her fellowship?"

"She'll be leaving for Lausanne right after the playoffs."

"Jeez," I said, still not fully awake, "I thought you two were about to make your move, get married and all."

He turned away sharply, and I realized I'd said something dumb. My wife was certainly right about me.

"Not now," he said slowly. "Not for a while, anyway." He paused. "Said she'd write."

He went back to the window and did a deep-knee bend so he could look out. "All those people down there," he said.

" 'Scuse me?"

The kid wandered over toward the door. "Roxanne—that fellowship meant everything."

"I know, Bru. Hey, man, be cool! She'll be back." I hoped I sounded convincing, but I doubted it.

"Did what she had to do, I guess," he muttered.

"Who doesn't?" I said soothingly.

Massy smiled and nodded. "Get better, hear?" he said and ducked into the hall.

Just as I finished a bath the telephone rang. I picked it up and heard the irritating voice of Tex Pecos. The sound bored straight through my cranium and out my wound and made the blacksmith start pounding again. "Forrester!" he said. "Good job!"

"Huh?"

"Clean, solid copy. Professional job."

"Thanks?" I said fuzzily.

"Just one criticism. The next time you mention police?"

"Um-hmm?"

"Don't call 'em pigs."

"I'll watch that," I promised.

"Well, keep up the good work," he said.

"Mr. Pecos," I said, feeling a pang in the back of my head and mistaking it for a conscience, "I was out cold——"

"Well, you usually are," the old man interrupted, and the line went dead.

8

That night I put the DND sign on the door, but it didn't keep somebody from knocking. I woke up and looked at my watch. It was midnight.

"Go 'way," I said drunkenly, even though I hadn't had a drink in two days. "Lemme sleep Chrissakes. . . ."

The knocker knocked louder, and I staggered out of bed and cracked the door. The long and the short of it was that Broussard Massy stood outside with a middle-aged man who barely reached his belt. "Feelin' better, Mr. Forrester?" Massy said in his hollow voice. "Uncle Leon said he just had to see you."

A sharp-faced ornamental bird of a man shoved into the room and waved the kid out. "I'll leave you two to visit," Bru said.

Leon Massy took my hand and pumped it hard and told me in a Mississippi river of words what an honor it was to make my acquaintance, he'd heard so much, he couldn't get the nephew to listen but maybe with my help, because Broussard respected me so highly, if I would just warn the kid. . . .

"Whoa, there, Mr. Massy!" I said, putting up a hand and flopping heavily on the bed. "I'm still asleep. I was injured, you know."

Leon Massy had the same bald head as his brother Mike and the same white-on-white skin of the whole Massy *famille.* Apparently nobody in the clan went out in the sun. His face was garnished with a waxed moustache, probably the only one west of the Place Vendôme, and he was dressed in bayou hip: shiny white plastic shoes, matching white belt, plaid pants, bright red sport shirt with a penguin on it, and a pink sharkskin jacket. He looked like a retired pimp.

"Interesting," I said, tapping my own upper lip and trying to pretend I admired his work of art.

"Good for my bidness," the little man said in that same rapid-fire delivery. "I'm a barber. In Thibodaux?"

Leon Massy didn't wait for a comment. "Mr. Forrester," he sputtered, "the boy cain't play no more. I tol' him he be killed, but he won't listen."

I wondered why Leon didn't have the same tortured cajun vowels as his brother. He'd probably spent the last 20 years prattling with customers in the barbershop. The process must have wiped out his cajun *Franglaise,* but it hadn't wiped out his southern accent.

"Slow down, Mr. Massy," I begged, wide awake now. "Broussard's safe in his room. Just take it easy."

Already the dapper little man had been in and out of a chair at least three times. Now he was standing up again, poking a stubby finger at me. "Mr. Forrester, he been lucky so far! Or else they didn't really want to do it. *But now they ready!*"

I wobbled to the dresser and poured a splash of J & B. "Here," I said. He downed it in a gulp. "Now back up," I said. "I'll sit with you all night, listen to your story. Don't worry. The kid's safe. The hotel's secure."

Leon plopped back down, licking his lips and watching me with busy little eyes. He held out his empty glass for an encore, as though assuming I would serve him, the way people *in extremis* assume that the whole world wants to help, because they *have* to assume it.

"It come down to this," he rattled on. "Either that boy gone hide out till this thing over or that boy be dead, one."

"Does he realize that?" I asked as I poured myself a slug to match my guest's.

"Course he know! Boy's stubborn, always been." I nodded agreement. "Talks about his commitment, his commitment, over and over. I say, 'Broussard, son, you ain't got a commitment to get kilt, son, heah?' And Broussard, he say, *'Oncle,* I got a commitment to the team, the coach, the owner, I got a commitment to my girl, to the fans.' Says 'I cain't let them folk down, *Oncle.* They dependin' on me.' I says, 'Broussard, *cher,* your papa's gone now, it's up to me to protect you.' And he just say, he says, 'God'll protect me.' God'll protect him, you heah that, Mr. Forrester? *Cain't he give God a little he'p?*"

"Mr. Massy," I said, trying to sound calm, "I've been close to your nephew, as close as he'd let me, but the more I learn the less I know."

"That's his style," Leon said, shaking his head in a quick tempo. "Poor child. A whole lot to hide." I waited for him to go on, but he stopped.

269

"Mr. Massy," I said, determined to open up the whole nest of snakes right here and now, "why would the Klan try to kill this boy? They can't bury their secret with Broussard. Somebody'll talk some day, and the whole crazy scheme'll come out. You don't really think they're demented enough to kill?"

A puzzled look on my visitor's face told me what a stupid question I'd asked. Did Arisaka rifles grow in the Garden ceiling like magnolias? Of course they were crazy enough. Look at their history: a bunch of lunatics running around in bedsheets, burning crosses and spouting racial theories that would have made Hitler envious. And occasionally hacking off a black man's balls. People like that could commit three murders and then sit down to breakfast.

"I'm sure Bru doesn't realize it," I went on nervously, "but Bru's helping their cause just as much as if the whole steroid scheme had worked. I mean, he's a big white man dominating a game of big black men. Isn't that what Labas and the Research Kommittee wanted?"

Leon Massy looked as if I'd been speaking Taki-Taki. He knitted his chalky forehead and ran a finger around the halo of his sparse hair. "Mr. Forrester, sir," he said in that polite Massy style, "I'm sorry, sir, but you done lef' me behind someplace."

"I'm talking about the danger to this boy's life!" I said heatedly.

"Well, so'm I!" Leon snapped back, drawing himself up to his full height. "But it ain't no Ku Klux Klan after him, man! My God, why'd the Klan want to kill that child? Why, shee-it, I don't even think there *is* a Klan no more!"

Go ahead, I said to myself, do the old cover-up. Maybe you'll be President someday, waxed moustache and all.

He walked briskly to the door, opened it, and looked up and down the hall. Then he stuck his nose into my closet and my bathroom and returned to his chair. "Mr. Forrester," he said evenly, "I thought you knew what's happenin'."

"I know one thing," I said defensively, thinking back to my Sunday adventures in Marcilly. "I know the Klan shot that boy full of anabolic steroids and plastics and chemicals, and I know. . . ."

"Hold on rat there," Leon said, stabbing his index finger at the air. "All Doc Labas give Broussard was vitamins. I seen some of the injections myse'f."

"Did you or Michel ever analyze what was in the needle?"

"In Doc Labas's needle?" the little man said, the tips of his waxed moustache quivering. "Our family doctor for twenty, thirty years? Why, shee-it, no, we didn't."

"Should have," I said.

Leon lit a smelly cigarillo and flipped the dead match on the floor distractedly, as though he were back in his barbershop. "I'm askin' you again. I need your he'p. That's why I rushed up here, not to talk about Doc Labas."

"Well, how the hell can I help you if you won't even admit what's going on?" I said.

"Look, mister, let *me* tell *you* what's going on!" Leon jumped up from his chair again. "Goddamn, I know somethin' too!"

He proceeded to give me a concise *histoire* of the Massys, *père et fils,* and unless he was the greatest little actor since Jean Gabin, no one in the family had ever suspected anything about the Klan's plan or the anabolic steroids.

Their own scandal was worse.

"Michel sold the boy out," the uncle said in a hushed voice. "Not to the Ku Klux Klan. To the mob. The Outfit. Gangsters. Whatever you want to call 'em."

"When?" I tried hard not to show my surprise.

"When? Why, at the beginnin', man! When the boy was eleven, twelve year old. Soon as ever'body in Loozana could see how good he was."

"But *why?*"

"Mr. Forrester, the Outfit, they looked around New Awlyins and they seen the whole city goin' plumb crazy over the Superdome, right? Almost two hundred million dollars in it, and new hotels bein' built, old ladies callin' up bookies to get down on the Saints and the Jazz and the horses, and you know how the Outfit is, Mr. Forrester—they don't want to be lef' outa nothin'! So they see my nephew and they say, 'This is it, man! Six, eight years, this kid'll be the most important thing in basketball. If we own him, we control the game.' Man, they looked at Broussard the way they looked at Vegas, back when it was nothin' but sand."

"It's happened before," I said. "Mostly, it's gentle persuasion. The great players don't knuckle under. That's one reason they're great players."

"Well, my nephew didn't knuckle under, neither," Leon said. "But the mob, they got their hooks into his papa. Mike, he was ripe. Never was enough money in the world for Michel."

He paused for a gulp of whisky. "Me and Michel, we're not alike no way." He spoke as though his brother was still alive. "I can cut fifteen, eighteen heads and have a couple beer after work and I'm okay. Mike, he need more. The Lord give him a son to make a man proud, but that ain't enough. Had to sell the child out, cash on the barrelhead. I don't know how much the Outfit give, but whatever it was, a hundred or a million, Mike lose it right back. Hot-seat poker games on Decatur Street in the Quarter. They set Mike up, Mr. Forrester. They set him up *good!*"

"What about the kid? Did he know?"

"My brother, he promised the capo complete control over Broussard, and he said it goes for life. But people like my nephew—they got somethin' inside 'em. *Nobody* control people like Broussard, not even their papas. You heard about the boy gettin' sick? His nerves?"

I nodded.

"Well, after he come back from the hospital he got kinda hot and heavy in a church on Melpomene Street. St. Crispin's parish? Father Moaty? He didn't care about nothin' else after that. The church and the piano, one or the other." The little man fell silent.

I looked at my watch. It was five after two, the shank of the evening for a basketball writer, but pretty late for a barber from Thibodaux. We'd been talking for two hours, and for the first time since I'd laid eyes on Massy at training camp, I was just about out of questions. "Leon," I said, "how'd Bru happen to pick the Wasps? Why not the Jazz, right in his own backyard? Why not some glamor team?"

"He figure it in his own head," the uncle answered wearily. "Wanted to go someplace he'd make a difference. Did he pick right?"

I had to laugh at the irony. "He picked right." For the first time ever, a player had selected a team on the basis of hardship. Not the player's, the team's.

"Protectin' Michel," Leon said, suppressing a yawn behind his waxed moustache. "Always worryin' about his papa. Way down in Marcilly. Helpless."

"Yeh, well. . . ."

"That boy *love* his papa! Don't ask me why, God rest his soul. That kid, he never ask nobody for help. He went back to basketball when his papa needed money, and then the hoodlums, they come down on the kid hard. 'Come on, punk, we bought you six, seven year already!' Pushin' him to miss a few shots here, play extra hard there, get sick, take a few games off. And my nephew, he jes' went about his bidness."

"Not healthy," I said grimly.

"No, it ain't. Now his papa's gone. The Outfit can't hold him over the boy's head no more. Broussard can go to the *po*-lice. That's the trouble."

"They can't afford to let him talk?"

"*Never!* He know ever'thing. Them hoodlums, they been on him all season, ever since he plays good. He tol' me back in the room. Plus I hear they got some kinda bettin' deal goin'. What'd it be worth to know that Broussard'd get his legs broke in the middle of the playoffs?"

"Not more than ten million," I said, throwing out a figure that someone had thrown out to me, "give or take another ten or twenty."

Leon shook his head sadly. "The Outfit," he said. "They'd kill a hundred men for that."

"Yeh," I said, "or one man eight foot two."

9

I dialed Massy's room. Now that I knew the whole story, I wondered how he'd ever withstood the pressures: The KKK, using him as a wedge against "nigger" athletes; his father, peddling him to criminals; the Outfit, trying to bludgeon him into fixing games; the Wasps, exploiting his height; King Crowder mailing him threats; all the other stresses and tensions. Too much for one man, no matter how strong.

For once, the kid answered the phone himself. "Bru," I said, "I know the whole story now."

"Yes, sir, I'm glad you do," he said in a low voice, as though Justin might be trying to sleep. "I was fixin' to tell you myself, now that Papa's gone. How you and Uncle Leon getting along?"

"Fine," I said.

"Hey, would y'all walk over to the chapel with me? Both of you? I'd surely feel better if somebody went along."

"What?" I said. He was full of surprises. "At two in the morning?"

"Didn't have time earlier. Uncle Leon and me, we talked four, five hours. I been waiting for you two to finish visiting. Gotta light a candle for papa."

He knocked on the door in a few minutes, and Leon and I bombarded him with protests. It was late, we told him. We were tired. We'd had a lot to drink. Besides, the streets weren't safe. Why make himself a target? The candle could be lighted in the morning. His father's soul would rest.

The kid just sat there impassively, the way he always did when his mind was set. He appreciated our concern, "but you're not realistic," he said calmly. "Nobody's gonna shoot me on the streets of New York."

"Broussard, *cher,* I'm beggin' you," Uncle Leon said, grabbing the boy by the arm. *"Don't go out!"*

"Y'all come along," the kid said, gently pulling away. *"Oncle?* Mr. Forrester? Papa'd think highly if you would."

"Deal me out," Leon said, scrunching down in the chair as though it would take a derrick to remove him. "If you want to risk yo' life, I cain't stop you."

"Mr. Forrester?" the big man said.

I dressed and stepped into the bathroom and used the wall phone to make a short call downstairs. Within a few minutes a pair of beefy cops knocked on our door. "Ready?" I asked.

"It's rainin'," the younger cop complained.

"Anything you say, Mac," his elder said.

The kid shrugged his shoulders and followed them to the elevator bank. When we reached the street, two more cops fell in behind, and our little task force moved off toward the chapel. You couldn't get much safer. Let Massy be brave on his own time. Dulcy was too young for widowhood.

The streets of Manhattan are busy even at 2:30 A.M., and soon a small group was in trail, straining for a look at the big man. "G'wan!" one of the cops shouted. "Give him a break!" The group fell back.

"Bru," I said, trying to keep my voice down, "why tonight?"

"God's will be done," the kid murmured, "just like it says in the Lord's Prayer."

"Okay, kid, but like your uncle says, don't you think God can use a little help sometimes?"

Massy peered at me with a patient look. "If He needed help," he said with the complete assurance I'd often noticed in the devout, "He wouldn't be God."

Years ago Dulcy and I took a Newspaper Guild charter to Italy. After we'd dodged a few drivers on our side of the autostrada I asked why Italians drove so fast and recklessly and every one gave me the same reason: God had already chosen their time of departure, and nothing could alter the schedule by as much as a second. Christian fatalism, I guess you'd call it. But too many were picked up on blotters. I could never see God as such a tyrant timekeeper.

But this wasn't the place to argue theology with the grieving Massy. We were at the point of no return, halfway to the Athletes' Chapel, about two blocks away. The night air was damp and penetrating, and wisps of steam lifted up from manholes like cobras from their baskets.

I saw the car when I turned to check our rear escort. A dark Chevy Nova, one headlight dimmer than the other, crawled along about 50 yards behind. "Hey!" I said. "Stop!"

"Whatsa mattuh?" one of the trailing cops asked.

"My shoe," I said. "The laces."

I bent to the sidewalk and looked backward through my legs down the puddled ribbon of asphalt. The Nova had stopped, and I could make out the heads of a driver and a passenger against the glow of a passing truck.

Hit squad!

I tried to alert our escort, but the words wouldn't leave the Mojave Desert of my mouth. I kept seeing a movie scene in two vivid colors: black and red.

ACTION: A long machine-gun blast slams Forrester and Massy and the cops through a plate-glass window. Their mangled bodies are flung across a display of Shell Scott paperbacks.

SOUND: One final tinkle of glass.

CUT TO: Widows mourning.

I jabbed my finger toward the assassins in the hit-car and made gargling noises till one of the cops got the idea and spun around, hand on holster.

He laughed out loud. "Don't worry," he said. "Them're friendlies."
He tapped a creepy-peepy, hanging from his belt. "I called 'em in."

I took a deep breath and exhaled loudly. "Well, gotta stay on the old *qui vive,*" I said. Cool McCool speaking.

"Yeh," the policeman said. "I knew you was shook when you leaned down to tie your loafers."

At the chapel, one of the cops started to go up the steps with Massy. "A little privacy," I whispered, and the cop smiled agreeably and dropped back.

"Bru," I called out, "light one for me, kid." He nodded and disappeared inside. An extra candle wouldn't hurt. The dead man hadn't meant no horm.

Sporadic traffic broke the silence as we huddled at the foot of the steps. A taxi marked "off duty" idled directly across the street, its driver reading a newspaper. Now and then a truck rumbled by, headed for a West Side warehouse and a postmidnight delivery. The sound assaulted my aching head and murdered small talk.

"I don't know how anybody sleeps in this neighborhood," I griped, and one of the cops said, "You get used to it, buddy."

Another one said, "I can't sleep *without* it," and we all smiled politely.

After a few minutes, a man of average height came out of the chapel. He seemed surprised to see four policemen, but he said politely, "Beautiful service. He's lighting a candle. For his father?"

I thought, How nice of the guy, a complete stranger. Must have seen Massy and recognized him. Every sports fan in New York knew about the kid's loss by now.

"Excuse me, podna," the man said calmly, squeezing between me and a cop. He walked lightly across the wet street and climbed into the idling taxi. As it drove off, he waved.

"Beautiful service?" one of the cops was repeating. "They don't hold real services here, do they, Rico?"

"Negative," a swarthy policeman answered. "It's just an all-night chapel."

I ran up the stairs and slammed into the oak doors so hard I almost cracked my shoulder. "Hey, take it easy!" one of the cops said. "They open out, cap."

The chapel was bathed in yellowish light, and at first my eyes didn't adjust. A faint scent of incense and wood hung in the air, and at the head of the narrow aisle I could see the props of faith: rows of candles flickering in stubby garnet-colored glasses, a dark silver chalice on the wooden altar, creamy white hangings embroidered in faded gold. High on the wall a polished wooden Christ looked down, seeing everything and nothing.

I relaxed when I spotted Massy kneeling in the second pew, his head deeply bowed. Otherwise the chapel was empty. I stood against the back wall and waited.

Then the acid-man's words came back to me from that spooky night in camp. "Better play it our way, podna."

A curious word: "Podna." You heard it often in Louisiana, but almost never in the North.

As I watched, Massy slid from sight. All I could see were his size 28 Pumas, jutting into the narrow aisle and slightly canted toward the altar.

For a second, I wondered if the Catholic ritual included prostration, like some of the Middle Eastern religions, but I knew better.

I ran to the front and looked down at the kid. Three lines of blood welled out from under his curly black hair.

He was smiling.